Treacherous Campaign
Tales of the Kashallans: Book Eight
By
Celu Amberstone

TREACHEROUS CAMPAIGN

First edition. October 31, 2023.

Copyright © 2023 Celu Amberstone.

ISBN: 978-1990581151

Written by Celu Amberstone.

Prologue

In the Dream, Tessa floated relaxed and at peace. Comforting images of old friends and family back home among the stars came and went in the patterns of rainbow mists swirling about her. Gone were the torment of pain and the disfigurement of her burns that haunted her in the Waking World. Here she could forget and remember how things used to be, before they were stranded on Timorna—before her bond with a demon—before the battle at Red Rock...

In spite of everything in the Waking World she tried her best to hide her misery from those who needed her help, but her injuries, her weakness and disfigurement were a constant ache, like a rotting tooth that needed to be extracted. It was always there to remind her of her duty—and her failure.

Determined to remain engrossed in the patterns of ever-changing forms and colors she resisted the nearby other, demanding her attention. Beside her in the mists lay another being, a twin. An image of her once lovely heart-shaped face with its high cheek bones and dark eyes stared back at her. The other's full lips curved into a smile. <<Hello, My Jewel. Did you think to avoid me by staying so long here in the Dream?>>

A note of sadness coloring the mental voice, Tessa said, <<Swe'a'sa, is it time to leave this beautiful place already?>>

<<Not yet, My Jewel, but soon,>> the Sweh'an demon who was her bondmate said. The Demon reached out a ghostly hand and took hers. <<But first, My Han'si you must choose.>>

<<Choose? I don't understand.>>

The demon chuckled and raised them both to their feet. <<Yes you do, My Treasure. I've told you before; you just don't want to understand.>>

A mental sigh of acknowledgement of the truth of her bondmate's words, finally Tessa said, "You are right Swe'a'sa, you have shown me—tried to tell me, but it's so hard. Everywhere I turn there is suffering and death. Even here in the Dream I can feel the echoes of the pain that torments me when awake.>>

The demon put a ghostly arm about Tessa's shoulder and drew her close. <<I know, My Jewel. Pleasure, pain, ah the joys good and bad of your corporeal existence. I have never had a human host, or felt so ensnared in the world of Physical Form before. Being bonded to one of you has been a—fascinating experience.>>

Tessa laughed. <<Not what you were expecting, not like your former contracts with Avairei priestesses, eh?>>

The demon smiled. <<No, not at all. I have learned many new things from you and your people, but as I'm sure you are also aware, our time together grows short.>>

<<Yes, I do know. If it wasn't for your magic and Phillip-Yoey's medicines, my frail human body would have perished after our last encounter with the Ghostland wizards' cabal.>>

The Sweh'an grimaced. <<Yes, the Ghostlanders' cabal... You are right your human body isn't able to channel as much of my power as I would wish, but we can take a terrible vengeance upon them nonetheless, before we must part, My jewel.>>

<<Vengeance,>> Tessa said in a dreamy voice as images of mutilated bodies and blood flowed across her vision. <<I would like that, Swe'a'sa, vengeance.>>

The demon chuckled. <<Yes, My Treasure, we will make them pay for our suffering and so much more, but alas, we aren't strong enough to destroy the Enemy completely. We are coming to a point where the path of the future for your people forks. And because it is with you that I have made my contract it must be you who must choose our path forward—how we direct our magic.>>

<<Me? But, but I can't! It's too much,>> Tessa protested.

<<You can and you must,>> the demon growled, a note of irritation coloring the mental voice. <<As I've told you before, I can't make that decision for you; the terms of my service forbid it. You are the only one, Han'si, that can choose for your people—all Timorna's peoples.>>

Tessa's etheric image shimmered. She wanted to wake up—even if it meant returning to the pain of her unhealed injuries—put off her decision for a while longer—as she had done before. This time, however, the demon wouldn't let her.

With a wave of its graceful hand the demon caused her trance to deepen. <<No, My Jewel, not this time, there is no escape until you choose. In the Waking World the future divides and battle is coming to both paths. All those you love will be affected. You must choose.>>

<<I can't stay here—Moraga said we would be moving on soon,>> she protested. <<I have to wake up; I will think more about this later.>>

The demon's gaze hardened. <<Now, My Jewel, or I will become cross with you. And, you wouldn't like that, would you, My Treasure, now would you?>>

<<N-no I would not,>> she stammered, recalling other times when she hadn't been strong enough to defy the demon's will.

<<Besides my slave Atahru will carry our body if the column begins to move before we are ready,>> the Sweh'an added with a smirk.

Trembling Tessa gave her agreement. <<So be it, Swe'a'sa, I will choose.>> feeling as if her heart was being torn in two, she watched again as the demon showed her the possible futures for the Speir'dina she cared about and how the future of the Kashallan Alliance would unfold, depending on her choice.

<<We have only enough power to aid one of the two paths unfolding before us. Which will it be, My Jewel? Shall we lend our aid to the one, or the many, My Treasure. There is only a single path for us before our time together ends.>>

Oh, Nathan love; Phillip we have been through so much together, she thought privately. *Why did it have to come to this? I'm so, so sorry.*

To her bondmate Tessa said, <<I will choose, but I would also like to know that whatever I choose will bring peace and a chance to survive on this alien world for my Speir'dina people. That is the gift I hope my life will give them—my sacrifice will be my legacy to the generations to come upon this world.>>

<<It will, My Jewel, I can promise you that, whatever you choose. Your people will survive in some fashion on this world.>>

<<Good. That makes what is to come easier to bear. But Swe'a'sa, but can we help—warn the other I don't choose in some way without violating the contract?>>

The demon thought about it for a moment, then smiled. <<Yes, My Treasure, I think we can.>> The demon let out a mirthless laugh. <<Perhaps there is one among the Alliance who has enough power and can be persuaded to help—in spite of himself.>>

When the demon showed her, Tessa, too, laughed. "Oh my, Swe'a'sa, if he agrees what a change to his world that will be.>>

Part One
Chapter One

"Greetings, Members of the Council, Imas, Atas, this is Jojo Tepring, your man on the scene, reporting again on our noble warriors' trek north into the enemy territory of the Ghostlands."

The Speir'dina holding the pocket recorder adjusted the screen away from his smiling golden-skinned green-eyed face topped by its thatch of curly red hair. He turned the recorder to show the waiting viewers back home the tawny ridges and rocky path leading through the clumps of purple thorn and sourwood. Ahead of him the recorder revealed a line of warriors their identities almost unrecognizable through the clouds of red dust kicked up by the column of the allied forces spread out before and behind him.

Jojo coughed. "Take a good look, People. For most of you viewing this it will be your first glimpse of 'the Ghostlands' in living memory. As you can see it's quite dusty—and hot, too, let me assure you. Not much different than the terrain around Tragar, actually. Well maybe a bit dryer, less vegetation—and more dust." He coughed again before continuing.

"This is our first day out into the open. Most of our travel North before now has been through the labyrinth of tunnels, used to great advantage by the Enemy on prior raids South into our home territory.

"Now that we've come out of the gloom the talk among the warriors is that there is a sizable complex of farms and slave breeding pens a few days' march ahead of us. It's not confirmed by the Alliance commanders, but the talk going around camp at night is," he confided in a low tone, "that the place is one of the major breeding facilities for the terrible monsters created by the Wizards' Cabal to ravage our innocent families in the South.

"And with the combined force of our brave Warlinga, Speir'dina and Western Clan Warriors we will destroy it, as we have already done with the enemy warbands we encountered in the tunnels. So far our casualties have been light, thanks in part to the superior skills of our warriors, and the noble efforts of our medical corps."

Jojo zoomed in for a closer look at the dust-caked tired men trudging nearby. "Among whom I am travelling at the moment." He focused on a pair of black-clad men with heavy packs on their shoulders walking nearby. "And here is our brave Speir'dina warrior Armachd Chang and his student and one of our most experienced young medics, Ata Timma."

Without slowing his pace, Jojo bounced over and held his recorder up to Armachd Chang. "Care to give the people back in the Yeyen your thoughts on the coming engagement or how the war is going in general?"

Chang pushed the recorder out of his face, causing Jojo to nearly drop the precious item. "Fuck off, Dymarian, I don't have time for your nonsense."

"Be careful, Armachd this recorder is only on loan to me. I have to return it to Tomas Chambers with a copy of my notes to the Council." Chang swore in Caldoni and quickened his pace. Jojo's face reddened. "Ah, for those who don't speak Caldoni, I'm not going to translate that for this recording. Let's just say the armachd has no further comments at the moment. I'll ask him again later."

Undeterred by Chang's rudeness Jojo waited for the grim-faced armachd to pass, then stuck the recorder in front of Timma. "And how about you, Noble Medic? Any comments for the Imas?" a sly smile curving his full lips when Timma remained silent, he added, "Want to say hi to that pretty wife of yours waiting for you back at Tragar Keep?"

Startled Timma opened his mouth as if to speak, sorely tempted, then he glanced at Chang's grim expression and stiff back, closed his mouth and without a word hurried to keep pace with his mentor.

Behind him the reporter heard a soft chuckle as he paused his machine. "Give it up, Jojo. You know the Hunt Leader has told the warriors not to comment to you about the coming engagement."

Plastering a friendly smile on his face Jojo turned, walking backwards a few steps till he could come alongside the kashallan. "I wasn't asking him to disclose the army's secret military plans, Kashallan-Phillip, I was just looking for some human interest quotes—something to help Tomas and the players create new dramas depicting our exploits when we get back to the Yeyen Banai Valley."

"Mm, perhaps, but now isn't a good time, not when everybody is tired—maybe later."

Jojo thought about it, then nodded. "You're probably right. When we are in camp and we've eaten and rested—" He brightened as a new thought came to him. "And then will you give me an interview?"

Phillip-Yoey pointed to his clan branded face and Umwira ponytail and laughed. Switching languages he asked in Galactic Standard, "Getting desperate, Jojo? Do you really want to send back as one of your first reports the thoughts of the 'Renegade Umwira's Kashallan?"

Jojo grinned, taking his meaning. A mischievous gleam in his green eyes, he said, "Why not. I believe history will prove that you and Maker Tinguss are the visionaries that began the process leading to a lasting peace on this world."

Sobering Kashallan-Phillip nodded. "I hope you are right, Jojo, for in order for Speir'dina to grow and prosper in our adopted home we desperately need peace and an end to the wars and hatred that has been festering between the Khutani peoples and the Umwira for centuries."

Jojo smiled, showing lots of teeth. "So does that mean you will talk to me this evening, Kashallan?"

Phillip-Yoey smiled as well, displaying his alien, sharp Khutani teeth. "No promises, but we will see."

Cheered up considerably, Jojo next turned to the Avairei slogging along dejectedly just behind the kashallan with a heavy pack of medical supplies on his back. Turning the recorder back on, he held it out. Caught on the screen was a disheveled young Ata his dirty matted braidlets pulled back into a ponytail like the clan warriors and the Speir'dina man walking nearby. "And how about you, Ata Crowis, any comments on what you are learning as one of the army's medics and your brother-in-law Phillip-Yoey's assistant?"

Torn out of his misery by the mention of his real name, Crowis raised his eyes from the ground and blinked. When he finally understood the question being put to him he shook his head and looked down as if where he placed his foot for the next step was the most important thing in the world. "Jojo, please," he mumbled, "don't torment me."

Jojo frowned, puzzled by his friend's reaction. Glancing back at the grinning pair of Clan warriors just behind them his mood improved again. "Ah, Nytaka, Qwayku, how are you doing today. I heard from War Leader Tesulu that you young warriors fought bravely in that last skirmish before we left the tunnels. I also heard you helped carry several wounded men out of the fighting." He held out the pocket recorder. "Want to talk to me again?" The Cousins nodded and eagerly moved alongside Jojo so they could see themselves on the little screen he held out to them.

Noticing Jojo talking to the Cousins they were quickly joined by other young warriors fascinated by Jojo's off world technology. "Ah, greetings Athala, Cho, how are you doing today...."

CROWIS ADJUSTED THE strap of the heavy pack on his shoulder and coughed. The excited voices of the little monsters who had been appointed his so-called teachers in the "survival arts" by his newly discovered relatives, Sensei Chang and Kashallan-Phillip, barely penetrated the misery of his situation as they lagged behind him. Well at least with Jojo to amuse them the ones whom he thought of as his personal tormentors would leave him alone for a while.

A cloud of red dust whipped up by the trudging warrior's feet seemed to hang over the column in a malignant haze. He wished they would stop, let him rest, but he dared not complain—no one else was. And if he did try to explain that he was a scholar and that they should have left him back at Tragar, because he wasn't cut out for this kind of life, the warriors and even the Begta traveling with the warbands would only laugh at him and call him Brat and other foul names.

How much longer till they would stop and camped for the night? he wondered. His feet hurt. But why did he care when they stopped; he couldn't rest even then.

"Feeling sorry for yourself again, Ata?" Phillip-Yoey said, glancing back at him.

"No," he lied.

The kashallan laughed. "Cheer up, Ata. The sun is sinking towards the horizon. We will be making camp for the night soon."

Maybe you can rest then, but I will have to haul water and gather fuel for the cook fires. I won't get any rest; I will have to keep working or Sensei Nytaka or Sensei Qwayku will be there with their switches, calling me a lazy Begta and making sure I don't dawdle.

In a part of his mind still thinking clearly he knew he wasn't being fair. Phillip-Yoey wouldn't be lazing around; he would be right alongside him hauling water or filling up the jars of kavay medicines that were always in demand. No, he wasn't being fair. Everybody in the Teh'lachs worked together to set up and take down the nightly camps. He was just tired—and frightened—if he was honest with himself.

THE CAMP THAT NIGHT was a wide sandy area off the trail with no looming rocks or thorn thickets that could offer shelter for a surprise attack. Crowis belonged to a Teh'lach made up mostly of the medics like Kashallan-Phillip, Timma, the Speir'dina Medics Williams and Ruan, their assistants Nurse Anilah, several Begta and Loti volunteers.

Sensei Chang, though not officially apart of their group, did spend quite a lot of time with them, being in charge of the ongoing training of the young warriors like the Cousins, their friends Athala and Cho, as well as the Warlinga Chi'am Tragar and two young Meh'gach hunters who were also a part of their Teh'lach. Crowis, too, much to his dismay was forced to join the nightly training sessions.

Nobody expected him to take up the spear and become a warrior, but his attendance was still required. *"You need to know the basics in case you are attacked or your patients are in danger, Crowis,"* Phillip-Yoey kept saying to him, *"and if you don't like getting bruised and bloody, then you will have to try harder and learn how to defend yourself."*

There was little fuel in this barren spot available for cook fires so the camp settled for an evening meal of water from the nearby creek and a handful or two of pemegas, a trail food made of pounded meat, masa root mixed with obeylem fat and rolled into balls. Before coming on this journey he'd never heard of the stuff, but it was a common ration known to both the Clans and the Warlinga hunters.

Choking down the last of his portion Crowis had just pulled his blanket out of their packs and swaying like a drunkard was looking around for a comfortable spot to curl up for the night when Nytaka's sharp voice cut through his fatigue like a knife.

"Where do you think you're going, Brat?"

Crowis froze, mentally he ran through the list of camp chores assigned to him—had he forgotten something? By the Mother, he had helped sort and repack medical supplies after Phillip-Yoey and Kashallan-Nathan refilled the kavay medicines they might need. He had checked on his patients, fed a man with a broken arm, and bathed another whose wound had started to bleed again. He shivered as a cold wind blew off the mountain looming to the north of them. He couldn't think of anything else.

Crowis sighed and faced his tormentor. "Sensei Nytaka, I've done my chores; I'm tired. I was going to sleep now."

Nytaka smacked the kavalpa wand he held against his leg. "We will need water for the morning. Go fill our buckets and the net of jars before it gets too dark to see and you fall and break something, Lazy Begta."

Begta, Crowis looked wistfully at the Begta shamanka Masonja sitting by the packs pulling her blanket and Phillip-Yoey's from the folded mass the Loti had deposited by their site. Before coming on this journey the only Begta he had known were slaves. It was their job to haul water and dig privy holes, but not here. Masonja was a shamanka and healer in her own right and more likely to order him to dig a privy hole and carry water than to do it herself.

Everybody took turns hauling water and he didn't remember being assigned that duty tonight, but arguing with Nytaka about it would only get him a whack or two from his wand, which his battered body didn't need. Sighing he picked up two buckets, slung the net of empty jars over his shoulder and headed for the creek. "Yes, Sensei."

It was probably the Cousins' turn tonight and the little monsters were taking advantage again, but it wasn't worth complaining to Sensei Chang or Phillip-Yoey about it. He might win a temporary reprieve from a distasteful task, but the Cousins would find a way to get back at him—later.

There were four containers setting by their packs, so he would be expected to make two trips, but to his surprise Phillip-Yoey gave Nytaka a warning stare and followed Crowis to the creek with the other two buckets.

The blue snows had melted earlier in the Sun-Season so the water in the creek bed was barely more than a trickle. To avoid getting sand in the containers along with the water was a slow business. It was nearly dark by the time they had finished. As they were carrying the heavy buckets and nets of stoppered jars up the bank, Phillip surprised him by stopping at the top and turning to face him. "I wanted you to know that we are pleased with how you are doing on this journey. Ma'lu says you could try a little harder in your combat lessons, true, but you are doing much better than Yoey and I expected you would with the healing knowledge we are teaching you."

Confused and too tired to decide whether his kashallan brother-in-law was joking with him, Crowis glanced up, trying to see his face in the dim light. Kashallan-Phillip met his gaze and nodded. "I'm not teasing you," he said, then laughed as Crowis continued to stare. "Keep it up and Ishka may even want to name you her brother again by the time we return to Tragar."

Crowis snorted a laugh, in spite of himself. So afraid he would tell their mother that she hadn't died when she was captured by the Umwira if he was allowed to return to his studies at Riath. She had been angry enough to have her two husbands bring him along on the expedition up into the Ghostlands. "That might be too much to ask, but thank you, Holy One," Crowis murmured, dropping his eyes once more to the sand.

"We shall see—" Phillip-Yoey might have said more, but he broke off as a shadowy figure loomed up on the path in front of them. Nearly bumping into the kashallan who had stopped abruptly just ahead of him, Crowis choked back a frightened cry.

"It's all right, Crowis," Phillip said quietly. "There's no need to be afraid." Recognizing the dark figure, he said, "Good evening, Atahru. Is your Mistress well? Does she need my help with her healing?"

As the Umwira stepped closer, Crowis too recognized the demon's slave and shivered. Back at Tragar the demon and her Speir'dina host had secretly bound him to her service. Had the Wa'chassey'ul come because she needed him for some reason? He shivered again.

As if the demon was able to see them through Atahru's dark eyes, she focused her gaze on him alone, the Wa'chassey'ul's mouth curving into a cruel smirk. "Your service is owing, Priest, but I haven't come for you yet." Dismissing him in the next moment the demon and her slave returned their attention to Phillip-Yoey.

Phillip-Yoey bowed and repeated his earlier question. "Tess-weh, are you well; how may I serve you?"

"My Mistress is well, Khutani," Atahru said in a hollow voice. "I come with a message, Khutani, Heed it well. Your life will depend on it."

"Mm, I understand."

Atahru let out a mirthless laugh. His voice taking on the tambour of the demon as he said, "Do you, Khutani? I wonder."

Phillip sighed. He hated her games, and didn't enjoy playing them for her amusement. "Just give me your message, Honored Spirit. It grows late as you can see."

Speaking in Galactic Standard Atahru said, "Beware, Dr Singey, for you are known and expected. If you swallow the bait offered you by the pale men in the North you will be enslaved and bound in a net of your own making. When specters of ancient evil whisper upon the northern winds, deception cloaks a great evil. Have a care, My Jewel. Flattery and illusion are powerful lures set to unearth old habits best left buried and forgotten. Heed the warning you are given and don't allow the malice awakened by ancient wrongs to whisper in your ear.

"But if you, in your arrogance, ignore my warning and they ensnare you, then surrender to the sweet hunger. The Little One leads the way and will guide you to the Ancestor who will give you the missing pieces of the puzzle needed to obtain your freedom."

Chapter Two

The warrior bowed to the dried-up old priest shrouded and veiled against the blistering sun standing in front of him. Bred and enhanced from his original stolen Warlinga ancestors, the Changeling Drucas Segoi and pride of the Ghostland wizard's breeding program was a tall muscular man with piercing red eyes and a dark mottling pattern on his back and arms.

While still an infant the small pair of extra limbs, a trait of his true Umwira ancestry, had been surgically removed from his torso. The phantom limbs ached on occasion, but he had learned to ignore the pain. He was a child of the Real People; he knew his purpose, to infiltrate and help destroy the Enemy from within. The pain and his sacrifice would one day be rewarded when the Khutani-held lands of the South flowed deep in a river of blood.

After a long moment of silence the old priest spoke in a voice roughened by the harsh land in which he dwelled. "Speak, Warrior of the Real People. Why have you made the long journey to the Plain of Fires?"

Plain of Fires, Drucas glanced at the not so distant conical mountains, some of their peeks belching plumes of dark smoke and flames into the sulfurous air. Lazy streams of molten lava rolled down mountain sides to spread out upon a stone-covered plain of glassy black rocks. If his petition was granted he would have to walk upon those rocks down the Trail of Death to the Well of Poison Fire.

Drucas bowed again choking back his fear and strengthening his resolve. *I will reach out my hands and take what is mine—by right. I will not be satisfied to be a slave to the weak grey worms of the Cabal any longer.* "I come seeking guidance and the gift of power that only the Unseen Ones in such a holy place can grant to the worthy."

The priest chuckled, the sound like dry leaves crackling under a clawed foot. "And are you worthy, Changeling? I wonder."

Drucas gritted his teeth, swallowing down an angry response. It was always the same thing when he had face-to-face dealings with any of these pale little Ghostland worms. These four limbed priests and wizards of the elite class claimed their descent pure and untainted from Timorna's ancient inhabitants, tracing their lineage from the ancients before the Great Wars. They thought themselves so superior to those of the People in the West born with six limbs and even more so than a half-bred changeling with Khutani slave blood, such as himself.

Was the Begta Puke baiting him, hoping he would do something rash, so he would have cause to refuse his petition? If so, the priest was mistaken. Drucas would do nothing to give the priest cause to refuse him. Even if it meant prostrating himself on hot rocks till his scales charred.

"There is a new alliance among the Hated Enemy. Our land has been invaded, Holy One." Drucas waved a clawed hand to the fiery mountains on the horizon. "As a trusted war leader of the Cabal, I seek guidance and the magic needed to defeat them."

"A noble purpose," the priest said, "if undertaken for the good of the People and not for personal gain."

"I wish only to serve," Drucas lied, his hard eyes meeting those of the priest, daring him to challenge that statement. Unable to completely erase the tone of arrogance and contempt from his voice when the priest remained silent, he added, "As a small token of my humility and faith I bring gifts to the keepers of the shrine—and to the Unseen Ones they serve."

By this time the old man had been joined by three other individuals, their age and sex indistinguishable in their voluminous veils and robes.

"The sincerity of your words isn't for me to judge. Your worthiness will be up to the Dwellers of the Poison Fires to decide, not me." The old man waved to his subordinates to come forward and take charge of the dusty and exhausted Loti slave and his heavy packs. After the Loti had been led away, the priest motioned for Drucas to follow him up a steep trail to the cool darkness of the temple cut into the cliff above.

Passing through the doorway the priest pushed aside the head coverings that protected his colorless, pale skin from the heat and light. "Enter and refresh yourself, Warrior, before you walk the Trail of Death. You have come a long way—and in haste. If what you say is true about the Enemy, then your need must be great.

"I wonder why the Cabal was able to spare you for this pilgrimage. How many will die because they are deprived of your knowledge and strength at such a critical time?"

The sly Begta Puke, had he guessed that Drucas's pilgrimage wasn't known or authorized by the new leadership of the Cabal? He had claimed to his superiors to be heading South on an extended scouting mission. No, they would definitely not be pleased if they knew his true destination—and its real purpose.

"Whatever deaths may occur in my absence will be compensated for by the guidance and power I will obtain when the Unseen Ones favor my quest," he growled.

"A favorable end to your quest, hmm." There was that rasping chuckle again. "Yes, Warrior, let us hope it is so."

Drucas was led to a small chamber by the younger of the shrouded priests. He was instructed to rest in its cool dimness until the elder had cast the bones and determined the proper time for his descent into the valley to walk the path to the Well of Fire.

When the obnoxious minion had gone, he drank long from the jar of water on a small table and then crossed to the nest prepared for guests and lay down upon its thin lumpy moss. Coming here had been a gamble. The Place of the Fires was a sacred and holy place to the People, but the gifts of magical power it offered weren't granted without a price.

To walk among the Holy Flames, to feel the burning power that had appeared after the ancient wars inside his flesh, such power could either kill or transform. To face the fear and withstand the torment took not only courage but strength of will. Body and mind must be united and strong enough to endure the pain of Transformation. If not, if he lost control for even a moment, then he would die—and most horribly.

But he was strong his natural gifts already enhanced by secret training offered to him in his youth by others among the elite class, who hadn't been content with the limited uses their rulers had seen in him. The rebels suspected he could be, with the right teaching, far more than just a ruthless and violent tool.

A smile curving his dark lips he closed his eyes and willed his tense body to relax. Fortunately for him the ones who had shared with him their special "gifts" were all dead. Barak had seen to that, but he had never learned of Drucas's conspiring with the rebels, or the changeling's enhancements.

ONE OF THE PRIESTS came for him in the cool, murky twilight. His guide instructed him to leave behind his spear, crossbow and any other weapons. He could keep his belt knife in case a blood offering was required. He was also to remove any foreign articles he carried on his person, including the death strand he still wore as was the custom among the Warlinga of the Yeyen Banai where he had lived for so many years.

Without a word he removed everything and laid them atop the moss of the nest. Turning to the priest with head crest flattened, and showing his fangs, he warned, "All my property had better be right here when I return."

Silently the priest stared at him from the concealment of its veils for a long moment. Finally it said in a low voice that still managed to convey contempt, "If you return, Warrior, your possessions will be here as you left them. Have no fear." Drucas grunted and followed the priest from the room.

Once outside the temple Drucas stopped and took a deep breath of the sulfurous air, trying to calm his nerves. Though the sun had gone below the horizon some time before, it was never truly dark in this place. The glowing red and gold streams of molten lava pouring down the mountainsides and pooling on the plain below cast grotesque shadows upon the nearby rocks, and illuminated their way down the trail with a flickering red glow.

When the gray sky of twilight had turned to the black of true night the priest stopped by a cairn of rocks the height of a tall man alongside the path. At the top was a cross. On its horizontal pole hung several ragged prayer flags and other offerings.

"This is as far as I go with you, Supplicant." The priest pointed to a winding trail leading down into a rocky ravine from which occasional clouds of steam and flame issued from a deep pit. "We will come back in three days to this holy marker. If your petition is successful we will bring you back to the temple and care for you until you are well enough to travel. If you are not here," the priest pointed to the cairn, "we will add another stone to the mound. Fare well, Supplicant." The priest turned and without another word headed back to the temple.

Gritting his teeth Drucas watched the pale figure disappear into the gloom, his barbed tail curling and uncurling in agitation. "I'll be waiting; have no fear of that. Just make sure you come back for me," he shouted after the retreating priest.

When his guide had disappeared into the darkness Drucas took a deep breath, refusing to surrender to his fears, and started down the trail to the Well of Poison Fires. His magic was strong. The Unseen Ones would grant him the power he needed to destroy the Khutani-bred slaves that threatened his people, and his enemies within the Cabal as well.

The arrogant wizards would understand how dangerous it was to under estimate him when his powerful jaws closed around their scrawny necks and he drank the life from their puny bodies. It would be too late but they would learn that he was no groveling slave to be used and thrown away—yes, they would all learn to fear and obey K'San Drucas Segoi.

He was well into the ravine and nearing the well when the buzzing in his head and the burning sensation under his skin became nearly unbearable. Choking on bile Drucas doubled over and vomited a stream of gray acid onto the path. The poisons were inside him now. There was no turning back; Transformation or Death were his only choices now. Falling to his knees he raised his face to the sky and roared.

It had begun. The poisons from the old wars that claimed him were invading every cell of his body. He was on fire the pain forcing him to the ground. He writhed in unbelievable agony, but refused to give up—refused to die. Unable to stand he crawled towards the pit.

He would not surrender to the pain; he would be found worthy of the blessings the Transformation would give him. Even though he had always been told by the gray worms that he was only a half-bred creature he was not. He was strong and his breeding true, a son of the Real People. This world belonged to him and his kind, not the alien invaders and their mutated slaves.

The heat of a blazing sun passed into the cooling dimness of another night while Drucas crawled towards the pit, oblivious to the passing of time.

Only the pain was real, and only the pain reminded him that he was still alive. Reaching the rim of the well at last he peered down into a pit of fire. In his torment, it seemed as if fiery demons laughed at him and danced in a swirling mist of changing shapes and colors.

Hoping to dispel the mocking vision, Drucas blinked and rubbed a hand across his dry and burning eyes. Damn them all! He pulled himself up into a sitting position, staring into the Well. He had come this far he would finish it. Taking the Speir'dina knife from his waist he made a deep gash on his arm and allowed his blood to drip into the inferno below.

"Ancient Ones, Holy Ones, I come seeking the Magic I need to defeat my enemies and the enemies of all the Real People of this world. I come seeking Power so I can help destroy the Khutani invaders and all those who are alien to our world once and for all. I come seeking your guidance and I offer you my Blood Gift. Hear me and grant me Power, Holy Ones of the Mighty Fires."

Drucas allowed a large amount of his blood to fall into the well before he felt too dizzy and weak to continue. He waited, but no vision appeared before his eyes, no voice spoke holy words of wisdom into his mind...

Tears of weakness and frustration pooled in his red eyes. Damn them! What more did they expect of him? In spite of his mixed heritage surely he was worthy? He had risked his very life to come here. Hadn't he paid their price in blood and pain? "Unseen Ones, speak to me. I have sacrificed much to come here. What more must I do to receive your favor and blessings?"

As unconsciousness threatened to overwhelm him Drucas sank to the ground his head slumping over the rocky edge of the well. It was only then that a blast of scorching heat caressed his face and a deep voice whispered into his mind. <<Sacrifice.>>

Sacrifice, what more could he sacrifice? He'd come here against orders, endured the tortures of the path..."What more can I give and still survive? Greedy, ungrateful Spirits! What do you want from me?"

<<if you want Magic and Power to defeat your enemies then you must sacrifice,>> the rasping voice repeated.

"Sacrifice, eh?" he said bitterly, suddenly wondering if it had been a mistake to come here. "And if I 'sacrifice' more, what guarantee do I have I will receive from you the magic I need to defeat my enemies, hmm?"

<<You will gain the Power that you seek. Your enemies among the Cabal and many in the South will die by your hand, Warrior, never fear. But unless you sacrifice something you greatly value in payment, you will join them in death, Arrogant One.>>

A grim smile curved the changeling's cruel mouth. He believed the voice; he would triumph. But what more did the Holy Ones of the Fires want? "I still don't understand what do you want; what must I sacrifice to win your blessing?"

<<The Gift is up to you, Warrior,>> the Voice finally said. <<You must decide. You will know if your Gift is accepted, because you will live—not die.>> The voice remained silent after that in spite of his angry demands for clarification or more information.

Drucas lay panting on the lip of the well for a long time his mind lost in confusing visions of battle and torment. Somewhere in the Ghostland tunnels the Great Avenger and other monstrous warbands of the wizards' creation were fighting the warriors of the Kashallan Alliance—and dying. He saw in the flames Warlinga he knew from the Yeyen Banai Valley like the Meh'gach brothers, as well as some of the Western Clan War Leaders he knew by sight, but not by name. The Alliance vermin raised their spears drenched in blood to the sky and rejoiced in their victories.

And then, in among the sulfurous fumes and shifting flames were visions of the flat-faced mutants with their magical weapons, who some of the more moderate factions among the elite whispered weren't mutants at all, but another alien species like the Khutani vermin, invading their world from the stars.

Feeling something jab into his hip, he smiled, now certain he knew what to offer. Aliens and their fearsome weapons! He would give the Unseen Ones their *sacrifice* and be a part of the force that destroyed the invaders once and for all.

"All right, I will 'sacrifice' something more. I will give you something I greatly value!" he said, his mouth too dry to do more than croak. Pulling the black and lethal Speir'dina blade from its sheath Drucas hurled it into the fiery pit. As the blade disappeared he heard a rumble from deep in the ground and a tower of sparks shot high into the air.

His lips curled back in a death's head smile. The blade was a fitting sacrifice, a symbol of death awaiting all invaders. How many of the foul creatures had been ensnared by Khutani lies and become hosts for the Makers unnatural children? It didn't matter; they were all going to die.

Drucas lowered his head and weakly began to crawl up the path to the cairn and the waiting priests.

Chapter Three

Creeping through the rocks above the trail that the main column of allied forces had used about a half day ahead of them, Tesulu motioned for the other members of his patrol to halt when he spied the two men he'd assigned to guard their back trail hurrying up to join them.

Dressed in black, a long brown four-ply warrior's braid down his back, when the Speir'dina man named Murda was close enough to be heard without shouting, he said, "War Leader Tesulu, there is a number of unknown Warlinga coming up behind us."

"What do you mean unknown Warlinga?" Tesulu said. Glancing over the dry barren hills through which they had come, he shaded his eyes with one of his four hands, but could make out no details in the red dust cloud near the horizon. Motioning for his band of nine to crouch down among the rocks so they couldn't be seen, he repeated,his voice harsh as he vented his frustration on the unsuspecting warrior under his command. "What do you mean unknown Warlinga?"

He hated being assigned a patrol at the rear of the march today, a position away from the glory of battle should the column be attacked once again. His long-standing rival Ogwy was at the front this time his Teh'lach and Goro's in a position to win honor while he remained at the ass end of their force. But maybe he should have more faith in the Unseen One's and their purpose.

Ingazi, waring the clan markings of a Rock Salt man in his Teh'lach had come up to the group by then, adding to his partner's tale, "They are no Warlinga we saw at Tragar, so maybe they are Ghostlander Changelings."

"They also have with them some Avairei and a few Loti carrying heavy packs," Murda said, "So they have either been raiding in the Yeyen, or the Avairei are more of the Dingay Changelings seeking refuge, and the Warlinga are escorting them North."

"They would be changeling hunters," Chelka said as she and her combat partner Marti came near. "The Avairei are probably Ghostland-bred, too, but I doubt if the poor Loti would have gone with them willingly."

Tesulu didn't care about stupid Loti, they were good for nothing better than to be made slaves. And the women were most likely right the people coming up behind them were Ghostland bred and then sent back south to infiltrate the Khutani held lands. Ah but how could he, Tesulu, use this information to best advantage, both for the Kashallan Alliance, and to win glory and honor for himself?

"We need to let the Hunt Leader know about this," Murda said, breaking in on his concentration.

Tesulu made a cutting motion and the man fell silent. "We will," he finally said, "but first we will use this information to our advantage."

"And glory," Juba said, tossing his dark brown ponytail back over his shoulder and smiling. He suspected he knew the mental trail his war leader was following.

Mar flattened his head crest and curled his lip, showing the tips of his canines. "Information isn't the most important thing here, Clan Warriors, for what would these misbegotten fools know. No the safety of our people is more important than information—or glory in battle."

Tesulu had no head crest to drop in a threat display, so he contented himself by showing his canines in a warning grin. "No reason we can't do both when the Unseen Ones hand us the opportunity, eh, Warlinga?"

Mar turned green then growled, "What are you talking about, War Leader."

"What was the War Council talking about last Night, eh?" Tesulu countered.

"Lots of things," Mar grumped, a puzzled expression on his scaled face. "I don't understand."

"Think, Stupid Begta!" Tesulu said, meeting the eye of every warrior under his command.

The patrol thought about it for a long moment, finally the youngest among them, Armachd Boughthy, pushed a snarl of red hair off his forehead and hesitantly said, "I overheard Hunt Leader Tizu talking to K'San Tobrach about us needing a way to get inside that fortress to open the gates.

Otherwise we might lose a lot of good warriors in a frontal assault. But I still don't see—"

Tesulu gave the young man an approving nod. "But I do, Warrior." his smile widened. "But I do."

"What are you talking about?" Chelka said, not liking the expression of smug satisfaction on the war Leader's scarred and grinning face.

Before she could react, Tesulu reached out and snatched the colorful headband off her forehead, revealing the sigil of possession the Changeling Drucas Segoi had carved into her forehead when she and Marti had been his prisoners in Riath.

With a snarl of outrage Chelka leapt forward with teeth bared. Still grinning, he leapt out of her way and landed a powerful blow of his tail across her shoulders dropping her to her knees. Before her cousin Mar and Qwi'ach the other Warlinga in the patrol could react, his Second, Juba was beside them, growling a warning.

"None of your insolence, Woman, I am War Leader here, so have a care how you challenge me," Tesulu snarled all teasing forgotten.

Once the Clans knew about the sigils that the women concealed under their headbands, they were considered bad luck and no one wanted to have them as a part of their patrols. Only some of the Speir'dina and the Warlinga who were her relatives included the women without being ordered to do so.

In spite of assurances to the contrary they were considered a danger, because the magic in the sigils created a link with the one who made them. Familiar with such magic compulsions, the Western Clans feared that at any time Drucas could seize control of one or both of the women's minds and bodies to create chaos among the Alliance.

Most thought they should be killed or at least sent back South, but they had convinced the Khutani elders to let them come and nothing the Western Clansmen could say would change that. But now maybe he could take advantage of the situation if he dared—

What are you thinking, Brother?" Juba said.

Smiling, Tesulu uncoiled some rope from around his waist and reached for Chelka's wrists. "I'm thinking it's time we return the K'San Changeling's property to him."

Over roars of outrage and cries of traitor from her Warlinga relatives Tesulu grabbed a startled Chelka and tried to force her hands behind her back.

Before everyone took sides and started their own little war, Marti hissed a warning. "Calm down, you shit for brains amadans," she snapped, using Hunt Leader Tizu's favorite expletive. "You want those changelings to come over here and kill us?" When the Warlinga and Speir'dina stared at her, she chuckled and took off her headband and handed it to a startled Murda.

In the confusion Chelka snatched her hand away, but a warning growl from the war leader stopped any further protest and he roughly grabbed her arm again and reached for the other he still held.

Ignoring Chelka's pleading look, Marti gave the War Leader a flirtatious smile. "Great idea, Handsome." Then noticing Mar and Chelka's angry glares, she said, an exasperated tone coming into her voice. "Think you two; it's a perfect way to get inside that fortress if we let our Clan brothers bring us in as their captives. Once inside we can overpower the guards and let our warriors in."

Murda scowled. He recalled that in their old life in Lann Gheal her superiors in the corps were always disciplining her for being too reckless and taking unnecessary chances—chances that could get herself and other people killed. "Nathan isn't going to like this, Marti," Murda said in a low voice as she handed him her sidearm and knife.

Marti grinned, her eyes bright with excitement. "Nathan isn't here, and I'm merely obeying my appointed commander's orders, right?"

Murda snorted. "My ass you are, Armachd" Marti grinned and tossed her beam rifle to a startled Boughthy. "Catch, Infant, here's another toy for you to play with. Nathan says you're getting to be a good shot."

To everyone's surprise, it was a thoughtful Juba who counseled giving more consideration to Tesulu's plan. "True if we meet up with the Changelings there is a good chance they may not know of our new allegiance to the Kashallan Alliance. We could say we captured the women, saw who they belong to and decided to bring them north, hoping to gain favor, but if K'San Drucas chooses to come to them before we spring our trap, either in person or through his magic then—"

Marti shook her head and held out her hands to Juba. "That's not going to happen, Sand Mountain Warrior."

"How can you be so sure?" Juba said, still reluctant to bind her.

Marti glanced at Chelka, then lightly touched to sigil on her forehead. "I can't really explain it, but this thing—I know—we know he's somewhere far from here and has been for a while, right Sister-Warrior?"

Reluctantly Chelka agreed.

"And besides," Marti continued, her eyes sparkling, "The Khutani are guarding us in the Dream; that black-hearted devil Drucas can't mess with our minds. He won't mess up the war leader's plan."

"No maybe not," Murda said. "But that doesn't mean it won't go sideways anyway. We need to think this through carefully—contact Command—"

"I am Command," Tesulu said, folding his top set of arms across his scarred chest while his lower set still held on to Chelka's tether. His grim expression dared anyone to challenge his authority as their leader.

When no one challenged his leadership, he unbent enough to explain further to her kin and the Speir'dina. "I have no wish to die on a Ghostlander spear today. We will wait and study them before we make contact—if we make contact."

Sensing Chelka's hesitation, Marti coaxed, "Come on, Sister-Warrior, this is our big chance to prove to these macho amadans that a woman is as good as a man at war. We can do this—truly we can."

Chelka sighed and over mar's protests she agreed to the plan. Tesulu nodded and then removed both her Speir'dina sheath and knife. Smiling, he drew it half out of its sheath to admire its lethal metal, before placing it on his own belt. "Prisoners have no need of such a fine weapon," he announced.

Chelka bared her teeth and snarled, "You will give that back when this is over, Umwira!"

"Maybe." Tesulu said, ignoring her name calling insult for the moment. "Though I don't understand how a mere woman could be found worthy of a blade fit for a war leader. Did you use your woman's magic to get it, I wonder?"

"She did not, War Leader," Mar snarled his head crest flat atop his head and teeth bared. "She was given the knife by a kashallan when she killed a Ghostland changeling agent who planned to slaughter his wives."

Tesulu gave her a mocking bow still smiling. "My apologies, Sa."

Stroking his drooping mustache, Murda glared at the Clan Warriors, his blue eyes troubled. "I still don't like it. Especially the idea of the women being bound and unarmed in an enemy fortress," he grumbled. "There's too much that could go wrong. What if the warriors in the fortress don't believe you and imprison you as well—then what?"

"Then me and Chelka will have to rescue them, too," a grinning Marti said and showed them the black razor-sharp garrote she had hidden among the curls of her hair, "because we aren't going in there unarmed. Chelka has one too hidden in her death strand."

Tesulu threw back his head and laughed. "I like you, Speir'dina; you are sly like an Oko."

"Not sure what an Oko is but thanks." She held out her wrists for Juba's tether. "I'm ready when you are, handsome. But tie the rope lose so I can get out in a hurry if I have to protect you from the big bad Ghostlanders, eh?"

"Ha! Not going to happen, woman. Don't flatter yourself," Juba said.

Marti cocked her head and grinned. "Anything is possible in war—and love, Warrior."

Juba snorted and wound his cord loosely around her wrists.

Tesulu narrowed his eyes, giving the Speir'dina female a speculative look. The woman had exaggerated female charms that could tempt a man of any species with the right type of equipment to couple with her. Was she another like the demon possessed female of her species? Maybe he would have to find out—later.

Returning his attention to the situation at hand, he said, "One more thing needs to be left behind." The War Leader pointed to Chelka's bone-scaled apron. "A prisoner has no need of a warrior woman's armor."

Chelka's face and torso turned a bright shade of green with embarrassment. Whether of bone armor or just patterned cloth, a Warlinga woman's apron covered her vulnerable breeding pouch and protected her modesty. To let men not of her close family see her unclothed was a terrible humiliation. "No!" Chelka gritted her teeth and growled deep in her throat, Mar echoing her outrage. Tesulu waited patiently, still showing his canines.

"Oh, Chelka, I know it's hard for you after what happened in Riath, but Tesulu is right. You can't go into that Ghostland fortress with the weapons and armor of a warrior. And besides, the guards in there would only take it away from you if you did, and then you might not get it back. Best leave it with Mar."

"No, she can't leave her apron with me because if Chelka is going in that fortress, then I'm going, too." Mar said.

"No you are not," Tesulu said. Juba, Ingazi are of the People. "Those changeling warriors will accept that we have come to join them, but you," he shook his head, "they would never believe it."

"I could say I was changeling bred—"

"And no one would believe you, Warlinga. Besides some of them might recognize you—is that not so?"

"He has a point, Mar," Boughthy said. "Right Sa Chelka?"

Lost in her own misery Chelka hadn't been paying attention and now everyone was staring at her.

"Sa Chelka, what are you thinking," Murda said in a soothing voice.

Words sticking in her throat, she shook her head. Couldn't they understand how hard this was for her! Recalling the taunts, the unwanted touches—the soul-destroying humiliation she had endured in Riath at the hands of Drucas and his men—she couldn't go through that again. "No—I can't do it."

Tesulu swore a Caldoni oath and glared at her. "I knew you were just a weak woman with no true warrior's spirit. Like all women from the South pampered and lazy. I think you may be good only for cooking and taking care of babies after all."

"Leave her alone." Marti swore at him in Caldoni. "She does have the spirit of a warrior, you macho asshole." Turning to Chelka she said, "Forget about men—all the stupid men. You can do this, Sister; I know you can. Tesulu's plan is a good one and if it will make you feel any better I'll strip down too. I shouldn't be wearing Lann Gheal garb either." Putting action to her words, she began climbing out of her clothes.

"Marti, what the fuck are you doing," Boughthy cried, dropping his eyes.

Marti snorted a laugh and continued undressing. "Get over it, Oglach (youngster). This isn't the first time I've gone without clothes since coming to this world."

Brave Marti. She was both her sister-warrior and her inspiration. The Speir'dina warrior woman had encouraged and stood by her when her family and most everyone she knew and loved had discouraged her from following her dreams. How could she disappoint her friend now? Taking a deep breath Chelka agreed and allowed Tesulu to remove her apron.

Tesulu glanced back at the growing dust cloud, they wouldn't arrive near here for another sun-mark or so, but his runner back to the main column needed to go soon. The war council needed time to plan. "Murda, you and Qwi'ach will go find the main band of our allies. Tell the Hunt Leader what we do. Juba, Ingazi you come with me and the women."

He studied the rebellious Mar and the younger Speir'dina armachd. What to do with them? "Mar, Boughthy, you will keep hidden and follow us. I also have heard you are good with the star weapons you carry. We may need you."

Murda sighed and nodded, then before he turned to leave, he took a small black object from a pouch at his waist and secured it in the tangled mass of Marti's braids. "Don't lose that. If you need us we'll be on channel six." He glared at Boughthy. "Got that? So set your own com to channel six." The young man nodded. Returning his attention to Marti and the War Leader, he said, "Let us know when you're in position to receive company."

Marti grinned and touched the miniature com device nested in her hair. "Tell my Sweetie I'll have tea ready when he comes calling."

Murda snorted and made a face. "If he doesn't spit that black goo on me first for letting you do this crazy stunt."

Marti laughed and blew him a kiss as he hurried up the trail to catch up with the main column.

Chapter Four

The Hunt Leader raised his eyes to the dun-colored rocks and thorn covered hills surrounding the halted column. The golden sun of this world had already sunk below the high purple mountains on the horizon.

"We should make camp soon and send out scouts, then discuss our plans further after we hear their reports." Hunt Leader Tizu turned his gaze on Tobrach and Warega, but spoke to the entire group gathered around him during their short rest break. "Anybody been this far north or know of a good campsite nearby?"

"There's a good-sized spring just inside a cave entrance a sun-mark from here, Hunt Leader, I believe," Warega said. "In my youth I traveled this way with a pack of Tragar hunters."

"Good. Send a small party of hunters to check it out, San Warega."

NOT KNOWING MUCH ABOUT military matters, Kashallan-Phillip was surprised to be summoned to attend the Alliance War Council when they made camp that evening. When he expressed that opinion to his co-husband Ma'lu Chang who'd been sent to collect him, Chang shrugged.

"I guess you'd be the head of our medical corps, so what they decide will concern you and the medics as well. Besides the clan wizards will be there," he added.

Phillip chuckled. "Does the Hunt Leader need someone besides Nathan-Corha to speak for Khutani interests in whatever they're planning?"

Chang's lips twitched. "Though Kashallan-Nathan and his parent, Maker Qwaltamis, have agreed to the alliance and most of the suggestions made by the clan wizards, they aren't thrilled to call them allies even after they've demonstrated their worth several times already. Maybe he needs you and through you Maker Tinguss to balance things out."

Sitting around their Teh'lach fire Crowis, Jojo, the young Tragar Warlinga Chi'am and the Cousins broke off their own conversation, straining to listen.

Phillip-Yoey grabbed his cup of sourwood tea and through his fur cape about his shoulders and rose. As Jojo started to follow them, Chang scowled, giving the reporter a menacing look. "Sit, Dymarian you're not invited—"

"But I have to make my report for the Imas. I—"

"Sit!" Chang made a cutting motion with his hand, his voice commanding. "The Hunt Leader will tell you what you need to know to make your damn report when they're done—and not before, Dymarian, got that? Now sit and don't try to follow us."

Plastering an innocent expression on his face Jojo slumped and reached for his tea. "I wouldn't dream of doing that, Armachd Chang. whatever gave you the idea I would do something so despicable?"

"Because you've tried listening in on conversations when you were told they were off limits before—and I'm not stupid."

"Oh, yes well I've learned my lesson."

"If not, I'll be happy to give you a refresher course." Chang smiled showing lots of teeth, and followed Phillip-Yoey into the night.

Warlinga, Clan War Leaders, Wizards and Speir'dina officers, Phillip-Yoey took his place around the central fire among the other leaders of the alliance he'd played such a big part in making. Chang crouched at his side. Hunt Leader Tizu acknowledged their appearance with a nod then returned his attention to the map Tobrach had drawn in the dirt illuminated by the green chemical rock firelight.

"How much farther is this enemy complex from our present position, K'San?" Tizu asked.

"About a half day's march from our current encampment," Tobrach estimated. "If we leave at first light we should get there while the slaves and most other inhabitants are in the fields gathering the first harvest."

"Mm, that may be, but if this complex of farms and breeding pins for the wizards enhanced warriors is as large and as important as you suggest, then it will also be well guarded."

Tobrach dipped his head crest and nodded. "That is also true, Hunt Leader, but we can't go around it and have the warriors at our backs."

"And—even if young and half trained, for the most part, they are dangerous," Goro the Red Wind war leader said in his gravelly voice.

"I'm in no doubt of that, War Leader," Tizu said. "And I am also sure the Ghostlanders down there are as aware of our presence and are preparing for our arrival. So stay alert tonight in case they have a few surprises arranged to welcome us into their territory."

"Surprises," Aju'an mused. "With Speir'dina help we may have a few surprises of our own for them."

Tizu's frown deepened. He surveyed the three species of men of the leadership council gathered around him. Some sported minor wounds plastered with yellow kavay scabs, everyone looked grim. He caught Kashallan-Nathan's eye and received the barest nod of agreement. He, too, didn't like how much the native Timornan's were counting on their off-world weaponry to get the Alliance forces out of trouble if they were in danger of losing an engagement.

But the Speir'dina knew that their off-world weapons were only one tool at their disposal, and weren't invincible. Beam rifles, C9 charges, flame throwers, grenades and the homemade clay jar bombs they'd cobbled together over the Sorins could be lost, damaged, or used up. And save for the homemade fire bombs there would be no replacements of their star weapons in future. So their Speir'dina weapons needed to be conservatively used, not only for their surprise value but to ensure they lasted as long as possible for their protection on this primitive world that the humans now had to call home.

"Like any weaponry," Nathan said, "a weapon is only as good as the warriors who wield them, so don't get lazy and rely on our weaponry to rescue you if you are stupid."

Some of the Clan warriors bristled at his implication, but Tizu cut in changing the subject. "Surprises, eh? As our Clan Allies have mentioned in the past the Ghostland wizards claim they also have technical weapons similar to Speir'dina weapons.

"Now since no one here has actually seen those weapons or watched them being used their claims may be just a bluff used in the past to keep the brave Clans from prying into their affairs too closely, but in case their threats are true, we can't afford not to take the threat seriously.

"I'm not inclined to show them all our tricks unless absolutely necessary. Got that? So stay alert."

"Most wise, Hunt Leader," Goro said. "We will be sly like an Oko, hiding in the sand until we are ready to pounce upon our prey."

Tizu didn't know what an Oko was, but when he saw the nods of agreement from the Clan warriors and some of the more experienced Warlinga he decided to ask for more clarity later—privately.

"You say this is a big fortress; the largest we've seen so far," Tizu clarified. "That means it will be well guarded with maybe a lot of civilians in there as well. I don't like the idea of killing women and children if it can be avoided."

"Hunt Leader, there won't be any women and children in the way I think you mean," Tobrach said quietly. He glanced at the Clan Warriors who nodded in agreement.

"There are only slaves and monsters bred for fighting," Lubwey said. "They have no families or clans as we do. The warriors have no fathers or mothers. From the time they hatch they must fight. Only the strong survive. And when they are older and trained all they know is the struggle."

"My Blue Stone brother speaks truth," Goro said. "When I traveled with their warband I saw these things with my own eyes."

Tizu grimaced. "I don't doubt you, Red Wind War Leader. It just isn't to my liking to kill without mercy like Ghostlanders do to our people."

"We must destroy the fortress and all those inside it, no matter how distasteful," Varrod said. "Either with our spears or with your magic weapons, it must be done."

"I am aware of that, Warriors," Tizu's dark eyes raked over the council. "I will bow to your wisdom in this, so let's discuss how to achieve the result we need. Goro, Warega, you two seem to have the most practical experience with the Ghostland war bands. What type of resistance will we face when we get there? And Elder Qwasigara, Wizard Eilo, are we likely to face a Psy-Magical attack as well...?"

PHILLIP ALLOWED THE military talk to go on around him without paying it much attention. His mind was worrying on a thorny problem of his own. If he was honest with himself he would have to admit that Tess-weh's veiled warning the other night scared him, because if it were true—and he believed it was, then he wasn't sure he would survive to return to Ishka or his duties in the Great Swamp.

Beware, Dr. Singey, for you are known and expected. If you swallow the bait offered you by the pale men in the North you will be enslaved and bound in a trap of your own making. The Sweh'an's words echoed again in his mind. He wasn't sure exactly what she meant, but for the sake of the Alliance, he might have to place himself between the Ghostland Cabal's waiting jaws in order to save all he held dear.

Chang's touch on his shoulder made him jump in surprise. Coming out of his reverie he realized that the group had fallen silent everyone staring at him. Taking a deep breath, he stammered out an apology, "I'm sorry, did someone ask me a question?"

Tizu folded his arms across his chest and after a long moment, he said, "I asked you about our medical supplies and if you needed more help with the wounded." The Hunt Leader waved his hand in a dismissive gesture. "That can wait for the moment." Leaning forward, he asked, "What's going on, Phillip-Yoey? You look like a man mulling over a difficult problem. What's on your mind, if it's not too personal?"

Phillip sighed. "Sorry for not paying as much attention as I should have been. Several things are on my mind at the moment, some personal others do concern the alliance."

"Got anything to do with whatever the Wa'chassey'ul told you a few nights ago?" Nathan asked. When he saw Kashallan-Phillip's mouth drop open he laughed. "I saw Atahru follow you to the spring. When you returned a while later you didn't look so good. Care to share Tess-weh's message with us?"

Why should he be surprised that Nathan, and maybe some of the others knew her slave had sought him out for a private talk. In the close quarters of the encampment nothing could be hidden for long.

Phillip thought about it for a moment then sighed and agreed. "You're right the demon did have a message for me, but like all her predictions and warnings it was difficult to understand, and I've been driving myself and Yoey crazy trying to figure it out. I don't think her words have much importance for the Alliance but more for me personally."

"Let me be the judge of that, Kashallan-Phillip, "Tizu said. "Please explain further; what did she say?"

<<You might as well tell them,>> his symbiont bondmate Yoey grumped. <<You're thinking about it on your own all the time anyway.>>

Phillip grimaced and set down his empty cup, and met the Hunt Leader's eye. "She told me that the Ghostland Wizards know my name."

Nathan snorted, dismissing his fears. "Of course they know you, they probably know me too, for that matter. Any of the changelings escaping north could have told the Cabal that several Speir'dina now host Khutani symbionts. That's nothing—"

"Atahru said they know me as Dr. Singey, Nathan, not Kashallan-Phillip or Phillip-Yoey—Dr. Singey."

Nathan sat back on his heels. "Shi-it."

Looking at the puzzled expressions on the native Timornans faces, Phillip explained, "In my old home among the stars I was called Dr. Phillip Singey. Since my bonding with Yoey I have stopped using my family name of Singey. I am no longer that man."

"And for the Cabal to know that name means that Sadrew or some of that bunch of assholes that remained at the base after we left for Ticca were captured and made it to the Ghostlands," Tizu mused, thinking out loud.

"Shit," Nathan said repeating himself shaking his head. "If they know about you then they probably know about Dr. Bennett the Hunt Leader and Councilor Arishim, too."

"Good thing we didn't leave them anything in the way of weaponry but a few side arms," Chang said, "because those amadans sure wouldn't be singing our praises to the wizards. They probably have a bounty on our heads—wanted, dead or alive."

Ross snorted a laugh. "Dead most like."

Nathan shrugged. "Dead most like—all of us."

"I don't understand, Kashallan-Nathan," Aju'an said, his headrest lowered. "Are you saying that some of your own kin have allied themselves with the Ghostlanders and want you the Hunt Leader and Kashallan-Phillip dead?"

"Those assholes are no kin to me," Chang murmured so only Philip-Yoey could hear. Phillip's lip twitched, sharing his co-husband's opinion.

"Not exactly," Nathan explained. "When our ship was destroyed and we were stranded here, there were a few among us that wouldn't accept that a rescue vessel wasn't coming to take us back to our old homes among the stars. Even when they became sick with the kavay alignment they refused to believe they would never leave Timorna."

"We warned them about the Sorin Storms and wanted them to come with us to Ticca, but the stupid shits wouldn't listen—so we left them," Chang growled.

"When we got back to the base after the storm season we thought they had all died, but I guess we were mistaken," Nathan said.

"The old Begta shaman told me that a war band from the North came to the base with the first Sorin storms," Phillip said. "They must have found Sadrew and his bunch and took them North."

Well if any of them are still alive up there, they certainly aren't singing our praises to the Cabal," Chang said.

"No those shit for brains amadans would not be singing our praises. They'd more likely be out for revenge, most like," Tizu agreed. "But fortunately Dr. B and the rest are back in the Yeyen and safe for the moment." Focusing his black stare on Phillip-Yoey, he said, "but not you. I should send you back tomorrow—"

Phillip-Yoey shook his head, cutting him off. "No, you can't, Hunt Leader, because you need me—and I wouldn't go even if you tried to send me." When Tizu opened his mouth to protest, Phillip held up a hand to stop him. "Hunt Leader, please listen. You asked a while ago about what was troubling me and why I was so distracted tonight. My concerns are more than just personal they concern the wellbeing of all our forces, so please hear me out."

Tizu scowled at the challenge to his authority, but nodded for the kashallan to continue.

"I know our warbands are a match for the Ghostland monsters—I have complete faith in your ability to overcome them. And with Khutani and our Western Clan wizards fighting for us in the Dream, I believe we will win on that front too." Phillip-Yoey leaned forward and met the eye of every man on the Council ending up with Tizu, who caught his gaze and held it.

"But what really frightens me, and why I can't consider my personal safety, and why you can't afford to send me back to Tragar or the Yeyen is because there's a big hole in your defenses that you haven't even considered yet."

Startled Tizu leaned back as if he'd been struck. He glanced around the fire and saw other puzzled faces. Returning to Nathan Tizu raised an eyebrow. Nathan shook his head. He didn't know either what Phillip was talking about. "All right, explain, Phillip-Yoey."

Phillip sighed and nodded. "Neither Yoey or I know a word in the Timornan languages to name what I'm thinking, so I will say it first in Galactic Standard then I'll try to explain for our Timornan allies."

"Get on with it, Phillip," Tizu growled.

"Biological warfare. I think the Cabal has the potential to use neurotoxins or some other unknown biological agent against us, like the agent that caused the great plague that killed off so many seven hundred years ago, and the drug that almost killed Dunnagh-Tani when he was captured and tortured in Riath. That's what gives me nightmares, Hunt Leader."

"Damn, I hadn't thought of that," Nathan said. "They would have to have labs—or something like a lab where they experiment and make these toxins,"

"Yes, Amsi, they would have to," Yoey said, "because they can't make medicines or poisons like we can in our own bodies."

"And I am the only one among us with enough scientific background to possibly recognize those facilities," Phillip added. "And that's why you can't send me back to Riath. You will need me to help you find their labs and destroy them and all they contain."

"Damn, I think Dunnagh would agree with you," Nathan said. "When we were back at Sulas he was always worried about the Avairei putting something in our food that would make us their mindless slaves in truth."

"Yes, I remember that," Phillip agreed. "And our imagined threat from the Avairei is nothing compared to the real threat these Ghostland Wizards could pose to us now."

He turned to Hunt Leader Tizu and continued, "This world, as we well know, has little in the way of metal ores left after the old wars. And what might still be there is too deep in the ground for their technology to make use of. But all the Natives of Timorna are far more advanced in their uses of biochemical products and genetic manipulations than most societies out there among the stars. Hunt Leader I suspect that one of the surprises the enemy may have in store for us will be some kind of biological weapon. It's what I'd do in their place."

Tizu swore viciously in Caldoni. When he calmed down, he turned to the wizards and the warriors around the fire. "Do you understand what Phillip-Yoey is telling us?"

"He is speaking of plant and fungal poisons that can kill, cripple, or enslave a man's will," Eilo said into the silence that followed.

Tizu leaned forward to look the Red Wind Wizard in the eye. "And do you and your people know about these poisons—and use them?"

After some hesitation, Qwasigara nodded. "I know about—some things, but the Ghostlanders may know much more, but they won't share their magics with us."

"And I too know some things, but don't use them," Eilo finally admitted. "Because there is no need we can defeat our enemies with the war magics, so we rarely use—"

"The wise One speaks truth; we never use foul poisons, Hunt Leader," Goro said angrily, folding his upper pair of arms across his scarred chest. "Only a sniveling coward would use such a weapon."

"There's no honor in using such trickery to win," Ogwy, the Blue Stone war leader said with a toss of his head.

"As a newcomer to this world, I mean no insult by asking about these things. There may be no honor in using such a tactic, true," Tizu said, "but biological weapons, as we call them, are effective."

Tizu pointed toward the purple sky. "Up there the Lann Gheal forces under my command have faced enemies with biological weapons before—and won, but the problem now is that if we face that kind of threat we don't know Timornan poisons—or their antidotes—and we don't have any of the protections we've used in the past. So that's why we will need your help."

"Kashallan-Phillip," Ross asked, "are you thinking that this fortress we are nearing might contain one of these labs?"

Phillip suppressed a shudder. "That's a frightening thought, Armachd, but I have no way of knowing."

The dog-faced elder Qwasigara spoke with Eilo in a low murmur then he shook his head. "Anything is possible, but not likely."

"And why is that, Elders?" Tizu asked.

"The Cabal would want to keep such a powerful magics secret and protected from their enemies—all their enemies."

"Hmm, so what you are implying is that those who now rule may have enemies among their own people and not just us," Tizu mused, his expression thoughtful.

"That is exactly what we mean, Hunt leader," Eilo said. "Barak was a powerful Ancient. He had been granted magics from his many visits to the sacred places upon the Plain of Poison Fires. He ruled the Cabal with a will of the hardest stone. No one dared defy him. But now that he is gone—" the Red Wind Wizard shrugged. "Whatever knowledge he and his supporters have will be closely guarded from other factions among the ruling Cabal who might want to seize power for themselves."

"I doubt if there are any 'labs' as you call them at this fortress," Goro said. "We are too far away from Tiebarai; those who now rule couldn't be sure of the loyalty of those who run the breeding farms."

"The Cabal might give the warriors orders, but the little grey mushrooms would never share their secrets with those they feel are so far beneath them," Lubwey said and couldn't keep the tone of bitterness out of his voice.

There was a chorus of growled agreement from the Western Clan leaders to his statement. The council fell silent after that mulling over what had been said so far.

After a time of contemplation Warega said as if thinking out loud, "Tiebarai, I can remember Gormach's mighty father speaking of that place. He claimed it was like Riath in the Yeyen Banai. He never went that far north with his hunting packs, but swore it was the place where the rulers of the Ghostlands dwell. He always said we would have to go there and destroy it, if we wanted an end to the threat from the North."

"As much as I don't want to admit it the Tragar K'San was right," Goro said. "We will have to make war on and destroy Tiebarai."

"And in hidden tunnels near Tiebarai is where you will find the places where they make these powerful magics," Qwasigara said.

"If it is as important as you think, Elder, then we will have to take it and destroy the threat that it poses for all of us," Nathan said. He met the eye of each of the Western Clansmen. "Can you tell us more about the place; anybody been there?"

The Westerners looked at one another then shook their heads. "Years ago I was persuaded along with other Red Wind men to join a warband of the Ghostlanders," Goro finally said. "On my way home I went with them as far North as Fa'Hanzoi. Even though we had wounded with us the arrogant Ghostland pukes turned us away from that place and wouldn't give us food or medicines for our wounded. It was a hard journey back across the Shallow Sea," he added bitterly. "Though the slaves and booty were tempting, after that I wouldn't war with them."

Slaves and booty were dangerous topics to discuss in this mixed company, so hoping to distract the Council before old grudges could be unearthed, Phillip said, "Tiebarai, Fa'Hanzoi, they sound more like what the Speir'dina would call cities and towns, places where people live together all the year around, rather than just a Sun-Season meeting place like Riath is for the most part. And am I right in assuming these places are located underground?"

"Yes, you would be right," Eilo said, then smirked. "The little grey mushrooms hate the sun. Like any fungi you will find them in the caves and tunnels hollowed out under the mountains. Only their slaves and savages like us," he raised a hand to encompass the other Clan warriors around him, "are strong enough to live in the sunlight and air of the world."

"And when they do have to walk upon the surface world they shade their eyes and cover themselves completely in pale cloth," Goro added.

Ross laughed. "Covered in white, that must be why they got named Ghostlanders by the rest of you Timornans."

"If they have been living underground since the time of the Great Wars they probably have adapted to their environment with large eyes and pale skin and white hair—if they have any. The cave-dwelling creatures I've seen on other worlds have evolved in that way," Phillip-Yoey mused, thinking out loud.

Not realizing he had spoken for all to hear, he jumped when Qwasigara agreed with him. "In my youth I came across the body of one of their wizards near one of the holy places where I had come to pray." An expression of distaste crossed the Elder's face. "It had failed in its quest for power and lay stripped and dead upon the rocks. Colorless skin and big eyes as you said, Khutani, but no fur."

"That's interesting to know," Tizu said. "Their eyes can probably see much better than we can in the dim light of their tunnels, which puts us at a disadvantage."

"Maybe, but not perhaps as much as you think, Hunt Leader," Warega said. "Their warriors bred to fight and raid in our lands see no different than we do."

"That's true," Lubwey agreed

"That's good to know," Tizu said. Then, turning to Ross he asked, "Have we got enough night scopes with us to supply all the Speir'dina? Our eyes aren't as sensitive to low light as the Natives. We will probably need them if we are to fight effectively in the underground towns."

"I will have to check, Sir."

"Do that and get back to me."

Still thinking about the terrain in which they would be fighting, Nathan said, "I remember when we were fleeing the changelings at Sulas, Dunnagh-Tani led us on a trail that followed the River Magra. We passed several ancient ruins that looked like abandoned town sites. Would I be correct that Tiebarai and other sites would probably be located along underground rivers like that?"

"I have heard it is so, Khutani," Qwasigara said.

"Those inflatable boats you had me put in our supplies may come in handy after all," Ross said to Tizu.

"They may at that," Tizu agreed. "Too bad we don't have more of them."

"Good for scouting patrols at least," Nathan said. "They wouldn't expect us to be coming by water.

"That's a thought if we get that far, but for now let's focus on the enemy fortress we have in front of us," Tizu said, returning the talk to the problem at hand.

They were about to end the meeting for the night when McLaren brought a dusty and exhausted Murda and Qwi'ach to report.

Chapter Five

"Hey, Boughthy, you asleep up there?"

"No, Marti, we aren't asleep. What do you want?"

"Tell Command it's a go. We are making contact now."

"Affirmative, Armachd. Mar has you in the day-scopes. We got your back. Good hunting."

Tesulu surveyed the five warriors in his band. With a little creative disguising on his part, the women now looked like the bloody and battered prisoners they were supposed to be. And he and his men sported cuts and blood of their own, hoping to reinforce their story of being hunted renegades fleeing capture by the enemy.

Motioning for Ingazi and Juba to take up the women's tethers Tesulu led the band out of concealment and onto the trail just ahead of the enemy warriors. There were about ten to twelve of them accompanied by one curtained litter and a few more low ranking Avairei walking beside it. In the rear were some exhausted Loti with heavy packs on their backs.

As he stepped forward to meet the newcomers, Chelka murmured so only Tesulu and Juba could hear. "The Warlinga leading this bunch is K'San Glatu Sotok. The family is aligned with the Segoi by marriage. Not sure how they escaped the roundup of Dingay supporters."

Tesulu grunted and stepped forward a wide smile plastered on his face. "Greetings, Cousins, your company is most welcome."

Tesulu's greeting in the Ghostland dialect didn't lower the array of spears leveled at them, but the tall well-muscled Warlinga at their head did step forward to meet him. "What are you doing in Ghostland territory Western Savage?"

Ooh, savage, eh? Tesulu didn't let his anger show but inside he vowed to make this piece of arrogant puke pay for that insult—soon. "Why the same as you, no doubt, half-bred Khutani Slave. We've come to honor the ancient covenant sworn between our peoples. We are here to fight the Hated Enemy."

The Warlinga's head crest flattened at the insult, but Tesulu ignored his threat display and held his ground, still smiling. "You come out of nowhere and expect me to believe that, Begta Puke?"

"We didn't come out of nowhere; we've been watching you for some time now, not sure at first if you were friends or more of the Khutani's slaves hunting us," Tesulu growled in protest.

Glatu snorted looking down his snout at the slightly smaller man. "And why would the Enemy care about three ragged hunters?"

"They press us hard, because we took something valuable, and they want it back. It would be safer for us if we join you."

"What are you talking about? Why should I care if you are being hunted—or what you stole?"

"Because taking us with you would be to your advantage, Stupid Begta, are you blind?" Before the man could answer Tesulu's insult with tooth and claw, Tesulu walked to Chelka and jerked her head up to display Drucas's brand upon her forehead. "Do you see now? What we stole is not only of value to the Enemy, but the Segoi K'San as well."

Not sure if this was some kind of Enemy trick, Glatu hissed and came forward to examine Chelka's mark more closely. Lifting her head without being forced, Marti stared defiantly into the Warlinga's red eyes when it was her turn.

"We have come to return the K'San's property to him as I said," Tesulu repeated.

Glatu snorted and folded his arms across his scaled chest. "And be rewarded for your trouble, no doubt."

"Of course. The females are young healthy and strong. Offered as brides to our warriors, they will make us many fine children. Why wouldn't we expect some compensation for giving them away?"

Glatu laughed and drew his knife. "And what's to prevent me from claiming your prize for my own and leaving you dead upon the trail, hmm?"

"That would not be wise," Tesulu said, drawing Chelka's Speir'dina knife and putting it against her throat, Ingazi doing the same to Marti. "If you try we will kill them, and what do you think K'San Drucas will do to you when he finds out, hmm?"

"Enough, Warlinga, we waste time." While the warriors were arguing the ranking Avairei Ima had descended from her litter and come up to the group unnoticed. An imposing woman with a mottled pelt and grey around her mouth, she gave both the changeling warriors and the Clansmen a haughty glare. "K'San Glatu, if this fortress is as close as you think, then we need to get moving before the Enemy *does* discover us."

"But Ima, they might be spies."

"What of it? Are you saying you can't handle three savages?" the Changeling turned green with her implied insult. "Besides, I recognize them. And the savage is right, the Warlinga female especially K'San Drucas will want to reclaim unharmed." The Ima folded her furred arms across her chest and smirked. "Are you looking forward to your stay in the Ghostlands, Sa Chelka?"

"Not particularly, Ima Alimay, especially since a traitor like you is here and not dead in Riath," Chelka snarled. "I wonder what the Ghostland wizards will do with you, now that you're too old for a breeding farm—"

Chelka might have spat out more insults, but Tesulu hit her, but not too hard, only hard enough to shut her up before she said too much and they might have to defend themselves against the whole hunting pack.

"Your will, Ima" Glatu snarled. "You are right; we do need to keep moving." He motioned for Tesulu and his warriors to take places in the middle of the pack, surrounded by his men. Without further delay the column began moving again. There was no point arguing further now about the prisoners. The western vermin could be dealt with once they were inside the fortress of Te'gal.

Blocked by Ingazi on one side and Juba on the other Marti raised her bound hands to her face. While wiping the sweat and blood away she reached into her hair and tapped the com device in a silent code that not only turned it on, but sent out a silent message that everything was all right—they were going in.

"BOUGHTHY, THIS IS MAIN camp. Give us a report." Rhys's voice was a soft whisper next to the young armachd's ear.

In a low voice Boughthy answered, "War Leader Tesulu and his patrol have made contact with the changelings and are now travelling among them to the enemy stronghold, Sir. We are moving our position to keep them in sight in case they need us."

"I'll tell the Hunt Leader. We are moving into position for the frontal assault. Let us know if the situation changes on your end."

Turning to Nathan, Rhys said, "They've made contact with the enemy, Sir. It's a go."

Nathan-Corha grunted and held out his hand for the scopes. Rhys handed them over and he focused them in on the distant dust cloud of people heading at a rapid pace for the fortress built into the side of the mountain a click and a half downhill from their position.

<<Our Marti is so smart and brave, going with the Clan warriors to open the gates for us, isn't she, Kasha?>> Corha burbled excitedly.

Nathan snorted and patted his middle. <<Those wouldn't be the first words I would use to describe this risky plan she agreed to be a part of, Shalla, but we can't do anything about it now. But if that shit for brains, Tesulu gets her or Chelka killed with this crazy stunt, I'm not sure who will kill him first, me or Tobrach,>> he grumped.

Corha was silent for a long time, then it finally said, <<Kasha, why are you so angry? Our Marti is a warrior. She wouldn't like it if we were always sheltering her from danger. You know that, right?>>

Nathan sighed. <<Yeah, I know. You're right as usual, Shalla. I guess I'm angry because she might be killed and I would lose another I care about.>>

There was a pause as Corha thought about it. Finally it said, <<She could die even if we did everything in our power to keep her safe.>>

<<Yeah, maybe. But I'm still going to half-kill her when we see her again,>> he grumped.

Corha gave him a mental laugh. <<No, you won't, Kasha. We will hug her and tell her how much we love her, and that we are glad she's safe.>>

<<Yeah, all that and then I'm going to half kill her for being such a reckless amadan.>>

The Ghostland fortress he saw seemed to be built into the mountain with half of its bulk underground and sheltered from the poisonous radio-active storms called Sorins. These storms blew down from the dead continent to the north after the final harvest each year.

What they could see were the Sun Season quarters above ground and the maze of pens where the slaves and young monster warriors were trained and kept. Spread out along a small river, flowing out of the mountain were fields lush with food plants of various types. Most of what he saw was unfamiliar to him, but he did recognize the grey furry leaves of masa root from his own time spent as a slave at Sulas when they first came to this world. He felt a twinge in his back in sympathy with the exhausted slaves he saw bent-over laboring under the cruel eyes of Ghostland overseers.

"Rhys, let Command know the situation and ask if there are further orders." Concealed behind rocks and the wizard-cast illusions of rocks, several Teh'lach of the Allied army were in position along the surrounding hillsides. On a perch higher up an adjacent ridge Hunt Leader, Varrod and the Clan wizards stood surveying the action. Nearby crouched several young men to act as runners where the com units were in short supply or might be blocked by walls of rock.

"Turning to the runners, Tizu said, Cho, Nytaka, go tell Hunt Leader Warega and War leader Ogwy to take some of their warriors and harass that column coming up to the fortress down there." His voice became stern as he added, "The attack is just a trick, mind. You be sure they understand that. Some of our people are now among the enemy and we don't want them killed, got that?"

The young warriors nodded their understanding as he continued, "I want a diversion only, something to hurry them along and have the gate guards ask no questions before admitting them. When our people inside give us the go ahead, then—and only then we will attack in full force. You two understand?" they bobbed their heads eagerly, proud of the honor they were being given. "Repeat your message back to me so I know you got it right," Tizu said.

When the young warriors were gone, Eilo gave Tizu an approving nod. "Most wise, Hunt Leader, I think it is a good plan."

"I hope you're right, Wizard Eilo, and I hope those fools obey my orders and don't take it into their heads to do something reckless and stupid."

Eilo snorted a laugh. "Warriors. Yes, we can only hope."

Chapter Six

"Hunt Leader Tizu is going to send some of our warriors to create a diversion to help us get inside without the guards asking questions. So tell the War Leader, and when they attack don't kill anybody on our side, got that?" Marti murmured to Juba and Ingazi on either side of her,

The warriors' expressions never changed, but Juba moved slightly forward to give Tesulu her message.

It wasn't long after her warning that Warega's men followed by Ogwy's came roaring out of concealment, one down the slope to the side and the other slightly behind them.

Confusion broke out as the Avairei screamed in fear and the Loti began kicking out wildly, unable to distinguish friend from enemy in their panic. The ones carrying Ima Alimay's litter dropped it with a splintering crash and took off at a stumbling run back down the way they'd come.

Over the dust and the chaos Marti could hear K'San Glatu shouting orders to his men. Moving off to one side Tesulu placed the unarmed women between the three allied warriors, forming a protective shield around them. Occasionally they thrust out their spears as if fending off an attack but made sure not to wound their pretend adversaries. At one point Warega maneuvered himself close enough to call out to Chelka in a low voice, "Are you all right, Sa Chelka?"

Looking up at the sound of her name, Chelka blinked finally recognizing Tobrach's hunt leader. Knowing he was seeing her un-aproned she turned green with embarrassment.

"She's fine, Tragar Hunt Leader," Tesulu said and aimed a spear thrust in the man's direction, which Warega blocked easily. "Tell the K'San I will keep her safe for him; he need not worry."

"You had better," Warega growled and aimed his own thrust at Tesulu's middle.

Tesulu laughed and hopped nimbly out of the way. "Go now, Old Hunter, before I have to seriously hurt you to maintain our disguise."

Warega might have said more but at that point their sparring caught the attention of one of Glatu's men. As he rushed over to attack the Warlinga, Tesulu stepped in close and under the cover of the choking dust, slipped Chelka's long Speir'dina blade between overlapping scales and into a vulnerable organ under the changeling's arm.

The man dropped without a sound at a startled Warega's feet. "That's one less of the vermin for us to worry about," he said and smiled as he wiped the knife clean and then sheathed it. As Warega just stood there staring, Tesulu snarled, "Go, Hunter, before you undo our plan. The woman will be fine; I give you my word. Go!"

Fortunately an alarm horn sounded from the guards at the fortress at that moment and orders were shouted for the Allied warriors to make a hasty retreat. Warega looked back once and caught Chelka's eye for a moment then leapt up hill following his men.

Tesulu motioned for his patrol to move forward, away from the dead changeling, so no one would suspect he had a hand in his death.

As they were surrounded and hurried into the outer courtyard of the fortress, Marti looked back and saw some of the Ghostlanders giving chase to the Allied warriors racing for cover among the rocks up the slope.

As they drew near the Ghostlanders were met by a volley of crossbow bolts from the men hidden among the boulders and hastily retreated back down the slope.

Glatu had stopped just inside the gate to watch the combat as well. At last he turned to Tesulu, and said, "It seems there may be a seed of truth in your story after all, Savage." He broke off as a disheveled Ima Alimay began angrily berating him for his incompetence. Her litter had been smashed in the skirmish and she had been forced to run along with the hunting pack for the safety of Te'gal.

Chelka's lips curled into a mirthless smile. She had enjoyed seeing the haughty Ima choking and struggling to keep up with the Warlinga. Glatu had refused to have one of his men carry her, claiming they were needed for their defense should the enemy stage another attack.

Knowing that many of the Speir'dina and even some of the Avairei travelling with the Speir'dina often sat astride willing Loti's backs, Chelka had laughed and told her to ride a Loti. Alimay sent her a dagger look and ignored the suggestion which caused Chelka and Marti to exchange smiles.

It didn't matter anyway most of the Loti had taken the opportunity to escape, led to safety by some hunters from Warega's pack. With the added supplies they carried they also might provide the Alliance with valuable information about the Enemy.

The gates closed after the last of the Ghostland warriors were inside. With whips and goads their burly handlers returned them to their enclosure, where they continued to howl for the enemy's blood.

Marti turned away from the clamor and looked toward the steps that led to the inner keep. There she saw a Pale six-limbed creature dressed in a long robe flanked by two leashed warriors emerging from the shadows of the doorway. The creature's head was draped in pale fabric with part of the garment's folds also covering the lower half of its face. The Ghostlander's face not concealed behind veils was shaded by a tinted glass visor of some sort that masked its eyes from view. Clustered behind the three on the steps she could detect several more curious onlookers, but could tell little about them in the dim light coming from inside the fortress.

Currents of power and unknown danger swirled about this veiled being. Marti shivered as a Psy warning ran down her spine. They had done it; they were inside, but things weren't going to go as smoothly as Tesulu planned. An image of Nathan's face appeared in her mind. He looked worried and frightened. *Oh love*, she thought. *You always said I was too impulsive, too reckless. I'm sorry. I hope I will live to see you again.*

As the creature paused at the top of the steps and surveyed them behind its impenetrable eye shield, Marti cursed colorfully in Caldoni.

Through the bone conducting communication device tucked against her skull she heard Rhys say, "Marti it's Rhys here; what's wrong?"

"Nothing—yet. I just saw one of the ghosts from the Ghostlands, and the bacach gives me a creepy feeling. I think it might be the one in charge here," she murmured under her breath.

"Describe it so I can tell Command, Armachd."

"Later, too many around right now for me to talk much."

"keep this channel open so we can come in if you need us."

Marti tapped her cheek in response. It eased her mind somewhat to know help wasn't far away if needed, whether they all survived this mission, even with help so near was a whole other matter, however.

Hearing her mumbled cursing then her talking to someone through her com Tesulu glanced at her, and said just as quietly, "What did they say to you, Speir'dina?"

"I just told Command that we made it inside the fortress. They said if we needed help they would come in to rescue us."

Tesulu snorted. "We won't need their help—" He broke off at a whispered warning from Juba, and then looked in the direction in which he was staring. He hissed. "A true Ghostlander has come out to greet us," Tesulu murmured so only his patrol could hear. "What an honor for us," he said, the irony clear from his tone of voice. "You are seeing one of the pale mushrooms, a member of the exalted elite class, but not a very high ranking one, I think."

"He looks like the one in charge here, that's elite enough for me," Marti said, "but how can you tell his rank, War Leader?"

"I have heard it said that the true rulers in the North, the ones in the Cabal, are creatures small and slim with only four limbs not six like us. They say they are descended from the Ancients of Timorna and all those with the extra limbs are low-born mutants, but it's a lie. My people in the West are the true descendants of the Ancient Ones. Only we are strong enough to live in the sun, and brave the Sorin storms and survive."

Glatu had also noticed the personage on the steps and moved forward to greet the Ghostlander, the rest of them following as well. When he arrived at the base of the steps he surprised Marti by sinking to one knee and bowing his head. The rest of his hunters and even the proud Ima Alimay did the same.

Marti blinked. This was the first time she had seen this kind of behavior since coming to this world. That of course left Tesulu and his warriors still standing and exposed.

"Kneel, Savage," came a snarled command from one of Glatu's hunters nearby.

Tesulu tossed his ponytail back over his shoulder and looked down his nose at the kneeling changelings. Then in a voice loud enough for the

Ghostlander to hear, he said, "No, why should I kneel? I'm no sniveling half-bred Khutani slave. I'm a son of the Sand Mountain lineage of the Real People." He bowed to the personage on the steps. "I offer you honor and respect, Excellence, but I do not grovel at the feet of anyone."

Through half closed eyes Marti saw the Ghostlander focus his gaze in their direction. "Ah, you speak a civilized tongue. What is your name, *Son of the Real People?*"

Arrogant prick. Was there a hint of mockery in that soft papery voice?

Tesulu must have thought so, too, because he puffed out his chest and glared at the slim robed figure. "I am Tesulu, a war leader of the Sand Mountain clan of the People. I speak many languages; all of them 'civilized.' So who are you?"

His words were stated boldly, not caring if he gave offense to the person so clearly in charge. Glatu cursed under his breath—something about the dim-witted savage maybe getting them all killed, and a few of the Avairei moaned in fear. Tesulu and his men ignored them and continued to stand their ground, waiting for an answer. The chained warriors at the Ghostlander's side growled deep in their throats, their A-symmetrical faces twisting into grotesque shapes and they flexed their long claws in a threat display.

Nearby Marti heard Chelka murmur, "Have a care, War Leader or your arrogance will get us all killed." Tesulu ignored her, too, and folded his upper set of arms across his chest, waiting.

At last the Ghostlander barked a harsh laugh and silenced the monsters with a gesture. "I am The Distinguished Commander Calahar. You have courage, I will give you that, but understand this as well. It is I who command here at Te'gal, *Western Cousin*. And from now on, I will tolerate no challenge to my authority. Do you understand me, Savage."

Tesulu smiled showing his canines and held out his upper set of arms away from his sides. "I have no desire to challenge your authority, Distinguished. I came here only to fight the enemy as was pledged in the Ancient Covenant between our peoples."

That earned him a derisive snort from K'San Glatu. "You came to fight the enemy, eh? And just exactly what enemy would that be?"

"Why, the Khutani and their slaves, Changeling K'San."

Glatu snorted again. "I saw today that many Western Clan Warriors fight with the Khutani-bred slaves, so are you traitor to your own kin or are you a spy."

Tesulu drew himself up to his full height and bared his teeth in a snarl. "I am neither, Begta Puke, I am no slimy spy. True many of my kin have chosen to fight alongside our Hated Enemy, but we chose to keep faith with the Ancients and join our kin in the North. And as proof—"

Tesulu stepped aside so that commander Calahar could see his prisoners. "As we traveled North we surprised a small party foraging for food. We killed the men but took these two captive." He stepped forward and squeezed Chelka's bicep and grinned at her when she bared her teeth at him. "As you can see, distinguished, they are young and strong. They would give us many healthy children. But then," he raised Chelka's head and touched a clawed finger to the sigil on her forehead. "I saw this and I knew I couldn't keep her—both females belong to K'San Drucas Segoi. So, my men and I decided to bring them to him.

"But the Enemy discovered our trail. They pressed us hard, because this one is claimed by one of their leaders, she tells me." Tesulu laughed. "She also says he will kill me horribly if I don't let her go."

Tesulu thumped his muscular chest and laughed again. "I am a warrior of the Real People. I care nothing for the puny threats of the Khutani's slaves. So we keep her and the other one."

"An admirable sentiment, Cousin. I'm sure the K'San will be most *grateful.*" Then noticing Marti for the first time, Calahar let out a startled hiss, and then walked closer to have a better look at her.

"Ah, is this one of the strange mutants I've been hearing so much about? Well, well, Savage, I have no need of more unknown warriors. My own breeding stock is quite adequate for our defense, but the mutant—you may indeed have brought us something of value to pay for your keep after all. Our Breeding Master will want to see this one."

Tesulu put a possessive hand on Marti's shoulder. "Perhaps—in time, after K'San Drucas and I discuss our payment for these fine healthy females." He motioned with his lips to her sigil. "She too is the property of the K'San. I think it would be wise to wait and let him decide what is to be done with his property—after he pays us, of course."

"K'San Drucas obeys the will of the Great and Exalted Master Barak, and the Master has ordered any of us to seize and examine any mutants that we find," Calahar said. "You have done the Master a great service, Western Cousin. You will be suitably rewarded, I assure you."

"Don't you know? Barak is dead."

Calahar reeled as if Tesulu had delivered him a mighty blow.

"That's a despicable lie, Western Vermin," Glatu shouted leaping to his feet."

Tesulu allowed his hand to rest lightly on the Speir'dina knife at his hip, through back his head and laughed. "I do not lie, Changeling Puke. All in the west know it is so. Barak was killed at Red Rock by a demon the Khutani bound to their service. Your Great Master was killed as were many others in the Wizards' Conclave during the battle."

Tesulu smirked, warming to his tale. "Of course the creature's host and her protector were killed in turn, so his death didn't go unavenged. But that is why my men here and I decided to come North to fight. We didn't like how so many of the People sided with the Khutani after that."

In the silence that followed this revelation Chelka let out a taunting laugh. "This half-bred Begta speaks true—damn him to the Black Pit. Who will protect you now, K'San? You failed in Riath and the cabal may not be so forgiving. Sorry you came North, Changeling, Ima Alimay?"

Tesulu raised a fist and cuffed her. "Be silent, Woman!" Tesulu had restrained his blow, but it had been hard enough to hurt and she bared her teeth and made a lunge for his throat. Juba cursed and pulled hard on her tether as a grinning Tesulu hopped out of range.

Chest heaving and still muttering curses, Chelka allowed herself to be brought back under control. Turning once more to the onlookers, he said to Calahar. "Strong and healthy as I said. K'San Drucas will enjoy taming her, but until then, the females—both females remain our property."

Calahar remained silent, surveying his guests behind the shade of his coverings. At last he said in a falsely soothing voice, "But of course, Western Cousin. It will be as you say. But you must be tired. All of you must be tired." The Ghostlander waved a hand to include Glatu and the other dusty and exhausted changelings still clustered about the steps.

"Come inside out of this blistering light. I will have my Second Nasrid and our slaves prepare food and comfortable nests for your rest.

It was impossible to see the creature's eyes through the tinted glass covering them, but Marti shivered as if it could see right into her mind and knew their secrets. Trembling she reached out with her bound hands as the Ghostlander turned to go back inside and grasped Ingazi's hand and held on tight. He covered hers with one of his lower hands and squeezed gently to reassure her.

As they started forward, she whispered, "Tell Tesulu to be careful. I don't trust these people to keep their word. I've had—a sending."

Ingazi glanced at her sharply. "You have the magic?"

She nodded. "A little. Sometimes I see—I know things—and this is one of those times. Please tell the war leader and be careful—all of us need to be very careful."

Chapter Seven

After giving instructions to Nasrid, his second in command, to arrange quarters for the changelings and the westerners, Calahar returned to the cool dimness of his own apartment in the inner keep and closed the door. He took off the face coverings and the outer robes of his office that concealed his narrow shoulders and thin build. Removing a lidded box from a wicker cabinet, Calahar sank into the padded chair at his work table.

With trembling hands he removed a small clay bowl, the jars needed to make the chemical green fire mix, a lump of dried brown fungus, and set them on the table in front of him. Measuring out small amounts of the two rock powders carefully, he heard a hiss as a bright green flame appeared in the bottom of the bowl as he mixed them.

When the flame burned with an even light, Calahar broke off a piece of the brown fungus and placed it atop the flame. When a thick gray smoke appeared, Calahar bent low over the bowl and covered his face and head with a heavy cloth. In the darkness he took in several deep breaths, allowing the fumes to flow deep into his lungs.

Ah, Malloneen, the Tempting Smoke. He could feel his body relax under its fragrant caress. He had needed this. Though he didn't want to admit it, the savage's revelation about Master Barak had both angered and frightened him. If it was true—and he was reasonably sure it was true—then that would explain the lack of communications coming to them from Tiebarai lately. No it was true; there was no gain for the western savage in lying about such an important thing. Barak's death was something that could be easily checked and terrible consequences would befall whoever dared to spread such a lie.

An ironic smile played about the corners of his thin-lipped mouth. The ruling Cabal must be in turmoil, everyone trying to gain a place in the new order. Calahar took another deep breath and held the smoke in his lungs for as long as possible. Idly he wondered who would succeed the Great Barak, and how many would die in the struggle.

No matter, what did he care stuck in this putrid frontier posting. The affairs of the Exalted were none of his concern. Whoever assumed power he would still be cursed with the job of overseeing the breeding of monsters, and slaves. Oh his position here was one of power and authority, true, but damn him to the Poison Fires, he still lacked the power to recall himself to the Capital and a civilized posting elsewhere.

His frustration mounting as his mind traveled down this familiar trail, he gulped in more of the fragrant smoke, hoping to find peace and oblivion in its alluring visions for a time. In a sane corner of his mind he knew he was playing a dangerous game with himself. He'd been resorting to the Smoke with increasing frequency the longer he remained among the monsters and the degenerates resident at Te'gal.

Malloneen had its addictive qualities. He had seen the tortured bodies of those who had gone too far and allowed themselves to become slaves to Malloneen's seductive allure. Big eyes red and weeping, gaunt as reeds and bleeding sores covering their pale skins, they haunted the dark alleys of Tiebarai and Fa'Hanzoi. They would do anything for another taste of the seductive Smoke.

Calahar shuddered and told himself he would never be one of them. Malloneen helped him relax that was all. It helps ease the bitterness that was eating away at his insides for being stuck in this back water fortress so far away from civilization. He could control his need—his hunger. Now if he used Crivo, The Enslaver, or Thaufda, the one they called the Sweet Hunger, then he might have to worry, because if overused, or in the wrong hands the unsuspecting could be enslaved against their will.

Ignoring his duties and the threat posed by the Allied Force outside his gate, Calahar leaned back in his chair and was drifting into a pleasant dream when a knock on his door jerked him back from the edge and into wakefulness. "Enter," he growled, annoyed by the interruption.

Nasrid came in and closed the door behind himself. A tall muscular man with a bald head, and the big eyes of his people, his mixed heritage was evident in his pronounced muzzle, heavy jaw and the darker coloring of his skin, a light brown from his work in the sun. Like the commander he had discarded his outer garments, but still wore a long bladed knife at his waist and a thickly braided whip coiled about his chest and back.

As he entered he breathed in the remnants of the Malloneen in the close air. Nasrid put fist to heart, then receiving a nod from Calahar he came over to the table and sat down in the chair facing his commander.

Calahar pushed the bowl and the lump of fungus within reach of his hand should he wish to indulge. Nasrid dropped a large chunk into the bowl and covered his head, breathing in several deep breaths. With a long sigh he pulled off the cloth from his head and slid the bowl and the Malloneen back across the table.

The two men traded the bowl and its contents back and forth until the green flames died and the lump of Malloneen was less than half its original size. Lost in their individual musings and dreams they allowed the silence between them to lengthen as the first delirious rush of the drug made conversation nearly impossible. They drifted, urgent matters such as the threat the allied enemy posed outside the gate and the day to day activities of the fortress forgotten.

Sometime later when the effects of the drug were waning Calahar roused enough to ask his Second, "What arrangements have you made for our *guests*?"

Nasrid blinked finding it difficult at first to focus on the question his commander put to him. At last he said, "All the new arrivals were settled before I came to report to you. The changeling Ima gave me the most trouble with her loud complaining. She thinks she deserves special accommodations because of her high rank while among the Southerners and her loyalty to Master Barak and the North."

Calahar grimaced. He had expected as much. "Mm, and what did you do with her?"

A lazy smile played across Nasrid's lips. "I put her, and the other half-bred Avairei, in the quarters with the servants and female pleasure slaves."

Recalling the haughty woman's demeanor, Calahar chuckled. "Can I assume her new accommodations are not to her liking?"

"Yes, you can assume that, Distinguished. She and the Dingay brat we've been forced to shelter until K'San Drucas has time to collect him for Master Barak want to see you—immediately."

"Too bad, I am unavailable."

Nasrid chuckled. "Forgive me if I over stepped, but I took the liberty of telling them so."

"Mm, quite right, and what of the others?"

"The changeling K'San and his men I lodged in one of the guest quarters near the entrance. K'San Drucas may want them for one of his hunting packs. If you recall, Distinguished, we received a message that he would be coming our way with more warriors to fight the Enemy that has now arrived from the South. I'm not sure what has kept him, but he should be here soon."

Soon yes, the arrogant changeling K'San should have been here to reinforce Te'gal more than a moon ago. But if Barak is truly dead is he coming at all? Calahar felt an unreasoning stab of rage. Why wasn't Barak's pet enforcer here? Why had he been abandoned and left to deal with all these major problems. He wasn't trained—it wasn't his fault if...

Tamping down his rage, he took a deep breath and nodded his approval to his Second. It wouldn't due to show weakness in front of this one. "Satisfactory. If he doesn't want them we can always feed their bodies to the young ones in the pens."

Nasrid's mention of K'San Drucas brought to mind the westerners and the captive women. He would gladly hand over the Warlinga female to Drucas, but the mutant—now that was another matter entirely.

With the aid of the Malloneen Calahar's mind was exploring new possibilities, possibilities that would include escaping this terrible place. With or without Drucas and the Westerners' approval he was going to keep the mutant and bring her to Tiebarai to bargain for his freedom.

"And our western cousins, where have you placed them?"

Nasrid smiled. "They are also in guest quarters, but in an interior passage nearer to the springs and the Breeding Master's work rooms. They refused to be parted from their 'property.' So, for the moment the females are there with them."

"Most Exceptional Nasrid, you have done well. We shall have to separate the women from their protectors—eventually, and dispose of our western cousins, but for now they can stay where they are. In a while the warriors from the west and the changelings can be given a tour of our fine facility. And while they are busy elsewhere the females can be given a quite different tour and new accommodations found for them."

"A tour of Master Unar's breeding pens perhaps?" Nasrid said and laughed.

No not that. Master Unar was an enemy and the last thing Calahar wanted was to give the mutant into that sadistic pervert's care. But why did Nasrid suggest that—and right now of all times? In spite of his careful cultivation of the man was Nasrid changing his loyalties? He must be careful here.

"Perhaps, but don't be too hasty, Exceptional. The Warlinga is of little consequence. If K'San Drucas wants her he can have her, but the mutant female we need to protect and send her to the Cabal. Whoever gains ultimate power in Tiebarai they will want her—and reward those who bring her to them—in good condition, of course."

Nasrid grimaced. "I understand. Master Unar often plays rough with his toys."

"Exactly. And in this case we don't want that, do you understand? Master Unar has friends here—with powerful connections in Tiebarai. So for the moment it might be best if he remains ignorant of our special *guests*."

Nasrid rose and put fist to chest. Ready to take his leave, he bowed. "I understand, Distinguished." Crossing to the door he opened it then jumped back with a curse. Dressed in an embroidered kilt, his slim neck and chest draped with a variety of necklaces, an Avairei stood in the doorway with a hand raised as if to knock.

Without being invited to enter, Tunial Dingay brushed past the head overseer and strode boldly into the Commander's office. Not giving either man time to respond Tunial started talking. "Distinguished Commander Calahar, my aunt, the honored Ima Alimay is being treated with the gravest disrespect. She is no base-born Khutani slave. Her breeding is true; she is loyal to the People and has served the Great Master Barak all her life. I really must protest and deman—strongly recommend she and her entourage be rehoused in accommodations better suited to her rank and dignity."

"Oh, really, Ata. You demand, is that what you were going to say?"

Tunial made a point of loudly sniffing the air, then wrinkled up his nose at the smell of Malloneen smoke heavy in the small room. He folded his arms across his chest and curled his lip in a threatening smirk. "Master Barak will not be pleased when he learns—"

The smoke coursing through his blood Calahar felt his anger threatening to overwhelm his reason again. How dare the half-bred puke dare to judge him—an elite son of the Real People? Damn all these accursed changelings to a terrible death in the Place of Poison Fires!

Now that Barak was gone he didn't have to suffer anymore threats and abuse from this one. He placed his hands on the table and leaned forward to glare at the arrogant upstart. "Master Barak is dead, Ata. Would you like to join him? Then you can tell him anything you like. I can arrange that, if you want."

Recognizing the threat in Calahar's words, he froze with his mouth open. At last he closed his mouth and then stammered, "I-I d-don't believe the Great master is dead—and nor should you, Commander. My aunt told me the savages had with them a mutant and disgraceful Warlinga woman who flaunts convention by joining a hunting pack like a man." Tunial made a disgusted face. "It was a traitorous mutant who killed my mother Tomina. You can't trust anything they might say. I thought you had more sense than to believe such a lie."

"Have a care, Khutani Slave, or I will feed you to the young in the pits. It isn't for the likes of a sniveling Puke like you to decide whether I have sense or not or what I should believe or not believe! Why would the savage lie about something that could so easily be checked? There would be no purpose in it." By the end of his speech Calahar was almost shouting. He slumped back into his chair taking several deep breaths to regain his calm and glared at the now trembling Avairei.

"Get out of my sight, Puke, and you can tell your hag of an aunt that she remains in the slave quarters until I receive further orders from Tiebarai. And she can work for her keep, since she is too old for pleasure or breeding."

Sullen and still rebellious Tunial Dingay turned on his heel and stalked out of the room without another word.

Calahar wiped a hand across his face and let out a deep sigh. "That probably wasn't the smartest thing I've ever done."

Nasrid gave him a noncommittal grunt and crossed to the door before speaking. In the doorway he paused and said, "We shall have to watch that one. The Dingay puke could still make trouble—especially if K'San Drucas chooses to favor the family. He worked alongside his relatives for many years while in Riath."

Calahar snorted, displaying bravado he didn't totally feel. "With his relatives bungling so badly the takeover in the South and now with Master Barak dead, how likely is that?"

Nasrid smirked. "Not very likely, Distinguished. And it would be a terrible shame, nonetheless, if another unfortunate accident befell members of that troublesome family."

"Perhaps. We must warn the good Ata and Ima to be careful. Tunial has talked of seeking vengeance against those who killed his mother in the past. It would be a shame if he did something foolish. Our savage kindred can be unpredictable and violent if provoked."

Chapter Eight

"**N**ot sure how much you Boyos heard of all that, but tell Command we are going inside the fortress now," Marti murmured. "Don't know how clear reception is going to be once we're inside."

"Not sure either," Rhys said. "There aren't any satellites up in the sky to help magnify the signal. It might depend on how deep underground you go." Rhys murmured something unintelligible to a person nearby, then said, "Marti, the Hunt Leader is going to hold off on launching our attack till we hear back from you about the conditions in there. So let us know everything you can find out as soon as possible.

"Did you notice as you approached that there is a large stream or river coming out of the cliff near the east side of the fortress? The Hunt Leader says it might be easier for us to blow up the main gate like we did in Riath. They probably won't expect that.

"There must be a gate the slaves use by the river to haul water or empty wastes. We could use that to get inside and attack their rear. Focus on letting us in by the river. And If you get into trouble and need to escape we have a couple inflatables the Hunt Leader plans to have posted over there in case we can bring warriors in from that side while the main force is occupied at the front gates."

"Affirmative, Command, I'll tell the War Leader." Continuing speaking in Caldoni, she kept up a low-voiced monologue describing what she saw as they were led inside and down the dim passageways to their new quarters.

As Rhys feared, her voice began to fade as they traveled deeper into the mountain. "Marti, if you can still hear me; we'll hold off the assault till tomorrow to give you some time to report back. Good luck."

He thought he heard a faint reply, then the com went silent. Turning to the anxious Nathan-Corha, his Second Aju'an, and others of the Allied

War Council standing nearby, Rhys related what Marti described to him as Tesulu's patrol was led deeper into the fortress.

When he finished, Aju'an scratched his jaw with a clawed finger and mused, "I remember elder hunters speaking of these pits where the Ghostland monsters are often kept. If we can surprise the fortress before they can release these creatures we could kill them all at once, maybe. We would lose fewer men that way."

"A beautiful dream, Warlinga, but not so easily done in the waking world," Ogwy said.

Before Aju'an could take offense, Nathan said, "it's risky, true, but if Tesulu's warriors can secretly get some of our men inside with those fire bombs we made during the Sorins we could toss them into those pits, before the defenders have time to release their monsters on us."

Ogwy grunted unconvinced, but let the subject drop.

"Sounds like a real rat's maze of tunnels in there. Lots of places to set up an ambush or get behind us for a rear attack," Chang said.

"Yeah, we will have to watch out for that," Nathan said. The Native Timornans agreeing with him.

Still mulling over what Kashallan-Phillip had revealed at the last war council, Ross said, "I wonder if they have one of those poison-making labs in there. I wish we had a few of our protective suits down here instead of leaving them to be blown up with Bennett's ship."

"Yeah, well that's water under the bridge now. We'll have Phillip-Yoey check after we have the place secured," Nathan assured him.

TESULU PAID CLOSE ATTENTION to his surroundings as the Ghostlander called Nasrid led them deeper into the bowels of Te'gal. He took note that Glatu and his men were ushered into a large room down a side passage close to the outer doors.

To his amusement, the haughty priestess that Chelka disliked so much was led away to other quarters down a side passage from which unpleasant smells of rotting bedding and unwashed bodies wafted. The woman's irate shouts when she discovered she was being led to the fortress slave quarters could be heard for some distance before the door to her chamber was closed and barred. He saw the Warlinga's lips curve into a malicious smile.

Don't be too quick to gloat, he wanted to tell her, now sharing Marti's misgivings. *The Unseen Ones only know what this Ghostland mushroom has planned for us.* Turning, Nasrid led them down another hall and paused outside a large room, bowing them inside.

If this was a prison cell, at least it was a big one, he thought. A box-shaped nest piled high with dried moss took up a large portion of a side wall. Opposite the door sat a poorly made wicker table and a couple battered stools. On the table was a lamp and sacks of the rock powder needed to make the green fire used to light the inner rooms of most keeps on Timorna.

In the corner by the table a small stream of clear water flowed into a stone bowl cut into the wall then disappeared back into the rock when the water reached a certain level in the bowl. There was also a hole in the stone floor for waste near the front wall past the door, and high up near the ceiling by the far wall were two slim windows to let in air and the occasional ray of sunlight.

So, they weren't deep enough in the mountain for this to be a true dungeon, he thought, but far enough from the front gate to make opening it for the Allies, or gaining their escape if things went wrong nearly impossible.

When Nasrid had left with a promise to the Clan Warriors to come back later and give them a tour of the fortress and talk to them over a meal about setting up some practice bouts, Tesulu motioned for Juba to check the door.

Juba moved quietly to the door and tried to open it. The door opened with a little effort, but when he poked his head out he saw two guards down the hall. Spying him they growled and flexed their claws. Juba closed the door and reported this information to the patrol.

"Well at least it isn't barred, that's a hopeful sign," Marti said and held out her hands. "I think somebody can take our bindings off. Your poor defenseless prisoners aren't going to run away now."

Juba snorted a laugh, but at a nod from Tesulu untied her hands, then did the same to Chelka. When she was untied Chelka crossed to the water bowl, drank, then walked to the nest and lay down, turning her back to them.

Marti stared at her for a moment, then hesitantly asked, "Chelka, you all right?"

"Just tired," came the mumbled response. Marti doubted that, waiting for her to explain further. When she said nothing more Marti shrugged and turned back to the men who were crouched on the floor examining and cleaning their weapons.

Tesulu looked up as Marti came over and crouched down beside them. He pointed with his lips to the com unit nestled in her hair. Then in a low voice, barely above a whisper, he asked, "Can you still speak to them, Speir'dina?"

Marti shrugged. "I'm not sure. I lost them at the end. Before that I was telling Armachd Rhys what I was seeing as we came in. I spoke in my own language so the Ghostlanders and the changelings would think I was just mumbling gibberish if they heard me."

Juba and Tesulu exchanged looks. "Sly like an Oko," Juba said and Tesulu agreed.

"I've heard you clan men say that before," Marti said. "Isn't it time somebody tells me what an Oko is?"

Tesulu chuckled and gave her a piece of dried Obeylem meat from a pouch at his waist as he told her about the tricky little creature, so a part of Clan folk tales.

Sometime later they were sitting together, when Tesulu asked, "Can you speak to the Speir'dina on the hill or hear them talk to you while we are in this room?"

"I've heard nothing for a while, but I don't know if they are just quiet or I can't hear them."

"Try now. I want to know what they are planning and how we can help them. I don't think we could make it to the front gate to let them in, even if we killed those guards out in the hall," Tesulu said.

Marti told them about the plan for them to look for a back door to let warriors inside, and then tried to contact Command. She thought she could hear—something but the signal was too faint to make out clearly.

When she told Tesulu, Ingazi looked up at the window slits high on the wall and asked, "Stone is hard and the walls are thick. If you could get closer to those windows could you hear them better?"

"Maybe," Marti said slowly as she thought about it. "But how would I get up there? The wall is too smooth for me to climb."

"You could climb on my shoulders," Ingazi offered. "Maybe that will be close enough to hear better."

Liking the idea of this strong and cunning female brushing his body with her so openly displayed female charms, Tesulu said, "It is a good idea, Rock Salt Brother, but I am taller and stronger. I will lift her." Ingazi scowled, but agreed. Tesulu was the leader; it was his right.

Motioning for Ingazi to listen by the door, Tesulu placed his hands on her smooth cinnamon-colored legs and crouched for her to climb on his shoulders.

It took a few tries, but finally she managed to balance on his shoulders with one hand braced against the wall. Tapping the com device, Marti said in Caldoni, "Hey Boyos, can anybody hear me?"

"Boughthy here, Marti. It isn't real clear but I can hear you, thank all the gods of Caldon and Timorna. Where are you?"

"Where are *you*, Infant?"

"Ha, ha, I'm lying behind some boulders above the stream about a half klick from the fortress," Boughthy said. "I will relay any messages to Command up the hill, Armachd. Seriously, where are you, and what do you have to report?"

"Tesulu is bargaining for the best price for his valuable prisoners, so for the moment we are being kept together in a large room down a maze of dark corridors. Not sure how long that's going to last—gotta bad feeling about this. Don't trust'em."

"Be careful, Marti and call if you need us."

"I will, Boyo, to be sure." A touch on her leg reminded her to translate for the rest of them. When she told Tesulu she'd made contact, he said, "Tell them that the one in charge here is a middle-ranking member of the elite class named Calahar. I think for some reason their communications with Tiebarai have broken down. They were unaware of Wizard Barak's death until I told them just now."

"That's—interesting. I'll tell Command. Do they believe you?"

"Some do, some don't," The War Leader replied. "Their commander does, even under all his protective veils I could sense his surprise—and fear. The changelings that escaped from the Yeyen, however, do not, so they will try to convince him that we are lying."

"Do you think they will be successful?"

"Probably not. They aren't well liked here and now they know the wizard is dead Barak's pets may have a harder time here than they bargained on when they ran from the hunting packs sent to kill them."

The War Leader might have said more, but Ingazi hissed a warning that someone was coming and Marti ended the call. Jumping down, she hurried to the nest and lay down next to Chelka with her back to the door.

She tossed a few armfuls of the moss over the both of them so anyone entering couldn't see that they were now unbound. Tesulu sat down on the bed beside her and as the door opened, he placed a possessive hand on her ample hip.

Coming into the room flanked by the two warriors that had been stationed down the hall Nasrid took in the tableau in the nest and smirked. "Ah, Western Cousin, sorry to interrupt your—nap. I would like to give you and K'San Glatu the tour of your new home I promised."

Tesulu rose slowly from the bed and gave Juba a sign to follow him out into the hall. Ingazi he motioned to take his place on the edge of the nest and stay with the women.

"Your property will be perfectly safe here, Cousin," Nasrid said when he saw that the third man hadn't followed them out of the room.

Tesulu grinned, showing his canines. "I believe you, Cousin, but that one is tired. It is his turn to take—a nap, as you put it. The lazy Begta can stay with *my property*."

Nasrid glared. Tesulu kept smiling. Finally the head overseer shrugged and motioned for them to follow him back down the hall.

When they were gone Ingazi lay down beside her and stretched out a hand to touch her. Still with her back to him, Marti said, "You'd better keep all four of your hands to yourself, cause if you touch me, Amadan, Chelka and me are going to beat the shit out of you."

Ingazi slowly drew back his hand and grinned. "I was only going to do what my war leader ordered me to do—take a nap."

Marti snorted a laugh and sat up, dried yellow moss cascading off her shoulders. "Yeah right, not a chance, Amadan. Now go make yourself useful and see if they've barred the door this time."

Ingazi rose without further protest and went to the door. He tried the handle and when it opened to his touch, he peered out into the corridor. In another moment he withdrew his head and shut the door. When he walked back to the bed both women were sitting up and staring at him.

"Well?"

"As you can tell, Speir'dina, the door has not been barred from the outside, and there are no guards I can see lurking in the shadows down the hall. We seem to be alone here."

"Appearances can be deceiving," Chelka said.

"That is true, Warlinga. I don't understand this. Do they hope we will try to escape?"

"Without the rest of the patrol—not a chance—and besides where would we go? They'd catch us in a heartbeat," Marti growled. She got up and started to pace the room, trying to figure it out. "I agree that ghosty bacach in charge here has some devilment in mind, but what?"

"Maybe he wants us to try and escape so he can kill us," Ingazi suggested.

"That's a thought, but if so, why separate us? He could have killed us at any time, but he didn't, so why now?" when no one had an answer for that she thought about it for a moment, then said, "And besides, nobody took away your weapons. I would think that would be the first thing they would do if all they had in mind was killing us."

The three remained silent, each lost in their own thoughts. Finally Chelka ventured, "I don't think Ingazi was supposed to stay with us, Marti."

Marti stopped her pacing and turned to face her. "What are you thinking, Sister Warrior?" Ingazi paused rummaging in his belt pouch for a piece of dried meat and glanced her way as well.

"I think—somebody— wants us to be separated from our male protectors, and it may not be the Ghostlander in charge."

"I don't understand, why would anybody want that?" Ingazi said.

Ignoring him for the moment, Marti came over and sat down in the nest beside her. "What are you thinking, Sister?"

"You said it yourself, Sister. Some believe Barak is dead while others don't. Well what if that isn't the only disagreement to form up sides about in this fortress amongst the ruling elite? What if there are no guards because someone—or someone's want to take us away from the clan warriors, either to kill us, spite the commander, or hide us away to bargain for favors from Drucas or the Cabal in Tiebarai."

As the chill of another sending ran down her spine Marti shuddered, knowing Chelka had the right of it.

Chapter Nine

N asrid's tour seemed to be quite thorough and Tesulu wondered why. The Ghostlander either planned to accept their story and make them a part of his fighting force, or he planned to kill them and it didn't matter what they saw, because he was only toying with them.

He showed them the warriors' barracks, and the deep pits where the youngest that still lacked any control over their murderous rages were housed. Pointing down a dim corridor filled with unfamiliar unpleasant smells which they didn't enter, Nasrid explained that area was the lair of their breeder, Master Unar and his apprentices.

With a smirk playing about his thin lips Nasrid waved a hand at the pleasure slaves' apartment, then moved on to the slave pens, the storerooms and the hall where they would be served their meals. Tesulu and Juba shared a quick glance. Smelling rotting river weed and sewage coming out a dark tunnel near the slave pens, they suspected the back entrance the Hunt Leader wanted could be found down there.

"I have notice several others of the elite class as we've toured the fortress today, Exceptional Nasrid," Glatu said. "Where might your own and the Distinguished Commander Calahar's accommodations be?"

Nasrid seemed startled by the question, but smiled and said, "Why on a higher level a little further down the hall where you and your men are staying, K'San. The breezes off the river are most cooling on hot days in that portion of the keep."

Knowing that the clansmen were being kept in a less favored part of the fortress, Glatu looked down his snout at the Westerners and smirked. Tesulu would like to cut that smirk off the Begta puke's face with the Speir'dina knife at his hip, but he could wait to repay the insult. He had no plans to take up residence in Te'gal, so what did it matter.

His eyes a light with some inner amusement, Nasrid said, "Since you are both men experienced in the weapons of war, unlike myself who is but a mere guard in this well-defended fortress, I'm sure you would like to see more of how we train our fighters and perhaps demonstrate to me some of your own skills—in a practice combat, of course."

Well, if the Begta Puke thought to get rid of his unwanted guests by having them slaughter each other in a *practice bout*, he was going to be unpleasantly surprise, Tesulu thought. He had no intention of dying today. He smirked and agreed, as Nasrid led them toward the training ground.

IT WAS GROWING LATE; the light coming through the window slits had turned a deep rose pink, and still no Tesulu or Juba had returned. The three of them had been taking turns throughout the afternoon, catching some well needed rest. Marti had just relieved Ingazi and was pacing back and forth in the center of the floor, when without warning the door to their room was flung open and several hideously scarred guards rushed in. Marti sprang to the attack, but one of them grabbed her from behind and a hood stinking of some unknown substance was flung over her head. She took in a breath to shout a warning to the others and then she was falling into a well of blackness.

When she awoke she was lying on rotting moss in the dark, the stink of old dung and blood in her nostrils. Marti swore and rolled onto her side as she tried to heave up the contents of her stomach. Thank the gods the Ghostland pricks hadn't fed them yet so there was little to cough up into the moss. Damn, she hadn't liked this movie when she had endured it while lying in a dungeon in Riath and didn't need a repeat performance.

Well, at least she now knew what the nasty bacach had been planning when they separated them. Separate! Shit where were Chelka and Ingazi? She couldn't see a damned thing in the blackness. "Chelka, Ingazi, you in with me here, too?"

No one answered her, so she began crawling around on all fours letting her hands search for her missing companions. It was hard, because her head felt like it was going to burst it hurt so bad, but she kept searching and at last touched a scaly leg. "Chelka, are you awake; are you hurt? Speak to me, Sister Warrior! Ingazi, are you hear, too? Somebody answer me, damn it!"

Crawling to the length of her tether in every direction, she touched no other body. Ingazi probably wasn't with them then. It was just her and Chelka as the Warlinga predicted. They'd been successfully separated from their male protectors—purpose unknown. Gods, she hoped Ingazi wasn't dead.

"Chelka, talk to me if you're awake, damn it. We need to start planning how to get out of here."

Finally a tiny voice spoke from the darkness. "There's no escape, Marti. I've tried so hard to defy him—to fight him—resist, but just like in Riath this is my punishment for wanting—for being a disgrace to my family. He's here—in the darkness—and I, we belong to him."

Marti scooted over as close as she could to her friend, but she could only reach as far as her scaly hip. Chelka was right, this was like a replay of what they had endured while being held at Riath. Maybe she shouldn't have been so quick to talk her friend into this crazy mission. Though Chelka had seemed all right in the months after their ordeal, maybe she'd been hiding how truly unwell she still was. And now...

"That bacach Drucas is not here; I would know it if he was. Damn it, Chelka I'm not going to let you do this to yourself—and me too. You can't give up; I won't let you, you hear me? So smarten up. We have to get out of here and find those crazy warriors so we can get the fuck out of here!"

In the darkness she heard Chelka sit up. The Warlinga gasped. "Eyah! My head hurts."

"Mine, too, they must have drugged us when they threw those hoods over our heads."

"I wonder what they've done with Ingazi and the rest of the men."

"Me, too, and their situation worries me the most at the moment," Marti said.

"...I hope they haven't killed them."

"Me, too," Marti agreed. "Tesulu is an amadan sometimes, but he's a good man and war leader, too."

Chelka snorted, not sure she agreed with that statement. Marti laughed then swore at her aching head. A while later, Chelka asked, "Marti, can you speak to our people outside; tell them what has happened?"

Marti tapped the com, but as she feared there was no response. "We must be too deep in the mountain. They can't hear me."

"So we are on our own."

"Yeah, but not like in Riath, Chelka. The boyos are just outside this fortress. And we have to help them take it down."

With a quiver in her voice she couldn't control, Chelka said, "How?"

"You still got that garotte hidden in your death strand?"

The Warlinga raised a hand and felt among the bones around her neck. Inside a hollowed out bone she had hidden the coiled razor wire of the garrotte Marti had given her. "Yes, it's still with me."

"Good. Take it out and come closer to me. See if you can saw through the tethers restricting my movements and I will do the same for you." Knowing nothing of what was happening outside the darkness of their cell, the warriors focused on the task. Unable to get a proper grip on the razor wire they persisted anyway, but when their hands became slippery with blood the process slowed even more.

Marti was sawing through the last of Chelka's bindings when a disturbance outside the door warned her to conceal her weapon and pile moss over the severed cords. "Chelka, hide your garrotte and pretend you are still asleep. Look away from the light when they open the door," Marti whispered.

She had just covered her own body when the door was flung open and bright light enveloped the room.

TIRED FROM THE PRACTICE bout, and proud of himself for besting the changeling, Tesulu was looking forward to a wash and a good meal back in their quarters. He was not impressed with the fighting skills of the Ghostland warriors he'd seen that afternoon—even the few mixed bloods like Nasrid who were not bred in the pits and were in control of the monsters used to strike terror on raids into the South. The Ghostland creatures were bred for their hideous appearance strength, and ferocity, but overall they were stupid. Today he had gained a new appreciation for the advantages his training among the Speir'dina had given him.

Nasrid came over and slapped him on the back. "Well fought, Western Cousin. I am somewhat impressed. The changeling will have to take lessons from you when you both join K'San Drucas's hunting packs."

Tesulu glanced over to where Glatu's side was being bandaged by a slave trained in the healing arts. He longed for the small jar of orange kavay tucked away in his pack that his adopted brother-in-law Phillip-Yoey had given him. Though in part he hated to admit it—even to himself, the Khutani's medicine would be a soothing balm for the pain of his own wounds. Unfortunately for him, damn the Ghostlanders, he couldn't use it while here in the enemy fortress.

"The day comes to a close," Nasrid was saying. "My personal slaves have prepared a special meal for us back in my quarters."

How 'special'? Tesulu thought, wondering if he and Juba were meant to survive it.

Glancing at the changeling holding his side and being led away by one of his men, Juba asked, "And what of the changeling K'San. Is he coming, too?"

Nasrid smiled, but there was no mirth in his expression. "To the victors belong the rewards of combat, Western Cousin. K'San Glatu will not be joining us, I'm afraid."

So they were probably not meant to survive the coming festivities.

"Come let us go and take our ease. With good food and drink, and later perhaps we shall send for some of the pleasure slaves to join us, eh?"

Tempting. What 'savage' could resist? "A most generous offer, Cousin, but first I need to go to our quarters, collect my brother—and check on my property—then if all is well, perhaps."

The Ghostlander's smile never wavered, but his big eyes hardened. Tesulu ignored his displeasure and picked up his weapons. He'd learned what they needed to know this afternoon; it was time to find that back door and get out of here. But first... "We won't be long, Cousin, but if you don't trust us, or think we might get lost—come with us."

For just a moment Nasrid let the mask slip and showed the fury he was concealing behind his bland smile. "That won't be necessary, Cousin, I will

go ahead and make sure my orders have been carried out to my satisfaction."
He motioned to the two body guards that had been with them all afternoon.
"These two will accompany you and see that you and your men find your way
safely to my quarters."

AS THE DOOR OPENED the women could hear a rasping male voice
say, "Ata Tunial, you had better not have dragged me away from my valuable
work on a fool's errand—"

"It isn't a fool's errand, Brilliant Master Unar," a slimy-sounding Avairei
voice pleaded. "My aunt, Ima Alimay, has been cruelly treated by our
Distinguished Commander, but she assures me that she saw many of the
mutants while in Riath. She knows their look. One of the prisoners is truly a
female mutant, and our commander is deliberately keeping her presence here
a secret from your brilliance to further his own advancement."

"Hmm, we shall see; show me, then."

The door was opened wider and a brutish guard stepped into the room
holding up a green flamed lamp. Behind him entered two smaller figures, the
fourth stayed in the hall just outside the door.

Her eyes closed to mere slits, Marti saw one of the Ghostland elite for
the first time without all the concealing veils. Dressed in a stained kaftan
this newcomer was pale-skinned with only four limbs rather than six like
the commander and his guards. The Ghostlander was a small creature of
indeterminate sex with a round belly and narrow shoulders. Its face was
closer to an Avairei—or human likeness, rather than having the heavier jaw
and longer nose of most Timornans she'd seen. The Ghostlander seemed
hairless in the poor light, with a bald head wrinkled forehead and large dark
eyes. Eyes that with only a quick glance at Chelka focused completely on her.
Knowing the threat this creature posed to her personally, Marti trembled.

The Ghostlander must have seen her fear, because a cruel smile played
about its thin lips. Motioning for the guard to hold the lamp higher, the
Ghostlander stepped closer to examine her more carefully. Pretending to still
be suffering the effects of the drug they had been given Marti didn't move.
"Ah, Ata Tunial, your aunt was correct in her surmise. From the descriptions

I have received the female does indeed appear to be a product of some traitorous Western Wizard's conjuring as the Great Master suspects."

"I spoke true, yes? It is I told you, Brilliant Master Unar."

"Indeed." Coming closer the Ghostlander reached out a tentative hand and touched her leg. "And I would dearly like to know how he achieved it," Unar said, as if to himself. "And I shall definitely have to find out. And there's no time to dawdle. When that Malloneen-enslaved Calahar finds out...."

Stepping away he motioned for the guard to precede him back into the hall. "Come, Ata, I have much to do before our addle-brained commander finds out the females are missing. You and your aunt will be rewarded for your service and loyalty."

"Brilliant Master Unar, may I stay here while you prepare for your—guest?"

Startled Unar paused in the doorway. "Whatever for, Good Ata?"

"I want to ask her some—questions—while she is still sluggish from the drug you had us give her. You see one of the foul creatures killed my mother and I want to find out who, so that when our warbands are victorious I can—"

"Have the pleasure of his punishment, no doubt." Unar laughed, but there was only menace in the sound." Unar considered for a moment then motioned for one of the guards to remain. "All right, Ata, you may stay here to help *guard* the mutant while I prepare for her."

When the Ghostlander was gone Tunial took the lamp from the slave and motioned for him to remain by the door. He crossed to stand at Marti's side, shining his light down at her. He watched her for a long moment, then finally asked, "Do you know who I am, Traitorous Slimeworm?"

Marti opened her eyes, taking in the guard hovering by the door and Chelka silently crawling through the inky shadows towards him. What she saw in the lamp light was a mottled brown-furred Avairei with a growing paunch, spilling over the belt of his richly embroidered kilt. His mane was neatly braided with lots of ornamentation, and his thick neck seemed choked with the weight of more gaudy necklaces.

She'd better keep everyone's attention focused on her while Chelka got in position to make her move. She yawned and gave him an insolent smile. "No, Begta Puke, who are you?"

The fat little pus-boil was finding it hard to control his temper. Marti smirked, closing her hand tighter around the handles of the garrott she'd hidden in the moss.

The Avairei opened and closed his mouth several times while he fought for control. At last he choked out, "I am Tunial Dingay, traitor." Then he surprised her by drawing a lethal bone knife from the folds of the kilt at his waist. "And you are going to tell me who killed my Mother Tomina."

Recalling that long ago day when Tomina Dingay had nearly killed Dunnagh-Tani, Marti smirked. "Dingay, eh? We didn't know she had a son, and such a fat ugly one at that." Marti's eyes widened as he cursed her in a variety of languages. She could appreciate someone who was creative with his cursing—even if he was a shit for brains changeling.

Tunial waved his knife in a threatening gesture. "Tell me who killed her before I lose my temper completely," he warned. "Master Unar won't mind if I cut you, as long as I keep you alive for his purposes, Traitorous Witch. Tell me—now!"

Ignoring his threat, she continued to smile as she tensed for an attack. "You really want to know, Puke? It was me."

With a cry he lunged for her. Startled by his quickness, Marti barely had time to knock his arm away, the blade running down her chest in a shallow arc. "Fuck!"

Marti scrambled out of reach and while he was off balance she came up behind him. Gritting her teeth against the sudden pain, she flung her garrote around his neck and pulled the ends tight.

Hearing the commotion in the cell, the guard just outside the open door rushed in. Seeing Marti crouched over the dying Ata he never noticed Chelka pull her own razor wire weapon around his throat until it was too late. Dropping his spear he began clawing at his neck, the two swaying back and forth in a macabre dance.

Breathing heavily from the effort Marti dropped the limp body at her feet and retrieved her garrotte. Damn that drug—whatever it was—was still slowing down her reflexes. Then spying Chelka still struggling with the burly guard, Marti lurched over, picked up his dropped spear and plunged it into his belly. With a strangled cry the guard died. Chelka let him fall to the floor.

While her partner caught her breath, Marti hurried to retrieve Tunial's knife from his dead hand. Tossing the spear to Chelka, she said, "Guess we have to go rescue the men, so we can find that back door and get out of here. Come on, we have to move—now! That other one will be back with more guards any moment."

"But where shall we go?"

"Anywhere but here. Come on!"

Chapter Ten

The moment they stepped inside their quarters and saw the empty nest and a comatose and bloody Ingazi on the floor, Tesulu whipped around and plunged the Speir'dina knife into the nearest guard. The warrior let out a strangled cry and fumbled for the blade at his own hip. Not giving him time to draw it, Tesulu pulled out his knife and slashed across the man's throat. Fountaining blood, the guard crumpled to the stone floor without another sound.

Nearly as quick as his war leader Juba bounded after the other guard who ran back into the hall to sound the alarm. Hurling his spear he buried it in the burly slave's back. He staggered and would have fallen, but Juba grabbed him and half-dragged, half-carried him inside the room and closed the door. Leaving the man slumped just inside, he hurried over to the nest where Tesulu had laid out Ingazi and was plastering his wounds with the yellow kavay from their packs.

Breathing shallowly Ingazi stared up at them, at last focusing on Tesulu's face. When he saw he had the wounded man's attention, Tesulu snarled. "What happened, Half-Bred Begta? Where are the women?"

"Gone," Ingazi croaked and motioned for water. Juba when to the wall and filled a bowl from the water trickling out of the rock basin there.

Well that's obvious, Tesulu thought. Tell me something I don't know.

"They betrayed us. Warriors came—drugged the women—I fought—then one covered my face, and, and everything was black. I woke up just before you came..." He touched his wound, surprised to feel the hard crust of kavay forming atop it. "Khutani magic here, how?"

"Don't be stupid, Phillip-Yoey gave it me before we left. Can you walk? We need to find the women and get out of here right now," he said impatient to be gone. "Do you know where they took them?"

Ingazi started to shake his head, then clutched it instead. "No, War Leader, they were gone when I awakened."

Tesulu cursed. He expected some kind of betrayal; that was why he'd left Ingazi here to stand guard, the lazy Begta, but what he hadn't expected was for Nasrid and his men to steal the women away before they had disposed of him.

Juba touched his arm and pointed with his lips to the bleeding man by the door. "He is still breathing. Want me to finish killing him?"

"Not yet." Crossing to the man, Tesulu studied him for a long moment. Tall muscular build, heavy jaw, but with little hair and big eyes, the bleeding man was of mixed breeding and probably intelligent enough for Calahar or his Second Nasrid to trust him with their secrets—at least some of them anyway. Crouching down the war leader flipped him over and glared down at the Puke. He was in pain, but still aware enough to answer questions.

"Where has your lying master taken my property? Tell me and I will give you magics for your wounds that might save your life. Tell me; where are they?"

Hope coming into his eyes the man licked his lips and focused on Tesulu's angry face. "Don't know. Master Nasrid wouldn't—"

Why not? He planned to kill us at this dinner we were invited to attend, yes?"

"Yes," the man agreed in a breathy voice. "But with you dead the women were safe staying here—no reason..."

"Who then? Speak quickly now if you want my magics."

The man was breathing raggedly now he hadn't much time. "Breeding Master—Dingay Brat maybe told..." Then with a final gasp the wounded man died.

Tesulu met Juba's eyes. Everyone in the West had heard the stories... If this unknown Ghostland wizard got his hands on the women—especially the Speir'dina—if he went back without them that crazy kashallan or the Warlinga K'San would want to kill him. He wasn't worried, he was Tesulu, the Pride of Sand Mountain; he could handle them.

But he had given his word to the old hunter that he would keep the women safe—and Tesulu didn't like breaking his warrior's word. "Ingazi, can you walk?"

The Rock Salt warrior staggered to his feet. He swayed and might have fallen, but Juba steadied him. "I will manage, War Leader."

He would have to, Tesulu thought eyeing him critically. "Good, my brother. We don't want to leave you for the enemy to find. We need to grab what we can carry and go, before Nasrid sends someone looking for us."

"Where shall we go, War Leader?" Juba asked, throwing the last of his kit into the sack on his back.

"We will start by looking down that smelly hall where the Ghostlander said the Breeding Master has his lair."

AFTER STRIPPING THE guard's bodies of anything useful, Marti poked her head out to see if the hall was still empty. It looked clear, so Marti dimmed the lamp's flame and crept into the corridor, Chelka at her back. When they came to a T intersection she paused. Not having been given the grand tour like Juba and Tesulu, she had no idea where she was or in what direction escape lay.

"We need a guide," Chelka murmured next to her ear.

"That we do, but not sure where to find one."

"Maybe one of the slaves," Chelka suggested, but Marti could tell by her voice she wasn't hopeful. A slave was just as likely to sound the alarm as help them. But Marti wasn't above using fear and pain to get what she wanted right now.

Which way to turn? The quiet corridor forming the top of the T gave her no clue. Hearing the sound of distant voices to her right, Marti instinctively turned into the dim shadows of the left passage, Chelka following without comment.

They continued on in silence ears straining for any sounds of pursuit. Only the drip of water somewhere up ahead and the muffled sounds of their own footfalls broke the stillness.

Becoming aware of the silence and noticing that the light in the lamp was beginning to dim Marti stopped. Shining the light onto the floor ahead, she noticed that no tracks were visible in the dust of the passage. She sighed and turned around. "Chelka we have to go back. I'm sure this isn't the way out."

"But if we go back they will find us—and maybe kill us."

"Maybe so, but I'd rather die fighting than die starving, and lost in these dark tunnels."

Chelka thought about it for a moment and then agreed. The darkness and deathly chill was too much like the unsettling visions K'San Drucas often sent into her sleeping mind when he wanted to torment her dreams. Hastily they retraced their trail through the dust, before the flickering light of the lamp faded completely.

They turned right this time when they came to the T intersection, but veered into another side passage just as the lamp blazed one last time and then went black. Marti mumbled a curse and set the empty lamp down in a hollowed out niche on the wall.

When their eyes had adjusted to the gloom she could see a dim glow of lamps ahead and hear the sounds of—laughter? Yes laughter from a room further down the hall. The merriment seemed to be coming from more than one person, one high-pitched like a female/woman the other lower more like a male/man's voice.

Where the fuck were they? Marti wondered. Where ever it was, it was better than that stinking room, too much like a prison cell where they'd been left after being stolen away from the clan men. It kind of even smelled nice around here, the scent wafting down the hall had a flowery aroma mixed with lemon. Nice, she hadn't expected something like that in a warrior fortress.

Pondering on the riddle as a distraction from the growing ache of her wound, she was unaware of the voices coming their way until Chelka touched her shoulder. Marti stepped boldly up to the next door they came to and opened it. Having a quick look around and spying no one, she quickly pulled Chelka in after her and quietly shut the door behind her.

Marti flattened herself on one side of the door, Chelka taking the other. "Do you think anyone saw us?" Chelka murmured barely above a whisper.

"Not sure. Guess we'll know in a moment—be ready."

When the voices came no closer, Marti breathed a sigh of relief and looked around her. The room was illumined with a soft green light, coming from several carved lamps resting on wall shelves on opposite sides of the room. Colorful tapestries hung on the wall above the lamps. Comfortable pillows in bright colors were piled atop a low couch. Placed in front of the couch was a low wicker table with a tray holding drinking bowls and a stoppered jar. On the wall opposite the outer door hung a beaded curtain dense enough to leave the inner room in shadow.

"Marti, what is this place?"

"Not sure."

Hearing the beads rustle as the curtain was thrust aside Marti dropped into a fighter's crouch, reaching for the garrot in her hair.

"Welcome Noble Warriors," a sing-song high-pitched voice said as a slender figure dressed in a gauzy kaftan entered the room. "My mentor and I weren't expecting any of our brave protectors to favor us tonight. But, of course you are always wel-come." Coming further into the room, she broke off her rehearsed speech, when she got a good look at them.

And what a shocking pair of visitors they must seem, Marti thought, two strange women crashing into the room, both armed, naked, and covered in dust and blood. "Uh, hi," Marti said. She grinned showing lots of teeth. "I'm Marti and this is my sister-warrior Chelka. Glad to know we are, uh, welcome."

The kaftaned figure stared, eyes wide, and mouth agape. But at least she wasn't screaming the alarm. The person had an androgynous figure, but Marti thought from the sound of her voice that she was probably female—though she wasn't positive. Through the sheer fabric she could see tiny rounded lumps that were probably breasts.

She had a strong Avairei-featured face atop her slim neck. Though her body fur was a pale cream, her face had been shaved, the smooth skin painted bone-white. On her cheeks and forehead geometric designs in red and black had been painted. Her eyes were the usual rich brown of the Avairei, but she had enhanced their size with more skillfully applied makeup. Her golden mane she wore in a curly topknot held in place by a woven band, not unlike the way Marti had taken to wearing her own shortened curly hair since her ordeal in Riath.

"Don't be frightened," Chelka soothed. "We aren't going to hurt you. We're just—" she broke off unsure how to finish that sentence.

Coming further into the room to study them, the Ghostlander looked from one bedraggled woman to the other. Finally she said, "I am Lovely Kitha. You are warriors, yes?"

"That's right. we are warriors," Marti agreed.

Glancing from Chelka and her spear to the full-figured Marti and her bloody knife, a puzzled frown crossed her face. Kitha's voice now deeper than the phony sing-song one she had greeted them with, she said, "But you are both female, yes?"

"Yes, we are women."

"I don't understand; a woman cannot be a warrior. How can you be warriors?"

"Among my people, the Speir'dina, a woman can be whatever she wants to be," Marti explained. "I chose the Warrior's Path." She motioned to Chelka and added, "Though Warlinga, my sister and battle companion Chelka has chosen to become a warrior as well."

Sensing the other woman's skepticism Marti sighed and admitted, "Though to be honest, her family wasn't thrilled about it at first. But her betrothed Tobrach settled her father and brothers down, because he values her as a warrior and his love."

Marti's hand holding the knife twitched as another kaftaned figure brushed aside the beads and stepped into the outer room. A true Ghostlander, this personage was taller and plumper than Lovely Kitha. She had smooth pale skin, her silver hair woven into a braided crown the plat strung with several large gems. And, Mother Timorna, were those three rounded bumps on her chest breasts? Had to be; she could see their elongated red-painted nipples pushing out the thin fabric.

Like the other woman she had but two arms. Marti suspected the reason was that her Ghostlander bloodline was purer than the mixed race Kitha. Marti wished she knew more about the elaborate geometric designs painted on her face. They probably signified her family and rank.

"Ah, Noble Guests, this is my sister and wise mentor, Enchanting Cochinna," Kitha said and bowed.

Cochinna smiled acknowledging the other's introduction and walked over to examine their guests. Standing in front of Marti she studied her closely. At last she said, "You have been injured, Warrior Woman, come into the inner room and we will clean and bandage your wound."

Marti shrugged, dismissing the injury. "It's nothing, only a scratch." She glanced at the outer door. "We should go, before we get you in trouble—we have to find the rest of our—people—and go."

"They are still searching for you; you should wait a while," the Ghostlander counseled.

"Why would you want to hide us if you already know there are men in this fortress searching for us?" Chelka asked.

"Because you intrigue me—" Cochinna started to say.

"And we don't like Breeding Master Unar. He is a very bad man," Kitha finished for them both.

"So you know who we are then." Marti said as she allowed Kitha to lead her into the other room.

Not sure how far to trust this strange pair, Chelka stationed herself by the wall inside the beaded curtain where she could watch Marti on the bed and also see anyone opening the front door.

"I heard you call yourself Sper'duna. Is that the name your wizard has given your people?" Cochinna asked as she cleaned Marti's cut with a warm, strangely scented rag.

"It's Speir'dina," Marti corrected, "and we aren't mutant Timornans—as everyone thinks who see us for the first time. In my native language Speir'dina means sky people. We call ourselves that because we aren't from Timorna originally but from other worlds out there." Marti pointed up to the sky above with a free hand.

"That's an interesting story, but difficult to believe," Cochinna said.

Remembering her brother's hunting pack's desperate race for Ticca, a Sorin storm nipping at their heels, Chelka laughed as she recalled her first meeting with Marti's people. "It wasn't easy for my people to believe the Speir'dina either, I assure you. My brother almost got me and the whole hunting pack killed because he found it hard to accept that they weren't Umwira mutants. It was only when he was forced into a Khutani pool and met one of the Ancients of that species that he believed truly."

"A Khutani demon," Lovely Kitha gasped, nearly dropping the bowl of bloody water.

"How fascinating." Her expression unchanged, Cochinna steadied the bowl and continued washing the wound. The two women exchanged looks. "You have met one of the Ancient invaders of our world."

Marti snorted a laugh, then winced as the Ghostlander probed a particularly deep part of the cut. "I don't know anything about the Khutani being invaders. All I know is that my Sweetie has one of the little ones coiled in his middle and I myself have talked to its parent many times."

"And you were not afraid of this ancient being?" Kitha asked.

"Well maybe a little—at first," she admitted, "but now not so much." Then lowering her voice, she confided, "And the sex in the pools with my man and his symbiont is—amazing!"

Kitha's eyes grew even larger at that revelation.

"Marti! Don't talk like that." Chelka's head crest dipped in embarrassment.

Marti frowned, then nodded. Why was she gossiping about Nathan like this. These women though friendly were still enemy—until proven otherwise. What was a matter with her? Was she still suffering from the effects of the drugging, or was there something in this scented water that was drugging her now? She had better be more careful from now on.

Studying Chelka, Cochinna changed the subject and asked, "I know little of your people, but I don't think from my studies that it is common for your women to take up the warrior's Path, as your sister has. You are—Warlinga, yes? Do you have a husband?"

"Not yet," she admitted reluctantly. "we plan to wed—soon."

The women might have asked more questions, but suddenly there was shouting and the banging of doors out in the hall. Marti sprang from the bed and took up her position on the wall opposite Chelka by the curtain. Cochinna motioned for Kitha to get rid of the bowl and bloody water. As the Dorr from the hall was flung wide, Cochinna calmly stepped through the beads, a wide smile curving her painted lips.

"Welcome, Noble Warriors. My sister-student and I weren't expecting guests tonight, but of course you are welcome."

Whoever was in the doorway hesitated, then growled, "We have no time for pleasure, Comely. We are searching for two escaped slave women and three savages. Have you seen them?"

Cochinna had stiffened when the man had called her Comely. Marti wasn't sure why, but obviously Cochinna considered the word an insult.

"I have seen no escaped slave or savages, Warrior. Only warriors have visited here tonight."

The man swore. From out in the hall someone snarled, "Where could they have gone? Master Unar will toss us into the pit if we don't find his precious mutant. Then the door slammed with a bang and they heard no more.

Marti let out the breath she'd been unconsciously holding. "Phew, that was close."

While the two women were occupied cleaning up, Chelka came over to Marti and whispered next to her ear, "Sister, who are these strange women?"

Marti gave her a low throaty chuckle. "They are the Ghostland's version of whores."

Chelka dipped her head crest. "I don't understand what that word means in your language. What's a whore?"

Marti sighed, she'd forgotten how sheltered Chelka's life had been before coming to Ticca and meeting the Speir'dina. And, as far as she knew, in the southern lands where the Khutani held sway she didn't think they had sex trade workers of any kind.

She might have explained further, but at that moment the two women came back into the room, Cochinna carrying strips of damp scented cloth in her hands. "We should finish binding your wound before we are interrupted again," she announced.

Catching a whiff of the unfamiliar scent on the cloth again, Marti held up a hand to stop her. "What's on the cloth, Enchanting Cochinna?"

Cochinna frowned, surprised by her question. "Why just a little Crivo to ease the pain, that is all. There's not enough in the cloth to cause harm, I assure you."

Marti shook her head and backed away. "No, if we have to fight our way out of here that Crivo—whatever might slow my reflexes down getting me killed. Whatever that crazy bacach drugged me with when they took me and Chelka is still giving me a headache. I don't want any more Ghostland drugs, but thanks all the same."

Chelka flattened her head crest. She didn't like the idea of being drugged again either, and she still wasn't sure she trusted these two anyway. "We should go, Sister. Our companions will be looking for us."

"Yes you should, Cochinna agreed, "and Lively Kitha and I will show you a way to leave that the warriors won't think of to look for you."

Marti folded her muscular arms across her chest and scowled down at the painted Ghostlanders. "And why would you do that for us? Why would you risk so much for strangers? You would be killed if we are caught."

"Because we don't like it here; the men here are cruel and hurt us," Kitha said. She stepped forward and boldly ran a soft hand down Marti's muscular arm, then brushed the same hand lightly over a sable nipple teasing it to erectness. "We want new protectors, kind protectors. We are clever and experienced pleasure slaves, never lazy or sullen. We will be good to you—and your man, too, if he wants us. Will you—and your people be our new protectors and benefactors?" she cooed.

Pleasure slaves, eh? Oh, Holy Mother Timorna, what will Nathan think about this! Marti swore under her breath and gently removed Kitha's hand. "That's a generous offer, but not how it works for us, Kitha.

"I don't know what kind of garbage you've heard from the changelings coming north, but the Speir'dina are a people who value freedom. We don't own slaves—any kind of slaves. We could use your help getting out of here, true, and if you want to take the risk we will take you with us. After that you can decide for yourself about how to live your life."

"Decide for myself with no Benefactor to tell me what I must do. That is a delightful thought—if true, Warrior," Cochinna said, still not totally convinced. She glanced at her student, who gave her a nod. "We will guide you and come with you, and may the Unseen Ones bless our venture."

Chapter Eleven

Tesulu and his men ghosted down the quiet halls. It was a meal time and most of the fortress's inhabitants were occupied elsewhere. Reaching the corridor with the unpleasant smells, they heard shouting at the far end and slipped into the shadows to listen.

From what they could make out an irate Ghostlander was screaming at his minions for losing something—or someone... Juba and he exchanged looks. Could it be the women he'd—mislaid? Tesulu smiled and Juba returned it. Sly like an Oko, those women were.

Or maybe Nasrid or his commander found the women first and stole them back. Tesulu could feel his temper boil. Had the women escaped on their own, or had they been hidden away somewhere else—by someone else. Tesulu doubted that Nasrid had known about the women's disappearance before allowing them to return to their quarters. Their escort would have been more alert for trouble if they'd known. Instead, their guards had seemed as surprised by the empty room as he was.

He needed more information before running off and getting the rest of his warriors killed. And the Ghostlander down the hall just might have a few answers for him. Signing for the wounded Ingazi to act as sentry, he motioned for Juba to follow him down the corridor. Posting themselves on either side of the open lighted doorway they waited for the men inside to be dismissed and leave.

Muttering under their breaths about how unfair it was to blame them, the angry warriors were paying no attention to a possible menace waiting for them in the hall. As the door closed, Juba and Tesulu plunged their spears into their exposed backs. A smaller Ghostlander dressed in a wrinkled kaftan had been hidden between his burly escort. When he saw his escort fall he let out a startled squeak and then raced down the hall.

Ingazi stepped out of a doorway and slit his throat before he could sound the alarm. He gave Tesulu an all clear gesture and dragged the body into a shadowy alcove. Tesulu grunted and flung open the door behind him and walked boldly in, Juba at his back.

A plump Ghostlander bending over a work table swung around, his pale hairless face still mottled with anger.

"What now Belam, I told you don't come back until—" he broke off staring openmouthed at his unexpected visitors.

Tesulu glided closer grinning, displaying his canines. "Not to worry, Wizard Puke, he won't be coming back—ever."

The breeding master backed up a step, his whole body trembling. "W-what do you want?" he stammered.

Tesulu took a step closer. "I want my property back, of course, Wizard Slime."

"I-I don't know what you're talking about, Savage. Now get out of here before I call the guard," he said and edged a little closer to a shelf of bottles on the wall behind him.

Tesulu gripped his spear a little tighter. The creature was trying his patience. Out of the corner of his eye he saw Juba with his knife drawn, creeping along the wall, hoping to get behind the fat man while he focused his attention on Tesulu. "I think not. Then you would have to explain to Commander Calahar where you've hidden the women. Do you want that, eh? No, you will not call for the guards, but you will tell me where they are."

His eyes going to the spear, the breeding master swallowed hard and cringed, moving ever closer to the shelf. "I don't know where they are—m-maybe the commander or, or his Second have them now. I don't know—I swear I don't. But I intend to find out," he snarled. "When you're dead." Whirling, he snatched a bottle off the shelf at random and hurled its contents in Tesulu's direction.

His trained warrior's reflexes saving him from the worst of the attack, only a few droplets of the stinging acid peppered his arm. Before the Ghostlander could launch another missal Juba stepped up from behind and slit his throat.

Tesulu gritted his teeth furious at himself for his carelessness. That had been close! The burning in his arm was a painful reminder of his arrogance and inattention. The burns now frothing with an ugly yellow foam, Tesulu hurried to a basin in the corner, and plunged his arm into the cool liquid. The tiny wounds stopped their foaming, but deep down he could still feel the penetrating ache of the acid.

Refilling the basin he immersed the arm again. The water was helping, but the water's cleansing was taking too long. He gritted his teeth and removed his arm when the worst of the Wizard's poison was washed away. He would just have to endure the pain and hope for the best. Maybe one of the kashallans could finish the healing later. They still needed to find those crazy women and get out of here. But not before doing more damage to this hateful place. No sense leaving many lethal weapons laying around to be used on Allied warriors when they broke into the fortress, he reasoned.

"Juba, you and Ingazi drag those bodies in here." Tesulu began snatching things off shelves at random and smashing them atop and around the dead Ghostlanders his warriors placed in the middle of the floor. Adding to the mound, they piled any writing materials they found and other items the three thought could be used against them in the coming battle.

At last deciding they'd spent enough time here, Tesulu and Juba took a couple lamps and tossed them onto the pyre. When the flames were burning nicely they closed the door on the inferno and raced down the hall.

"I hope we haven't created a fire that will poison the air and kill us all," Juba muttered as they turned the corner on a different hall and ran smack into some of Nasrid's men looking for them.

ENCHANTING COCHINNA put her head out the kitchen door that led into a passage used mainly by servants and slaves. She checked to see if the corridor was empty, then she closed the door and said, "There is no one out there; we should go. Mistress Lareusha, the Gaishinay in charge here may come soon to check on us.

Now dressed more sensibly for travel both women had changed their revealing garments for modest long dresses and thick outer robes. A bulging bag crossed each one's shoulder and Cochinna carried a small ornamented bag in one delicate hand.

Marti's eyes had widened when she saw them. Had these two been planning their own escape before they conveniently came along to act as their armed escort? Motioning for Cochinna to step back so the warriors could precede them, Marti paused before opening the door as a new thought came to her. "This escape tunnel you are leading us to, is it near enough to the surface that I can let our people know we are coming?"

Cochinna frowned thinking. "If you call out or draw attention to us by signaling to your warriors, the Honored Nasrid's men will capture us."

Marti shook her head and showed the two women the tiny com device nesting in her hair. "In the stone like we are now, it is nearly impossible for them to get my signal. But once I get close enough to the surface for this to start transmitting again I will tap out an emergency code that will bring them running. I have no need to cry out."

"Speir'dina magic," Kitha breathed.

"No magic, My Lovely." Cochinna shook her head studying Marti in a new light. "Your wizard must be very clever if he has given your people access to some of the old technology of this world without the Cabal in Tiebarai knowing."

"I don't know anything about what technology you Ghostlanders managed to save or recreate from your destroyed civilization. As I said, we aren't mutants from the West. We have our own tech that we brought with us when our craft was destroyed, leaving us stranded here." Marti opened the door, ending the conversation.

"Sister, wait," Chelka said. "I can't believe I'm going to say this, but shouldn't we try to find the war leader and the rest of our men?"

"Yes, we should," Marti agreed. "But I haven't a clue how to find them." She glanced at the Ghostlanders. "Do you know where Nasrid and his men were holding us before that slimy fat bacach stole us?"

"No," Cochinna said, answering for both of them. ""Maybe when we get near the slave gate you can signal your warriors to come for them."

Marti scowled. She wasn't sure Cochinna was speaking the truth. She seemed to know much of the gossip whispered among the slaves in a place like this. But the woman was right, they needed to be on the move. She hoped they might recognize something familiar on the way. Cochinna once more taking the lead, the four women crept out into the corridor and hurried down the dark hall.

They had traveled unnoticed through several branching corridors, when a cloud of noxious air coming out of a side passage caused them to choke and cough. Eyes stinging they beat a hasty retreat.

Hurrying towards cleaner air the women leaned against the stone wall gasping for breath. "Ik, what is that horrible smell," Chelka said when she could speak without coughing.

"I have no idea, Cochinna said. "Breeding Master Unar's work rooms are down there. He is always working on some nasty project or another, but it's never been that bad before."

Master Unar, eh? Marti shivered guessing what horrors he might have had in mind for her. "We should keep moving. Whatever is going on will attract the guard's attention soon."

"But just past the master's workrooms is the hallway leading to the slave gate we plan to use," Kitha wailed. "What will we do now?"

"We will find another way, stop sniveling, Student," Cochinna snapped. Then addressing the warriors, she said, "There *is* another way to the slave gate, but it is more dangerous, because it is closer to the barracks, but we have no choice now." Her mouth set in a hard line she lead them down another confusing corridor.

Their plans changed once again when turning into a deserted passage, they heard roaring erupt ahead. Through the flickering lantern light near the next intersection they could see the shadows of men in combat. "We need to go back," Kitha hissed, "before they see us."

Marti was about to agree with her when amidst the clash and bam of spears she heard someone utter one of Lann Gheal's favorite curses. Marti swore herself and started down the corridor.

"Marti, where are you going?" Chelka hissed urgently.

"Warrior, no we have to go back—find another way," Cochinna echoed.

Marti turned walking backwards a few steps. "Chelka, it's the rest of the patrol. I knew those amadans would get themselves into trouble left on their own—come on. We have to hurry before that fool war leader gets himself killed."

Chelka growled but leapt after her partner. "Warriors, Please. What are you doing—come back!" Kitha cried.

"We'll be back, Ladies. Just keep out of the way," Marti called over her shoulder as the sister warriors raced towards the struggling men.

The pleasure slaves looked at one another in frustration. "What do we do now, Mentor?" Kitha whispered. "Should we go back to our apartment and wait for another opportunity?"

Cochinna frowned, her painted face a mask of disapproval. What should they do indeed? Warriors of any species and sex were always unpredictable creatures. "We will wait a while and see what happens."

"But what if we are seen—"

"If we are discovered," Cochinna broke in before she could finish. "We will say the alien warriors forced us to help them, and cry grateful tears to those who rescue us." She motioned for Kitha to follow her down the hall. "Right now, they are still our best chance of escape from this place. Come, I want to see. Then we will know better what to do."

Kitha followed, but muttered under her breath, "Mistress Lareusha will punish us severely if you are wrong, Wise Mentor."

"Then pray hard that I am not, Doubting Student."

TESULU KNEW THEY HAD to kill their adversaries and escape before the sounds of combat drew the attention of more enemy fighters. Unfortunately, the Ghostland officer facing him wasn't cooperating with his plan. The man was one of the elite class and a more skilled opponent than Tesulu would have liked. Plus his still burning arm was causing him to favor that limb and slowing down his reactions. He was hard pressed—and knew it—damn the man to the Poison Fires.

The enemy warrior seemed to sense his advantage and pressed Tesulu mercilessly, a smile curving his lips and triumph gleaming in his hard eyes.

Then suddenly the man staggered and dropped to the stone at his feet, blood spewing from his still smiling lips. His own mouth open wide in surprise Tesulu glanced up to see Chelka pulling a spear out of the man's back and then she whirl to face another opponent.

Knife in one hand and a captured spear in the other Marti laughed at his astonished expression. Returning to the task at hand, she feinted with her knife and plunged the spear into another enemy's unprotected guts. "I knew me and my sister warrior were gonna have to come rescue you boyos before we could get outta here."

Tesulu snorted, but now wasn't the time to argue the point with her. Without conscious thought, the five allied warriors fell into the battle formations they had practiced so many times while preparing for this war.

Leaning against the wall after all the enemy lay dead around them, Marti grinned and said, "I'm ready for our noble protectors to take us back now. My sweetie will have to make his own tea when he comes. "

Juba snorted a laugh. Then spying the two pleasure slaves heading down the hall towards them, he cursed and leapt forward, bloody knife in hand to grab them before they sounded an alarm.

"Don't hurt them, warrior," Chelka called. "They are friends."

Tesulu stared, two Ghostlanders their friends? He wasn't so sure about that. But by then Chelka had placed herself between Juba and the women.

"They are our guides out of here," she repeated.

"We have no need of Ghostlander 'guides,'" Tesulu said. "I know a way out, too. Juba, kill them."

"No," Marti snarled and stood beside Chelka, clutching her spear. "We can't do that. They saved our lives, War Leader. The warriors here will torture and kill them horribly as traitors if we don't take them. They don't deserve death from you or anyone for helping us," she insisted.

Tesulu snarled at her challenge to his authority as war leader, but more shouting from behind them in the darkness ended the argument. He motioned for Juba to put away his knife. "All right, Speir'dina you can keep your toys. This way. Come!"

Hurrying to catch up with Tesulu, Marti gasped, "Cochinna there," she pointed to the taller woman Chelka was helping along, "she was guiding us to the gate the slaves assigned to work in the fields use."

The sounds of people discovering the dead they'd left in their wake and pursuit were coming closer. Tesulu shook his head and quickened the pace. "No time to find it now, we will go to the one I know about."

Entering another smelly passage at a dead run, Marti gasped, "Ugg! War Leader, where are you taking us?"

Tesulu didn't stop to answer; there was no time for an argument. The enemy was too close. She would find out soon enough.

"Fuck! A sewer hole?" Marti gagged.

The entrance looming ahead of them was a shallow tunnel ending in a steep incline. Near the edge of the slope several recently emptied buckets were stacked against the wall, waiting to be cleaned. The incline was covered in a dark slime running down to a wide hole, muddy water lapping at its rim. Good thing the slope was covered in slime; it was going to be a tight fit for some of them she thought and shrugged.

Pausing at the edge, Marti tapped her com. "Hey Boughthy, if you're still out there we are coming your way hot. Tell Command we need back up. We are in the river—need the boats. And we found the Hunt Leader's back door." *Though the boyos weren't going to like it much*, she thought.

"War Leader, you are such a shit. The women's way would have been—drier and cleaner. Couldn't you find a better way out?"

Tesulu snorted a laugh. "Soon I won't be the only one who's a shit eh, Speir'dina?" He motioned for Juba to help the wounded Ingazi down the slimy incline and into the river. He waved for her to follow when he saw they were clear of the opening. Letting her captured spear fall to the stone Marti took some deep breaths, held her nose and slid on her rump feet-first after them.

"Wait! Don't leave without me!" Not wanting her new protector to disappear out of sight, Kitha followed her without being told. Her mouth twisted into a mew of disgust, Cochinna lifted her robes, clutched her bags and followed her student into the foaming brown water.

The sounds of pursuit were coming closer. Lifting his bow from its case, Tesulu glanced back the way they'd come. The Ghostlanders were close, probably following Ingazi's blood trail. When he returned his attention to the sewer outlet he saw Chelka frozen at the edge, staring blindly into the dark water. "Go Warlinga!"

Chelka ignored him, continuing to watch the foaming water. Cursing Tesulu grabbed her roughly, and spun her around to face him, demanding, "What's wrong with you, Woman we need to go."

She looked at him quivering, her red eyes moist and pleading. "I don't know how to swim, War Leader—no Warlinga does—we never—"

"Then you will have to learn fast, Woman," he snarled and gave her a mighty shove. Losing her balance Chelka fell heavily and slid down the slimy incline head first and into the river.

"Stupid Warlinga," Tesulu muttered. At a shout he spun around and fired a few darts at the first men coming into view down the passage, making them dive for cover. Taking several deep breaths Tesulu followed his patrol down the sewer.

HOLDING HER BREATH as long as she could, Marti allowed the current to carry her as far as possible before she surfaced. Pushing hair and river water out of her eyes she glanced about trying to figure out in the dim light of twilight where she was. Not far from her one of the clan warriors was helping the wounded Ingazi into one of the black inflatables. Owyn was steering, Medic Ruan already crawling over the seats to have a look at the wounded man as Juba pulled himself into the boat.

Coming her way was the other inflatable, with Boughthy at the controls. Marti submerged to make sure any offal wasn't still clinging to her before reaching for the hand Lubwey stretched out to her.

Fanning a hand in front of his face Boughthy complained, "Maybe we should throw you back in the river. You stink like a privy."

Marti laughed. "Sewer pipe actually. That crazy amadan Tesulu's way out was out a sewer."

"Yuck, go sit in the bow will ya," Boughthy said turning the boat around, heading for the far shore.

Marti snorted and splashed water at him. "Get used to it, Infant, the sewer is the way in and you might be in the first patrol."

"Speaking of Sand Mountain, where is War Leader Tesulu?" Lubwey asked.

All mirth forgotten Marti searched the water for the rest of the patrol. She didn't see Tesulu or Chelka in the other boat. A cold chill ran down her spine. Had they stayed to cover their retreat and then fallen to an enemy spear? After all she and Chelka had gone through together both here and back in Riath—to lose her now... No, Mother Timorna, please not that, she prayed silently.

Then spying the two pleasure slaves struggling to stay afloat in the current she pointed. "Boughthy, over there those two women are with us. We gotta get them before they drown."

Spying the floundering swimmers, Boughthy expertly steered the boat in that direction. Leaning over the side Lubwey reached out and grabbed the closer of the pair, and dragged the female into the bottom of the boat. Face paint smeared and dripping, the whimpering Kitha crawled to Marti and flung herself into the warrior woman's lap, throwing her arms around Marti's neck. Boughthy blinked, his mouth dropping open in surprise.

"Ghostlander pleasure slave," Lubwey explained, also staring at the bedraggled woman.

Boughthy allowed the boat to drift, continuing to stare. Finally he murmured to Lubwey, "You mean here in the North these guys have whores?"

Lubwey frowned. "I'm not sure what that means in your language, Speir'dina, but if you mean slaves who are trained to offer a man pleasure, then yes, the wizards and the elite classes in Tiebarai keep such slaves."

Still watching Marti and the whimpering slave, Boughthy said thoughtfully, "Damn, wait till McLaren and the boyos hear about this. They are going to love it when we take Tiebarai."

Marti's head shot up. "You two, stop being amadans and find the other Ghostlander." They turned back to the river, but by then there was no sign of Enchanting Cochinna.

Still in the river and weighted down by her clothes and bags Cochinna felt her head sinking once more below the surface, and this time she wasn't sure she had the strength to claw her way up to the life-giving air again. So this would be how it will end, she thought. Her gamble for freedom had been only a wistful dream after all. Ah, well maybe the warrior Kitha fancied would be good to her. Cochinna hoped so.

Then a sinewy body wrapped a coil about her waist and swam with her towards air and light. Some distance away from the safety of the boat, she immerged, gasping for air, still confined tightly in the creature's coils. Once on the surface, it swiveled its head around to face her. Cochinna stared into assessing yellow eyes and felt her blood run cold. She was now helpless, ensnared by a Khutani, the ancient enemy of her people.

Black kavay... Swallowing down the terror that was threatening to overwhelm her reason, Cochinna lay still awaiting her fate.

This powerful being was one of the invaders that came to her world at the time of the Great Wars. The Khutani Makers had claimed they came to help save their world, but all they had done was to drive her people out of the lands that had once been their ancestral home, so they could breed and repopulate those favored lands with slaves of their own making.

The Khutani bent its head and brushed sensitive mouth tentacles across her face. Finding a small open cut at the base of her neck, the Khutani inserted a tentacle and formed a link. An amused colorless voice spoke directly into her mind.

<<Well, Ghostlander, you were not what I was expecting to find when I caught you and helped you to the surface. I thought at first you were one of the Speir'dina related to our cousin Nathan-Corha.>> The Khutani rumbled a laugh. <<It has been a long time since we have tasted one of this world's ancient destroyers. The question is now what do I do with you?>>

<<Whatever you wish, Khutani, I am powerless to stop you.>>

<<That is true.>> it agreed. <<But I taste in you none of the ancient taint that nearly destroyed this world, or the wizard's vengeful malice—only fear. Fear of me and of the warriors in Te'gal. You want to escape them. Why is that Ghostlander? I am curious.>>

<<Because I hate them....>> Unaware of the compulsion the Khutani had sent down the link they now shared, Cochinna felt the anger and frustrations of her life boiling to the surface of her mind. Unable to stop, she found herself reliving and sharing much of her life experiences with a being her people named enemy.

Sometime later when she lay exhausted and trembling in its coils, the Khutani spoke once more. <<You have given me much to savor, Enchanting Cochinna. If you still wish to seek shelter and protection among the Kashallan Alliance I will not kill you. Instead I will take you to shore where my people will care for you as they are now caring for your student.>>

<<Yes, please take me to join my student, Khutani. I swear I will not betray the trust you have shown in me. I will help your people all I can in the war that's coming.>>

<<So be it then, Little One. Now that I have tasted you, I will know if you betray us. And I will punish you with the death you fear if you do, wherever you might try to hide in future.>>

TESULU SURFACED AND looked around searching for his patrol and the boats he hoped were hear to rescue them, before someone on the fortress wall started shooting crossbow bolts at him. Ahead he saw Marti and one of the Ghostland toys, being dragged into a Speir'dina boat. Juba and Ingazi were already in the other. He didn't care much about the missing Ghostlander, but where was the stupid Warlinga?

That Tragar K'San was going to be very angry if he lost her now. He tread water looking for her. Ah, there she was floundering, her head once more disappearing under the surface. Cursing, he swam in that direction.

Diving under the water he peered through the gloom and finally saw her sinking to the bottom. His tail whipping the water to increase his speed, Tesulu dove after her.

Coming up behind her he placed a strong arm around her neck and swam for the surface. Pulling both their heads atop the water he held her face above the surface as he took in several deep lungfuls of air.

Gasping, a choking Chelka panicked, trying to claw out of his grip.

"Stop fighting me, Woman, I have you. I won't let you drown." He chuckled. "Your man and his old hunt leader would never forgive me if I did that. Then, to his surprise several eel-like creatures surrounded them, gurgling happily.

Khutani. He gritted his teeth, forcing himself to ignore the ancient fear that had been such a part of Clan traditions for countless generations. After all, he told himself, he now had a Khutani relative in Phillip-Yoey, so he might as well get used to the new order of things.

Instead of guiding him to be picked up by one of the boats the pod headed for the shoreline far out of range of the fortress weaponry. When they reached shallow water, the Khutani urged them onto the beach with gentle nips.

Helping Chelka to her feet, Tesulu led her to shore where anxious Speir'dina and the rest of his patrol were waiting for them.

Chapter Twelve

Looking up as she tried to comfort the sobbing Kitha, who had noticed her mentor wasn't among the people waiting for them, Marti saw several dark figures heading towards the group on the river bank. The two Warlinga with them were probably Aju'an and Tobrach. And though it was hard to tell in the dim light one of the taller Speir'dina must be her sweetie, Nathan-Corha.

Hastily getting to her feet she extracted herself from the clinging Lovely Kitha and bounded over to fling her arms around a startled Nathan.

Holding her at arm's length Nathan glared down at her, trying not to show how relieved he was to see her. "You're a crazy Amadan for agreeing to be a part of the war leader's risky stunt. I ought'ta—" He broke off and pulled her into a bone-crushing hug. Marti laughed and hugged him back.

Releasing her at last he held her out at arms' length. Noticing the knife wound still leaking a little fresh blood, he asked, "You all right?"

Marti shrugged. "Sure, that's just a scratch. Ran into one of the Dingay brats, hiding out in the fortress. He's dead now, but there's still a few more in there."

"Mm, Dingay, eh?" Wanting to be sure Corha extended its tentacles and slid them into the flesh of her arm. Nathan closed his eyes to allow the symbiont's senses to dominate their awareness.

<<Marti's wound isn't serious, as she claims, Kasha, but she tastes—strange.>> Corha said, and Nathan could sense his bondmate's puzzlement.

<<What do you mean, Shalla?>>

<<Someone has given her something—maybe more than one substance that I can still taste in her blood.>>

Thinking about Phillip-Yoey's warning about biological warfare, a cold chill of fear ran down his spine. <<Is she going to be all right, Shalla?>>

<<Yes, I believe so. The substance is fading, but now that I have its taste implanted in my memory I will ask our Amla later to be sure.>>

<<Yes, do that, Shalla.>> Well that was a relief, but he would have to ask her about what really happened in the fortress when there was more time. Opening his eyes Nathan smiled down at her. "Yeah, you crazy amadan, I guess you are all right." Holding a hand to his mouth, he spat out a thick yellow paste and plastered it over the long cut.

"Hate to break up this happy little reunion," Murda said as he handed Marti her clothes and weapons, "but Command needs your report." Then spying a sobbing Lovely Kitha for the first time, he blurted, "Who is that?"

Nathan turned to stare as well, Marti still held in one arm. A bedraggled and shivering mixed-race Ghostlander with pale fur and Avairei features stared back at them. Marti detached herself from Nathan and pulling on her clothes and weapons she hurried to put an arm around the stranger's shoulder. Leading the woman over to introduce her to Nathan-Corha, she said, "This is Lovely Kitha. She and her mentor Enchanting Cochinna were helping Chelka and me find our way out, after we got separated from the rest of the patrol. They—uh—wanted to come with us."

Lovely, eh? Well the poor shivering creature didn't look so lovely after being half drown in the river, Nathan thought. Then her dripping make up and ornamented clothes registered in Nathan's awareness. Speaking in Caldoni, he said, "Uh, Marti, is she—"

"Yeah, she's the Ghostland's version of a sex trade worker—or in this case a slave. She and her mentor didn't like the way they were being treated so," she shrugged. "They came to join the alliance."

Nathan bobbed his head in a greeting to the wide eyed Ghostlander now clinging to Marti's arm again. Speaking once more in the Northern dialect so she could understand, he said, "Greetings. I'm Marti's—friend, Nathan-Corha."

Kitha studied him for a long moment and then smiled. "I am happy to meet you, Warrior. I have already heard about you. I am very skilled and I can also give you much pleasure. Will you be my Protector, too?"

Out of the corner of his eye he thought he saw Murda smirk. Not all the Allied Forces spoke the Ghostland language. There'd not been enough time during training to share with everyone the language patterns they would need. Had he understood what she was saying? Damn it had Phillip-Yoey shared the Northern dialect language patterns with him?

Nathan could sense Corha's awakened interest. He was glad it was almost dark so nobody could see his blush. Deciding to change the subject, he asked Marti, "You said there were two of them; where is the other one?"

Marti sighed, and turned to look at the river, barely visible in the growing darkness. Her voice thick with sadness, she said, "We lost her in the river; guess she drowned."

Nathan and the others nearby turned to look in that direction. Then suddenly Kitha, whose eyes were keener in the dim light, let out a glad cry. "No, My Honored Protector, I see her. The river has given her back to us. Praise to the Fire Gods she didn't drown. You still have two pleasure slaves here to see to your comforts."

Breaking away from Marti, she hurried to embrace the pale figure being helped onto the gravel beach by a grinning Boughthy.

"Protector, eh>" Murda said, trying to suppress a chuckle and not doing a good job of it. "What were you and the patrol getting up to in that Ghosty Place, I wonder?" he asked Marti.

"Shut up, Amadan, it's not what you think," Marti protested. Nathan rolled his eyes. "It's not! and both of you are amadans."

<<Ghostlanders, I want to taste them,>> Corha burbled in his mind. "And if they were nice to our Marti I won't kill them.>>

<<No, we won't kill them,>> Nathan agreed. <<They may have valuable information for the alliance—provided we can trust them.>>

<<And I will know that after I taste them,>> an exasperated Corha said. Then thinking more on the topic of the Ghostlanders, the symbiont added, <<What kind of pleasure do you think she was talking about, Kasha?>>

Nathan sighed. <<I don't know and we aren't going to find out right now. We need to get information for Command, remember?>>

STILL A BIT SHAKY ON her legs, Chelka didn't resist when Tesulu continued to help her up the beach. She could see an anxious Tobrach and her brother Aju'an coming to meet them. Aju'an handed over her warrior woman's apron and she gratefully put it on. Now modestly clothed again, she turned to smile at her betrothed. "Hello, Dear One, I am back."

Tobrach dipped his head crest and returned the smile. "Yes, and thank Mother Timorna and The Great Hunt Leader for that." He wanted to take her in his arms and lick her neck and other special places, but here on this riverbank with battle at hand, he felt too shy to do so. Instead he turned to a smiling Tesulu and offered him his hand. "Thank you, War Leader Tesulu. I am in your debt."

Still smiling Tesulu took the offered hand. He liked the idea of having this Warlinga K'San in his debt. "It is as I told your old hunt leader, K'San, I keep my warrior's oaths."

"War Leader Tesulu," Rhys said stepping up to greet them. "Command wants a report from you and the rest of your patrol. As soon as things quiet down in the fortress we will begin the attack."

Tesulu nodded, starting to walk away, calling for the others to join him. Further up the slope he could see someone had just lit a fire, so he headed in that direction. The night air was a chill in his still damp fur.

"War Leader Tesulu, aren't you forgetting something?" Chelka marched up to him, her expression grim and held out her hand.

Tesulu feigned puzzlement. "No I am not forgetting anything."

Chelka gritted her teeth, still holding out her hand. Bemused Tobrach and Aju'an followed to stand on either side of her. Finally she broke down and growled, "I want my Speir'dina knife back—right now, Warrior."

"Your knife, such a beautiful weapon. I think I will keep it in exchange for not letting you drown in the river. Is that not a good trade your life for the weapon?" He was looking at Tobrach by the time he finished his little speech. Tobrach was inclined to agree with him, he could see that in the Warlinga's red eyes, but a growl from Chelka made him focus his attention back on her again.

"No, it is not a good trade, because I saved *your* life, too, remember?" she held out her hand again. "I figure that makes us even, so I don't owe you anything, Warrior—especially my knife."

"You did promise to return it," Aju'an said, his expression grim. "Mar told me."

Sighing, he took the knife and its sheath off his belt and handed it to her. She had a point—damn her—and he *had* promised.

NATHAN SENT BOUGHTHY to find a couple blankets for the shivering women and then hurried everyone over to where Murda had lit a small fire. Tucked up amongst the boulders and behind a thicket of thorn, they would be sheltered from the cold wind blowing down the valley, and out of sight of the fortress.

Gesturing for the women to come close to the fire, he took the blankets from Boughthy and placed them about their shoulders. Grateful for the fire and the added warmth over their damp clothes, the Ghostlanders pulled the blankets tight and stared into the flames, aware of the curious attention focused on them by the surrounding warriors.

After he saw to the comfort of their unexpected visitors Nathan sat down beside them and motioned for the rest of the men to gather and report. Rhys set a black box-shaped device on the sand and several warriors jumped when they heard Hunt Leader Tizu's voice coming out of the tiny device. "All right, people. Rhys tells me everyone's back safe. Good to know, so let's hear what you found out."

Tesulu began, Marti and Juba chiming in with added comments when necessary. When they'd finished Hunt Leader Tizu summed up, "Marti, you told Boughthy to relay to me that you found another way into the fortress. The main entrance will be heavily defended and we might lose a lot of men, so we're gonna blow the front gates, but it would help to have some of our people come in from behind and surprise them. "

Marti laughed. "I'm not sure if we can get people back in the same way we came out. Don't know if Boughthy told you, but we were hard pressed at the end so we had to use the sewer. Getting back that way would be hard, because the incline is steep, slippery and a tight fit for men with gear and weapons. And we might have to swim part of the way. The Warlinga would find that hard."

"We plan to use the Warlinga troops on the frontal assault for the reason you mentioned. Some of the Clan warriors and Lann Gheal would come in from behind. The sewer entrance is another matter, however. Anybody got a suggestion about that?"

Juba grinned at Marti and Chelka. Then in a low voice, he said, still grinning, "Ask your little toys, Speir'dina, didn't they say there was another way in or out, eh?"

"What did you say, Warrior," Tizu said, "speak up."

Marti shot Juba a murderous glare, but before she could open her mouth with something cutting in response Nathan said, "Uh, Hunt Leader, the patrol brought a couple civilians with them when they left the fortress. The women told Marti and Chelka they know another way in."

"What! who are these women?"

"Uh, they're slaves, Hunt Leader, and they, uh, agreed to help our people escape. They were going to get them out by this back door Marti mentioned to Boughthy, but the plan had to be aborted in favor of Tesulu's way at the end."

There was a murmured conversation at the other end; Tizu obviously conferring with the other leaders. Finally he came back and said, "Have you tasted these women, Corha? We need to make sure they haven't been sent to us as spies."

Well why not? Nathan thought. That was exactly what Tesulu's patrol had been doing in the fortress after all. Taking the startled Cochinna's hand, he glanced at Marti, who shook her head no.

"Not possible, we came to their apartment only by chance when we were looking for our guys."

Still just holding her hand Nathan turned back to study the women. The younger one, who didn't seem to be translating the conversation completely, watched him through half closed eyes, unsure what was expected of her.

The other and older woman, who seemed to be a true Ghostlander now that he could see her more clearly in the firelight returned his stare calmly with no attempt to pull away, or divert him with coquettish flirting. At last taking a deep breath, she said, "I will help you Khutani, I have already sworn to your kindred in the river that in exchange for my life I would help your people."

Nathan's eyebrows rose at that unexpected revelation. Extending his tentacles he slipped them into the skin below her wrist and apologized, "I'm sorry, but my Hunt Leader will want me to verify your claim," Nathan said.

Cochinna stiffened at his touch, then relaxed when she realized he wasn't going to hurt her. "Do what you must, Khutani."

<<She's right, Kasha, one of the Amsi has tasted her. I think it was K'amsi Sika.>> Corha was quiet for a while, exploring, tasting, then finally the symbiont said, <<Kasha, she isn't lying. She will help us, but she too has the strange taste like Marti—only much, much stronger.>>

<<Good to know she isn't lying or a spy, Shalla, but about this unfamiliar taste—>>

Breaking in on their internal conversation, Tizu demanded, "Nathan, what's going on?"

"I'm tasting one of the Ghostlanders right now," Corha said.

"Good. Ask her about this other way in," Tizu said

Taking a deep breath Cochinna said loud enough for the voice in the box to hear, "There is an entrance where the overseers bring the slaves who work in the fields. It is near the river and not usually guarded once the slaves are asleep in their quarters at night. It will probably be barred from the inside, however."

"That's good to know thank you," Tizu said. "Rhys, you and Tesulu can head up the mission, send Murda back to me to help coordinate communications. Everybody stay on channel six, got that?"

"Hunt Leader, I would like to go with the squad going in the back way," Marti said. "I saw a bit of the interior in case we need to split up, and I think our guide would feel more comfortable with me along."

"Good point, Armachd, you can go then."

Nathan opened his mouth to object being left out of the mission, but as if reading his mind Tizu said, "No, Nathan. You aren't leading up a squad. You're more use to this operation if you are working in Medical with Phillip-Yoey."

"But—"

"No buts, Nathan, I'm still in charge here and I said no."

Staring over Nathan's shoulder, Murda's eyes widened in surprise. Then turning back to Nathan, he smirked. "I seem to recall many a time when you told Dunnagh something similar after he made a career change. Pay back's a bitch, eh Nathan?"

"Shut up, Murda, you amadan." Turning to see what Murda had been staring at, Nathan saw the Wa'chassey'ul standing silently behind him. Waiting to escort him back to the medics, no doubt. The Demon was taking the 'protect all kashallans,' part of her contract seriously these days. He sighed; Tess-weh would give her slave the power to *make* him obey if he tried ignoring Tizu's orders. Might as well give in gracefully and not make a fuss. Muttering one of his favorite Caldoni curses, he unslung his rifle and tossed it to Aju'an.

Then noticing the wounded Ingazi, he said, "You're with me, too. All right, Atahru, I'm coming."

Chapter Thirteen

As the one called Nathan-Corha motioned for Kitha to follow him, she desperately grasped Cochinna's hand. In a voice barely above a whisper, she said, "Mentor, I fear we have made a bad mistake. In our apartment the warriors were so dirty and bloody—I didn't see the sigils—but they must be agents for Mighty Drucas. He might be angry with us for helping the enemy when he reclaims his property."

Were these warrior women indeed spies working for the changeling and the Cabal in Tiebarai? Did the enemy alliance know? How could they not? There were Western Clan warriors in the Alliance, surely they could read and sense the magic implanted in the marks. What game was actually being played here? Cochinna suddenly feared that in their attempt to escape their despotic Gaishinay Mistress and the brutal and debouched warriors in Te'gal, they had placed themselves in a far greater danger.

An image of being ensnared and confined within a Khutani's coils, flashed before her mind's eye. With a sinking feeling she knew the enemy owned her body and soul. There was no escape for either of them. Handing her bags to Kitha she prayed their new masters would be kind.

"Be silent, Foolish Student. It is too late to turn back now. I did notice the glyphs, but things may not be as they appear. Use the lessons I've taught you and try to find out more information we can use to our advantage wherever they take us."

"LOVELY KITHA WILL BE fine," Marti said, coming up beside her. "She will be away from the fighting and no one will hurt her."

Unlike me, Cochinna thought. More warriors were gathering in the darkness just outside the firelight. Speaking in low voices, they checked their weapons and waited for their leader's signal. Unlike the creatures bred to defend the North who roared and boasted of their might, these warriors needed no whips or goads to make them fight. The alliance warriors were alert, disciplined—and deadly.

Cochinna shivered and took several deep breaths, trying to calm her nerves. Acting on impulse Cochinna said, "I know about the glyph you and your sister warrior wear. Are you here to spy on the enemy for him? Don't kill us, please. We won't tell them if so."

Marti turned, her face a dark blur in the guttering firelight even to Cochinna's night-sensitive eyes. Her voice a somber murmur, she said, "I was wondering when you or Kitha were going to ask one of us about the glyphs we wear. To answer your question, no, we aren't his willing agents. Quite the opposite is true. We took an oath to kill him for what he did to us when we were his prisoners—and the Khutani are helping us keep that promise."

Cochinna would have liked to ask more questions, but at that moment the one called Rhys came over to them. He handed Marti a pair of round shields like the ones covering his own eyes. Studying Cochinna, he said, "Sa, I'm assuming you can see to find your way fine in the dim light without any technical aids like we need, correct?"

Taking another deep breath, she said, "Yes, I believe I can."

"All right then, you and Marti will come with me so you can show us the way. Boughthy, Sietriga, you cover us with your rifles; we will take point. When we get in position you pick off anybody on the wall while Owyn and Tesulu go in and set the charge if this side gate is barred like the lady suspects." Turning to the one named Tesulu, Rhys said, "If your men are ready, let's move out."

"HELLO AGAIN, IMAS, Council Members and everyone back in the Yeyen Banai Valley. This is your man on the scene, Jojo, speaking to you from a thorn thicket on the slope above the great northern fortress of Te'gal." Jojo turned the recording device away from his face and showed the viewers the massive silhouette of a forbidding fortress across the narrow valley from his current position.

"That is the Ghostland fortress of Te'gal you are seeing. This is the place where the Umwira breed most of the frightening monsters that the wizards send south to terrorize our people." Adjusting the recorder's camera to a wider view that showed the warriors getting ready around him, he continued his voice-over narrative. "As you can see the fortress presents a formidable menace for a lasting peace, but the allied leaders are confident that our noble warriors can destroy this threat once and for all."

There was a murmured conversation in the background, then the camera showed a formation of dark silhouettes quietly moving down the dimly lit hillside, keeping under the cover of boulders and bushes as much as possible. "There goes the first wave," Jojo announced in a breathless whisper. "Command plans to assault the front gate with both Speir'dina weapons and the spears and crossbows of our native Timornan warriors. Meanwhile a contingent of our troops will come in from a side gate to assault them from the rear. Now that it's a bit safer we will go closer to the action," he burbled. The camera's images jumped about as Jojo followed the advancing column down the hill.

Suddenly there was a shout from a guard on the fortress wall. "Ah, our warriors have been discovered by Te'gal's defenders," he explained. "Hopefully they are close enough to send the men in to blow the gate."

There was a loud whooshing sound and then the night sky burst into light as several flaming balls exploded above the fortress.

"And, there go the first flares. Soon we will be able to see much better. Well, that should even the odds a bit," Jojo explained. "I've been told that Ghostlanders can see better in dim light than our warriors, but the flares should blind them somewhat, giving the allies an advantage."

The recorder showed running warriors of several species yelling war cries and racing towards the fortress gate. The recorder bounced up and down as Jojo kept pace just behind them. Ahead of the allies the defenders shouted their defiance and abuse as they hurled down stones and crossbow bolts at the approaching warriors.

"Oh look, everyone, our warriors have formed a shield barrier to protect our people from the Ghostlander's deadly missals. This is a tactic my Speir'dina ancestors used in our prehistoric past to storm a fortress," Jojo explained, shouting to be heard over the clamor.

Just ahead of him a man dressed in black raised his beam rifle and began picking off Te'gal's guards. The recorder caught an image of a snarling defender, and the portion of the wall behind which he crouched, suddenly they both vanished in a geyser of flame. Jojo could hear screams of anger and fear as other burly figures on the ramparts were also vaporized.

In the midst of the chaos a Speir'dina man guarded by Warlinga and Clan warriors, holding aloft shields had crept to the massive gates to set the explosive charge that would blow it open. Once it was in place at the edge of the gate, they ran for cover, shouting at the allied warriors to get back. Thinking that they had discouraged the attack, the defenders atop the wall crowed with victory and hurled abusive taunts and stones at the fleeing allied warriors.

Covering the army's retreat several of the Lann Gheal Armachda, Aju'an proudly among them with Nathan's rifle, knelt to continue picking off targets showing themselves on the wall.

Suddenly there was a loud boom, and then a fiery cloud of great stones, dust, and mangled bodies exploded into the night sky. As the dust was settling a great roar erupted from the Allied Warriors.

"Oh Viewers, did you see it?" Jojo exclaimed his voice gleeful and triumphant. "The gate is down and we are going in!"

Nearly knocking him to the ground, a wave of warriors rushed past Jojo, screaming their war cries. Using a device to extend their reach, the first men to enter Te'gal threw in ahead of them clay jars filled with homemade Timornan chemical substances that burst into flame upon impact with a solid surface. Leaping through the chaos, the allied warriors followed this frightening barrage with an attack that left Te'gal's defenders retreating before them.

Allowing the hatred festering for hundreds of years to fuel their battle frenzy, the hunters of Tragar led the charge into the heart of the Ghostland fortress, Aju'an and Chelka among them. This was what the Khutani had bred them for and they reveled in the slaughter of the enemy monsters they saw rising out of the chaos to challenge them.

RHYS AND THE PATROL crept through the fields of vegetation heading for the side entrance Cochinna told them was used by the slaves working in the fields. Studying the vegetation as they passed, Rhys murmured to Marti, "That masa root looks about ready for the first harvest. If it survives the battle we should have some of our people harvest it. We could use the extra supplies as we travel north."

"Our people?" Marti let out a quiet chuckle. "I notice you aren't volunteering yourself for that job, eh, Boyo?"

Rhys snorted. "No chance, I had enough of a slave's work when we were at Sulas."

"We'll get Boughthy to do it. The Infant could use the experience." Overhearing them, Sietriga smothered a laugh. "And you can join him, you big blond amadan."

"Be quiet, gossiping women," Tesulu hissed. "We are near enough they might hear us."

Not a chance, Rhys thought as the sky blossomed with light and they heard loud war cries coming from somewhere out of sight. Here we go, he thought. "We're visible now, so stay alert, Armachda."

The Ghostlander let out a startled cry, trying to shield her eyes from the light.

Marti put a hand on her shoulder. "Don't be afraid. Those are just flares to help us see the enemy."

"Unfortunately, it is the opposite for me. Without an eye shield for protection from the light, I am nearly blind right now," she wailed, trying to cover her face with her hands.

Marti swore and looked at Rhys helplessly. Rhys took a square of printed cloth from a pouch at his waist and put it into the squinting Cochinna's hand. "See if this will help shield your eyes. I'm so sorry, Sa, we didn't think of that. Maybe you can just tell us how much farther to this gate and we can leave you here for now."

Cochinna tied the cloth over her eyes and shook her head, pleading, "No, please don't leave me here alone. I can see through the cloth somewhat, and I'd rather come with you."

Snarling with impatience, Tesulu said, "It doesn't matter if the woman can see to direct us or not; I can see the gate myself, it's over there." He pointed with his chin to a sheltered door in the stone wall on the edge of the field they were currently crossing.

Unfortunately the light in the sky had also made it easier for the few defenders assigned to keep watch on the slave gate to find their targets, too. Sietriga swore as a crossbow dart nicked his arm and buried itself in the ground behind him. Cursing, Marti pushed Cochinna to the dirt as Rhys shouted for everyone to take cover. In a field of knee-high vegetation that wasn't an easy task, however. Ignoring the blood dripping down his arm, Sietriga fired several beams in the wall's direction and smiled when a body plunged to the ground along with the exploding rock.

"Where's some of the famous 'war magics' you Clan warriors keep boasting about?" Boughthy cried as he aimed his beam rifle at the enemy. "Hide us with an illusion while I fry some of those Begta Pukes up there."

Happy to oblige him Juba linked his war magic with two other men to create an illusion of fleeing warriors in another part of the field, drawing the crossbow darts in that direction. While the enemy was diverted, Tesulu cloaked the patrol's approach to the gate.

To their surprise, the door was not barred from the inside when they reached it. Fearing something unpleasant might be waiting for them just inside, Rhys motioned for Tesulu to wait as he reached to open the door.

"In case they've set up a trap for us we will surprise them with a little Speir'dina magic first." Rhys took a rounded object from the belt pouch at his waist and twisted the protruding knobs on one side.

Tesulu came closer to look. "What is that, Speir'dina?"

"It's called a boomer in our language," Rhys said as he moved to the opposite side of the closed door, facing the way it would open. "Everyone, keep back; this might be loud," he warned.

Knowing what was about to happen, Marti pulled Cochinna down to the ground with her, and directed her to cover her head with the blanket she still wore. When Rhys saw that everyone was prepared he motioned for Tesulu to open the door. As the opening widened, Rhys tossed the boomer inside and yelled for the War Leader to shut the door again.

Inside there was a loud boom and then a bright light shown around the edges of the door. A moment later the armachd shouted to open the door and with Tesulu at his side they led the charge through the billowing clouds of smoke past several torn and bloody corpses into the fortress. The acrid stench of blood, offal and charred flesh formed a choking cloud in the thick air through which they ran.

Hurrying down a passage, the warriors saw several barred cages containing field slaves. Ignoring their terrified cries, the allied warriors pressed on, encountering little resistance from the guards stationed there. At first sight of the enemy most ran, disappearing into the gloom ahead. The Allied warriors finally stopped to catch their breath when they came to a clear intersection. Echoing out of the gloom, they could hear the sounds of combat from somewhere ahead.

Rhys motioned for Marti to bring their trembling guide forward. Studying the disheveled Ghostlander for a long moment, he said in a gentle voice, "I'm sorry, Sa, I know this must be difficult for you, not being combat trained, but we need to know how best to stage a rear attack. What might we encounter between here and the front gates?"

Cochinna swallowed hard . Never in her life had she been so frightened as she was at the moment. Though impatient for her answer, she also heard the compassion in the man's voice and was amazed. No wizard or warrior of her own people would have given any thought to her wellbeing under the same circumstances.

Taking a deep breath, she pointed to the right hand corridor and said in a shaky voice, "That way will lead us to the upper apartments where the masters of this fortress are housed. The passage leading to the outer courtyard by the front gate is off a side passage that way. As a Gaishinay, my companions and I live in quarters down another side passage in that direction—though not so close to the fresh air and the outer courtyard as the Elite stationed here."

She pointed to the left intersection. "That way leads downward to the barracks where the lower ranks of the trained warriors stay, and their dining hall. Deeper in the mountain are the breeding master's work rooms and our Sorin quarters."

"I have been to the passages near the barracks," Tesulu said. "I also saw the wizard puke's workrooms." He smirked. "We won't have any trouble from that quarter. We killed him, his assistant and a couple slaves in his work area when we were looking for the women."

"Good to know," Rhys said as he started down the right passage. "Juba, Sietriga, you cover our rear in case the warriors in those barracks aren't all fighting out front."

As they neared the upper passage and the great hall by the main entrance into the outer courtyard they quickened their pace. They could hear the screams of the dying and wounded and smell the stench of blood and awful in the smoky air.

Suddenly from a side passage K'San Glatu and his changelings stepped out to confront them. Recognizing Tesulu, Juba and Marti among the newcomers, he snarled, as he leapt forward, aiming his spear at Tesulu's gut. "I knew you half-bred Begta were spies all along."

Tesulu leapt aside, bringing up his own weapon to ward off the next attack. As the men squared off for single combat, Rhys growled, "We haven't got time for this, War Leader." Ignoring him, the men continued to circle one another feinting and jabbing with their weapons, no one gaining a quick advantage.

Muttering a curse, Marti drew her side arm. "Damn macho amadans. Rhys, do something. The boyos out there may need us!" Noticing out of the corner of her eye one of the other changelings stealthily reaching for a crossbow dart, she turned and shot him. With a piercing scream the man burst into flame, crashing to the stone.

The distraction gave Tesulu the advantage he needed and he plunged his spear into his enemy's chest. Choking on the blood suddenly spewing from his mouth, Glatu toppled to the stone at his feet. As the other changelings broke and ran back down the passage from which they'd come, Boughthy and Sietriga shot them. Loping back to the main squad in another moment, the column headed for the entrance, the clamor from outside goading them to hurry.

Recalling their guide at the last moment, Marti paused, looking around to see if she had been hurt. Cochinna was flattened against the nearby wall, trembling. Marti hurried over to her and touched her arm. "I'm sorry, Cochinna. I have to go with my people now, but I will come back for you when it's over. Try to keep out of sight—and thank you for everything."

Cochinna swallowed hard a couple times, then stammered out, "I will go back to my apartment and wait for you." Marti nodded, patted her arm one last time and raced off to join her patrol.

When she was gone and the hall was quiet Cochinna took several deep breaths to calm herself and then crept back to her apartment. She definitely needed something to steady her nerves and she prayed none of the others had discovered her hidden stash.

Chapter Fourteen

"All right, Atahru, I'm at the Med station—and so is Phillip-Yoey," Nathan grumbled. "We aren't gonna go anywhere else. You can go now; I'm sure your Mistress must have something else for you to do than babysit us kashallans." The Wa'chassey'ul's blank expression never changed, he just turned and walked back into the night.

Nathan suppressed a shiver and pulled open the tent flap with more force than was necessary. Motioning for Ingazi and Kitha to precede him, he stepped inside and closed the flap behind them.

The structure was a large dome-shaped tent, its skeletal frame covered by a dark fabric. In its center a square stove on legs gave off a pleasant warmth to ward off the night's chill. Atop the stove were steaming pots and a pipe that allowed the smoke from inside the box to escape through a hole in the top of the dome. Narrow cots surrounded an open central area in a circle. In the central area several people crouched talking and drinking some kind of hot liquid. When the newcomers entered they turned to stare.

Nathan directed Ingazi to sit on one of the cots. "Me or one of the other medics will be here in a minute to have a look at your wounds, but first I need to—" Taking the shivering Kitha's arm he walked over to the stove and sat her down by its warmth, handing her a cup of Phillip's notorious sourwood tea.

"What is this place, My Protector?" Kitha murmured as she took the cup he handed her.

Nathan grimaced at her form of address, but decided this was no time to argue the point. "It's what we call in our language a Field Hospital. It's where they will bring the wounded once the fighting starts. You are safe here; no one will hurt you—I promise. These people are all healers gathered here to help the injured," he sighed, "as am I now."

He straightened and turned to face the curious onlookers. "This is Lovely Kitha. She and her mentor helped our guys escape the fortress. They've come to join the Alliance. Will somebody have a look at Ingazi's wounds for me? I need to talk to Kashallan-Phillip for a moment."

A dark-skinned Speir'dina wearing Western Clan brands and a curly topknot rose and followed her new protector to another part of the tent away from the people by the fire.

The ones left by the warmth were a mixed lot. Several Speir'dina were there, both men and women she thought, but there was also a Begta, some younger clan warriors and two pure-bred Avairei.

One of the Avairei was dressed in black clothing like most of the Speir'dina she'd seen so far. He also wore his mane in a tight four-ply braid down his back like the Speir'dina wore their own manes. The other was dressed in a ragged Avairei kilt, his traditional braidlets stuffed into a fiber net at the nape of his neck. Kitha dropped her eyes suddenly shy under his open mouthed stare.

The dark haired Speir'dina, who said his name was Medic Ruan, playfully swatted the back of the Avairei's head as he passed him heading for Ingazi. "Close your mouth, Brat, you're acting like you never seen a pretty woman before."

PHILLIP TRIED TO SUPPRESS a smile as he sat down on a cot facing Nathan. "I saw Tess-weh's slave out there as you came in. Guess she had to send the Wa'chassey'ul to get you, eh?"

"I was coming—eventually. I got busy that's all," Nathan grumbled.

Phillip chuckled. "Sure you did."

"I did, damn it," Nathan protested. "And that's why I needed to talk to you." Taking Phillip's wrist he formed a link.

All teasing set aside, Phillip-Yoey formed his own link with Nathan's other hand. "What is it, Amsi; does this have something to do with the Ghostlander you brought with you?"

"Yeah—sort of, and more importantly the biological warfare stuff you mentioned at the war council that night."

"Go on; you have my full attention, Amsi."

Nathan glanced to where Crowis was now offering Kitha a steaming bowl of porridge from the big pot on the stove. "When Marti and Chelka arrived with Tesulu's patrol on the beach outside the fortress I discovered that they'd been drugged. Thinking she was a mutant one of the wizards in there stole her and Chelka from our guys. While fighting her way back to the patrol she was injured. It was nothing serious, but when we tasted her Corha noticed there were two separate substances in her blood.

"The two pleasure slaves acting as their guides decided to come with them when the patrol escaped. In the river they were separated. Kitha's mentor was saved from drowning by one of my pod. When she got to shore she claimed K'amsi Sika had tasted her and that she had sworn the oath to help us. She went back with Marti and the squad going in the back way to help them get in position for a rear attack.

"Hunt Leader asked me to verify her claim and make sure these two weren't spies. It was while in the link with her we tasted one of the same substances that Marti came into contact with. We haven't had time to taste Kitha over there to see if she also has the drug but you needed to know about this. As we speak, Corha I'm sure is sharing with Yoey what it has discovered, in case you come across the substance in future."

"Hmm, when there's more time we will need to taste them thoroughly and explore the meaning of this further." A smile curving his lips again, Phillip asked, "Pleasure slaves? Did I hear you right?"

Nathan sighed. "Don't you start, too. The word is already going around that the women are Ghostland whores, thanks to Boughthy and Murda, the shit for brains amadans. Sietriga has already asked me if Marti will let me play with her new toys, too."

Phillip laughed. Then their joking was abruptly cut off as the night sky outside exploded with light from the first flares. In silent agreement they rose and walked to the tent flaps throwing them wide and tying them open. The assault had begun.

Chapter Fifteen

"All right, Boyos," Medic Williams said to the group of young warriors lounging around the stove. "Athala, pick your men and come with me. The rest of you go with Medic Ruan. I can see our Loti stretcher bearers already gathering by the fire out there. Grab your gear and head out. We will be needed soon." Eager to be a part of the coming battle, the young warriors hurried to gather what they would need, glancing out the open tent flaps at the flickering light in the sky.

"I should go with them," Timma said as he started to put jars of kavay in his medical bag.

"No, you should stay here," Nathan said. "We will need your help with the severely injured. The Brat can go with Williams and Ruan if you think they need a third man to ready the wounded for transport or to patch up the warriors who don't need more than a kavay dressing to stop bleeding."

Timma looked up and opened his mouth to protest when Phillip-Yoey said, "Let Crowis go with them, Timma. He can do that much; you've taught him well and he's a good student. *You* are needed here."

Noticing Crowis's shocked expression, Ruan laughed. "You heard the kashallans, Brat. Get your med kit; you can talk to the pretty slave later."

"WE ARE GOING INSIDE the destroyed gates of Te'gal fortress now, Viewers," Jojo said, his voice a breathless whisper as he played the recorder's camera over a scene out of someone's worst nightmare.

The mangled bodies of both enemy and allied dead sprawled among the fires and burning rubble. Jojo coughed as the stench of blood and offal blew his way in a smoky cloud. "As you can see, Viewers, the fighting was pretty bad here, but our noble Allied warriors are moving forward into the fortress. The enemy is in retreat."

Then from a charred pile of bodies almost directly in front of him, an enemy monster covered in blood and half crazed with pain rose up to confront him. The warrior's hideous face distorted with rage, it snarled and charged with claws extended. With a squeak Jojo stumbled backward a few steps, then tripped and sprawled in a dead man's bloody entrails. Clutching the recorder close to his chest he scrambled backwards, barely dodging the murderous swipe aimed at his head.

The warrior roared and lunged again, but its cries were suddenly cut short as blood fountained from its open jaws, covering Jojo. The monster crashed to the ground, almost burying him under its weight. Rolling out of the way just in time Jojo saw a nearly unrecognizable Varrod, covered in blood and gore wrench his spear out of Jojo's now-dead attacker's back.

Red eyes nearly as crazed as the enemy warrior he'd just killed, it took the Warlinga a moment to focus on Jojo and notice he was a friend. "What are you doing here, Stupid Begta?" Looming over the smaller man, trying to get to his feet, Varrod shoved him to the ground again. Jojo yelped in protest and scooted backwards through the awful before he managed to get up. Following him Varrod bared his fangs and snarled, "You were told to stay out of Te'gal until we said all was safe."

Barely able to control his fury Varrod extended his own clawed hand and made a swipe at the frightened Jojo's face. "You could get one of us killed trying to protect you, Begta Puke. Now get out of here before I cut you up myself!"

"All Right, K-K'San Varrod I'm g-going right now—and I won't come back till I'm told it's safe—I promise," Jojo stammered, carefully stepping away from the enraged Warlinga, never taking his gaze off his face.

By this time Varrod's roaring abuse had caught the attention of other Allied men in the outer courtyard. As Jojo staggered towards the destroyed gate Medic Ruan caught up to him.

"Jojo, wait up. Are you hurt?"

Just outside the fortress Jojo stopped. Looking down at himself covered in blood and gore he shook his head, bewildered. "I-I don't know," he said in a shaky voice.

"Let me see then." Ruan came up and examined him with an expert's eye, trying to determine if any of the blood covering his clothes actually belonged to him. Lifting Jojo's arm Ruan pointed to a tear in his shirt the flesh underneath leaking fresh blood. He showed it to Jojo. "Better stop by the Med Tent and have someone look at that. Now get out of here; I got work to do." Ruan motioned for Jojo to follow some Loti stretcher bearers carrying a wounded Clan warrior heading in that direction.

When Jojo arrived at the Med Tent, he found it a very different place than when he had looked in earlier on his way to the battle. He could see through the opened tent flaps that many of the cots inside now held the severely wounded, some moaning in pain, others comatose, lolled into sleep with kavay medicines.

Outside the less severely injured, their bodies a patchwork of different colored kavays, sat about a fire drinking tea and talking in low voices. Others lay on the ground nearby, or sat leaning up against the tent frame with eyes closed. Jojo played the recorder's camera over the scene without adding any further comment, then feeling suddenly exhausted he shut the recorder off and followed the stretcher bearers inside.

The two kashallans, Timma and Nurse Anilah were all busy with patients, so he lurched to the center area and sat down by the stove, suddenly grateful for its warmth. Now that it had been brought to his attention, he was aware of the blood dripping down his arm. Closing his eyes he took several deep breaths; he could also feel the pain, now a nagging goad to torment his mind.

Sometime later he was startled back to reality when a harsh voice said, "Well, Begta Puke, how much of that blood and mess on your clothes belongs to you?"

Opening his eyes Jojo stared up at a scowling Timma, his arms folded across his furred chest. "Not much I think. Medic Ruan said I just had a claw wound here." Jojo showed him the tear in his filthy shirt.

Timma sighed and reached for his med kit, still lying on a low table between two cots. "Take that shirt off so I can see. Masonja, Kitha, somebody bring me some warm water and a clean cloth."

Jojo struggled to remove his shirt, grimacing at the stench and the pain. A strange Avairei with almost white fur came over to Timma and sat down a basin on the ground in front of the kneeling Timma. Still focusing on his kit he thanked her without looking up. Jojo's eyes opened wide, his pain suddenly forgotten. When the stranger had stepped away to help Kashallan-Nathan, Jojo whispered, "Timma, who is that stranger?"

Totally focused on cleaning Jojo's wound Timma glanced up. "What stranger?"

Jojo motioned with his chin to the pale furred Avairei helping Nathan ease a cursing warrior onto a cot on the other side of the circle. "Oh, that's Kitha. Tesulu's patrol brought her back with them when they left Te'gal."

Jojo gasped. "You mean she's a real Ghostlander?"

"Yes, Stupid Begta, now hold still."

Jojo shut up and held still while Timma finished cleaning his wound, and plastered it with yellow kavay, but all the time his mind was racing down new and exciting pathways. A real Ghostlander, here, and just maybe he could talk to her. What a story that would be to send back to Tomas and the Kashallan Players! As Timma finished and was packing up he said, "Timma, what's her story? Who is she?"

"Don't know much," Timma admitted. "But I did hear one of the wounded Speir'dina teasing Kashallan-Nathan about him now having an Umwira whore slave to play with—whatever that means to you Speir'dina."

Jojo's eyes bugged wide. "Oh my, how fascinating! Does she speak our language?"

"Not well, but she's getting by. One of the kashallans will have to give her the Southern Language patterns when there's time."

"Yes, indeed." He would definitely have to talk to her now. And he was so glad he'd coaxed Phillip-Yoey into sharing the Northern Dialect language patterns with him earlier on the march North.

TRYING TO IGNORE THE horrors of the battle scenes around him, Crowis was mindlessly plastering yellow kavay on a cursing Clan warrior's shoulder wound when he heard a frightened voice shouting for a medic.

At first he ignored the call, thinking Medic Williams or Ruan would see to the new emergency, but when the cries continued he found there was something familiar about the frantic voice. It sounded like it belonged to

Qwayku, and it registered through the shock and fatigue of his awareness that his sensei and Teh'lach brother sounded desperate.

Finished with his own injured man Crowis glanced around to see why one of the more experienced medics hadn't answered Qwayku's shouts. Williams was nowhere to be seen, probably with the warriors rooting out the last of the resistance retreating into the bowels of the fortress. Medic Ruan was nearby, but totally occupied trying to stop the fountaining blood from a downed Warlinga's leg.

Crowis stood up peering through the smoky haze of small fires still fogging the air. Qwayku shouted again and finally Crowis saw him near a pile of rubble and sprawled bodies just outside the main entrance. He was crouching over someone but from this distance Crowis couldn't tell who it was, or the extent of the wounded man's injuries.

Hurrying over, Crowis crouched by the injured warrior, already rummaging in his kit bag for supplies. "What happened?" he asked, without looking up, still focused on his kit.

Ignoring his question Qwayku continued to shout frantically for a medic, his hand still pressed to the bubbling wound.

Ah, it was Nytaka; no wonder he was so frantic, Crowis thought. Those two called, 'the cousins,' by almost everyone had been close since their babyhood Phillip-Yoey had told him once. "Qwayku, move over and let me see,"

"No," Qwayku snarled, continuing to shout for a medic and blocking Crowis from the injured young warrior. "He needs a real healer—not you, Begta Puke!"

Frowning and trying to see anyway, Crowis felt a stab of doubt pierce his resolve. Qwayku was right—sort of—he was still just a student, and a not too experienced one at that. Maybe he should let someone else—no there was no one else, and he needed to assess the situation further, before he gave up.

"Qwayku, everyone is busy. Let me see how bad Nytaka is hurt."

Qwayku still hesitated. "If you kill him I will kill you, too. I don't care if you are related to the Khutani!"

Startled, Crowis sat back and stared at the frightened warrior. Insulted he said in a low angry voice, "Sensei Qwayku, I would never do anything like that—especially to a Teh'lach brother. Would you do that to me if you were in my place?"

Qwayku had to think about it for a moment then said, "No, I would not. But you might after we—"

"Don't insult me by thinking I would be so petty and cruel." When Qwayku opened his mouth to argue further, Crowis snapped, "Stupid Begta, yes, I know you and Nytaka often make me do chores assigned to you, and I know you discipline me more harshly than is called for when you think Sensei Timma or Sensei Chang isn't around to stop you, but I would never risk someone's life to get revenge for having to do extra work, or a few more slaps with a discipline rod. Now let me see him, before you kill him with your own foolishness!"

Reluctantly Qwayku moved to one side, still nervously glancing around to see if one of the more experienced healers was free to come help, in case Crowis needed it.

The cauterizing powder ready to hand, Crowis removed the cloth Qwayku had been pressing on the wound in Nytaka's upper arm just below where it attached to his shoulder. Wiping the blood away, he could see where the bone had been broken in more than one place. One of the pale shards was poking through the torn flesh.

"We were trying to pull some of the warriors out of the rubble," Qwayku explained, motioning to the mound of debris around them, "when some of the pile shifted and fell on him. I think he hurt his head, too—and the Warlinga was dead anyway," he added, his voice choking on a sob.

"Mm, that's too bad," Crowis said, his mind distracted by the wound he was examining. Sprinkling a light dusting of powder to slow the bleeding, he sat back on his heels to study the brake. His training so far hadn't included handling anything like the injury confronting him now.

What to do? He had to put the pieces of bone back in place, but how to keep them from moving again? That was the first question he needed to answer—then he would tackle the head injury. Right now he was grateful that Nytaka was unconscious and unable to curse him out for his inexperience and the pain.

Rummaging through his kit again, he came across a dark gelatinous kavay he knew was often used like glue. If he painted the ends of the bone with the kavay and held them together till the glue gel hardened a bit... But he would have to be careful not to use too much, or it could impede blood flow to the affected area as it healed.

Dabbing the edges of the bones with the dark kavay he directed Qwayku to pull Nytaka's arm straight, as he guided the pieces back into alignment and held them steady till he felt the kavay start to gel and hold the bone on its own.

Taking another jar with a different colored kavay inside he next applied it to the torn flesh and pulled the gaping wound closed, covering the whole with a yellow kavay seal. Someone handed him a leather thong to bind the wound to the young warrior's chest as he finished.

"Good job, Crowis," Medic Ruan said, squatting down beside him.

Startled Crowis looked up. Face streaked with soot and blood, his curly hair coming out of its warrior's braid. How long had the Speir'dina medic been there and watching him? Shyly he looked down at his handy work again. "Thank you, Medic Ruan." He was also amazed that the man had called him by his real name.

Ever since he'd been forced to come on this expedition by his sister and her two husbands everyone, but Jojo—and sometimes his brother-in-law Phillip—had been calling him, 'The Brat'.

And, if he were honest with himself, knowing what he did now, he probably deserved it. A spoiled, privileged child was exactly what he was—or at least what he had been when he headed to Tragar Keep on a drunken dare. Now, he wasn't so sure what he was, and at the moment there was no time to ponder the matter. "Qwayku says he has a head injury as well, but I haven't had time to examine that," Crowis explained.

"Let's check him out and see," Ruan said. His fingers already discolored with the green kavay, those not Khutani used to diagnose an injury among the Allies, Ruan placed his hands at the back of Nytaka's skull near the cut still oozing a little blood. Closing his eyes he allowed the green kavay to aid him in 'tasting' the wound, as the kashallan healers did.

After a time he opened his eyes and said, "He has a concussion and will need to rest, but as best I can tell right now his skull isn't broken."

By this time Nytaka himself was starting to wake up, fighting against the strap confining his arm, and wanting to sit up. "Ly still, Nytaka, you've had a head injury and you will re-break that arm Crowis worked so hard to fix if you keep messing about."

Nytaka stopped struggling and stared, trying to understand what the medic was telling him. He glanced down at his arm and shoulder. "Hurts," he said and lay back, closing his eyes.

Crowis made a shallow cut in the injured arm and applied some orange kavay to the wound. "That should ease the pain, Sensei Nytaka, before too long."

Turning to Qwayku, Ruan said, "Go find some of the boyos to help you put him on a stretcher. He needs to go to the med tent, but with that head injury he shouldn't be walking. Crowis, you come with me. We need to see if anyone else needs us."

Chapter Sixteen

Kashallan-Nathan flopped down beside Phillip-Yoey and sighed. Masonja put a steaming cup into his hand, then handed the other cup to Kashallan-Phillip. Nathan made a face, but took a sip of the sourwood tea anyway. He was exhausted and the tea could help with that, even if it tasted vile, to his way of thinking. They had been working with the wounded all through the night; the sky outside now turning salmon pink with sun rise.

It was over—or seemed to be. They'd had no new casualties in quite some time. He would like nothing better than to curl up on one of the cots in here, but they were all full and there was too much to do to think about sleep yet. Nathan sipped his tea and closed his eyes.

Then a woman's quiet laughter made his eyes fly open again. Glancing around he saw Jojo and Kitha huddled together over his recorder. Though their voices were no more than a murmur she seemed interested in whatever he was showing her on its little screen.

Studying the pair as well, Phillip chuckled. "The man never gives up, does he? He asked me earlier if he could interview her. I told him he would have to wait until it quieted down around here. Right then we needed her help with the wounded."

Nathan snorted. "When did you share the Northern language patterns with him? I doubt he'd get much out of her otherwise. She doesn't speak the Southern tongue well."

Kashallan-Phillip shrugged. "Oh, you might be surprised. Our Jojo is very resourceful. But I've been sharing them with anyone who asks—when there is time. I wasn't sure of his reasoning, but he asked me a while ago. Now he's ready for anything."

Too ready and too eager to take more risks, Nathan thought and grimaced. Then changing the subject he said, "Speaking of sharing and time," Nathan glanced once more at the pleasure slave. "One of us needs to taste her and take her oath."

Focusing on something over Nathan's shoulder, Phillip said, "I'll do that for you, because right now I think you may be needed elsewhere."

Nathan sat down his half-filled cup and turned. Armachd Murda had just walked in and was heading their way.

"He doesn't look injured, so he must want you for something."

Murda walked up to them and saluted Nathan. "The Hunt Leader asked me to bring you to the fortress. We found some Avairei slaves who claim they were stolen from the Yeyen. They want us to free them, but Sa Chelka says they are lying. Hunt Leader Tizu wants you to come—uh—taste them, Nathan."

Sighing again he got to his feet. "They probably are lying. Marti already told us about some Dingay in there when she gave her report after the patrol escaped Te'gal. But Tizu and the war council will want a report on the wounded, so I can do that while I'm there, too."

"Try to get some rest afterwards, I'll taste the slave and stick around here in case someone needs a kashallan," Phillip said.

His words seemed prophetic, Nathan thought as he and Murda ran into Juba and another Sand Mountain man hustling a growling Tesulu, clutching his arm, towards the med tent.

MURDA LED THE WAY PAST the piles of bodies, rubble, and smoldering fires into the main reception hall of the fortress. Hunt Leader Tizu was there talking to Wizard Qwasigara, Wizard Eilo and the Meh'gach brothers. He didn't see Ross, Tobrach or Chelka anywhere.

Tizu noticed him and beckoned him over, the others stepping aside to include him and Murda in their circle. "Ah, there you are, Nathan-Corha."

Giving the two wizards a curious glance, Nathan said, "Hunt Leader, Murda says you got a problem that needs a kashallan to solve?"

Following his gaze, Tizu said, "Our Warlinga say you are better qualified to take care of this little problem and the Elders agree with them."

Nathan doubted that, but he decided not to make a fuss—he was curious. Folding his arms across his chest, he said, "All right, here I am; what's the problem?"

Tizu motioned for Nathan to follow as he headed further into the fortress. "We have some civilians, slaves mostly. They are a mixed lot, field, house, cooks—whatever. Most you can see are some wizard's breeding experiment, like the warriors, but a few are pure Avairei and they claim they were stolen against their will and brought North.

"Chelka and her brothers say that most of the Avairei slaves are from a family related to the Dingay and are lying changelings. The Avairei, on the other hand, say the Warlinga are lying because of an old family feud." Tizu shrugged. "The Meh'gach kids say they want you to taste them and take their oaths—not the wizards." Stepping in front of a guarded door, Tizu motioned for Aju'an to open it and precede them inside.

The narrow window slits high on the far wall let in enough light to reveal several disheveled Avairei sitting in the middle of the floor. The dry masa cakes and water someone had been kind enough to give them lay untouched on a tray just beside them.

Aju'an closed the door, the two Speir'dina standing on either side of him. An Ima with some grey around her mouth rose stiffly to her feet. Voice quivering with indignation, she addressed Aju'an directly. "This is an outrage! I told you, Meh'gach that I wanted to speak to the person in charge of the Southern hunting packs and not to come back otherwise."

Aju'an's head crest flattened at her insulting arrogance, but he remained silent. "Person in charge, eh? That would be me, Ima," Tizu said and folded his arms across his chest. "What do you want?"

The haughty Ima looked down her nose at the Hunt Leader and sniffed, letting him know that she wasn't sure she believed the claims of such a small individual. "Why out of here, of course. I am Ima Alimay and I will need an escort to take me back to my home in the Yeyen Banai Valley—tomorrow."

"You want out of this room? That can be arranged, Ima. But first there is the small matter of taking the oath to the Kashallan Alliance, and proving that you are not a changeling and working with the enemy," Tizu said. "Sending you back to the Yeyen is another matter altogether, however."

Ima Alimay took a deep breath, then said, "If an oath is what is needed to gain my freedom, and that of my servants, then of course I will do it." Kneeling, she clutched a small figurine of Mother Timorna in one hand, and held out the other to Tizu. "I am ready, Hunt Leader; what is the oath you wish me to swear?"

"The Hunt Leader isn't the one you need to assure of your sincerity," Nathan said. "I will take your oath, Ima, but all your people will need to swear to the Alliance," Nathan showed her his tentacles. "And I will do it while you are in the link with me, so I can 'taste' your sincerity."

Her eyes bugging wide she rose to her feet, dropping her hand back to her side. Swallowing hard she shook her head, then stepped closer to Nathan. Drawing a knife from the folds of her kilt she screamed, "Never, Khutani Slime!" and charged.

Nathan hopped out of the way as she hurled her knife, and then Tizu pulled his sidearm and shot her. Ima Alimay crumpled to the floor in the next moment as the beam from his side arm found its target and killed her. Not giving the screaming people another chance to launch an attack, Aju'an leapt among them with tooth and claw.

Before Tizu and Nathan had him settled down, more broken bodies and puddles of blood covered the floor. He might have killed the rest, but he agreed to let Corha taste them after making sure no one else had any hidden weapons.

Two frightened and bewildered young people Ima Alimay had been fostering and brought with her as slaves were actually from other families in the Alliance, not changelings at all. He tasted them and then spared their lives, promising to send them home as soon as it was possible.

The others were all changeling bred, and though confused and probably harmless Corha refused to take the chance; and so they had to die as well as the Ima who led them.

"Well, that was—unpleasant," Nathan said as they headed back towards the main hall. "Got any more prisoners you need me to taste?" he yawned. "If not, I should get back to the med tent and help Phillip-Yoey, before I fall over."

"Stay with me a while longer, I could use your opinion on some other matters," Tizu said. "And I do want you to have a look at some of the other prisoners who managed to survive last night's battle."

Suddenly feeling the presence of his parent in his mind, Nathan said, "Maker Qwaltamis has just joined us. And yeah, we'd like to do that, and question some of them, so we have a better idea what we will be facing when we march on Fa'Hanzoi." Nathan thought about it for a moment, then added as if thinking out loud, "I suppose the commander of Te'gal and his top officers all died in the fighting, or escaped down the tunnels before we sealed them off."

Tizu bowed, acknowledging the presence of the Maker, then said, "I'm not sure who all we have, but as to Te'gal's commander, Juba and Marti say we *do have* him." Tizu snorted in disgust. "The piece of worthless shit was still in his quarters so out of it and high on some foul-smelling fungus that we couldn't wake him. One of the Warlinga tied him to his bed and then we posted a guard outside his quarters till we figure out what to do with him."

"Why not just kill him?" Corha said. "I will do it now if you want."

"That's a tempting offer," Tizu said. "But I'd like to get what information we can out of him first—and you can certainly help with that." As he finished speaking Tizu stopped beside a closed door guarded by two Clan warriors Nathan knew by sight but not by name.

"Is he sober enough to make sense if we try to talk to him, Tahasi?" Tizu said, addressing the man with Red Wind brands on his face.

Tahasi snorted, his lip curling to show his contempt. "He is awake, but how much sense you will get from him is another matter."

Tizu grunted and opened the door, Nathan and Tahasi right behind him as he stepped into the room.

Breathing in a lungful of the fetid air Tizu gagged. "What is that horrible smell?"

Using Nathan's voice the Elder answered him in the Southern language, "I believe it is called Malloneen. Many of the Umwira were addicted to the smoke of the fungus in the past and it would appear the habit exists among the foul creatures to this day."

Detecting the smell of bodily waste amid the fumes of Malloneen in the room, Nathan thought the disheveled Ghostlander tied to his bed was both a disgusting and pitiful sight. With the threat of the Allied troops outside his gates, as Te'gal's commander he should have been on the walls directing his fighters, not getting high in his quarters.

At the sound of their voices Calahar turned his head, his red-rimmed eyes trying to focus on them. When he was sure he had the man's attention, Tizu came closer and said, "I am Hunt Leader Tizu; I am in charge here now." He glared down at the bound Ghostlander, his lip curling with his contempt. "You're a disgusting piece of shit, Umwira. What kind of commander neglects his duty and gets intoxicated when an enemy threatens his fortress?"

Calahar gave a rasping laugh. "A poor excuse for one it would seem. But in my own defense, I'm no military man, just a civil administrator. I thought there was little danger. Te'gal's walls are thick and in the past they have always been invincible to the Warlinga hunting packs raiding this far North. I had no reason to believe this time would be any different."

Nathan snorted. "That's a piss-poor excuse for your cowardly behavior."

Calahar grimaced. "So it would appear, Mutant. But if Drucas and the reinforcements from Fa'Hanzoi had shown up like we were promised the outcome might have been different."

Tizu directed Tahasi to untie the prisoner so he could sit up while they talked to him. Pulling the wicker chair from Calahar's work table closer to the bed, Tizu sat, shaking his head. "I doubt it. Him being here probably wouldn't have changed anything, but we would like to catch up with that one very much. He is at the top of our list of enemies needing killing, now that Barak is dead."

Calahar nodded. "So it is true what your spies told us. The Great Master Barak is dead?" Tizu nodded. Calahar grimaced. "I suspected as much. Your spies aren't fools; they wouldn't lie about something that could so easily be checked. What do you plan to do with me now?"

His expression stern and unyielding, Tizu stared at the man for a long moment, as if he was considering the matter. "That might depend on the answers you give to my questions and what kind of mood the Maker who has joined us for this interview is in," Tizu said.

Without warning, Nathan sat down on the bed beside the Ghostlander and took his arm, Corha jamming its tentacles painfully into the flesh above the man's wrist.

Calahar jerked in surprise. A Khutani demon! His large eyes grew even wider as he realized he was now in a link with one of the ancient enemies of his people. His mind paralyzed with fear and despair, he suddenly regretted not being up on the fortress walls to die with Te'gal's defenders. And with an ironic insight he also knew he was going to get his heart-felt wish to leave Te'gal, just not in the way he had hoped.

"And now, Umwira Puke," Maker Qwaltamis said, "you will answer all the Hunt Leader's questions—and mine, before I give you the painful death you deserve."

WHEN THEY FINISHED and were about to leave, Murda who had come in during the questioning, said, "Hunt Leader, Armachd Ross found a room that seems to have maps and other documents. Problem is that they are written in script nobody can translate." He glanced hopefully at Nathan. "Can you—"

Nathan-Corha shook his head, cutting him off. "I have in my memory the spoken language patterns for Timornan languages," Corha said, "but we didn't learn either the Avairei glyphs or the Ghostlander script. We can't help you there. I'm sorry, Hunt Leader."

Tizu shrugged and stepped into the hall, Nathan and the others following him out. "Then we will have to find someone left alive in the fortress to help us read them before we leave this place."

"What about the wizards," Nathan suggested. "I don't think the Western Clans write much, from what Phillip-Yoey says, but the Elders with us, being more learned, may be familiar with their script."

"Hmm, that's a good idea, but I have another," Tizu said. Dismissing the guard at Calahar's door, he turned to Murda. "I'm going back to the main reception hall to check on things. Tell Ross to secure all documents and papers he and the warriors find. I don't want any stray defender not in custody to destroy them before we have a look.

"Then see if you can find Armachd Marti and her—friend. I want to talk to them. Bring them to me there."

Keeping pace with him Nathan said, "What are you thinking, Hunt Leader?"

Tizu waited until they were nearing the main reception hall before speaking again. "From what I've been told the slaves Marti and Chelka brought out of the fortress are women who have been trained to offer their patrons pleasure. And, if their training is similar to the training a courtesan or geisha might receive elsewhere in the Galactic Union, then part of the training offered to a patron will possibly include music, dance, and a versatile education in poetry and other forms of literature."

Well, the Gaishinay had given them her allegiance; it was worth a try, Nathan thought.

"And while we are waiting," Tizu said, breaking in on his thoughts, "You can give me a basic report on the condition of the wounded in the Med Tent."

Nathan was just finishing up, when out of the corner of his eye he saw Marti leading a transformed Cochinna towards the group. Evidently while the battle was raging in other parts of the fortress, Marti had had the presence of mind to tuck the Ghostlander away in a safe enough place where she could fix her hair, change into fresh clothes and put on new makeup. Marti smiled when she saw him, and taking Cochinna's arm quickened her pace.

Following the direction of Nathan's gaze, all the Speir'dina in the hall gaped, their mouths hanging open. "Close your mouth, Amadan, you look like a fish out of water," Nathan murmured to the nearest man.

Well he couldn't blame the armachd for staring, the Gaishinay was transformed. Though not exactly beautiful by human standards, her confident bearing, richly embroidered dress, jewels and elaborate face paint told the story of someone held in high regard by her society.

Tizu broke off what he was about to say when he caught sight of them. Coming to stand beside him Marti saluted and said, "Hunt Leader Tizu, this is Enchanting Cochinna. You wanted me to get her for you?"

"Yes, Armachd, thank you." Tizu turned to Cochinna and gave her a deep bow. Focusing his piercing black eyes upon her, he studied the Gaishinay for a long moment, as she did him. At last he said, "Honored, Sa,

I'm sure you must feel very overwhelmed by what you have witnessed and what has happened. My warriors and I are very grateful for the assistance you have offered us."

Cochinna bowed her thanks in return. "I have given the Alliance my oath, Hunt Leader, it is no more than my duty to serve you."

"Mm, that's good to hear, Enchanting. There are a few other things you may be able to help us with, perhaps."

"Of course, Hunt Leader, you need only ask." Being not much shorter than Tizu himself, Cochinna studied him carefully for a moment, then looking him in the eye, she said boldly, "Hunt Leader, may I be permitted to say that you seem tired. I would like to offer you and your officers some refreshment in my apartment. There I can see to your comfort and you can tell me how best I can assist you further."

Startled, Tizu blinked. "That is a generous offer, Dear Lady." Receiving a nod from Marti, silently telling him no treachery was planned, Tizu stepped forward and took her arm. "I would be delighted, Enchanting."

Nathan followed in their wake, not sure he liked the idea of the hunt leader eating and drinking whatever the Ghostlander had prepared for them. He knew she was using something—and probably it was addictive, he just wasn't sure how it affected Speir'dina. If the substance was commonly used in the North, she may have added it to the refreshments with no malicious intent.

After only seeing destruction and misery since entering Te'gal the Gaishinay's apartment was a marvel to the tired men entering it. Before taking advantage of Cochinna's suggestion that they be seated, Tizu looked down with dismay at his filthy and blood-stained uniform and then around at the plush room with its bright tapestries on the walls and embroidered cushions on the couch.

Sensing his reluctance, but unsure of the cause, Cochinna said, "What's wrong, Exalted Hunt Leader, how have I displeased you?"

Startled Tizu focused on her and chuckled. "You haven't displeased me, Enchanting, this room—it's beautiful." He looked down at his filthy clothing again. "But I'm afraid if I take you up on your most generous offer I will spoil its beauty forever." It was difficult to tell behind her elaborate makeup, but

Tizu thought he detected her momentary surprise, quickly masked by a deep bow.

"You honor me with your concern, Hunt Leader, but a dirty cushion is nothing compared with your comfort."

When he still hesitated, Marti laughed. Disappearing through the beaded curtain she returned in a moment with a sheet which she tossed over the couch. "There. That better, Sir?" Tizu gave her a grateful look and sat down heaving a great sigh of relief. Leaning his head back he allowed himself the brief luxury of closing his eyes.

Nathan sat down on a nearby chair, Marti sitting on the floor by his feet and leaning her head against his thigh. Aju'an and Murda remained standing on guard by the door.

Sitting down beside him on the couch Cochinna said, "May I offer you some refreshment, Hunt Leader? I have some lamra brandy, some kaiso, and various types of tea."

Tizu opened his eyes briefly then closed them again. "I'm not sure what kaiso is, but no brandy or other liquors. They would put me to sleep for sure. But if you have some sourwood tea I could use a cup. There's still a lot I need to do before I can rest today."

Cochinna frowned, thinking. "I'm not sure I have any sourwood. But if you wish something that has a mild stimulant property like the Western Tea I'm sure I can find something in our supplies to suit your need." Without opening his eyes, Tizu thanked her.

Rising once more she inquired what her other guests, including the guards at the door, might like.

When she was gone, with his eyes still closed Tizu said to no one in particular, "I'm getting too old for all this."

Nathan snorted a laugh and got to his feet. "We all are, Sir. Let's hope we can put an end to this threat once and for all this time." Then excusing himself he followed Cochinna behind the beaded curtain.

Chapter Seventeen

Hearing the sounds of talking ahead, Nathan caught up to the Gaishinay in a small kitchen area where she was instructing an old slave to heat some water for tea. Cochinna herself was rummaging through a wicker chest, several selections already laid out on a table in front of her. When she noticed him leaning against the doorframe watching her, she gasped, a hand covering her mouth to stifle a scream.

Pushing off the doorframe, he came the rest of the way into the room and crossed to the table, the old slave cringing away as he passed. "Sorry, I didn't mean to startle you. We need to talk and maybe this is as good a time as any." Addressing the slave, he continued, "Don't be afraid, Elder, I'm not going to hurt you. Please leave us for a while. I want to talk to Enchanting Cochinna—alone." With a quick glance at the Gaishinay the slave scurried from the room.

Trembling, Cochinna grasped the table for support and forced herself to meet his cold grey stare. "H-have I done something to displease you, Khutani?"

"I don't know yet; have you?"

Cochinna swallowed hard and shook her head. "I don't think so; I wish only to serve."

Nathan sighed and took her hand. He could taste her growing fear even without forming a link. "I'm sorry, Enchanting, I don't mean to frighten you, but it's been a particularly long and troubling night and day, and we do have some—concerns."

Allowing Corha to speak for them both, the symbiont continued, "When I tasted you before I became aware of a foreign substance in your blood. This foul poison will eventually cause much damage in your body.

"My parent says the drug made from this particular fungus is very addictive. When I tasted our Marti I savored traces of the same flavor in her blood. My Khutani Elders and I will not tolerate any of our people to become addicted to this substance. Do you understand me, Gaishinay?"

By the time Corha finished oily tears were flowing down Cochinna's face, spoiling her make up. "It's called Crivo the Enslaver. When my crèche parent traded me to my benefactor as a child I was fed crivo in everything I ate and drank. It is a common practice and part of the training for all Gaishinay—and many others who serve the Exalted.

"Crivo is a painkiller—along with its other properties. I meant no harm when I soaked the cloth that I used to clean the warrior's wound. It never crossed my mind that your people, Speir'dina, didn't use it, too. I'd never met anyone who didn't use it—even the Exalted in Tiebarai often are addicted, using it for simple aches and pains of the body and mind. Please believe me. I met no harm!"

<<She is telling us the truth as she understands it, Kasha,>>Corha said. <<Maybe not everyone in the North are to blame, but these Ghostland Wizards are truly evil. How could anyone do such a thing to a child?>>

<<Power,>> Nathan said. <<The fear of losing it and the greed for more, can warp any species that acquires a taste for it.>>

With his free hand Nathan handed her the cloth resting on the table. She took it gratefully and dabbed at her eyes. Nathan waved a hand at the various herbs and fungal teas spread out on the table before them. "And what of these. Do they all contain crivo?"

Blinking away the last of her tears Cochinna shook her head. "No. now that I am grown and have the taste for it, I can add it to my own food or drink as needed." She held up a cloth packet to show him. "I was planning to make this one for the Hunt Leader. Taste it; you will see its properties are similar to Sourwood—nothing more."

Nathan opened the packet and allowed Corha to examine the tea. While it did so, he asked, "I haven't had time to taste Kitha yet. Can I assume she, and the rest of the Gaishinay and other slaves we captured are also addicted to this crivo stuff?"

"Yes, and any of the Ghostland guards you may have captured will be addicted to crivo as well. It helps them endure the pain of their wounds."

"Mm, and what about Malloneen?"

She seemed startled he knew about that fungus, too, but answered him honestly. "Malloneen isn't as powerful as Crivo or Thaufda, but eventually it will ensnare the unwary user. I believe Distinguished Commander Calahar is losing that battle."

Nathan grimaced. "Yeah, we know. The stupid puke was so lost in the smoke he missed the battle to defend Te'gal." He handed her the packet. "Go ahead and make the Hunt Leader his tea. He shouldn't have any problems with this. And make enough for all of us—I'll pass on the brandy." As she reheated the water and allowed the herb to steep, he asked, "I would like to see and taste crivo and malloneen, too, if you have any."

Digging once more into the chest she handed him two more cloth-wrapped bundles much larger than the tea packets she already had laid out. Nathan unwrapped them one at a time and closed his eyes, allowing Corha's senses to dominate their awareness.

When he was done and had replaced all the packets back in the chest, he said, "Thank you, Cochinna. Now there is just one other matter to discuss before we return to the other room." Cochinna bowed and then waited for him to continue. "I gather from its name and what I have tasted, that crivo has a quality affecting the mind of the user that makes that person easier to control. For the safety of all those in the Alliance we need to take measures to prevent anyone needing either of these drugs from being used by the enemy in future."

Cochinna gasped, nearly dropping the heavy tray she had started to lift. Nathan quickly reached to steady it, placing it back on the table. "You mean to kill me then, Khutani?"

Shocked, Nathan hastily shook his head in denial. "No, that's not what I mean at all. I will need to consult with my Elders about this—and maybe Phillip-Yoey, but I would like to help you break free of this terrible drug so no one can force you to do their bidding in future. Are you brave enough to work with us and try?"

Cochinna put her hands to her face and began to cry again. Through her tears she said, "I would like nothing better, but they say that is an impossible dream, Khutani."

Nathan handed her the cloth again and then patted her shoulder. "That may, or may not be true. I won't know for sure until I talk with older and wiser relatives, but we will do all that is possible to free you and Kitha from this curse. We won't abandon you—I assure you. So be brave; I'm sure we can figure something out."

Sniffing back the last of her tears she reached for the tray Nathan was now holding. "Here, allow me; you are both a warrior and an Exalted Khutani. It isn't for you to do a foolish slave's work."

Nathan smiled but held on to the tray. "One thing you and Kitha will learn as you get to know us better is that, we Speir'dina don't stand on ceremony much. Work is work and anybody free does it. I've dug privy holes and pulled masa root from the fields as well as a mountain of other unpleasant chores."

Cochinna stared wide-eyed. "How is that possible, Exalted? Those things are a slave's work."

Nathan laughed and led the way out of the kitchen. "Because I've been a slave, Enchanting, so I know from personal experience what it means to be at the mercy of someone else's will."

"How is that possible?"

"When we were first stranded on this world, some of us were captured, Marti and I were among them. Unable to speak any Timornan language we were stripped of all our off-world toys and given as slaves, first to a brutal Warlinga K'San and then to the Avairei at Sulas. It was there that one of us gave himself to the Khutani and became the first kashallan. He freed us and from there we eventually were able to form an alliance with others to fight Wizard Barak's monstrous warbands causing so much misery among other peoples—including the Western Clans."

"That is a fascinating story," Cochinna said. "Sometime you will have to tell me more."

"Yes, sometime, now why don't you fix your make up while I take the tray out to your guests. Join us when you're ready."

WHEN NATHAN PUSHED backwards through the beads, he saw that Tizu had fallen asleep, his head resting on a pillow propped up against the back of the couch. Ross had also joined them and was now sitting in Nathan's vacated chair, a packet of scrolls and other materials at his feet.

As he set the tray down on the low table next to the couch, Murda smirked. "Deciding to take up a new career, Nathan? How much do you charge?"

Nathan straightened and gave him a sour look. "Keep it up, Amadan, and you'll be on the privy detail with the Begta till we reach Fa'Hanzoi."

Marti laughed, then gave him an inquiring look, motioning with a jerk of her head to the other room.

"She'll be along in a moment—not to worry."

"Cochinna all right?" she murmured as he sat down on the carpet beside her.

"She's fine—tell you more later."

With the sound of Marti's laugh Tizu jerked awake with a snort. Wiping a hand across his face he sat up and yawned. "Why didn't you shit for brains amadans wake me up?"

"Because you needed the rest, Sir," Ross said.

Before Tizu could frame a reply Cochinna, her makeup now repaired, came through the beads carrying another tray piled high with masa cakes and other food items. Setting down the tray next to the one Nathan had brought, she knelt and took off the painted earthen pot's lid, reaching for a dipper and drinking bowl. "May I serve you some tea and other refreshments, Exalted Hunt Leader?"

"Yes, Enchanting, thank you."

When everyone, including the guards at the door had been served and were munching on tasty snacks, Ross cleared his throat and pointed to the pile of materials beside his chair. "You wanted to see these, Sir?"

"Yes I did." Turning to the gaishinay, he said, "Enchanting, as a newcomer to this world I confess I know very little about your people, so forgive my ignorance.

"Though my people don't keep pleasure slaves—or any slaves at all, among the nations of the Galactic Union out among the stars, I am familiar with people who are skilled in giving their clients pleasure and entertainment of all kinds. Am I correct in assuming that you also are well versed in arts and literature, as were others I have known in the past?"

Puzzled Cochinna thought about his words for a moment, then said, "I am not a very good artist, Exalted Hunt Leader, but I can sing and dance—though my student, Lovely Kitha, is a better dancer, if I am honest."

Tizu waved a hand in dismissal. "I'm sure you are being quite modest. You couldn't have achieved the rank you now hold if you weren't very skilled. When there is more leisure time I would enjoy seeing you and your student perform very much, but right now," he motioned to the pile at Ross's feet. "I need someone who can read the Northern script. Can you do that for us?"

"I can read, to be sure, and I would be glad to do so, but I may not be able to interpret what I am reading if those papers concern military matters."

Tizu got to his feet, the others rising with him. Motioning for Ross to resume his seat, he yawned, but forced himself to follow the rest of his warriors to the door. "Reading will be a big help, Enchanting, I assure you. Armachd Ross will stay here and help you get started on the project."

Before he could leave Cochinna spoke, "Hunt Leader, Please come back later and join me. I will have my personal servant prepare a special meal for us."

Tizu glanced longingly at her comfortable couch and nodded. "I would enjoy that, Dear Lady, truly I would."

As Nathan started to follow, Ross called him back. "Hey, Nathan, if I'm to stay and do this, tell Murda, Rhys, or Chang—he won't argue with Chang, to make sure he does come back. He needs to rest, damn it. He can't do everything by himself."

"You're right he can't—though he'll try."

Chapter Eighteen

Kitha woke in the late afternoon with a growing concern for the fate of her mentor. She wasn't sorry to learn that the brutal warriors in the fortress were either imprisoned or dead, but she'd been so busy helping the kind healers in the Med Tent for the last few days that she hadn't been back to Te'gal to see for herself, nor had Enchanting Cochinna come to be with her. And she was worried, in spite of Exalted Kashallan- Phillip's assurance that her beloved mentor was fine and just busy helping the warriors with other matters.

Sometime that first day the Speir'dina, named Nurse Anilah had given her a blanket and taken her to a nearby tent where they could rest. Kitha was so tired and overwhelmed she'd fallen asleep without caring about the thin mattress of moss atop the cold ground.

But today was different. Her bodily cramps had returned and that meant she couldn't abandon her worries and get lost in her work caring for the injured. She needed to find Cochinna and maybe go back to Te'gal for more crivo. Unsure what to do to solve her growing problem, when she woke in the deserted tent hungry and disorientated, she had just wandered back to the Med Tent, because she was afraid to explore further into the Allied camp.

She hoped to at last see Cochinna—or maybe Marti—she could trust Marti! A quick look around told her neither woman was there to give her advice. Things hadn't changed much in her absence. The two Speir'dina medics were tending to the wounded. The Begta female was there, as well as the kashallan called Phillip-Yoey. Suddenly shy she paused just inside the tent flaps.

Though everyone had been kind to her she was uneasy alone without Marti or Nathan to protect her. Not that anyone had given her reason to feel that she needed protection; she just felt more at ease when the ones she had chosen as her new guardians were there with her.

Partially it was the language barrier, but more importantly, she was starting to feel the first painful side effects stemming from missing her dose of crivo for the past few days. Her supply had been ruined by their escape in the river. She needed to go back to the fortress to get more, because she had already discovered that no one here knew about, or used it.

That was an unsettling revelation, and one she and Cochinna hadn't counted on when they had planned in haste their desperate escape. In spite of her growing desperation she wasn't sure how to go about finding a source of more crivo. Could she just go, or did she need an escort? Would the warriors take her for an escaping spy if she tried to leave camp on her own—and with her poor grasp of the Khutani's language how could she explain? All these thoughts were going through her mind as she hesitated in the shadows, the cramps getting worse in her gut. Oh, what to do?

Then the one named Phillip-Yoey, eating a bowl of porridge by the stove looked up and beckoned her over. "Ah, Kitha, there you are. I was just going to send Masonja or someone to look for you. Come sit with me and have some food while things are relatively quiet in here."

She wanted to run, unable to cast aside the ancient fear of the hated Enemy bred into her people. And knowing that a Khutani demon was coiled in the middle of this man gave her chills, even though the two kashallans she had met had been nothing but kind to her.

Forcing her feet to move at last, she walked down the center aisle. When she stood near him he patted the ground beside him and she reluctantly sat. "Are you hungry?" he waved a hand in the general direction of the warming pot at the back of the stove. "Grab a bowl and help yourself. There's tea in the pot next to the porridge as well."

Kitha dropped her eyes and shook her head. Her voice barely above a whisper, she said, "Thank you, Exalted, but I'm not hungry; I'll eat later."

Kashallan-Phillip sat down his bowl unfinished and studied her carefully. "Are the cramps getting bad now?"

Kitha jerked her head up, eyes wide. "How—"

Kashallan-Phillip chuckled, "Cochinna has already spoken with Nathan-Corha about your crivo addiction. We have agreed to help her with the problem. We will help you as well, if you agree. But for now..."

He took one of her hands and made the link. Staring down at her arm with the Khutani's tentacles embedded in her flesh, she tried not to shudder; she didn't want to make him angry with her. The kashallan wasn't hurting her, but the teachings of a lifetime were hard to overcome...

Suddenly Kitha felt a cooling balm flowing down her arm and into her middle, easing the cramps and relaxing her tension. Startled, she looked up her eyes brimming.

"Does that feel a little better?" She nodded, unable to speak. "Good. What Yoey is giving you is only a temporary respite, but we are talking with our Elders and hope in time to have a more permanent solution to this addiction problem for all who wish to be free of it."

He sighed. "Unfortunately, finding the time to devote to the matter is the big problem at the moment. So, in a bit I will send you up to the fortress to get some more of your own crivo until we have the time to work on a permanent solution."

Kitha breathed a sigh of relief. Good, he was going to send her to the fortress where she could check on Cochinna and replenish her supplies. "I would like to be free of the craving, Exalted, truly."

Extracting his tentacles, the kashallan held onto her hand and looked her in the eye. "Kitha, it may be hard for you to believe right now, but you are no longer a slave. The Begta, Loti and all the members of the Kashallan Alliance are here because they volunteered to come with the warriors. They weren't forced to come. And the two you think of as your new protectors, Marti and Nathan don't have slaves—no Speir'dina does. Some of us, like me, Marti and Nathan, have been slaves. When our leader gave himself to the Khutani and became the first kashallan we were freed and now won't tolerate it among our own people."

His expression growing wistful, he added, "Alas, I can't speak for the Western Clans, but hopefully in time there, too things will change. And there's no need to call me or or Nathan-Corha, Exalted." He grinned, showing his sharp white teeth. "From one freed slave to another, just our names will do."

Kitha dropped her eyes, suddenly shy. Did Cochinna know about the kashallans once being slaves? She had so much to share with her mentor; she hoped to talk to her soon. "I will try and remember, Exal—" she broke off with a nervous giggle. "I will try, Phillip-Yoey."

Phillip chuckled. "Good that's all we ask. Now, before I send you up to the fortress," he took her other hand. "I think you will also feel more comfortable among us if I share the Southern language patterns with you as well. I've noticed you are having a hard time understanding the mix of languages we use around here."

When they were finished, Kashallan-Phillip arranged for her to accompany a group heading down to the fortress. Some people she already knew, like Jojo and the student healer Crowis, were among the warriors acting as escort. Now able to better understand the talk going on around her, she was amazed at how free and easy they were with one another. Loti, Speir'dina, Begta and clan warriors laughed and joked with each other as if they were all of the same rank and crèche.

HER SESSION WITH ARMACHD Ross finished for the day, Cochinna hurried back to her apartment to help prepare the evening meal. The Exalted Hunt Leader Tizu was favoring her with his company again this evening and she wanted to make sure everything was in order to receive him properly. In spite of his five fingered hands and other alien aspects, the warrior fascinated her. His alienness was intoxicating, like being given a new drug, to which she could easily become addicted.

Her mind running over the many questions she hoped to ask him this evening about his old life among the stars, Cochinna wasn't paying attention like she should have. Coming into her apartment she finally realized that there were no savory cooking odors coming from her tiny kitchen—and the bed hadn't been made... the apartment was deathly quiet. Calling her personal servant's name Cochinna stopped abruptly just inside the beaded curtained doorway a shiver running down her spine.

Cochinna called for the servant again, and when she received no answer she moved cautiously into the kitchen. The first thing she saw was Iefer's crumpled body lying bloody on the floor near the kitchen shelves. Cochinna gasped, her hand flying to her mouth. Hurrying over to the servant, she knelt and touched Iefer's shoulder gently turning zer over. "Iefer, what happened?"

"Finally decided to come back, Worthless Slave?"

At the sound of that harsh voice Cochinna stiffened, her heart pounding with fear. Mentally chiding herself for her inattention, she took a deep breath, rose to her feet and turned to face her adversary. Mistress Lareusha, with her pet Enchanting Afma, was sitting by the far wall, a pot of tea on the table between them.

"Why have you disciplined my servant so severely Iefer couldn't do the chores I assigned zer? I have a guest coming soon. I instructed Iefer to prepare a meal for us."

Mistress Lareusha got to her feet and stepped closer, her hands concealed at her sides. A tall imposing female in her youth, as she aged her body had betrayed her, making her bitter. Though she tried to compensate by always dressing in the fine robes and jewels that showed her rank, Mistress Lareusha never entertained guests any longer, her duty at Te'gal only that of an overseer of her younger charges.

"I am well aware that you and your half-bred student have been entertaining more than one of the invaders without my permission, Traitor," Lareusha snarled. "And that stops now."

She motioned to the smirking Afma now on her feet and coming to stand by her mentor. "Enchanting Afma will be entertaining your guest tonight—and from now on."

"You can't do that—"

"I can and I will. I decide which of my charges entertain—not you."

"Mistress Lareusha, please listen to me. These Speir'dina aren't like the warriors who are our usual guests. The Hunt Leader won't like—"

The Gaishinay mistress snorted a laugh. "Don't flatter yourself, Old Hag; he has no say in this matter. He will accept the gaishinay I give him, because warriors of any kind care only for themselves and their pleasure. One gaishinay or another, it won't matter to him."

With a sinking feeling in her heart Cochinna wondered if that were true. The Hunt Leader and the other Speir'dina she'd met seemed kind, but were they really?"

"Some of the Comelies have, at Mistress Lareusha's direction, already been entertaining some of these traitorous mutants, and I can assure you, all warriors are the same. He won't miss you," Afma said.

Though wearing the same facial markings and having the same rank among the gaishinay as Cochinna, like her mentor, Afma was a vindictive and spiteful woman who took out her resentment for being assigned to this frontier fortress on anyone whom she felt she could bully. She had picked on Lovely Kitha mercilessly for being of mixed ancestry until Cochinna had claimed her as her student and warned Afma with verbal and physical threats to leave the poor girl alone.

Afma chuckled, but there was no mirth in the sound. "I will entertain him and see to his needs as well as you could, Cochinna Dear, don't worry. I will feed him the sumptuous meal that my slave is preparing tonight and for the time he has left among us. But that won't be for long, of course."

Not long? Cochinna felt a shiver run down her back bone. "What are you talking about!"

Afma's painted mouth curved into a cruel line. "I'm sure you can figure it out, Old Hag."

Yes, well maybe she could and that made her afraid. More than her personal safety was threatened if they carried out their plan. Staring wide-eyed at the gaishinay mistress, Cochinna said, "If you try to poison the Hunt Leader or any of the other officers of the Alliance, the Khutani among them will know and punish every one of us! You can't do this terrible thing!"

Lareusha brought out the discipline cane she had been concealing and advanced on her. "And who is going to tell them, Gaishinay? Not you, Traitor, because after you receive my discipline you will be unable to entertain guests for a long time to come. If ever again. And when Mighty Drucas learns what you've done—you probably won't survive his wrath."

Cochinna stepped back groping for something to use as a weapon. "I've done nothing wrong, and I am no traitor. The Alliance was here long before I encountered any of their warriors. Commander Calahar himself allowed them inside our gates. You might as well call him the traitor by your reasoning."

"Calahar," Afma snorted, "that smoke-addled degenerate and most of the warriors in this fortress maybe dead, but that doesn't mean we surrender. The

Master's warriors are coming to reclaim what the enemy has stolen. So the more chaos we can create among them in the meantime the better."

Cochinna shook her head, stepping back without taking her eyes off Lareusha. "I am no longer a ward subject to your discipline. My student and I have given the Khutani and the Alliance our Oaths. You no longer have a say in what we do or don't do. I will tell—"

"You will tell no one, Traitor," Lareusha snarled and raised her cane as Afma stepped in to grab her from behind.

JUDGING BY THE MANY wounded she had helped to treat in the past few days Kitha knew that there had been a terrible battle, and yet when she saw the pile of rubble that was now the front gate and other parts of the outer wall she was shocked speechless.

Following the direction of her gaze Jojo, walking beside her said, "It's a terrible sight, Dear Kitha, even for those of us who have experienced war before."

Chi'am overhearing him snorted a laugh. "At least the piles of bodies are gone; they buried them before the stench got too bad."

Jojo grimaced. "Yes, there is that. Have they set a time for the honoring ceremony for our dead yet?"

"I haven't heard; you will have to ask my K'San, San Jojo."

"I will, thank you, Chi'am."

Kitha shivered, then deciding to change the subject somewhat, she asked, "Were you a warrior, Honorable Jojo when you lived on your world among the stars?"

Jojo shook his head and chuckled. "No, Lovely Kitha, I was the farthest thing from it. I was a poet and an actor," His face became animated as he asked, "Do they have theater of some type in Tiebarai?"

Kitha thought about it for a moment, not sure she was correctly interpreting his words. "If you mean people who perform entertainments for others then yes, there are such entertainments in Tiebarai. My mentor Enchanting Cochinna is a very skilled musician and singer. Distinguished Commander Calahar called for her to entertain him many times. My mentor would sing and play the uta and my partner Zalin and I would dance for him and his officers."

"How wonderful, I am truly looking forward to meeting her."

Te'gal was a hive of activity Kitha saw as they moved from the outer courtyard deeper into the fortress itself. Work crews of both Allied warriors and Te'gal's slaves were working to clear away debris and pile up the supplies the Alliance would be taking with them when they marched further north.

When Jojo bounced off to record the activity with his little recorder, Crowis shyly asked, "I've noticed you haven't resumed wearing your, uh, face paints. Were they ruined in the river?"

When Kitha stopped and turned to face him, he became suddenly shy. Dropping his eyes he stared at the floor as if the dust patterns were incredibly interesting. Finally he ventured, "I'm sorry, I meant no offence. I-I just think you are very beautiful without them."

Beautiful? Kitha had heard from older siblings in her crèche that her mother had been a captured slave from the Khutani lands, forced to conceive in a wizard's breeding program, but she herself had no memory of her. She'd never known a true Avairei until she'd encountered the few, like Crowis, who had accompanied the army coming North.

Growing up Kitha had learned to hate her mixed heritage, and though her mentor always tried to convince her otherwise Kitha herself knew she would never rise to a higher rank than Lovely among the gaishinay because of that. And, she also knew that as her youth faded, her Benefactor would trade her to a street brothel that serviced the brutish lower classes. And there she would stay until her death finally claimed her.

"I don't want to be a gaishinay anymore. I want to become a healer like Nurse Anilah—if your people will let me, that is," she surprised herself by adding, suddenly unsure.

Crowis looked up and smiled. "Really? That would be wonderful! My brother-in-law, Phillip-Yoey says there will always be a need for nurses and medics. Maybe he and Sensei Timma will let you work with me. I know I'm only a student myself—back home I trained as a scholar and historian. But now—" he broke off suddenly shy again. "I'm sorry; I'm babbling, aren't I?"

Kitha giggled. He was kind of cute in his innocent boyish way. "If you are a scholar, how did you come here?"

Crowis barked an ironic laugh. "It's a long story, but in short I came North through a series of stupid decisions made on my part that started by getting drunk and accepting a friend's dare—who was also drunk at the time he challenged me to come."

Kitha's voice taking on a coquettish lilt, she asked, "And are you sorry you've come now?"

Crowis answered her smile. "Not really, now that I've met you." Then sobering, he said, "I honestly don't know. I have learned so much about the healing art since we left Tragar, but I also hate the fighting and killing. I wish it would end—forever."

Kitha paused before turning into the corridor leading to the apartment she shared with her mentor. "My apartment is the third door on the right. Come see us when you finish your duties with Medic Ruan. I'm sure my mentor would love to meet you."

Chapter Nineteen

Yes, the Avairei was kind of cute, Kitha thought as she opened the door and stepped into the apartment. Still smiling to herself, Kitha froze when she heard the sounds of a struggle coming from the inner room. Punctuating the thwack of a discipline cane being applied vigorously, came the sounds of Mistress Lareusha cursing and someone else angrily crying.

Creeping slowly forward, Kitha peeked her head around the door frame. The sight that greeted her was terrible. The kitchen was a mess: broken crockery and food items scattered everywhere. Mistress Lareusha with cane raised for another strike was hovering over a bloody Cochinna being forcibly held down by her protégé Afma, their enemy.

Kitha gasped, a hand coming up to cover her mouth. At the sound Cochinna looked in her direction. "Run Kitha, tell the warriors they plan to kill the Hunt Leader!" Kitha hesitated, not wanting to leave her mentor alone with these fiends. "RUN, FOOLISH GIRL, TELL THEM!"

Her paralysis broken by Cochinna's shouts Kitha turned and raced for the outer door.

"Leave this one to me. Go after her, Useless Hag," Lareusha snarled to Afma. "We can't let her escape and sound the alarm!"

Screaming for help Kitha made it halfway down the corridor before Afma caught up to her. Grabbing a fistful of her golden hair Afma jerked her backwards, causing Kitha to nearly fall.

Crying out in fear Kitha pivoted, like the dancer she was, and raked her extended Avairei claws across her adversary's face. Blood dripping down her painted cheeks Afma screamed.

JOJO HAD FINISHED RECORDING the few scenes he wanted for his documentary and had decided to find Lovely Kitha when he heard a disturbance and saw a few of the off-duty warriors heading in that direction. Hailing an armachd he knew by sight but not by name, Jojo called out, "What's going on?"

The man laughed. "Man on the scene, eh Jojo?"

Jojo grinned and held up his recorder, repeating his question. "Don't know exactly. Someone said two of the whores are fighting. Yohkay is taking bets on who will win." The armachd motioned for Jojo to follow him to see the fun.

His guts suddenly twisting in knots, Jojo had a bad feeling about this as he followed the man down the passage where Kitha had told him she lived. When he reached the circle of shouting warriors, Jojo saw in their midst two disheveled females with hair tangled around their faces, their clothing torn and bloody.

Instead of breaking up the struggle the damned amadans were cheering their favorites and encouraging them on. Grabbing the nearest man's arm Jojo shouted over the clamor, "What are you people thinking? Stop them!"

"It's just a cat fight—probably fighting over a dress somebody borrowed without permission or some such. Let the boyos have their fun. We'll stop it before anybody gets killed." Jojo started to protest, but the warrior pushed him back and moved in closer to see the fight better.

Deciding he was getting nowhere like thi,s Jojo hurried back down the hallway, hoping to find an officer or someone else who could stop the fight. It needed to be stopped he was sure of it, because one of the combatants was Lovely Kitha.

Entering the reception hall he happened to see Marti and Chelka talking with Aju'an and Tobrach as they headed for the main entrance. Gasping for breath Jojo raced over to stop them. Puzzled they paused by the entrance and looked back at his shout.

When he caught up to them he managed to gasp out, "Marti, Kitha is in trouble—and maybe her mentor, too! There's a fight—and the boyos think it's funny. They are taking bets to see who will win!"

Growling a curse Aju'an demanded, "Where?"

Still trying to catch his breath Jojo pointed back the way he'd come.

"At the gaishinay's apartment?" Chelka asked. Jojo nodded. "I know the way," she said and bounded off in that direction Aju'an and Tobrach and then Marti right behind her.

As he followed at a slower pace, Jojo saw Nathan and Crowis staring at the retreating Warlinga. As he came up to them, Crowis asked, "Jojo, what's going on?" When Jojo told them, they too hurried in the same direction.

TAILS SLAPPING HARD at anyone stupid enough to be in their way, the three Warlinga waded through the gathered warriors with teeth bared and claws extended. Right behind them Marti and her foghorn voice bellowed curses at the lot of them.

Sensing trouble a Speir'dina man and a Red Wind warrior stepped into the circle and pulled the two women apart each man holding on to one of the combatants. Kitha quieted as soon as she felt the Speir'dina warrior's grip confining her. Afma, on the other hand was giving the Red Wind man a hard time, cursing and struggling to get free.

As Chelka and Marti pushed through the knot of warriors Kitha saw them and called out, "Protector Marti, Honored Chelka, help my mentor. The gaishinay mistress is beating her." She took a deep breath and continued, "And this one and her mistress want to poison the Hunt Leader. I was trying to warn you when Afma caught me; please help us!"

At her words in the Southern Tongue the group around her grew deathly quiet. This was far more serious than a simple fight.

Breast heaving Afma shook her head in denial, and then said in a badly accented southern language, "Bad slave lie. She want kill commander. Me stop!"

"No, that's not true," Kitha protested. "They want to kill the Hunt Leader!" Not sure who to believe the warriors began grumbling among themselves.

"You shit for brains amadans," Marti snarled. "That's Kitha. She's been helping patch up your sorry asses in the Med Tent the last few days. And her mentor has been working with Armachd Ross to translate the documents we found. Of course, she's the one telling the truth."

Coming to stand beside Marti, Nathan said, "Where is she, Kitha?" Kitha pointed to the open apartment door. "Aju'an, tie that woman up and put her somewhere very unpleasant. She stays under guard till I have time to taste her. Marti, Chelka with me, Crowis, check out Kitha. See how bad she's injured, will you?""

Tobrach folded his arms across his scaly chest and looked down his snout at the warriors still hovering about unsure what to do. "And as for the rest of you lazy Begta, I'm sure there is work needing to be done elsewhere. Do you need my help to find it?" No one dared answer that question. The crowd of warriors quickly deciding to a man, that yes indeed, they were needed—elsewhere.

The outer rooms devoid of people, Nathan followed his warriors through the bedroom and into the kitchen. The room looked like a Sorin storm had passed through, three crumpled bodies lying in puddles of blood upon the floor. Marti drew her sidearm and focused her attention on the gaishinay mistress struggling to sit up, holding her head. Nathan hurried forward to check on Cochinna.

He crouched and gently raised Cochinna to a sitting position resting her head and torso against his thigh. She was conscious, thank the gods of Caldon and Timorna, but she had taken a terrible beating. Long strips of raw flesh cris-crossed her arms and shoulders, but the gaishinay mistress seemed to have paid particular attention to her face, with an aim to permanently disfiguring her, no doubt.

There was a deep cut by Cochinna's right eye that worried Nathan, but the growing swelling for the moment made it difficult to determine the true extent of the damage. In his middle he could feel Corha's rage mounting.

Without opening her eyes Cochinna said in a voice slurred by pain, "You found me, Khutani, please tell Hunt—"

"Shh, it's all right, Enchanting, we already know. Kitha told us. Just rest now. I'm gonna give you something for the pain and put you to sleep. You're safe—everybody's safe; don't worry, just rest."

As she started to drift away, Cochinna managed to express her concern for another. "Please look after my servant, Iefer. Ze is hurt bad, I think. Iefer was here cooking for the hunt leader, before I returned and found..." Her voice trailed off as she drifted into sleep.

Without turning Nathan said, "Somebody check on her servant."

"Already did," Marti said. "The slave's dead."

Nathan cursed.

"How bad is she hurt, Corha?"

Nathan glanced up to see Tizu hovering over them. "Most of her injuries will heal with kavay and time," Nathan said for them both. "It's the cut by her eye that we are most worried about. She might lose her sight if it's too damaged. Corha isn't sure at this point—have to wait and see."

Nathan saw the flash of anger in his leader's dark eyes before Tizu regained some control over his emotions. Turning to Marti, he growled, "Marti, send for a stretcher. I want her and the little Avairei taken to our camp. Put Cochinna in my tent and tell them to have Phillip-Yoey see to them till I can arrange other accommodations for them."

Then to Nathan-Corha, he said, "You, are with me." Focusing his smoldering stare on the gaishinay mistress Chelka was now guarding, he added, "We have other business to take care of."

Even though Tizu had been issuing orders in the southern language Mistress Lareusha knew they were talking about her. When the Hunt Leader focused his glare on her she offered him a coquettish smile, the affect rendered ghoulish by the blood and smeared paint on her face.

"Warrior Commander, I want only to please you and offer you a better gaishinay to see to your comforts." She pointed to the sleeping Cochinna now being carried by Tobrach out of the kitchen. "I was only disciplining her, because she is jealous and evil. Whatever her little half-bred student told you it isn't true, I mean no harm to you or your men."

Nathan smiled showing her lots of his pointed Khutani teeth, and extended a tentacled hand. "You mean no harm, eh? Care to repeat that while in the link with me?"

As they stepped back into the hall to follow their prisoners, Nathan staggered and braced himself against the wall as an enraged Qwaltamis joined them again. Tizu glanced at him, eye brow raised. "You all right?"

Nathan grimaced, pushed off the wall and began walking again. "Yeah, I'm fine. Maker Qwaltamis came back—and it's pissed."

Tizu nodded. "Elder, I gather Corha has made you aware of our current situation."

Using Nathan's voice the Khutani said, "Yes, my child has told me. I want them, Hunt leader. Those enemy females have attacked women who gave us their oaths and are under our protection. I want them and anyone else who might endanger our cause."

Tizu continued walking, at last he said, "I gladly bow to your will in this matter, Elder. What do you plan to do with them?"

"Bring them to the sewer outlet and toss them down into the river like the garbage they truly are. We will take care of their punishments."

And they aren't going to survive what you have in mind, are they? Tizu thought and shuddered, but made no objection. Thinking of Cochinna's damaged eye, ruined face and her dead servant, maybe they deserved whatever the Khutani planned for them.

Chapter Twenty

Cochinna was aware of people coming and going around her, but the time blurred into a river of pain from which she occasionally surfaced. Kitha was by her side often when she woke, offering her food water and helping her take care of bodily functions. Kashallan-Nathan stopped by when freed from other duties as well as another dark-skinned alien with a Khutani symbiont coiled in his middle that Kitha called Phillip-Yoey.

Panicked at first by the hard patch over her eye, she had had to be restrained, not understanding at first how badly she had been injured by Mistress Lareusha's cruelties. Even though her eye hurt like poison fire, making her act a bit crazy, everyone she'd encountered in the Allied Camp had been so kind to her, soothing her fears and assuring her she would be just fine with a little more rest and the Khutani's medicines.

This time when she woke in the dim light it was different. Still feeling disoriented and weak Cochinna lay on the narrow bed, unsure where she was, or whether it was early morning or evening. No doubt she supposed she was somewhere in the Kashallan Alliance camp, but she had been in too much pain to know exactly what they had done with her.

The pain of her injuries was still a dull ache at the back of her awareness, but it was bearable for the moment. She took in several deep breaths trying to puzzle it out. Over her head the fabric covering of a tent of some kind billowed gently in the cool breeze off the river. Outside she could hear the sounds of men and a few women talking. Smells of frying meat and mushrooms made her stomach rumble with its emptiness.

She had some vague recollections of being placed upon a stretcher and carried out of the fortress, but after that Cochinna could recall very little until she awakened just now.

Hearing a rustling noise she turned her head in that direction and saw a Speir'dina man with a covered tray just entering followed by the Ally's exalted commander. Seeing that she was awake and watching him the man with the tray smiled. "Evening, Sa, I hope you are feeling better today."

"Just set the tray on my table, Owyn," Tizu said as he came through the tent flap and hung a lantern on a hook on the ridge pole. A soft green light suddenly filled the space, revealing the sparse furnishing of the tent's interior. The light illuminated her bed, a small portable table and camp stool, a moss-filled mattress by the far wall, with a dark colored blanket atop it, similar to the one under which she lay. Just inside the tent flaps a couple open packs with extra garments and other unknown articles spilled out from their shadowy interiors next to the other mattress.

Realizing that she was awake, Tizu came over to her bed and smiled down at her, his eyes searching her face for signs of pain. "I'm glad to see you awake. How are you feeling tonight?"

Struggling to sit up in the Exalted's presence, she managed to say with barely a tremble in her voice, "I am... well, Exalted Hunt Leader, but a little confused. This is no healing center. Where am I?"

Tizu noticed her difficulty and helped her sit up. Retrieving the pillow off the bed on the ground opposite hers, he placed it behind her shoulders for more height. "There, that should make it easier for you to relax. You are right; this is my personal quarters, not the med tent. It's too crowded over there at the moment. I had my people bring you here so I could personally see to your care and comfort till I could make other arrangements for you."

His personal quarters? Cochinna gasped and stared at the bed on the floor, now understanding its true meaning. He had given her his own bed and was now sleeping on the cold ground. Cochinna felt overwhelmed. The idea of a warrior, and a commander of warriors doing something so thoughtful was so foreign to her experience she wasn't sure how to feel or respond to such an alien act of kindness.

"Exalted Commander, it isn't right for you to sleep on the ground while a lowly slave lies here—"

Bending forward he brushed a quick kiss on her forehead above her injured eye. And then patted her shoulder. "Nonsense, it is perfectly all right for you to have my bed. As an old campaigner it isn't the first time I've slept rough. And it gives me great pleasure to see you nearby and getting better each day."

When she still looked unconvinced, he decided to change the subject, "Are you hungry? Nathan said you might feel well enough to eat with me, this evening when you woke, so I had the armachda cooking tonight serve up extra, just in case."

His words only added to her discomfort. Feeling suddenly deeply embarrassed Cochinna clasped her hands together under the blanket. This wasn't right, she should be up and serving him! He was an Exalted, one of the leaders of this invasion force, but still it wasn't right for him to be offering to serve a lowly pleasure slave. All her instinct and training rebelled against this exchange of roles.

But though she had the desire to slip into a more comfortable position, her body wouldn't obey her command. At last she admitted. "The food on the tray does smell delicious."

"That's good. I'll fix you a plate." He smiled at her again, moved the table closer and proceeded to fill a plate for her and himself from the food laid out upon the tray. Snagging the camp stool he sat down beside her bed and picked up his eating sticks.

After a couple bites he made a face, then said, "This food isn't nearly as delicious as the meals you prepared for me, but I hope it will serve." He took another mouthful. "We share the work around here, everybody takes a turn with whatever needs doing." He made a face. "And most of my armachda aren't known for their cooking skills. Fortunately for all of us their fighting skills are much better."

Cochinna chuckled, in spite of herself and ate another mouthful of the tasteless stew. She was aware that he was trying to put her at ease with his banter, and was awed by his concern. These alien Speir'dina with their strange ways were a wonder to her. None of the Elite among her own people would care about her feelings or needs. She was only a slave—bred to serve the Elite. That was her only purpose for being alive.

"The food isn't that bad, Exalted Hunt Leader,"

Tizu sighed. "I know very little about your people, Enchanting, I confess, but the Speir'dina don't care so much about titles. My personal name is Hukiyo, Hukiyo Tizu. Tizu is my family name. I would prefer—especially when we are alone like this that you call me by my name rather than a title. Could you do that for me?"

"I will try Hukiyo, and I will look forward to the day when I will be able to cook a meal for you myself like I promised you. My servant Iefer has a special recipe that we would love to make for you."

Sobering Tizu cleared his throat. "About your servant, Cochinna, I'm sorry to have to tell you that by the time my people discovered you, ze had already died of zer injuries."

"Oh, I feared it was so, but I hoped—" A lump of sadness clogging her throat Cochinna put down her eating sticks.

Tizu put down his own eating utensils and patted her hand. "I'm so sorry. Iefer must have meant a lot to you."

"Yes, I guess Iefer did. Too old to work as a pleasure slave any longer, ze came with me when my benefactor charged me to come and serve the warriors at Te'gal. Ze could have stayed in Tiebarai rather than come with me, but ze came anyway. And now Iefer is dead—and it's all because of me."

"No not because of you, because of that witch who beat zer to death—and that was not your fault, so don't blame yourself for that," he admonished her, his expression grim. "And those two have paid dearly for that murder I assure you."

His expression suddenly frightening her, she resumed eating , not wishing to anger him more by inquiring further about what had happened to Afma and Lareusha. Kitha could tell her about it later.

Changing the subject, Cochinna asked him about his home among the stars instead, and they passed the time together pleasantly until one of his men showed up to bring him to a meeting with his officers.

Kashallan-Phillip showed up not long after Hukiyo left with a Kitha decorated with kavay patches similar to her own, trailing in his wake. The kashallan inserted his tentacles and gave her a kavay that would take away her pain and let her sleep, and then Kitha helped her get ready for bed. Asleep nearly as soon as her head touched the pillow she didn't hear the hunt leader come back and crawl into his own blankets.

NEXT DAY, ENCHANTING Janixa and the hermaphrodite Lovely Zalin came to visit her while she was awake, but still recovering in Hunt Leader Tizu's quarters.

A small but commanding woman with beautiful purple eyes and silky silver hair Janixa fell to her knees beside Cochinna's bed and took her hand. "Please, Cochinna," she begged. "Speak to your new protector on our behalf. We want to go anywhere this army is going rather than remain abandoned here in these ruins."

A beautiful dancer with soft green dyed ringlets framing a delicate featured face, who often partnered with Lovely Kitha for entertainments, Zalin took a deep breath and added, "We will even let one of the Khutani drink our blood," Ze shivered, swallowed hard, and then taking a deep breath ze added, "We will give one of those kashallan aliens our oaths—but please tell it not to drink too much of our blood or hurt us."

Kitha, who had been persuaded to bring them gasped, "The kashallans won't drink your blood! And when they extend their tentacles to take your oath or do a healing it doesn't hurt—truly it doesn't." she insisted when they still seemed skeptical.

"I don't know anything about it drinking your blood. But what I do know, is that when the Khutani symbiont nesting inside its Speir'dina host 'tastes' you, as they say, it doesn't hurt." Cochinna assured them when they looked to her for confirmation.

"Which one took your oath," Zalin asked, zer eyes bright with curiosity. "Was it the tall muscular warrior, or the slim dark skinned one? I think they are both cute—even if they are aliens," ze confided.

Kitha gasped, putting a hand over her mouth to stifle a giggle. "Oh, Lovely, you are shameless!"

At a frown from Janixa, zer's face assumed a sober expression.

"To answer your question, Lovely Zalin, neither kashallan took my oath. I gave my loyalty to the Khutani who rescued me from drowning during our escape. It wrapped me in its coils, penetrated my skin with a mouth tentacle and spoke to me mind to mind. Helpless as I was, ensnared in its coils, it didn't hurt me. Much of what the elite have told us about our ancient enemy isn't true, I believe."

Cochinna laughed when she saw their mouths drop open in surprise. "But know this as well." She said, her voice suddenly stern, "don't try to lie to them, because while in the link with one of them they can taste your dishonesty and—"

"And punish it with a painful death," Nathan said as he stepped all the way into the tent, Tizu right behind him. He grinned, showing them lots of sharp Khutani teeth. With cries of fear Cochinna's guests dropped prostrate on the ground in front of him.

Tizu snorted. "You Amadan, smarten up. No need to scare her visitors half out of their wits. Brushing past the kashallan he took a seat by his work table. When the gaishinay remained quivering on the ground, he growled, "Oh get up. Like the Enchanting said, he isn't going to hurt you."

Rising to a sitting position they stared at the two men wide eyed and silent. An embarrassed look coming over Nathan's face he said, "Sorry. Though it is true that I can taste when a person lies to me, I didn't mean to scare you like that."

Focusing his attention on Cochinna, Corha said, "We came with the Hunt Leader, because I want to check on your injuries. We didn't know you had guest."

Cochinna, with Kitha's help raised herself to a sitting position on Tizu's cot. How long had they been listening outside? She wondered and held out her hands palms down for his link. "Maybe it is a good thing you've come, Kashallan-Nathan. This is Enchanting Janixa and Lovely Zalin. They say they want to serve the Alliance and go with us.

"They are also a bit frightened by the stories they have heard about Khutani and the Speir'dina. If you put me in the link to check on my injuries while they are still here, then they can see that there's nothing to be afraid of—if they sincerely want to join us."

Nathan nodded and sat down on the ground in front of her, taking her hands and forming the link. Knowing the gaishinay were watching, Nathan looked them in the eye and said, "Blood drinker, eh? Though it's true that young Khutani do require a blood supplement to their diet, Corha hasn't needed the Blood Gift for a while now. And we would never take the Gift from anyone who didn't offer it freely. Whoever told you about the Blood Gift didn't have their facts straight."

Then as Corha tasted her injuries, Nathan closed his eyes and allowed the symbiont's senses to dominate their shared awareness,

"See there is no pain," Cochinna said. Then she sighed as the healing warmth of the symbiont's pain killer traveled through her body. "Ah, thank you, Corha, the pain is waning now," she breathed.

"While he's doing that," Tizu said, interrupting. "if you two are sincere about joining us and Nathan-Corha there takes your oath, you need to know a few things about us before you decide."

He held up one finger. "One, except for the severely wounded, everybody walks and helps carry our gear. So, with that in mind you will be limited in what you can bring with you when we leave."

Tizu held up a second finger, "Two, everybody around here works to help set up and take down our nightly camps. You will be assigned to a Teh'lach. Each Teh'lach is made up of all the different peoples of the Alliance, Warlinga, Clan Warriors, Speir'dina—even the Loti and Begta, everyone in their Teh'lach works together and shares together, like—uh—family," he glanced at Kitha, groping for the right word in the Northern dialect.

"Like how the age-mates in a crèche work and share might be a better way to explain what you want to say, Hunt Leader," Kitha said.

"Thank you, Nurse Kitha, that's very helpful." Addressing the other gaishinay, he said. "You can ask Kitha or anyone you like about the Teh'lachs I won't take time to explain them further now."

He held up a third finger, "Though the Khutani's peoples in the South don't keep pleasure slaves, and when you join us you will no longer be slaves, I do know about people trained in your arts. Your knowledge of conditions we will encounter as we march north will be of great value to us, and I hope you will offer it willingly.

"If you have the energy after a long days march to entertain 'guests' you are welcome to do that. I'm sure those of my warriors with the appropriate biological equipment would appreciate your services. You may entertain as you like—as long as there is no trouble—I won't tolerate that. If anyone going with us from Te'gal causes dissention among my warriors, they will be killed or abandoned on the trail.

"And I will speak to my warriors on your behalf. Nobody in this Alliance will be allowed to force you to pleasure them sexually, nor will they be allowed to beat or abuse you either."

He glanced at the injured Cochinna lying on the cot with eyes closed nearly asleep. "And that also applies to one gaishinay abusing another. Do I make myself clear?" Both gaishinay nodded. "Good, I can see that Corha has given Cochinna something to make her sleep, so why don't you go back to the fortress, talk among yourselves and when Nathan-Corha and I come to Te'gal tomorrow you, and anyone else who is interested, can swear your allegiance if you still want to."

Cochinna had heard them offer their good byes as Kitha guided them back outside, but was too sleepy to even say good bye.

Chapter Twenty One

When Tizu and Nathan-Corha got to Te'gal the next day there were quite a number of people milling around the main reception hall, waiting for him to taste and take their oaths. After Tizu finished his little speech laying out his rules for any of the civilians left alive who wanted to join the Alliance and go with them, Nathan waited for them to decide.

After talking among themselves several of the boldest among the freed Ghostland slaves and recently captured Southerners agreed to let Nathan-Corha taste them and gave the Alliance their oaths.

They were about to dismiss the group when the air around them suddenly grew colder, Nathan shivered, knowing from past experience what the change in temperature meant. Glancing over his shoulder he saw that the expected robed and veiled figure with the Wa'chassey'ul at her side had just joined them.

Beside him Tizu muttered a curse under his breath. Face devoid of expression Tizu bowed in her direction. "Tess-weh, is there a reason that you have chosen to join us?"

"Yes there is, My Jewel." Tess-weh walked forward keeping eye contact with him. Tizu shivered, but held her gaze. "I've come to see your new recruits, Hunt Leader." Her cold dark eyes raked across the still kneeling inhabitance of Te'gal. She chuckled and there was no mirth in the sound. "Not a very promising lot are they?"

Tizu snorted as if sharing her joke. "They'll do."

"Will they? I wonder. Are you sure they will keep their oaths and be loyal to their new masters?"

Tizu made a face at her implication that Te'gal's people were only exchanging one master for another. "We don't keep slaves—as you know, Tess-weh. All members of the Alliance are free peoples."

Tess-weh chuckled again. "Don't keep slaves, eh? Does that apply to the Western Clan warriors, too?"

"I just tasted them," Nathan-Corha growled, interrupting, before her banter could cause an argument or worse. Returning the discussion to her original topic, he declared, "No Ghostland agents are among those who have just given me their oaths." Like Dunnagh before him, Nathan hated her little games.

Without warning she reached out a hand and patted his middle where the symbiont coiled. "Poor, poor, Little Khutani, so much responsibility for one so young—too much perhaps. Too bad your snaky relatives haven't shared with you my earlier warning."

Nathan felt a shiver run down his spine. What had the big worms neglected to tell them now? "What warning; what are you talking about?"

Eyes gleaming with a hidden amusement she shook a finger at him. "Ah, ah, ah, that would be cheating if I told you, you know. The rules of my contract, remember?"

He didn't have to see her veiled lower face to know she was smiling at him. Nathan's face flushed a deep red. She'd got him again—damn her. "Right, I guess the Makers forgot to mention something. What can you tell me then?"

"I will repeat myself—and only this once. Remember what was found at Ticca after Tomina's death. Are you sure you have tasted all of them correctly, Khutani?"

Think! Nathan commanded his sluggish mind, what had Marti and Marnez found that was so important that they needed to destroy it besides Barak's communication crystal? Think!

They had been speaking in the Southern language, not well understood by many in the fortress. Under the kashallan's renewed scrutiny, however, Te'gal's inhabitants shifted nervously glancing from one grimfaced warrior to another.

Tizu was also aware of the shifting mood and snapped an order to his men who were guarding the oath takers. "Nobody leaves here till we get this sorted, got that? Anybody tries to sneak away kill them on the spot."

Shifting languages he addressed the anxious people watching them, "This lady here thinks that there is an agent or two for the Cabal disguised among you. If you were truthful when you gave Kashallan-Nathan your oath, then you have nothing to fear right now, so stay calm while we sort this out."

With Speir'dina and Khutani senses straining Nathan-Corha studied the problem. <<I can taste them again, Kasha, if you believe the demon's warning,>> Corha suggested in a tiny worried voice. <<I've never made a mistake before—but maybe this time... I am young, like the demon said.>>

<<I'm sure you did your best, Shalla. I guess the Makers have been so busy with other matters they just forgot to tell us about Tess-weh's warning.>>

<<Could she be playing with us—or has she made the mistake and not me?>> Corha said hopefully.

<<No, there is something we've missed. She wouldn't make that kind of mistake or tease us in that way. We've missed something—important.>> he sighed. <<I guess we need to taste them again.>>

But where to start? Glancing over the thirty or so people enclosed in the circle of guards before them, he studied each one carefully. One of the gaishinay would be a possible spy or assassin. Men revealed a lot after a sexual encounter sometimes; he hoped it wouldn't turn out to be one of them. He hated to kill a woman, though he would if necessary.

Dismissing them for the moment, Nathan next studied the servants and field slaves huddled in groups apart from the gaishinay. Dirty and ragged with make-shift bandages covering minor wounds, Nathan's eyes narrowed, noticing that several slaves, who were unquestionably field hands, judging by the muddy red clay on their fur below the knees were crowding together as far away from him as the guards would allow. They were a motley bunch and they'd obviously been picking masa root today, he recognized the signs from personal experience.

Now, however, they seemed to him to be unusually nervous. Why? Singling out one muscular slave with an unusual amount of whip scars across his chest and arms he focused his gaze on him. The man hadn't seemed so anxious earlier when he took his oath.

Was he the one? The man met his gaze and held it. Slowly he motioned with his chin over his shoulder while still keeping eye contact. Nathan gave him a slight nod then continued checking the slaves. This group was standing very close together the larger slaves among them forming a protective barrier around—something—or someone. Nathan couldn't see into their midst, but sometimes when a man moved unexpectedly he caught a glimpse of a smaller person.

Without warning Nathan stepped forward, pushing aside two burley slaves and yanked the smaller man out so he could examine him. "Don't be shy; why are you hiding away? Come out where I can see you."

Trembling under his hand the little man blinked up at the tall muscular warrior still with a firm grip on his arm. "I'm not hiding—not really. I'm just a bit shorter than my friends—and-and you scared me talking about spies and traitors to the Alliance, that's all."

Nathan chuckled, firming up his grip when the Ghostlander tried to pull away. "Scared you, did I? Well, there's no need for you to be worried, because I already tasted you and you gave me your oath. So, you weren't lying. You couldn't be the one I'm looking for, right?"

Trembling, the small man shook his head vigorously. "N-no, Exalted, I'm not the one."

Nathan kept a hand on his arm but didn't extend his tentacles. This six-limbed individual was ragged and muddy—maybe too muddy. For a field hand he was unusually small and thin. He lacked the muscles sported by someone spending his days doing hard labor. And under all that dirt the patches of skin revealed were pale, not tanned by the sun.

He smiled showing lots of Khutani teeth, deliberately making the man cringe. The slave's face was covered with red clay, why? Unless an overseer knocked him down and jammed his face into the ground nobody got mud on their face like that from digging masa. And since the Alliance had taken over, no one had been forcing a slave to work with such cruelty.

"My, it looks like you have had a rough day today," he remarked. allowing sympathy to color his voice. "What *have* you been doing?"

"W-working in the fields digging masa root, Exalted Master," the little man squeaked.

Nathan clicked his tongue with disapproval and jammed his tentacles hard into the frightened man's flesh. "I warned you earlier when I took your oath not to lie to me—and you are lying."

"I'm not lying!" the man protested. "I'm loyal!"

"Ah, but the real question is to who?" Nathan shook his head and clicked his tongue again. "Because you are lying and that's not a smart thing to do, not if you want to live—not smart at all."

Nathan reached out his free hand and drew a line through the mud on the Ghostlander's face exposing the pale skin underneath. He grinned. "You see, I've been a slave and I know unless you're in credibly clumsy you don't get mud on your face digging root. You should have copied the slaves you were trying to imitate more carefully, Ghostland Puke."

<<Kasha, he tastes different than before when I took his oath,>> Corha said, breaking in on his talk with the Ghostlander. <<I don't know if he is the spy Tess-weh wants us to find, but he is definitely very afraid—and lying. He is no field slave.>>

<<Yeah, I figured that out already, but thanks Shalla, for confirming that.>> Now he recalled someone at Ticca saying something about the wizards having a substance that could mask their true essence for a short time while in the link with a Khutani. That was how the Changelings had managed to stay hidden for so long among the southern peoples.

"So, who are you, really, Ghostland Puke?"

The Ghostlander licked his lips and swallowed hard. "I-I'm just a lowly slave, Exalted," the Ghostlander stammered, trying harder to pull out of Nathan's grasp. "My name is Daz; and I'm loyal to the Khutani, truly!"

<<Definitely lying, Kasha.>>

"His name really is Daz," the man who alerted him to the traitor's presence," said into the silence. "But he is one of Master Unar's assistants, not one of us."

"Nieshu is right," another slave added. "The wizard threatened to kill us with his poisons if we didn't hide him" His comment was echoed by others in the group.

"Poisons, eh?" Nathan swore, and opening his mouth wide, he allowed Corha to spit a stream of black kavay into the Ghostlander's face.

Then the kashallan let go his prey. Unar's assistant fell to the floor writhing and screaming as the Khutani's acid dissolved his features.

"If there are any more spies among you," Tizu growled into the stunned silence when it was over, "you people had better speak up and tell me now, because I've had enough of this shit. If there's another Cabal agent concealed among you, tell me or I will throw the lot of you in the river for the Khutani to deal with."

Into the stunned silence following Corha's execution Janixa took a deep breath and ventured. "Kashallan-Nathan, Exalted Hunt Leader, I honestly don't know if she was lying to you in some way, but I think you should taste Comely Sanna again."

A plump figure with six limbs and long died pink hair gasped, glaring dagger eyes at the other gaishinay. "Evil Old Hag, are you still trying to get me in trouble for stealing your ruby ring?" turning to Nathan she pleaded, "I am no hidden agent working for the Cabal! All I want is to go back to a civilized place and not be left behind—please believe me."

"Janixa, using me to get personal revenge for a past wrong is just as dangerous as lying to me," Nathan warned.

"I know that, Exalted." Turning to Comely Sanna, she said, "I'm not seeking personal revenge for the ring; it was finished for me when you gave it back. Believe me I'm not trying to get you killed. I don't know if you are an agent for the Elite in Tiebarai."

Turning to Nathan she added, "But what I do know is that she was Daz's special pleasure slave. All I'm saying is that you check her again, because if anyone could be a spy, it might be her."

"Hmm... Comely, that's a very pretty crystal hanging around your neck. Did Daz give it to you—may I see it?" Nathan held out a hand and looked her in the eye.

Startled Sanna put a hand to her neck, clutching a crystal that had been revealed as she leaned over to accuse Janixa. Backing away, she shook her head. "No! My crystal is very special to me, Exalted Khutani; I never take it off."

"Nonetheless I would like to see it." Nathan repeated.

Sanna stared wide-eyed and trembling, then her fear took over and she bolted, twisting her way through a gap between two surprised warriors, racing for the tunnels below.

"After her, you shit for brains amadans," Tizu roared.

"Don't touch that crystal," Nathan called after the retreating warriors. "Sietriga, destroy it with your side arm, before it ensnares someone else. It's a Cabal communication device."

From the bowels of the fortress came a scream not long after the warriors left. A moment later the tunnel echoed with a flash of light and a loud boom.

The sound of someone clapping caused Nathan and the others to turn in that direction. Tess-weh clapped one last time then returned her hands to her side. "Well done, My Jewel. You are as clever as I remember, isn't he, Atahru?"

"Yes, Mistress, most clever. Your faith in an old love was well rewarded today," Atahru said in his toneless voice.

Nathan felt his cheeks go red again as Atahru led the way out of the fortress. Damn her—did she have to bring up the past in front of everybody? He thought.

Part Two
Chapter One

Fa'Hanzoi at last, Drucas thought as he stepped onto the pebbled beach. Above him loomed the stark, grey cliff that concealed the seaward entrance to the northern city. Here, and only here, the ruling Ghostland Cabal of wizards allowed some trade with the Western Clans. And it was also here that Ghostland war leaders carried on their recruitment of warriors from the West for their raids south into the Khutani lands.

Drucas allowed a cruel smile to play across his dark lips. The beach was nearly empty, only a few slaves lingering to put away the last of the equipment and supplies. The water gate was also closed at this time, the night's activity diminished, most workers and officials retreating into Fa'hanzoi's cool interior to wait out the heat and glare of the coming day.

His recovery from his ordeal in the Holy Place of the Fires had taken much longer than Drucas had anticipated. So instead of taking the land route as he had when going, he had gone west to clan territory to take the shorter sea passage back to Fa'Hanzoi. The three Twisted Grass warriors he had tempted with tales of slaves and plunder to ferry him across the Shallow Sea stood waiting for him to escort them to the recruiting officer—which he, of course, had no plans of doing. They were witnesses to his disobedience and they would have to be silenced. No one could be left alive to tell the true destination of his *scouting mission*.

"As you can see the gate to the city is closed at this time of day." Drucas pointed up the winding trail on the cliff face. "You will have to come with me to the smaller gate near the top of the cliff. We will enter and go to my quarters. There you may rest and refresh yourselves before we make the journey back to my war camp."

He had no luxurious apartment in Fa'Hanzoi—yet, and there was no smaller gate at the top of the cliff. Beyond the underground city and the shore stretched barren desert. Only his war bands and the Hated Enemy were waiting for him on the dusty trail to Te'gal.

Instinctual caution goading them, the three brothers passed a silent communication among themselves. The Ghostlanders were jealous of their secrets, never before had westerners been allowed to enter any of the northern towns. And now this half-bred southerner was inviting them into a forbidden place? "The trip was easy for us. We have no need of rest," the eldest of the warriors said. "You can pay us now. We have changed our minds about joining your war band."

Drucas snorted a laugh and held out his arms for them to see he carried no treasure." "Do you see the pretty jewels and shells I promised on my person? They are in my quarters in Fa'Hanzoi. Come if you want them, Little Begta."

They talked among themselves again, and then to Drucas's disgust one of the three turned back to the canoe. "Your property will be safe here, no need for one to stay," Drucas said.

"That one will stay with the canoe, the oldest of the three said, showing lots of teeth. "We go now." The warrior motioned for Drucas to lead the way up the cliff.

Cursing under his breath, Drucas started up the cliff, the Twisted Grass warriors in his wake. Drucas took several deep breaths as they climbed, drawing up power and searching for the correct moment to strike. He knew the two with him were on guard, though he wasn't sure why. When he let loose his magic he would have to be quick and deadly; he wouldn't get a second chance.

As they neared the top Drucas found the spot for which he'd been searching. A small land slide had caused several boulders and rocks to fall onto the trail, obscuring the way beyond. Drucas saw with his newly won magic the hidden flat place to one side of the trail where he could land safely. Though not visible from their side of the slide, the footing directly beyond the rocks was treacherous with loose sand and gravel.

A leap straight over would leave the jumper off balance for a few moments before he could sink in his claws and regain his footing.

Drucas planned to take full advantage of that fact. When the Westerners hesitated and considered turning back, Drucas called them sniveling, cowardly Begta.

Without pausing to check Drucas blindly leapt into the air and cleared the crest of the rocky mound, knowing the others would follow rather than be named coward. Secure of his footing as soon as he touched the ground on the other side, Drucas whirled and lashed out with his whip-like tail, catching the first man over the slide full in the chest and flinging him off balance.

The warrior cursed, dropping to hands and knees, scrabbling for a purchase on the slippery gravel-covered slope. Following up his first attack Drucas slammed another hard blow to the side of the man's head with his spear butt. With a cry the man fell backward over the cliff into the inlet water below.

The second warrior hearing his companion, looked down and saw him falling into the bay. Knowing the fall was no accident the man turned and ran back down the trail. From a boulder at the top of the slide Drucas watched him run. The cruel smile back on his lips he raised a hand, and power shot from his fingers. The ground under the running man's feet melted away and he, too, tumbled from the cliff trail.

The third brother watching from the shallows saw what had happened to his relatives and hastily pulled up the anchor and clumsily began paddling the war canoe into deeper water. Drucas watched the vessel pull away from the beach, but felt little worry about the young warrior left alive. One man alone couldn't manage the big war canoe. The Shallow Sea would claim the western savage before he could reach a safe refuge to tell of the Changeling's treachery. That one would be feeding the Dhuura before nightfall.

DRUCAS WAS HOT DUSTY and hungry by the time he reached the Ghostland war camp sprawled across a narrow valley on the way to Te'gal. His approach had been noticed by a sentry posted on the slope, and to his disgust, a reception party was waiting for him as he walked into camp.

His Second Sanglaz and a few of his best hunters were there, but the party also included The Great Avenger. Though spawned in the pits like most of the northern warriors, this monster was the pride of a rival wizard's breeding program. In spite of his fearsome A-symmetrical visage and elongated body and the sharp teeth and claws bread into all the dull witted creatures of the birth pits, the Avenger was intelligent and there for a threat to K'San Drucas's domination of the army's leadership.

"So, half-bred Khutani slave, you have finally come to join us?" The Great Avenger greeted him when Drucas stopped in front of them. "What do you have to say for yourself?"

Drucas's head crest flattened at the insult. Refusing to be baited by the Slime, Drucas addressed his Second instead. "Get one of the slaves to bring me a meal. You can give me your report while I eat."

"Where have you been?" The Avenger snarled. "Do you know the Hated Enemy has taken Te'gal while we waited for you, Lazy Begta! Why weren't you here to lead your men? I was called away from other duties to take over in your absence."

"I am here now, Begta Puke, so you can return to your duties in the cesspit , *Great Avenger,*" Drucas snapped. The Great Avenger roared in outrage and dropped into a fighter's crouch. Drucas ignored him. Turning his back on his rival to show his contempt, he motioned for Sanglaz to lead the way to his headquarters tent.

Te'gal taken! This news—if true, was a great shock. Drucas felt a knot of unease tighten in his gut. Cohbruel and the cabal of wizards who had survived the power struggle after Barak's death would be furious that the Enemy had gotten so far into Ghostland territory unopposed. And, they of course, would blame him for Calahar and the fort's defenders failure.

Sanglaz led him to a round tent staked out near the center of the encampment. Once inside and away from prying eyes Drucas dropped his weapons and pack by the door and sank gratefully onto a padded stool by a portable work table. Stopping to order his K'San a meal and posting a guard, Sanglaz stepped back inside and closed the tent flap behind himself. Clawed hand to his chest, he stood waiting further instructions from his leader.

Drucas would like nothing better than to plaster his aching burns with stolen kavay and sink into that welcoming nest across from the table, but he knew that wouldn't be possible for some while yet. He sighed and said, "Is it true that Te'gal has fallen to the Hated Enemy, or was that half-bred puke toying with me, trying to make me angry?"

"It would appear to be true, K'San. A Ghostlander named Nasrid, claiming to be Second in Command at Te'gal showed up here several days ago with a few wounded warriors. Their story is that the fortress commander and most of Te'gal's warriors are dead. They say the Enemy destroyed Te'gal's gates with their magics, much as they did at Riath, I suspect. Nasrid and his men escaped through the tunnels before the Enemy closed them, and are probably all the fighters that are left from Master Unar's breeding program."

Drucas snorted. "Cowardly Begta, escaped through the tunnels, eh?"

"Perhaps they are K'San—and stupid." Sanglaz said. "There first question to us was whether it was true that Master Barak was dead."

Damn all wizards to the Black Pit. Drucas felt a stab of unease at the news. Had things gone awry so badly in Tiebarai that the new Cabal hadn't even thought to inform the commander of such an important fortress as Te'gal of Barak's demise? It would appear so.

"Where is the Hated Enemy now? Are they still dividing up their plunder and slaves at Te'gal?"

"No, they are coming this way, marching towards Fa'Hanzoi the scouts The Avenger sent out say."

"Hmm, how close are they?" Drucas asked, his mind suddenly overwhelmed with a cascade of possibilities.

"The Avenger's scouts say three days, maybe."

"Better have some of our own trusted men verify that."

"Your will, K'San; I will see that it is done," Sanglaz said.

"Yes, do that."

Three days, Drucas felt the knot in his gut tighten a little more. If the Enemy was that close they needed to get out of this narrow valley where they could so easily be trapped. No—better yet—leave much of the camp where it was and conceal the warbands under clouds of illusions on the higher slopes. When the stupid fools swallowed the bait and attacked the empty camp then his warriors could fall upon them like hungry vistri.

Ah but what of the Speir'dina's strange weaponry that some in Tiebarai claim come from another world. Well, if that was true then the damned

Cabal better bring out some of the old weaponry hidden away from the time of the Great Wars, if they really have such weapons—if they really want to win this war...

Breaking in on his speculations, Sanglaz said, "Wizard Cohbruel informed us that he and the Cabal want you to contact them as soon as you returned. The wizard said he didn't authorize you to be gone so—long."

Sanglaz hadn't come right out and demanded an explanation, but in the face of the disaster that had happened in his absence, he should offer the man something. It would be in the best interest of his future plans to keep Sanglaz and the rest of his men loyal.

"I was gone over long," he agreed, "but not from choice." Drucas drew Sanglaz's attention to the charred and blistering patches on his scales. "While scouting, as I told the wizards I was going to do, I was discovered and recognized by some of the Khutani's warriors," he lied. "They wounded me with their magics and pressed me hard. I had to circle far around to avoid their hunters."

Sanglaz seemed to except his story, and then held open the tent flap for the slave who arrived at that moment, bringing his meal. Knowing he couldn't put off his meeting with the Cabal much longer, The Great Avenger had probably already contacted them, Drucas stopped Sanglaz as he started to leave.

"Have our priest come. I need him to check my wounds. After he does that, I will ask him to prepare The Drink for me. When I've eaten and had my wounds looked after, I will swallow his potion and go into trance to make contact with Cohbruel and the Cabal."

ALLOWING HIMSELF THE luxury of a brief rest to organize his thoughts and strengthen his personal shields, Drucas at last drank the priest's foul potion and sank into the deep trance needed to project himself into the depths of the Dream. His spirit-body flowing down the familiar dark pathways of the Cabal's magical construct, he passed into the wizard's hidden council chamber where they were waiting for him.

Bracing for a series of hard questions concerning his long absence and his failure to report to them as soon as he had returned, Drucas was surprised when they got right down to business instead.

<<It's time,>> the new Master of the Ghostland Cabal, Cohbruel said as he rose to confront him. <<You have two items of your property in the Enemy's camp, we command you to use one of them to further our plans for the Alliance's destruction. The Hated Enemy Vermin are getting too insolent. Now that they've taken Te'gal they think they can come into our territory unchallenged and annihilate us.>>

K'San Drucas dipped his dream-body's head crest in acknowledgement of the wizard's order. <<Yes, it is time, Exalted,>> Drucas agreed. <<My hunters have told me the Enemy is marching on Fa'Hanzoi. What service can my agents perform for the Cabal?>>

The bald, grey-skinned wizard studied the big Changeling with brow furrowed, as if he sensed a change in the warrior after his unexplained absence, but couldn't define the difference. At last, he said, <<You have told me that the two women wearing your brand are well respected among the Hated Enemy.

<<The Warlinga female is the consort of one of their Hunt Leaders and often attends their strategy meetings, is that not so? It is time to eliminate some of their leaders. It is time to spread confusion amongst the Alliance, before our combined force attacks and destroys them.>>

Combined force, did the slimy little mushroom mean he would have to share the leadership with his rival, The Great Avenger? Were the wizards still unsure of his loyalty because of his mixed bloodlines? No matter what he did, no matter how hard he worked to win their approval, always it was the same. Drucas felt the old resentments awaken anew. He strengthened his shield so the Cabal wouldn't detect his rising frustration and anger.

Work alongside The Avenger? That wasn't going to happen. Their hatred for each other ran too strong and too deep—no matter what the damned Cabal ordered. He would kill, or be killed, before he agreed to that!

"...Use the crystal I gave you to enhance your power,>> the wizard was saying. <<Take full control of one of the women—the Warlinga perhaps—she is the strongest of the two. Have her kill her consort and as

many of the traitorous Khutani's slaves and the new aliens as she can before they kill her in return.>>

Kill her? kill Chelka! The wizard's bloodless command sparked a rebellious rage in Drucas that he quickly tamped down to smoldering embers. <<I see the beauty of your plan, Exalted Master,>> Drucas hastily lied, hoping his silence hadn't been taken for opposition. <<While they are recovering from that blow we will fall upon them and crush them between our mighty jaws.>>

Arms folded across his narrow chest Cohbruel's penetrating stare studied him for a long moment before he nodded. His voice dripping with menace and promised pain, he warned, <<We remember Riath. Don't fail us again, Half-Bred Slave.>>

<<Your will is my command, Exalted Master. I will complete the task you have assigned me, never fear.>>

Oh he would do the task assigned to him—for now—but in his own way. Drucas bowed low, hiding his eyes, a tight shield on his private thoughts that even one, such as the sniveling coward before him couldn't break without risking injury to himself.

Watching the pale, bald-headed creature take his seat among the others, Drucas vowed that one day there would be a reckoning between them. He had hidden it well, but along with the known enhancements bred into him by Barak's rivals came a few other 'gifts' he'd managed to keep secret. His prayers at the Holy Place had also born their power-enhancing fruit—he could feel it.

Drucas would like nothing more than to kill the sniveling half-bred Begta Tobrach that was now sharing her sleeping nest. And it would be a sweet, sweet irony to make her do it for him. She would be his forever when he told her that fact in all its gruesome details. But no, he couldn't let her do it. The Tragar upstart would die but so would she in the process—and he didn't want that—not that at all costs.

But in spite of what he had boasted to the wizards his control of Chelka wasn't as secure as he would like. To be perfectly honest her will to resist was proving stronger than he had expected from a mere Khutani-bred female. Truly she would make an excellent consort and mother of his children—when he at last broke her to his will. And after they were victorious and they had reclaimed the South for their own, she would be his, and his alone.

Unfortunately, after the Alliance had left Tragar Keep he had discovered she was now being watched and guarded. A Maker slimeworm, no less, often swam near her spirit, protecting her sleep from his torments. For now, however, the Speir'dina female would do nicely for his purpose, Drucas thought. True she was also guarded, but not as closely. Only a younger, less experienced member of the Khutani pod accompanying the Southerners was assigned to guard that one's sleep. When the time was right, the youngster would be no match for his enhanced power if his attack was swift and unexpected...

Chapter Two

The afternoon was hot and dusty. Even through the folds of the covering placed over her litter to shelter her sensitive skin from the light, Cochinna suffered in silence the heat and jarring movement as her Loti bearers carried the awkward litter around the obstacles encountered upon the path.

At last a break had been ordered and Kitha had come to help her from the litter and guide her to a private place among the rocks where she could relieve herself. After that Kitha sat her down on a padded stool set in the shade and offered her tea and a bit of cold food from their packs. The walk, the food and drink revived her, but all too soon it had been time to take her place once more inside the litter.

Kitha arranged the moss-filled pillows behind her mentor's head and shoulders and urged her to lie back in her makeshift bed. "I heard we will be moving on soon, so rest while you can, Mentor. Though I know the Loti carrying your litter try not to jostle you too much, this surface trail is rocky and narrow.' Kitha giggled. "It's a much more difficult path than the one we traveled through the underground pathways on our way to Te'gal, I fear."

Oh so very true, Cochinna thought, every inch of her wounded body could attest to that. Cochinna patted her hand to comfort her. "I know they try their best, Student—or should I say, Nurse Kitha now."

Kitha let out a nervous giggle and dropped her eyes. "It is what I would like to be—one of the nurses helping heal the sick and wounded." She glanced up and met her mentor's one good eye. "I hope you are not angry with me, Mentor."

Cochinna patted her again to reassure her. "No, Kitha, I'm not angry. I have no idea what the future will hold for us, and you have every right to reach for something that pleases you." Cochinna chuckled. "Including that shy young Avairei that follows you around whenever he can. Do you want him, My Lovely?"

Kitha's eyes opened wide, then she smiled, arranging Cochinna's blanket neatly across her chest and shoulders as she considered her answer. "Maybe. I find him easy to talk to—and interesting," she finally admitted. "There is so much I don't know about my mother's people—and he tells me—things—about the South... But it's too soon to know for sure what may happen between us. Honored Jojo says he has a betrothed waiting for him at home, so..."

"So don't give into him too easily. You need to consider your future security. Now that we are free and no longer have a Benefactor to provide for us, you must prepare for the time coming when you will no longer be able to count on your beauty to win sanctuary among these people."

Kitha nodded, her expression serious. "That is one of the reasons I am studying to be a healer. The kashallans say there will always be a place for me in the southern communities as a nurse. And as to a relationship with Healer Crowis," she shrugged.

"That's good, My Lovely. It eases my mind to know you still have your wits about you. I'm sure you will do well, whatever happens."

"And while we are on that subject, what about you, Honored Teacher, have you thought about what you will do after your wounds have healed?"

Cochinna sighed, the eye still concealed under the Khutani's healing patch suddenly throbbed with awakening pain. No, she had not—and she was trying hard to avoid thinking about it.

As if divining her private thoughts Kitha said, "I'm sure you have no cause for worry; a place will be made for you among them, too. The Exalted Hunt Leader will see to your continuing welfare, I'm sure."

As if her student's words had conjured him, Hunt Leader Tizu walked over to them at that moment, her litter bearers and another Loti, trailing in his wake. Stopping beside her litter, he crouched down and took her hand, giving it a comforting squeeze.

"We will be camping early tonight so my scouts can study the country ahead of us. This close to Fa'Hanzoi I want to take every precaution to preserve our safety. I know it isn't easy traveling at the end of the column with the rest of the civilians and our wounded, but it is also the safest place to travel in case of trouble. How are you doing?" Tizu asked, searching her face for signs of pain.

Cochinna smiled to reassure him, in spite of her discomfort. "I will be glad of the rest, but I am well, Hunt Lea—Hukiyo. Soon I will be able to march alongside the rest of your people, you will see."

He chuckled and squeezed her hand again. The bravado of her words seemed to reassure him somewhat, but his eyes remained concerned. "I'm sure you are healing well, but we will wait on one of the kashallans to pronounce you well enough to march with my armachda."

He let go of her hand and reluctantly turned to mount the back of the Loti volunteer who knelt to assist him. "They won't even let me do that these days. Kashallan-Nathan says it's too tiring for an old man like me."

Cochinna smiled. "I don't think you are too old, Hukiyo, but you do look tired. Will you favor us with your company for a meal tonight? Lovely Zalyn has been teaching some of the younger gaishinay coming with us the secrets of zer cooking arts."

"If there is time away from my other duties I would like that very much, Enchanting."

"Do come, Hunt Leader," Kitha chimed in. "My mentor is right, you do look tired. I will give you a massage to help you sleep after the meal, if you like." Then, as an afterthought she added, "Bring Armachd Ross and anyone else you wish, if it pleases you."

Tizu laughed. "Your offer is very tempting, Nurse Kitha, I just may take you up on that." Then giving them a final salute he headed up the forming column, shouting orders as he went.

When he had gone, Kitha said, "This Speir'dina commander from the Khutani lands is a wonder to me—as are many others among the Alliance. When you were first injured, I couldn't believe that the Exalted Tizu, the very one who was War Leader of the entire Kashallan Alliance, would give up his own bed to you to sleep on a pallet laid upon the ground, so that he could be assured of your comfort until other arrangements could be made.

"The kashallans told me that when I wasn't able to be with you he would even care for you himself, like any healer-trained slave. None of the exalted or the elite warriors of our own people would ever do something like that."

Cochinna grimaced, and a hint of bitterness colored her voice as she said, "No, they would not; you are right about that, Student. Their rank and dignity would be far more important to them than a wounded slave."

Hunt Leader Tizu giving up his bed and caring for her himself, the thought gave her a deep sense of shame even now. But when she had protested to him, saying that it was beneath his dignity to sleep on the cold ground while a mere pleasure slave had his bed, Tizu had kissed her hand and said, *"Rest easy, My Dear Lady, to know that you will be comfortable as I can make you is a true pleasure to me. As an old warrior it won't be the first time—or probably the last, the ground will be my bed."*

Breaking in on her thoughts again, Kitha continued her musings, "Oh, I know Hunt Leader Tizu can be fierce—I have seen that for myself, when we were ambushed the other day, but he is also incredibly kind and generous as well. His warriors all seem to love him and do his bidding without the need of whips or other cruelties."

Cochinna agreed and soon Kitha left to take her place among the members of her Teh'lach for the rest of the march that day.

When Cochinna was left alone in the swaying litter, she tried to sleep, but her mind kept returning to the unpleasant thought of her uncertain future. She had been told there were no pleasure slaves in the South. Kashallan-Nathan had reluctantly admitted to her that as a way of ensuring they maintained some control of their introduced species' breeding, his Khutani relatives had bred the southern peoples to be dependent on the red kavay for their sexual arousal and fertility. So if she followed the Khutani's war bands South after the war was over, what would she do back in their homeland?

The Hunt Leader seemed attentive now, because she had been useful to him and the Alliance when she had read Commander Calahar's files and offered him valuable knowledge about conditions further North. And she could still continue to do that—even with only one eye—but what if he tired of an ugly gaishinay once his war was won—what then? Surely he had another woman waiting for him in the South among his own people. He might abandon Cochinna in Tiebarai among those who might name her traitor, and go back to his old love.

Though no one would let her see a mirror, Cochinna was sure the gaishinay mistress had permanently scarred her, and no amount of skillful make up and paint would hide that fact if she stayed in the North to practice the trade she had been trained for since childhood. Though she couldn't claim the rank of a Gaishinay Mistress, she could probably enter a pleasure house as an instructor of Comelies and Lovelies, but did she really want that? No, she decided, she did not.

Well, she wasn't alone in her uncertainty; the few gaishinay survivors who chose to come with the Alliance faced a similar problem. As free agents, with no ties to benefactor or crèche, what were they to do to survive in this new world after the fighting ended?

Honored Jojo had mentioned to her and the others when he showed up at their tent one evening with a couple bottles of stolen brandy from Te'gal that the Speir'dina who weren't warriors faced a similar dilemma in the Khutani lands when they had been stranded on Timorna.

Those like Jojo, who had been entertainers in their old lives among the stars had formed a company of actors and musicians and dancers. They planned to entertain at Sun Season festivals and perform for the exalted families during the Sorin confinements as a way to earn their living.

"My director Tomas Chambers would be so excited to meet you," Jojo burbled to them when the bottle was nearly gone. *"Kitha says you are all incredible singers, musicians—and dancers. You could come back south with me and perform with the Kashallan Players. If you shared with us some of the Northern dances and songs we could sell our talents to the highest bidder among the Avairei and Warlinga houses. Everybody would be clamoring to see us. Everybody would be famous!"*

Cochinna laughed at that, which made her face hurt. Jojo had apologized and left them soon after, but before he left Cochinna and the others had promised to consider his offer.

Becoming a performer in his company would be something similar to what she had done in part as a gaishinay. It would be an easy and familiar transition for her. Maybe she *would* join them.

But thinking of her exalted, alien, hunt leader again, that wouldn't be her first choice. No, not at all.

Chapter Three

It was time. The enemy was nearing Fa'Hanzoi, and the Ghostland forces were veiled and in position for a massive attack. It was time to use the power of his sigil and loose his agents to spread chaos among the Hated Enemy.

Spurning the aid of the wizard's puny crystal Drucas drew upon his own enhanced magic and slipped effortlessly into the deep trance needed to travel the world of the Dream. Assuming the form of a Warlinga with large bat-like wings Drucas's dream-body flew easily through its turbulent etheric currents, guided by the glowing cords of the sigils he'd placed on his "property," to the place where their bodies lay among the Enemy.

Senses alert to danger he was able to shield his presence from the Maker coiled around the sleeping form of the Warlinga female. Inwardly Drucas raged. Its contact with the one he'd claimed for his own, was an unforgivable violation. One day he and the Ghostland Cabal would kill all these invaders. One day—soon—but for now, he prudently kept his shield and veil of illusions strong as he passed by her guardian.

Focusing his power on the weaker, Speir'dina female he came closer. To his joy, only a younger, less experienced member of the enemy pod guarded her sleep. This one would be no match for him, he was sure of it. But he would have to be quick and silent, so as not to alert the more powerful members of its pod, swimming within call, for as long as possible.

Concealed behind his veil of illusion Drucas floated on the etheric current, gently altering its flow to bring him near the youngster. Then as the violet cloud enveloped both Khutani guard and Speir'dina woman, Drucas leapt, clamping his powerful jaws around the Khutani, severing the silver cord linking it to its body in the physical world. Swallowing its power, Drucas attacked the unsuspecting woman, easily defeating her futile attempt to defend herself.

When her Khutani guard was dead and the woman's mind and body was in his control, Drucas took in several deep breaths allowing his spirit to get used to this alien flesh. Banished from her body by his power, Drucas was amused to see her spirit hovering nearby trying to reinter. Her ghostly face contorted with rage, she pounded her fists at his etheric wall keeping her out. If he allowed himself to listen he could hear her tiny voice cursing him in a variety of languages.

Opening his new eyes to mere slits he ventured a look around. The Enemy camp was quiet. The evening meal was over, night sentry duty assigned, the rest of the enemy asleep, like the man beside her, or nearly so. It was time.

Drucas directed this alien body to rise quietly to her feet. Through her eyes he glanced once more at the sleeping man beside her. He was a large male, well-muscled with a long brown mane. Drucas would have liked to kill him, but the woman's spirit assaulted his shield with such ferocity that he knew he would have to exert too much of his magic to fend her off before the warrior awakened and became suspicious. Knowing he had little time before the young Khutani's death was discovered by an elder pod member Drucas reluctantly focused his will on the more important task.

He had learned from the woman's shattered mind that the Great Hunt Leader of this combined force was sleeping in a tent nearby. Killing that one and anyone else who got in his agent's way would throw this bunch into chaos, easy picking for his warbands when they sprang their trap.

"Marti?" the man's sleepy voice said.

The woman froze, her hand unconsciously moving to the weapon she had strapped to her waist. Without turning around she said, in a hollow voice, "I'm just going to relieve myself. I will be back in a moment."

There was something wrong, Nathan could almost taste it. "Oh, all right then. Hurry back," Nathan mumbled, faking a sleepiness he no longer felt. Swallowing down his fears, he forced himself to pretend to close his eyes. *Relieve herself?* Nathan felt the chill of a Psy warning penetrate his being. Yes, there was something wrong. Marti was an armachd; she would never say relieve herself. Take a leak, take a piss, going to pee maybe, but never, "I'm just going to relieve myself."

<<Kasha, I don't think that was Marti talking,>>Corha said. <<Something is wrong with her.>>

<<I know, Shalla, quiet now; we need to see what she does next.>>

Corha was right, that voice didn't exactly sound like hers—and why did she need to strap on her sidearm just to walk to the waste pit? Watching her with eyes slitted to mere cracks, he saw she turned into the main part of their camp, not towards the privies. Easing out of the bedroll, Nathan-Corha strapped on his own weapon and followed her into the night.

HUNT LEADER TIZU SANK down onto the edge of his cot, letting out a long sigh. He set his weapons on the table next to the lamp and bent to take off his combat boots. In spite of his pleasant meal with Enchanting Cochinna and little Kitha's massage, it had been a long and tiring march today. He was getting too old for this. Grateful that someone had already made up his bed for him—in spite of his orders to the contrary—he was looking forward to just lying back and getting some rest.

Suddenly a scuffle outside the tent caught his attention. He froze with one boot off, reaching for the other. He'd been too exhausted to pay much attention to who was on duty outside his quarters tonight, but he could see dim shadows on the tent wall and then he heard a grunting sound.

Inwardly he groaned, Not tonight—please not tonight, he thought. The Sorins would be coming to the North in another moon cycle or so. After the overwhelming victory at Te'gal, there had been desertions and fighting, because many of his warriors were talking about going home. "What's going on out there, you mangy dogs? Do I have to—"

The door flat was abruptly thrust aside and the dark figure of a Speir'dina with a weapon drawn stepped into the tent. Instinct taking over, Tizu dove for the ground as the night exploded with a flash of blinding light above him. Hampered by having only one boot on, he scrabbled behind the tipped over, flimsy refuge of his bed.

He groped for his own weapon, but the table had been knocked over and his hand couldn't find it. His Timornan language failing him, he shouted in Galactic Standard, "Lann Gheal! We are under attack!"

The beam weapon fired again and this time the blanket just above him burst into flame, pelting his face and shoulders with burning fragments of debris. Who? Tizu wondered, then she turned and he saw that vacant-eyed stare. With a sinking feeling in his heart, he realized it was Marti. They'd been so worried about Chelka they'd been careless—and the damned Umwira had gotten her instead.

Finding the butt of his weapon at last he pulled it to him. "Oh Nathan, I'm so sorry..."

SEEING THE FLASH OF beam fire Nathan burst into a run. Not stopping to check out the crumpled form outside Tizu's tent for signs of life, he drew his weapon and leapt through the opening, dropping into a fighter's crouch.

Sensing the new threat Marti turned, her eyes focused on him, her face expressionless. Nathan's heart gave a lurch. No, not again, Tessa, Dunnagh, now another he loved lost to this cruel world! Trembling with rage and fear, he met the merciless hard stare of the Changeling controlling her. "I'm sorry, Mo Cri." Nathan fired.

PHILLIP-YOEY SAT AMONG the Healer's Teh'lach members by a small campfire. Some of his Sand Mountain relatives and Eilo from Red Wind had come over to join them for the evening meal. He was tired and tried to hide a yawn behind his hand. It had been a long day and he definitely wanted his bed, but also didn't want to insult Tesulu's long war story by leaving before its conclusion. Eilo across the fire met his gaze and smirked. Yes, the wizard could guess what was really on his mind and was amused by his predicament.

Suddenly Tesulu froze, the words dying on his lips as he stared at something or someone behind Kashallan-Phillip. A chill ran down his spine. Was it his imagination or had the air around them dropped in temperature. The circle of warriors reached for weapons, suddenly alert. He turned slowly to see what was wrong. Also turning, Crowis gasped. In the firelight Phillip saw the Wa'chassey'ul, standing expressionless at his back. "Good evening, Atahru, does your mistress wish to see me?"

"My Mistress wishes you to come—now, Khutani," the Demon's mortal protector answered in his deep hollow voice. Then turning to Crowis, he said, "You come, too, Cha'Han."

Cha'Han, that was the second time the demon's slave had called the young Avairei that in Phillip's hearing. If Tess-weh had bound him to her after Ata Doyan had been left at Tragar, Crowis had been very secretive about what service she demanded of him. Phillip-Yoey got to his feet a trembling Crowis beside him. "Is there trouble, Atahru?"

Atahru moved away without answering, expecting him to follow. "What's happening, Kashallan?" Crowis breathed as he followed them into the darkness.

"I don't know—" Phillip started to reassure the frightened man when the night's peace was shattered by the flash and boom of a beam weapon firing. Hurrying after the Wa'chassey'ul he was aware of other men shouting questions and racing in the same direction.

At Hunt Leader Tizu's tent Atahru halted. Taking up a guard position outside, he motioned for Kashallan-Phillip and Crowis to enter. Unsure what he was going to find, but trusting that it was now safe for him to do so, Phillip-Yoey reluctantly entered, Crowis at his heels.

In the dim light he saw Tizu grimly beating a scorched pillow atop the charred remains of his smoldering bed. Midway across the space lay the crumpled form of a body. When he saw it was Marti, he swore under his breath. Kneeling beside her he automatically reached for her hand and extended his tentacles for the link.

<<Is she dead, Shalla?>> Phillip ventured.

<<No, just deeply unconscious from the Speir'dina weapon,>> Yoey replied. <<But all isn't right with her either. I can taste—something—>>

<<To make her come here—like this, the Changeling must have used the power in the sigil upon her forehead to compel her.>>

<<I know, Kasha, but if she can be rescued from permanent insanity or death, the healing is beyond my power,>> Yoey moaned. <<I'm sorry, Kasha, I'm too young—and our Amsi—>>

Nathan... he felt the sadness building, threatening to drown him in a well of despair, too. Taking a deep breath he tried to reassure his young bondmate. <<It's all right, Shalla, I know. You are doing your best. Let's give her a bit

of a restorative, but not enough to wake her. We don't want the Umwira to come back. Our Amla, or one of the other makers can surely help her.>> Yoey seemed comforted by his reassurance and did what he suggested.

When he opened his eyes, he was startled to see Crowis crouching beside him. In the stress of the moment Phillip had forgotten about him. Outside there was a growing clamor, but for the moment the presence of Tess-weh's protector guarding the entrance was enough to keep the crowd from bursting in.

"Will you stay with this woman while I see to the injuries of my kinsmen, Student? Please let me know immediately if she wakes."

Stepping over the smoldering debris Kashallan-Phillip came over to the cursing Tizu. He'd given up on the bed and was pulling on his scorched boot, muttering in a variety of languages. Phillip could see a few angry red burns on his face and a gash on his arm, dripping blood onto the ruined bed.

"How badly are you hurt, Hunt Leader? Let me see."

Finally getting his boot on, Tizu stood and waved his hand in a dismissive gesture. "I'm all right; don't trouble yourself, Kashallan-Phillip. I'll get Williams or Ruan to patch me up—later." Tizu motioned to the huddled figure in the corner. "You'd better have a look at him; he needs you more than I do."

A haunted look coming into his black eyes, Tizu studied the comatose woman with Crowis sitting beside her, and asked, "Is she?"

Phillip-Yoey shook his head. "Dead? No just unconscious for the moment. I'm going to keep her that way if I can till I know how we can rid her of the damned changeling's magic for good."

"For Nathan's sake, as well as her own, I hope you or the makers can help her," Tizu said.

"I hope so as well."

Nearly to the entrance Tizu paused as a new thought struck him. "Now what do we do with Chelka?"

What to do about Chelka indeed, Phillip thought. "The Changeling may try again, using her this time, so we need to be on guard."

Tizu grunted. He glanced at Nathan again. "I'll send someone to keep watch outside so you won't be disturbed."

"No need, Hunt leader, the Wa'chassey'ul is already on guard." Tizu muttered something unintelligible under his breath and walked out.

"WHAT'S HAPPENING?" Chelka shouted to a running Speir'dina.

Without stopping he called back over his shoulder, "Somebody just tried to kill hunt Leader Tizu."

Chelka staggered, catching herself from falling with a slap of her tail. She had a sickening feeling churning in her gut. Where was Marti? The mark on her forehead lanced with pain. Gritting her teeth she refused to surrender, give into the pain, she would fight—she would kill—

"Chelka, My Love, there you are." Tobrach wrapped strong arms around her and held her close, licking her jaw and eyes with a sensitive brown tongue. "When I heard—I thought—"

Chelka relaxed, allowing herself to be comforted by his love and protection for a long moment then she pulled herself out of his embrace. "I'm all right, but where is Marti."

Tobrach's head crest flattened. Then in a hesitant voice he admitted, "I heard she's dead; she tried to kill the Hunt Leader."

"Is the Hunt Leader dead?"

"No I don't think so. I was just going to find out. Come with me and we both will know the news."

So it was true. "No I cannot—I dare not." Chelka shook her head, trembling. Poor dear, he didn't understand. Drucas had come for her and finding her guarded by the Maker and not easily broken to his will, he took Marti instead. But he would be back—and for her this time. *No escape,* he had warned her—promised her actually. She had no escape—except into death.

Chelka drew her blade and aimed it at the unprotected area under her jaw. Before she could plunge the blade in too deeply, a strong clawed hand grabbed her wrist and pulled the knife away. Wrenching it out of her hand, he threw the Speir'dina blade into the darkness and shook her hard enough for her teeth to grind together. "Chelka what are you thinking? What are you doing?"

She struggled in his grasp, her blood splattering his face and chest. "Let me go, Damn you. Let me finish it, before I kill someone—hurt you, too!" she cried.

"Chelka stop fighting me, stop! You aren't going to hurt—kill anybody."

"You don't know that," she insisted. "I'm a danger—to everyone while I'm alive and I wear his brand. Look what has happened to Marti."

"Marti hasn't been trained in the War Magics like you have. Before coming here to Timorna her people didn't use the magics like we do, they relied mainly on their weaponry. You know this—Dunnagh-Tani and Nathan-Corha have told you this—even Marti herself admits she has little skill with the War Magics. It isn't the same for you. You can fight him. And one day soon you will kill him just as you promised him."

Could she kill him—did she even want to anymore? Torn between unimaginable pleasure and pain, she doubted she knew her own mind. Tobrach didn't understand—none of them did—even the makers didn't know fully what it had been like for her all this time. Drucas wanted her. She belonged to him; there was no escape. Bearing her teeth she lunged for his throat.

Caught off guard, Tobrach jerked his head out of reach just in time. He would have fought back to defend himself, but suddenly the woman in his arms went limp, nearly dragging him to the ground as she fell.

Easing her to rest on the moss Tobrach stared up in bewilderment at a grinning Tesulu. "She is right, you know she is a danger to us. The Ghostlander's hold over her is strong. Maybe you should kill her."

"No. I won't do that. She is Warlinga; she can fight him."

Tesulu shrugged. "Do as you wish Warlinga, but tie her up while she sleeps to keep her out of trouble. The Demon has summoned the Khutani, and our wizards say an attack is coming—soon. You are needed elsewhere."

Wanting to deny the truth he knew was in the Clan war leader's words Tobrach hesitated, still crouching protectively beside his fallen consort. Tesulu shrugged and moved off into the night. "Suit yourself, Warlinga. If you're not too much of a coward to fight alongside the warriors of the Real People, leave your woman with the Begta shamanka, standing there, and gather your hunters." Tobrach looked in the direction Tesulu pointed and saw, to his surprise, the Begta shamanka watching him.

Masonja motioned with her lips to the fire outside the nearby med tent. "Bring womans to med tent," she instructed. "Masonja got big magics. Masonja keep safe. No bad Umwira find Chelka now." She waved her hand in the direction of the main camp. "Warlinga hunt leader must go fight Umwira, you go!"

As he hurried away into the darkness Tesulu smiled. The spirit of an Oko must be guiding him this night, he thought, proud of his slyness. The Warlinga female couldn't be trusted around such a fine weapon as the Speir'dina blade he now wore on his belt. No, no it was far too dangerous a weapon to allow her to keep in her possession after this.

CROSSING TO THE HUDDLED figure in the corner, Phillip placed a hand on his shoulder. Nathan was shaking so violently he could barely stay upright. "Nathan, Amsi?"

Unable to speak, the man snatched up Phillip's hand, like a life line, and jammed his tentacles in to form a link. Phillip winced. The torrent of raw emotion crashing down their shared communication was painful, violent, desperate, both Nathan and his symbiont were in a bad way.

He tasted the host, a frightened Caldoni warrior overwhelmed by a lifetime of abandonment and loss, and then there was the terrified young Khutani, also experiencing what Nathan had had to do to someone they both loved, and trying bravely to cope.

Hoping the contact wouldn't be too much for his own partner, Phillip eased himself into a more comfortable position and took Nathan's other hand. Gently forming another connection with the other kashallan, he said, "Nathan! You didn't kill her. Marti isn't dead. Not Tizu, not Marti, no one is dead, and the Changeling is gone. Stop tearing yourself apart like this! Corha is very frightened, please stop!" Damn it where was Nathan-Corha's Amla, Maker Qwaltamis—or his Amla for that matter? He was barely treading water here; he needed help!

It took a while, both Yoey and Phillip repeating themselves before Nathan and Corha were calm enough to listen and understand what he was telling them.

"But I shot her, Amsi I killed—"

"You didn't," Phillip assured him. "You must have put your weapon on heavy-stun rather than a killing setting. Truly, she isn't dead. I've tasted her; you know I'm not lying to you, Nathan."

Nathan glanced at Crowis sitting by Marti, holding her hand. With a sob he buried his face on Phillip's chest. "I warned them," Nathan complained. "Damned complacent, know it all big worms. I sensed they were underestimating the Changeling and his Ghostland wizard masters, and now look what's happened? Marti, too." he choked, tears streaming down his face, unable to go on.

"Gently, Cousin," Phillip soothed. His eyes flicked a warning to Nathan's middle where the young symbiont coiled. "You have to fight him for Corha and Marti's sake as well as your own, you can't give in to despair and let him win. I'm sure with time she will be all right and Chelka too."

Nathan released his portion of their communication. Phillip let go and rose as Nathan got clumsily to his feet. He walked over and looked down at the quiescent Marti.

"I thought it best to keep her asleep for the moment," Phillip explained. "The Changeling or his master won't bother with her further if they know she can't be manipulated to do their bidding."

Nathan nodded, and walked to the entrance. "Will you stay with her? I got to go see—" he broke off as both kashallans felt the currents of the ether around them change. In the next instant they heard screaming war cries echoing from out of the darkness. They were under attack. "Stay here," Nathan shouted as he pushed open the tent door, only to be shoved roughly back inside by the Wa'chassey'ul. In the demon's hollow otherworldly voice Atahru growled, "Stay here, My Jewel. You aren't needed out there."

Nathan cursed and jumped to his feet. "The hell I will, damn you!" expressionless, Atahru pushed him down again. Then reaching across his body the Wa'chassey'ul took Nathan's weapon out of its holster and tossed it across the tent. "You will stay, Khutani," he repeated.

When Nathan would have got up again, Phillip shouted, "Nathan, stop! Remember what you used to tell Dunnagh? You're a kashallan now; it isn't your job anymore to lead the warriors. Let Aju'an do it. Isn't that what you've been training him for?"

Yes, damn him, it was. He sat up but made no move to rise and argue further with Tess-weh's protector. "All right, you've made your point. I'll stay here." He waved a hand to the tent flap. "Go on, get out of here. Go back to your guard duty outside."

The Wa'chassey'ul watched him with a piercing gaze that seemed to penetrate into his deepest core. Then deciding he was telling the truth, Atahru turned without a word and when back to his post outside.

When he was gone Nathan got slowly to his feet and came over to where Phillip-Yoey and Crowis still crouched beside the comatose Marti. Sinking down he took her in his arms the tears unnoticed rolling down his cheeks.

Outside their protected sanctuary the battle raged. Shouts and screams punctuated by the flair of their off-world weaponry lit up the night.

Chapter Four

T he night was quiet; the evening's entertainments over and the gaishinay settling down for sleep when the tent flap was violently pushed open, revealing the dark silhouette of an armed Speir'dina warrior pushing into the tent. One of the Comelies let out a startled cry as the figure closed the flap and stepped into the light. Fully awake now everyone stared wide-eyed.

Fighting back drowsiness Cochinna sat up on her cot, staring like the rest. Who? Ah, it was one of the few women warriors among the Speir'dina. This one had pale eyes and golden hair she wore plaited in a long braid down her back like the other warriors. Cochinna wasn't sure of her name but she had seen her around, sometimes in the company of a mysterious veiled woman riding astride a Loti as some of the Speir'dina often did.

"Get up—now, Gaishinay, trouble is coming and you will be needed to assist the medics," she said in a stern voice.

"What's happening, Sa Moraga?" Kitha asked.

"No time to explain; you are needed, Nurse Kitha—everyone. Go to the med tent—hurry!" coming over to Cochinna, Moraga studied her for a moment then held out a hand to help her to her feet. "Sa, do you need my help to walk?"

"We will help her, Warrior," Janixa said coming over with Comely Nielu to take her arms.

"Good. I will see you safely to the med tent, then I am needed elsewhere." Taking her alien weapon off her shoulder Moraga crossed to the tent flap, check to see if it was safe, then stepped outside and held it open for the gaishinay to follow.

Trembling inside and trying not to scream, as her friends guided her across the uneven ground towards the med tent, Cochinna thought, "It's happening again. They were under attack—or soon would be."

As they neared the safety of the med tent several hideous Ghostland monsters leapt out of the darkness to confront them, roaring with claws extended. In the next moment Moraga fired her weapon, a beam of blue-white light cutting the first warrior in the pack nearly in half. As she aimed at another charging warrior, she shouted, "Run! Get to the Med tent—hurry!"

Looking back over her shoulder as Janixa hurried her along Cochinna saw their guard had been joined by another warrior with an alien weapon. Back to back they fought, creating a bloody circle of death around themselves.

Once inside the med tent Cochinna could see that the scene was one of controlled chaos. The two Speir'dina medics were there, as well as the Avairei medic and the other nurses like Kitha, checking their supplies and setting up cots. A few of the younger warriors hovered nearby some on guard duty by the opening, others helping get the tent ready for casualties.

But where were the kashallans? A dart of real fear stabbed her chest. Something bad must be happening for both of them to be missing. Her fears were only strengthened when she was directed to sit in an out of the way place by the stove and saw the bound and comatose body of Chelka lying nearby. The Warlinga didn't appear to be seriously wounded, though a long cut plastered with the colored kavay Cochinna knew from personal experience was a sleeping aid ran down one scaly arm. Her focus drawn to the sigil on the Warlinga's forehead Cochinna felt a shiver run down her backbone. Mighty Drucas must be here with his warriors to claim his property and take a terrible vengeance on them all.

WITHIN THE DREAM QWALTAMIS spat out the brilliance of its rage in a stream of blinding fire. The Ghostland vermin had dared—dared to kill one of its young. Fah had been a promising young one with the potential to become a Maker one day. Around the grieving parent several Makers alerted to the disaster, and the others of the dead one's pod swam in an agitated circle.

A nibble of fear twisted in Qwaltamis's gut. Not since the early days had the Hated Enemy become so bold. Not since the plague years had one of their number fallen to the enemy's machinations.

Suddenly a chilling laugh broke in on their grieving, freezing the pod in place. From the darkness of the Void Tess-weh floated into view, a mocking smile curving her full red lips. <<So, once again, you wallow in your grief when you are needed—elsewhere. Truly you are proving to be poor guardians of the world entrusted to you.>>

Snarling a warning Maker Sherigus raised its head from the coiled mass its mouth tentacles bristling with menace. <<How dare you chastise us! You swore to protect our Khutani children. It is you who have caused this—not us!>>

<<I warned you, Khutani Slimeworms, back at Tragar to have a care. The Ghostland Wizards have become far more dangerous during your Long Sleep than you imagined,>> she growled, her eyes flashing a dangerous black fire.<<I keep my bargains, Slimeworm! And my contract is to protect your symbiont children—which I have done to the best of my ability—though it has cost my host dearly. Don't question my honor again, Arrogant Worms, or I will claim my contract forfeit and abandon your kashallans in the battles to come.>>

<<What are you talking about, Demon?>> Sherigus grumbled, its golden eyes still alive with barely controlled anger.

Ignoring the Maker's threat display Tess-weh folded creamy arms across her full bosom and glared. <<I'm talking about the Ghostland warbands massing to attack the Alliance. Did you think your child had frightened the changeling away when he shot the Speir'dina woman the changeling claimed?

<<And what of the Warlinga female that he wants more than life itself—what of her? She is a dangerous threat if you don't find a way to stop him, Khutani, a danger, in your arrogance you haven't considered with enough care. And now another of your children has paid the ultimate price for your inattention.>>

<<And what of you, Demon, why are you here instead of helping our people if the danger is so imminent? >> another in the pod challenged.

For just a moment her dark eyes flashed with anger and resentment. Then she calmed. <<Don't try to bait me, Slimeworm. I am there when I am needed—as you should be.>>

As many in the pod waved their mouth tentacles wanting to argue, Qwaltamis spat out a placating spice into their communication. <<The Demon is right. We have no time for this—and there are limits on what she may do, according to her contract. We need to protect our own and hunt the Hated Enemy ourselves. The Ghostland Wizards have forgotten that we are a force to be feared on this world. It's time we show them the error of their ways,>>

AS TIZU HURRIED FROM his tent shouting orders, the night erupted with the blood-curdling screams of charging Ghostland warriors. Though their initial attack was fierce, it wasn't totally unexpected. Most of the Western Clan warriors as well as many of the Speir'dina and Warlinga had had time to grab their weapons and were able to meet their charge with equal force.

Amid the chaos Tizu shouted, "Owyn, Rhys, somebody launch some flares to even up the odds." Suddenly the night around them burst into blinding light as several flares exploded in the sky above the camp.

In the monochrome glare Tizu recognized Tobrach and the Meh'gach brothers racing in his direction. "K'San Tobrach, where is Chelka right now?" Tizu shouted over the din when he was close enough to hear.

"I left her tied up and asleep in the med tent." Then noticing Tizu in the flare's light Tobrach flattened his head crest with concern. "Are you all right, Hunt Leader?"

"Never mind how I look; I'm fine. Gather your hunters—where are those wizards—and that damned Tess-weh?"

Comforted by the Hunt leader's familiar bellow his hunters and warriors hurried to form their practiced battle formations and meet the Enemy swarming out of their concealment behind the Ghostland wizards' magical shields.

It didn't take Tizu long to realize that this attack was far more serious than the ongoing skirmishes they had been fighting ever since they'd left Te'gal behind. This close to Fa'Hanzoi the enemy had at last decided to seriously engage him.

Tizu hoped the Alliance troops were up to the challenge.

STILL IN POSSESSION of Nathan's beam rifle, Aju'an led a mixed squad of warriors up the far slope in the hope of circling around to attack the Enemy from behind. Senses alert to any war magic illusions the Ghostlanders might still use, they crept slowly down the slope.

Suddenly the lead Warlinga raised a clawed hand and the squad halted crouching behind any bushes or rocks that could offer concealment. Ahead of them appeared to be a line of enemy warriors massing for a charge into the Ally's camp.

Ah, but were there truly Enemy warriors below, or had they been discovered and the Enemy set up a trap to lure them into a fatal move? Aju'an hesitated; as the hunt leader here everyone was looking to him for orders, yet still he waited. Something didn't feel right about this...

At last knowing that the Clan warriors among them were growing impatient with his delay and would see any further hesitation on his part as a weakness that would cost him the leadership of the squad, Aju'an took the beam rifle off his shoulder and murmured for his warriors to be ready.

This squad contained no Speir'dina; so if they had been discovered the Ghostlanders wouldn't be expecting the off-world weapons here. Illusion or not, a beam aimed into the center of that shadowy mass would solve the problem—and in a way the Enemy wasn't expecting. Aju'an fired.

The momentary blazing light that followed showed no Enemy warriors sliced apart or bursting into flames. There was a pause, then a band of screaming hideously disfigured monsters brandishing spears and clubs charged out of the rocks above and to the side of them. Ululating their fearsome war cries, his hunters rose to meet them.

FINDING BOTH HIS AGENTS comatose and unable to be roused Drucas roared in frustration. Had the Speir'dina killed the Alliance leader? He wasn't sure; she had been felled by another Speir'dina before Drucas could be sure of the kill. Should he return to his physical body and begin the attack, assuming she had accomplished his purpose before she was eliminated, or wait for more information? What to do? His thoughts spun like leaves caught in a whirlwind.

He would need to report back to the Cabal's emissary soon. At such a distance the wizards could hold their illusion in place for only so long before the strain would cause it to weaken too much to serve its purpose. Oh what to do? In spite of his enhanced power gained at the holy place he couldn't afford to fail the Cabal another time.

As Drucas hesitated the decision was taken out of his hands when the emissary found him. The little wizard approached his aura blazing with anger and menace. <<So, Half-bred Khutani Slave, once again you have failed us!>>

Drucas bared his teeth and loomed over the smaller being his own aura radiating streaks of blue fire, causing the Cabal's minion to move back. <<I have not failed,>> Drucas bluffed, <<my agents among the Enemy have—>>

<<Have killed no one. There supreme commander still lives as do the rest of the vermin. The Great Avenger has told us of your failure.>>

<<He lies. I have not failed the Cabal!>>

<<The enemy commander lives—where are your agents, Bumbling Slave? The Enemy Wizards have discovered our illusions, so don't try to lie.>> the small grey man raised a hand and fire shot towards Drucas.

Startled that the wizard had resorted to punishment so early in their talk Drucas was unprepared and felt the magic as a sting of pain across his chest and face. He roared and threw up a shield to block a further assault. <<You sniveling little worm, how dare—>>

<<Dare? Yes I dare. You have failed us once again. You will go back to Tiebarai to receive your just punishment. The Great Avenger shall lead our warriors from now on, Worthless Khutani Slave.>>

<<Never! I alone will lead and triumph over the Hated Enemy not the Avenger. The Gods have promised me and neither you nor anyone else shall stand in my way.>>

<<Insolent grub it's time you learn your place.>>

This time as the wizard drew in etheric power to make good on his threat, Drucas was ready for him. The Changeling opened his mouth wide and blinding white fire shot from his gaping jaws enveloping the thin grey man in a ball of searing pain.

The wizard writhed, screaming, the sound dying at last to a choking murmur as the energy dissipated. As the light faded Drucas leapt upon his prey, clutching the dazed man in his claws. Looking down into the frightened grey face Drucas smiled showing his glowing fangs.

<<Did I surprise you, Little Mushroom? There is a lot that you and the rest of the Cabal don't know about me. I have been gifted power by your rivals and even more, I have taken power from the holy places for my own. Oh, I will go to Tiebarai, never fear, but when I return it will be as a victorious leader, not as a chastised slave.>>

He tightened his etheric grip on the struggling man and bent low to look him in the eye. <<But you unfortunately won't be there to cheer my victory procession.>> Then with a snarl he clamped his jaws around the wizard's neck and bit down, drawing into himself the weaker man's power.

Reveling in his victory, his head jerked up from his feast at an unfamiliar sound. Allowing the drained husk to fade away into the violet mists Drucas listened, his senses alert to danger.

This confrontation with the Ghostlander had forced him to remain too long in the Dream. And it was only a question of time before the Khutani discovered the death and came hunting him. He smiled to himself. Drunk with the thrill of vanquishing one of his tormenters so easily, he welcomed this new challenge. Let the slimeworms come, he thought. He would show them—all of them—and the Cabal, too. He was Mighty Drucas; he had paid with his blood and sacrifice to the Fiery Ones and they had blessed him with power—the Gods had promised...

Yes, he could see them now shadowy grey worms swimming behind and through the etheric clouds, trying to sneak up, coming for him. Spreading his bat-like wings he roared his defiance into the void. <<Here I am, Khutani

Slimeworms. Come. I'm the one who killed your child. Fight me, if you dare.>>

Chapter Five

"Hunt Leader!" Varrod called. With Tobrach in his wake, the two Warlinga ran up to Tizu's temporary headquarters on the far edge of their encampment. "Our scouts say that the Enemy has a large camp not far up the valley from here."

"Is it a real base or just an illusion set up to lure our warriors away from this battle?" Tizu said.

Varrod's head crest dipped in thought as he pondered his response. "The camp itself is real—I'm sure of that—but it also may be a trap to lur hunters away from the combat here. There are two guarded tents in the camp that the scouts could see, but other than that, they saw only slaves and a few wounded moving about the encampment."

Distracted by a messenger running up with a report, Tizu's focus was diverted elsewhere for a moment giving orders, then he returned his attention to the waiting Warlinga. "Hmm, those slaves could be disguised warriors... But I *am* curious what—or who, is in those guarded tents."

Standing nearby and overhearing the conversation, Ross said, "Our flares up there," he pointed towards the night sky where several flare still burned bright with no indication of their internal fuel running out anytime soon, "must be getting extra power from either Tess-weh or the Clan Wizards."

"And to do that," Varrod said, showing lots of teeth as he followed Ross's logic to its conclusion. "They usually leave their bodies and go into the Dream World."

"That's true, Hunt Leader," Tobrach agreed. "For the Ghostlanders it would be the same. And one of those in the tents must be the Changeling—Hunt Leader, I want him!"

Well it might solve a lot of their current and future problems if he let them destroy the changeling or a wizard or two working their mischief in those tents. But on the other hand, could he spare a squad away from the main conflict going on right here? Tizu wondered.

"Hunt Leader, please; I need to do this," Tobrach said. "I know Chelka has sworn to kill him, but I'm not sure if we dare let her try after what has happened to Marti."

"Chelka is my sister," Varrod growled. "I would go with him, too."

No fuckin' way, Tizu thought glaring at the both of them. He wasn't going to let them make this a personal vendetta, because next thing he knew he'd have the other Meh'gach brother wanting to join them as soon as he heard they were going. "I can't afford to lose both of you right now, so only one of you can go on this mission.

"Varrod, you are the more experienced hunt leader, I need you to stay here. Tobrach if you think Warega can lead your men, then take Sietriga, pick a patrol and go check out the enemy camp.

"Go in and get back out as soon as you can. Don't engage the Ghostlanders anymore than you have to. We can deal with the changeling later if you can't find him. His death isn't worth you taking the chance of losing your hunting pack—do you understand me, Tragar Hunt Leader?"

"I understand; your will, Hunt Leader Tizu," Tobrach said and dipped his head crest in salute.

KEEPING TO THE SHADOWS, Tobrach and his hunters approached the Ghostland encampment with caution, alert for any signs of danger. Nostrils flared to catch the faintest scent on the dry night wind, he paid special attention to the slopes just above the shelters. If this was indeed a trap the Enemy would be hiding behind their war magic shields up there ready to pounce. To the south, back the way they'd come, a faint glow colored the horizon, distant shouts and the boom of alien weapons punctuating the stillness.

"Maybe they got tired of waiting for us to walk into their trap and decided to attack us instead," the Blue Stone man named Ikuwi growled, putting into words Tobrach's thoughts.

"Maybe, but keep alert as we go in," Tobrach said as he gave the command for the hunters to spread out and follow him down the slope.

The hunters passed between several darkened tents as they crept among the Enemy dwellings. As best they could tell the encampment did seem to be as deserted as it appeared, except for a few posted guards near three shadowy tents clustered by a fire built up near the center of the encampment.

Several armed men sat around that fire talking quietly among themselves, one or more taking turns checking on the occupants inside the tents, or heading into the night to walk the grounds. These warriors Tobrach could see right away weren't the maddened deformed monsters that had been driven by their overseers and guards to attack the Alliance. No, tall, hairless, with a variety of facial features, these men were mixed race Ghostlanders, the pride of some wizard's breeding program. They were similar to some of the elite they had fought at Te'gal and they weren't going to be easily deceived or killed if they were alerted to their presence.

Moving quietly to the back of the tent farthest from the fire light Tobrach crouched his senses straining, trying to detect any movement inside. Wearing a pair of the Speir'dina night scopes, Sietriga stood guard with his alien weapon as the rest of the patrol crept closer.

From this shadowy place there was no way to see inside this tent, so after taking a moment to listen, Tobrach pulled his long Speir'dina knife from its sheath and made a cut in the leather wall big enough to see through. Only a dim glow from the fire outside the entrance illuminated the interior. All he could see was someone lying on a cot near the center of the space. The body on the cot appeared too small and slim for Drucas, so it was probably one of the wizards they were hunting lying there.

Tobrach opened the cut wide enough to allow a crouching warrior to slip in. He was about to do just that when Ikuwi touched his arm. He showed the Warlinga a bone talisman he removed from around his neck.

"Wizard Eilo said the Ghostlanders will probably guard their sleeping bodies with magical wards as well as their warriors. He gave me this to protect us," Ikuwi murmured close to his ear.

Tobrach nodded and stepped back, motioning for the Clan Warrior to precede him inside. The rest of his men he signed to check out the other dwellings but not to enter. Following Ikuwi, he crossed to the cot.

The body was indeed a Ghostlander and judging by his robes and appearance he was a Cabal Wizard. A wizard who appeared to already be dead. Tobrach's head crest rose when he figured that out. How could that be? Head crest flattened, he glared at his subordinate. Had Wizard Eilo's talisman done this?

Ikuwi shook his head and then shrugged. Just to be sure the Ghostlander really was dead and not in some unknown magical trance Tobrach drew his blade across the man's throat, nearly severing the head from the torso. Hurrying out, they examined the two remaining tents in similar fashion.

In the other two the wizards were deep into the Dream, but alive. His hunting pack made quick work of the killing then faded back into the night. Hurrying up the slope, they came to a place where they couldn't be seen and could talk. As they gathered Tobrach felt a mixture of frustration and anger threatening to overwhelm him. None of those tents had contained the Changeling K'San he so desperately wanted to kill.

Was there another encampment of the Ghostlanders further up the valley? Or had Drucas just returned to his body and physically taken command of the Enemy warriors now attacking the Allies. Where, oh where was the Changeling?

"This place is almost completely deserted," one of his hunters complained. "Too deserted, I think to be their main headquarters—even with most of their warriors down the valley attacking us. It must have been left here to entrap us. I wonder what happened to make them change their minds about using it for that purpose."

"Yes, I wonder about that too," Tobrach said, "especially since we found no evidence of the changeling here in the guarded tents."

"I could take Wizard Eilo's charm and go back to search some of the darkened dwellings in the outer circle of the camp," Ikuwi suggested. "He may still be here but concealed in some way we haven't detected."

That was possible Tobrach mused. "Sietriga, the Hunt Leader and Kashallan-Nathan have tried to explain to me exactly what your alien magics can and can't do, but I'm still not sure about somethings. Can those night scopes of yours tell if there are any Ghostlanders concealed by the war magics in the dark tents or up the slope across from us?"

The big Speir'dina thought about it for a moment then said, "Depends on how skilled the warrior or wizard is, and how far away they are. If close I can detect a heat signature, even if my eyes can't see anything. As far as for seeing up the slope," he shrugged. "I've never tried the scope's range that far on Timorna. Detecting someone not using your war magics, yes, not a problem—even up high on the slope."

"Hmm... I think the Ghostlanders must have another encampment nearby. Whether K'San Drucas is there or leading the attack on our base, that will be hard for us to know until we find him. But finding the Enemy's real hiding place would give us an advantage—especially if we could destroy it. Can you let the Hunt Leader know what we plan with your alien box?"

Sietriga nodded, agreeing with him. "Yes I'll do that, but maybe we should pick off the enemy here and fire this place, before we hunt further. I don't like the idea of armed warriors at our backs. I brought a few of the fire jars we made at Ticca with us. Then if we find the camp we can sure do some damage there too at least."

Could they find it indeed, that was the big unanswered question, Tobrach thought.

"The question is can we find it?" Ikuwi said, echoing his unvoiced thoughts. "Hunt Leader Tobrach I agree with my Teh'lach brother we need to destroy this place before we continue on."

Tobrach had to agree with both of them—as much as he wanted to race head long into the darkness to pick up the changeling's scent. Hadn't Hunt Leader Tizu warned him not to take unnecessary chances? They couldn't afford to have these warriors lurking at their backs.

VARROD ROARED AND BURIED his spear in the guts of another enemy monster. Spewing a river of dark blood, the warrior crashed to the ground at his feet. Ignoring his own bleeding wounds, he leapt over the body and spun to meet the charge of another enemy.

This creature was a big brute, his asymmetrical face rendered more hideous by the Alliance warriors he'd killed, blood and gore marking his features. Suddenly the monster's image blurred into two, then three warriors facing him as the creature invoked his powerful war magics.

In a hollow, otherworldly voice the images laughed. <<Come, Khutani Slave, which warrior is the real Great Avenger, hmm? Come fight me. You will find out and die,>> the images taunted.

Varrod wasted no time on idle banter that would give the Ghostlander the advantage of learning his weaknesses. He threw up a magical shield of his own. In spite of his injuries from earlier bouts, he allowed instinct and years of training to guide his attack. The two fought ignoring the larger combat going on in other parts of the encampment totally focused on their own interchange of magic and physical weaponry.

Stepping through a veil of flames, Varrod lashed out with his whip-like tail at the Ghostlander images lunging towards him. Two of the illusions leapt back while the one on his left came in low with a spear aimed at his side. Varrod felt its bite, managing to block most of its force and countered with a strike of his own that sent his opponent whirling away, a trail of blood marking his retreat.

As a Warlinga, Varrod had been bred by their Khutani makers to endure pain and injuries, continuing to fight the Enemy without faltering until the moment death claimed them. Unfortunately for him, that death might be soon. He could feel his body weakening in spite of his will to survive and triumph over this Hated Enemy. Forcing his tired muscles to respond without falter he fought the monster, determined to rid the Enemy of this powerful warrior—even if it meant his own death.

Block and thrust, whirl and jab, the fire of their hatred for each other fueling their combat, each warrior continued the fight in spite of their many potentially fatal wounds. Like himself, Varrod sensed his opponent weakening and pressed him hard, determined to kill this, "Great Avenger," before his strength failed him.

Suddenly the Great Avenger's war magics vanished in a shower of fragmented lights. Now before him there was only one wounded and panting bloody warrior facing him. Mustering the last of his strength Varrod charged, a roar of triumph already issuing from his throat.

Too soon, he suddenly realized as a shielded Enemy Warrior struck, burying a long bone knife hilt deep in his back. Varrod choked, a fountain of blood spewing from his open mouth in the next moment.

Slipping into the darkness his last conscious thoughts were for his wife and the rest of the family waiting at home. He hoped Aju'an survived and made it back to Meh'gach lands to carry on in his place.

The Great Avenger roared with mocking laughter. "Stupid Khutani Slave! You fell for my trick, and now you die, worthless Puke, like the rest of the vermin who challenge Ghostlander might." He thumped his chest, Varrod's own blood splattering his face. "I am the Great Avenger, Mightiest warrior of the North! Die knowing you have failed—"

"No, Begta Puke, you die!" Ogwy growled as he let go his own war magic illusion and drove his spear into the Avenger's chest. With a startled cry the Ghostlander crumpled to the ground at his feet. Crouching Ogwy drew his knife and cut off the Ghostlander's head. Raising it high he shouted his triumph for all to see. "Death to all Oath Breakers who turn against their own! May the Poison Fires burn you forever, Ghostland vermin!"

With a scream of fear and anger several Ghostland warriors saw his grim trophy and swarmed to the attack. Dropping his prize Ogwy faced the onslaught, several of the Alliance warriors hurrying to his aid.

Chapter Six

Crowis stood near the tent flap, trying to peer past their Wa'chassey'ul guard's shoulder into the night outside. He shivered as another loud boom sounded followed by angry screams from somewhere near the edge of camp.

Glancing in that direction from his place beside Nathan still cradling the comatose Marti, Phillip-Yoey rose and came over to join him. "The battle seems to be moving away from our portion of the encampment," he said quietly.

"Yes, I was just thinking that myself," Crowis said. "I hope the Alliance is winning."

Kashallan-Phillip chuckled. "I hope we are as well. I have no desire to become a Ghostland wizard's slave."

Crowis ventured a nervous chuckle of his own in agreement. Then sobering, he glanced at the grieving other kashallan and then back to the tent opening. In a hesitant voice, he ventured, "I wonder if Sensei Timma is all right? They are probably needing us in the med tent right now."

"Yes, they probably are—all of us," Phillip agreed. His expression grim Phillip crossed over to the other kashallan and stood looking down at the grieving Nathan with the tears traveling unnoticed down his cheeks.

"Nathan, Amsi, get up." Phillip motioned with his chin to Marti. "Can you carry her, or do Crowis and I need to help you?"

Nathan glanced up bewildered. Lost in his personal turmoil it took him a long moment to understand Phillip's repeated question. Finally he said, "Where are we going?"

"To the med tent. Crowis, you, and I—all of us are needed there to take care of the wounded. We can't stay here doing nothing while our people are fighting and dying."

"What about Marti?"

"We can care for her there just as well as we can here."

"Do you think Tess-weh's guard dog will let us out of here?"

Phillip-Yoey's mouth formed a hard line. "Atahru can guard us as easily there as here." He handed Nathan back his sidearm. "And I plan to argue that point with her minion if necessary." He motioned Nathan to his feet. "So come on; let's go."

When they joined Crowis at the tent opening Phillip opened his mouth to do just that, argue his point, but the Wa'chassey'ul surprised him by opening the flap wider and motioning for them to come out. Taking a position at the head of their little procession, he led them to the med tent and took up his guard post just inside the open door flaps.

Passing by the overflow of wounded waiting outside to be seen, as Phillip had expected all the cots were full. Medic Williams must be somewhere with the stretcher bearers collecting the fallen, he thought. Timma and Medic Ruan were here, busy bending over the wounded, the others—including the gaishinay—to his surprise, were scurrying to carry out the medics' orders as best they could.

Abandoning the kashallans when he saw Kitha helping Timma with a badly wounded Clan warrior, Crowis hurried over to them. Seeing him Kitha smiled, then focused back on the task Timma had given her.

Beside him Nathan surveyed the chaos, his expression grim. "Looks like our people are taking quite a beating out there."

"Yes, I expect so," Phillip agreed. Not allowing himself to be caught up in fear and sadness, he pushed his emotions to the side and focused on what he could do to help at the moment.

Noticing him, Masonja hurried over, her golden eyes troubled. "Good kashallans come." She motioned to a shadowed place by the stove where a bound and sleeping Chelka lay covered with a blanket. "Womans sleep there. Masonja guard with big magics. Kashallans need help warriors now." Leading the way, she directed Nathan to a place where he could lay the unconscious Marti next to her friend.

FIRES AND DEATH IN their wake, Tobrach and his hunters raced north into the darkness, the scent of the Enemy strong in their nostrils. One of the Ghostlanders admitted, before his painful death, that yes they did have another place further up the valley shielded by illusion.

Shielded by powerful war magic illusions, Tobrach prayed that between the added reinforcements Hunt Leader Tizu sent them, Ikuwi's charm and their own magics they would be strong enough to find and destroy the threat. They needed to put an end to this and soon. The Sorins were coming and no one liked the idea of being trapped in the Ghostlands until the storms abated and the blue snows freed them.

To the east the light of a new day was greying behind a thorn bush-covered ridge when the talisman Ikuwi held out blazed with white light and fragmented into burning shards.

"Well, I guess we found their shield," Sietriga said, stating the obvious. Ikuwi swore at him, glaring. Sietriga chuckled and held out a jar of burn salve from a pouch at his waist. Grumbling Ikuwi took it and plastered the goo across his palm and handed it back.

The way wasn't blocked—physically. They could pass through it easily enough—might not have even noticed—without Wizard Eilo's gift. Tobrach scanned the slopes above this narrow cleft in the valley. This would be a perfect spot to stage an ambush, lot of heavy rocks up on that cliff to push down on the unsuspecting enemy intent only on catching up to their prey. The question now was, what might be waiting for them if they continued ahead?

"Could be someone forgot to close the wards when they abandoned their earlier plan," Sietriga suggested, as he too studied the rock-strewn cliffs ahead.

"Hmm, maybe..." Tobrach agreed. "But not a usual practice, because such a shield would take the creator's personal magics to maintain."

"So what do we do, go back?" a hunter asked, "or, do we go—"

The Warlinga broke off as a cloud of violet mists engulfed them. Tobrach shuddered as he saw with his war magic several massive grey forms outlined in light, swimming through the cloud to encircle them.

<<Well met, Warriors of the Alliance, the Changeling has eluded us by returning to his body, hoping to escape our vengeance, no doubt. We would

hunt with you and together we will bring down our prey,>> the Maker in the lead said.

<<We would welcome the help, Ancient One,>> Tobrach said in the mind speech. <<But how would that be possible?>>

<<It will not be easy,>> the Maker admitted, <<but some among you are strong enough in what you call the war magics that if we exert enough of our own power, we can form a link with you—for the time needed for this hunt.>>

Not as fluent with this form of speech as the kashallans Tobrach wasn't sure he'd heard the Maker aright. He glanced at his hunters. Ikuwi, a few others, and to his surprise, Sietriga, seemed to be able to hear the Maker as well. Somewhat bewildered, the rest waited with weapons ready, knowing something unusual was happening, but unable to fathom it.

Addressing them Tobrach said. "Don't be afraid this isn't a Ghostlander trick. Some of the holy Khutani have joined us. We are talking to them in the mind speech. I think they want to help us with our hunt."

<<How would that be possible, Elder?>> Tobrach heard Ikuwi ask as he returned his attention inward. <<There is no water nearby in which you can swim.>>

The Maker focused its golden eyes on the man, studying him before answering. Ikuwi shuddered under that intense stare. <<Your power is strong, Blue Stone Warrior. I'm surprised one of your own wizards hasn't snapped you up and made you an apprentice of the ancient arts.>>

Taking a deep breath, Ikuwi bravely met its eyes and answered, <<They tried, but I like being a warrior protecting the People, so I resisted their efforts.>>

The Maker rumbled a laugh. <<I like your spirit, Young One. Now to answer your question, we can work as one being, with a little trust, on both our parts. If you allow us behind your personal shields we will form a link with you for a time. Through this link we will see, hear, smell and touch the surface world with your senses, and you in turn will have the added power of our magics when we encounter the Ghostlanders to guide and protect you as you fight them.>>

<<That would give us a big advantage,>> Sietriga said. <<But it might be hard to achieve—especially with time pressing. I doubt if any of us are used to sharing so completely with another being.>>

<<By opening yourselves to hear our voices you have already begun the process, Speir'dina,>> The Maker assured him.

<<Now let us finish it. We will be gentle and occupy no more of a place in your minds than you allow us,>> another in the circling pod said.

<<The Changeling thinks he has eluded us, not suspecting us to follow him into the physical world. If we are quick we can catch up to him before he runs back to his masters in Tiebarai,>> the eldest said.

<<Yes, time is passing, and his power has been weakened. But still, if we don't hurry the Changeling will slip through our net once again.>> a scarred Maker said, sounding impatient with the delay.

Taking a deep breath Tobrach said, <<I agree, Holy Ones, I will open myself. Come; I will try not to let fear rule me and resist your union.>>

FEELING BETRAYED BY his gods, Drucas wrenched himself out of the Dream with a burst of power that left him nearly drained. He had escaped the attacking pod—for now by retreating to the physical world where they couldn't follow, but at great cost. Well at least he had managed to kill another of the loathsome aliens before they swarmed him.

Taking in several deep breaths he lay still on his make-shift bed in the small cave up the slope from their hidden headquarters. To his surprise he could see the mouth of the cave clearly, a pale grey in the coming light of a new day. And there, nearly as motionless as the stone he rested against, crouched his faithful Second Sanglaz.

Too long away, and nothing to show for his effort, he thought. Fear and rage twisted a knot in his middle. Why was this happening to him? He had done all the gods of the Fires asked of him, hadn't he? They had told him that if he gave up something he valued greatly, they would bless him and give him the power he needed to triumph over his enemies—all his enemies.

Well, damn them, hadn't he done that? He'd delayed his recovery by giving them more of his own blood than was wise, and the fine alien blade—something he valued greatly and didn't want to lose, damn them. Why weren't they keeping their side of the bargain?

Tonight when he had gone into the Dream to do the Cabal's bidding the Gods of the Fires abandoned him to the Khutani. Feeling vulnerable and out of control he realized that events in the physical world had progressed on an unplanned and unknown course. Where was his deadly rival the Great Avenger, and the rest of the slimy little grey mushrooms that Cohbruel had insisted he bring with him on this mission.

Had they gone against his orders and directed the Avenger to lead the attack without waiting for him as the Cabal's minion he'd killed said? Possibly, the Avenger would have been eager—too damned eager to seize control and the weak-minded mushrooms—not the best the Cabal had to offer—would have been easy prey for his persuasions.

And if that were true—and their warbands moved too quickly—without sticking to their original plan—his plan, then the gods alone knew what might happen. Drucas felt the knot of fear in his gut twist a little tighter. If the Avenger failed—even though such a major disaster wouldn't be *his* fault—the Cabal wouldn't care. He would be blamed, his life forfeit to their combined rage.

Lying still and unnoticed, he listened to the sounds of the awakening day in the valley below. Unfortunately, there wasn't much to hear... wind rustling the dry leaves of the thorn bush, the cry of some creature killed by another, the sounds of a few slaves in the camp below making fires and cooking the morning meal.

It was too quiet. Where were the yowling screeches of the young chained warriors, clamoring for their breakfast of bloody meat and drugs to encourage them to fight when loosed on the Enemy? Where were the shouted commands from their keepers, promising them a great feast soon?

The question now was whether to run—run where—or stay, kill the Great Avenger and salvage what was possible from what he was sure was the disaster he feared? Delay could be fatal whichever course he chose.

With a deep sigh Drucas got to his feet and stepped to the cave mouth. Sanglaz saw him at once and rose to his feet, putting hand to chest in salute. Motioning for his Second to fall into step with him as he started down the hill, he said, "Tell me what has happened while I was in the Dream on the assignment for the Cabal."

CROUCHED BEHIND A LARGE thorn bush Tobrach and the Maker sharing his body peered down the slope at the large encampment below. Nostrils flared to catch the faintest scent of the changeling on the intermittent breeze coming towards them, he detected no sign of their prey.

<<He has to be here—or coming here,>> Maker Qwaltamis assured him. <<I doubt if he has the strength to run straight to Tiebarai after our battle last night. He is here.>>

Keeping low Ikuwi crawled over to him. Speaking in the mind speech, he pointed with his lips up the nearby slope and said, <<Hunt Leader, Elder, it is hidden by a fading illusion but the Khutani with me has detected a small cave up there.>>

<<Is he there, Thu?>> Qwaltamis asked the younger Khutani.

<<Not now, Maker,>> Thu answered for them both, <<but he and another were there, not long ago.>>

<<Good,>> Maker Sherigus with Sietriga said. <<He is within our reach. Probably making his way under an illusion to the cluster of Ghostland dwellings below us.>>

<<Yeah, and there's something about that camp that isn't right,>> Sietriga said, adding his thoughts to the conversation.

<<I agree,>> Tobrach said. <<There are many tents and cages down there but most seem empty—or nearly so.>>

<<Gone to attack us most like,>> Sietriga said. <<So maybe we should return the favor.>>

<<Not if it means losing the Changeling,>> Thu protested. <<He has killed two of us. I want vengeance—>>

<<We will have our vengeance, Young One, but not at the expense of losing more of the pod to the Changeling or the two wizards I detect among the Ghostlanders in that camp,>> Qwaltamis said.

Two more of the Cabal to deal with, probably here, and not in the Dream—no more easy kills. That was a sobering thought for all to consider, Tobrach thought privately.

<<Personal vengeance isn't the only meal to savor. Considering this problem as a whole, destroying their base here—or at least doing it some real damage is an important part of ending the Ghostland threat for good,>> Maker Gladdris said. There was some outraged grumbling from Qwaltamis's pod, but they quieted under the maker's golden stare.

<<If we split up we could do both,>> Sietriga ventured in the silence that followed. <<McLaren and me have our star weapons with us and some fire Jars. If most of the hunters come with us to burn out the camp and kill as many of the Ghostlanders as we can, the rest of you could hunt for Drucas. But don't forget to make sure those wizards you sense don't attack us while we are destroying their base. Working together we can accomplish both tasks.>>

<<Yes, that is a great plan. Then when Our warriors from our main camp send the lazy Begta running this way they will be caught between our powerful jaws and destroyed,>> Ikuwi said, radiating his excitement.

Chapter Seven

"Hunt Leader Tizu," a breathless messenger cried as he jerked to a halt in front of Tizu and the men at the command post. "War Leader Goro says to tell you that most of the Ghostland war leaders are dead and the crazy young ones that are left are running away. He wants to follow them—kill as many as he can—so they won't come back—ever!"

Tizu looked around the expectant circle; he could see the exhaustion written plainly upon the faces of the men standing there, and yet the news had given them a hope. There was a gleam of new excitement in their eyes. Won't come back ever? That was too much to hope for, but still...

"Murda, get on the com and let Sietriga know what's coming his way."

Then turning to the messenger he added, "Tell Goro he and Tesulu can take half there men and pursue the enemy. Chase them and make sure they don't regroup in the hidden base Tobrach found. Keep them running all the way back to Fa'Hanzoi if you can. But tell those amadans not to follow them that far. I need them back here to help sort out the damage to our own forces. *And bury all the dead*, he thought privately.

SIETRIGA TAPPED THE com box on his belt, listened through the ear piece, turned to Tobrach and the waiting men, and said, "Hunt Leader Tizu says the Ghostlanders are retreating and heading our way—fast. He wants us to destroy as much of this base as we can and keep any Ghostlanders left alive running for Fa'Hanzoi—but not follow them that far. He wants us back to base after we finish here."

"But won't they be harder to root out of their holes in the ground if we let them escape to an underground city?" one of the hunters complained. "This makes no sense; we should follow and kill them all while they are in the open."

"It makes perfect sense, Young One," Maker Qwaltamis said, using Tobrach's voice. "If the Enemy is running away, it will be because the Alliance has killed the overseers that direct the monsters they breed in the pits. And without that familiar goad, urging them on to fight you, the vermin will be without direction. They will be terrified angry, and out of control. If *we* direct them towards Fa'Hanzoi they will turn on their own and do some of our work for us. Now do you understand?"

Oh yes, Sietriga thought privately. Ruthless, savage, and brutally effective, most like. He understood quite well what the Khutani was saying. Seeing only the healing side that the kashallans presented to the world, he, and most other Speir'dina, probably weren't aware of this darker aspect of Khutani nature.

<<You disapprove, Warrior,>> Maker Sherigus said. <<You are trying to shield from me but I can still taste the sour flavor of your thoughts.>>

Slightly angry and a bit afraid, he said, <<Honestly, I don't know what I feel. I know we have to end this fighting, but in a big town like what I think Fa'Hanzoi is, there will be innocent civilians there too, women and children—slaves like the ones we saw at Te'gal. they didn't order those monsters to attack the South. What of them?>>

<<No they didn't, but they didn't stop the wizards either. And besides all in the North carry the ancient taint that nearly destroyed this world. We must protect our peoples and see that the Great Destruction never happens again. That is our charge, and we will fulfil it by any means.>>

<<And what of the Changeling?>> Thu added. <Are we going to let him go, after what he has done?>>

<<No one said anything about abandoning the hunt for the Changeling, Impatient One,>> Maker Gladdris said. <<He is near; we will find and kill him, never fear.>>

DRUCAS WAS NEARING a cluster of tents on the outside of the Ghostland base when his recovering magic warned him of trouble. Stopping abruptly he glanced around, nostrils flaring to catch any scent of danger.

"What's wrong, K'San?" Sanglaz murmured.

Impatiently Drucas motioned for silence, his senses straining. All seemed as before, the camp around them quiet, undisturbed, no one nearby, and yet... There was something different, a powerful illusion perhaps, masked something—someone; he was sure of it.

"Show yourself, Cowardly Puke. I know you are here," he snarled.

At his words the wizard dropped his illusion and confronted him with arms folded across his narrow chest. "Where have you been, Half-bred Slave?"

"Trying to carry out the assignment given me, Exalted."

The Ghostlander snorted. "And taking your own sweet time about it, too. When we had no word from you I had to send the Avenger to do the *other* task assigned you. So I ask again; where have you been?"

So, they had done what he feared and loosed the Avenger and the might of the Ghostland warbands on the enemy too soon, expecting the ferocity of their monstrous horde to gain the victory instead of following his carefully laid out plan. Damn them, damn them all! Drucas could feel the rage boiling inside him, barely controlled. "Fighting Khutani! I was discovered and have been hard pressed," he spat out, his whole body trembling with his fury. "But I killed two of the slimy alien vermin before the pod swarmed me and I had to return to my body."

The wizard snorted again, making no secret of his contempt. "Return with your assignment unfinished, Worthless Slave. Well no matter The Great Avenger will do what is needed to destroy the Alliance vermin once and for all. We will have the Southern land for our own as Master Barak always promised—in spite of you."

A cruel smile twisting his thin lips the wizard continued, "After two bungled assignments, however, you may not live to enjoy our triumph once the Cabal learns of your failure—once again."

Unable to control himself any longer, Drucas pounced with teeth bared and claws extended. Unprepared for a physical attack, the Ghostlander had no time to throw up a protective shield before Drucas was upon him and sinking his fangs into the small man's vulnerable throat.

With a twist of his head Drucas snapped the wizard's neck, the body spasming in his grasp. Looking up from his kill he stared into the shocked face of his Second. "Stop staring, Begta Puke. Go find the other slimy little mushroom, before he alerts the Cabal and I have no time to clean up the disaster they've created."

Sanglaz hesitated, staring at the body at his K'San's feet. "You just killed one of the Exalted. The Cabal will kill us both for such a crime."

Drucas snorted. "The Cabal will do nothing, because the Hated Enemy killed this one." He kicked the corpse at his feet in disgust. "And when I manage to achieve a victory for them they won't care about this or the other puke hiding somewhere in these tents."

Drucas pointed to the left, away from the empty cages. "Help me drag the corpse up the slope, then go check that way for the other little mushroom. I will go in the other direction."

"And what should I do when I find him?" Sanglaz asked, still uncertain.

"Kill him, of course. Then report back to me." Drucas could tell Sanglaz wasn't happy about his assignment, but he helped hide the body and went off to check on the other wizard without further question or complaint.

Drucas watched him go with narrowed eyes. He might have to kill Sanglaz. In spite of his years of obedient service, Drucas could sense the rebellion and mistrust that was now building between them.

When Sanglaz was hidden from view among the tents Drucas started back down the hill, then stopped abruptly as he saw some of the Hated Enemy creeping through the thorn, heading towards the camp.

So the Enemy had discovered their true encampment, Damn the Avenger and the bungling minions of the Cabal. The Allied warband seemed intent on attacking whoever was left among the tents and cages below, unaware of his presence. Alone and in his weakened state, his first thought was for his own survival. Drucas was willing to let them destroy the base if he could escape and later blame others for the disaster.

Keeping low and under cover as much as possible he headed back up the hill the shouts of alarm ringing in his ears, as the first of the tents and cages burst into flames below him.

Hoping to escape discovery, Drucas was making for his hidden cave, when Tobrach and another Alliance warrior stepped onto the trail to confront him.

"Running away again and leaving others to die in your place, Changeling Puke?" the otherworldly voice coming out of K'San Tobrach's mouth said as the Warlinga dropped into a fighter's crouch weapon raised. "He's mine," the voice warned the other warrior who nodded.

Tobrach! Drucas blessed his good fortune. "Not this time, Khutani Slave," Drucas snarled and launched a furious attack at his rival, his jealousy an added goad to the anger and frustration of many days.

Back and forth they sparred, the Khutani alert for magical intervention or treachery, but otherwise allowing its chosen combatant to follow his own instincts in the fight.

Whipping his tail across the younger hunter's chest, causing him to stagger and nearly fall, Drucas let out a mocking laugh. "Not so easy to kill me, eh, little Begta, is it? You will never have her; she's mine—all mine!"

Tobrach reversed his spear and slammed its butt into Drucas's unprotected leg. "I know Chelka has sworn to kill you herself, but I found you first, so I will have the privilege. I hope she won't be too angry with me for spoiling her kill."

Drucas aimed another blow at his opponent's chest. With a muttered curse Tobrach leapt away, the obsidian tip cutting a long furrow through scales and skin, dark blood welling up in the wound. Drucas laughed again.

"Are you sure she still wants to kill me? That's not what she says to me when I come to her in the Dream and give her pleasure—more pleasure than you give is what she tells me, little Begta. She won't be angry when I kill you; she won't even miss you at all. She belongs to me—me, Khutani Slave, me!"

For just a moment Tobrach's heart faltered. Recalling how she had attacked him without warning last night, a worm of doubt gnawed at his resolve. Was that true; did she want the Changeling after all? Tobrach loved her with all his being; he wasn't sure he wanted to live without her.

Drucas saw the seed of doubt he had planted flower, pressing the Warlinga mercilessly as he took advantage of his opponent's waning resolve. Tobrach now sported several deep gashes along his chest and arms. Though Drucas himself was wounded his broader combat experience had given him the advantage. It was time to finish this.

<<You must be strong, Warlinga,>> Maker Qwaltamis roared in Tobrach's mind. <<Whether what he says about your chosen mate is true or not doesn't matter. The Changeling has killed two of us; he must die for his

crimes, and you are the chosen vessel of our vengeance,>> Maker Qwaltamis said as it seized control of Tobrach's wounded body.

Using its power, the Maker resumed the attack with no regard for Tobrach's safety. "It is you who will die, Changeling. You will not escape our vengeance. Either here, or in the Dream, wherever you try to run, there is no escape. You will die today," Qwaltamis snarled, and let the changeling see its sinewy form wrapped around the Warlinga's physical body.

Suddenly Drucas realized his mistake. Upon seeing the Tragar K'San, his jealousy had lured him into the Maker's cunning trap. Even if he succeeded in killing his rival the Khutani would use their power and force the corpse to continue fighting until he lay dead on the ground.

With a choking clarity, once more he recalled the Fire Spirits' words in his mind.<<*You will gain the Power that you seek. Your enemies among the Cabal and many in the South will die by your hand, Warrior. But unless you sacrifice something you greatly value in payment, you will join them in death, Arrogant One.*>>

Arrogant One, yes that was who he was, he had thought the Spirits were satisfied with the gift of his blood and his Speir'dina knife, but the gift they wanted him to sacrifice was Chelka. As he felt his strength weakening he saw the glory of his possible future unraveling before his inner eye.

If he had done what Cohbruel wanted and sacrificed Chelka, he would have lost her when the allies killed her, but she would have killed Tobrach, the Alliance's Hunt Leader and many others before she was slaughtered. She was the sacrifice they wanted, not the knife.

With a cry of desperation Drucas used his magic and launched an unexpected attacked within the Dream, directing a spear of flaming light at the Maker's head. The Maker roared in pain as a fire, straight from the poisonous pit encircled it. In the next moment

Qwaltamis spat out a cool blue light quelling the fire. With a snarl of outrage Qwaltamis retaliated with a stream of violet light that made Drucas hastily fall back into his body. Damn the Khutani, the Alliance and the Cabal, too, for that matter. If he was fated to die and his glorious future denied, and if he couldn't have Chelka, then his last act while alive would be to make sure that sniveling Tragar K'San wouldn't live to have her either.

STANDING IDLY BY AS Drucas and Tobrach battled Ikuwi realized that Tobrach's strength was nearly at an end. He had lost too much blood, but the Maker was pouring its power into his torn body goading him on—to the death maybe. <<Thu we have to stop this. We have to help, or my Teh'lach brother is going to die.>>

<<I would like to do that, but Maker Qwaltamis will be angry if I interfere,>> the younger Khutani reluctantly said.

Ikuwi swore a Speir'dina oath and gripped his spear a little harder. <<Fine, then the Maker can be angry with me then.>> And before Thu could use its power to stop him, Ikuwi lifted his spear and drove the obsidian blade into Drucas's back. As Drucas began to turn to face this new adversary, Ikuwi grabbed him by his head crest and slashed his knife across the Changeling's exposed throat.

Allowing Tobrach's injured body to slump to the bloody ground, Qwaltamis flew out of its host and twisted itself into an angry coil of light , its hard yellow eyes glaring at the Blue Stone warrior.

Angry now himself, Ikuwi face the enraged Maker, and tried not to cringe. <<Yes, I ended your little game, Khutani; do you want to kill me for interfering? A child of the Real People would never be so cruel as to drive one who has given you trust and loyalty to his death to satisfy a lust for personal vengeance? Have you no shame?>>

Caught up in the moment and his indignation, Ikuwi thumped his chest and cried, <<Kill me if you want, Khutani Demon! Or leave me to take care of my wounded brother. I don't care which you choose, because the Warlinga will die soon if one of us doesn't help him. He is a good war leader and doesn't deserve to die. The Ghostlanders have killed enough of our people today.>>

The image of the Maker shimmered as Qwaltamis worked to bring its boiling emotions down to a simmer. At last it said, <<You are right, Young One, and wise beyond your years. If the Warlinga dies the Changeling slimeworm will have won, and I won't let that happen if my power can prevent it. Come we will care for him together.>>

Chapter Eight

Exhausted and feeling every year of his age, Qwasigara curled up in his fur blanket and closed his eyes. He needed to sleep and renew his vital energies while within the Dream, but though he tried, sleep eluded him. Though sheltered in one of the Speir'dina cloth dwellings he could hear the sounds of the restless encampment around him. He was exhausted, but like him, it seemed as if no one else in the camp felt like sleeping either.

Nearby several of his Sand Mountain relatives sat beside a small fire, talking in low voices as they roasted the cannibalized meat of their own dead to appease their hunger. He could see their silhouettes painted in the flickering shadows made by the firelight. Out in the darkness someone cried out with pain, only to be soothed by a woman's soft voice in the next moment. Coming from the direction of the mass grave the surviving members of a Teh'lach chanted a lament for their fallen.

With a clawed hand he stroked the soft fur of the Avairei blanket. Never could he have dreamed he would be aiding the old Enemy against the Ghostlanders, resting unharmed and free among them and lying in a covering made from the skins of one of the Real People's ancient enemies. The world had turned upside down and he was tumbling without an anchor in the maelstrom. Still angry and bitter, he wasn't sure how he felt about the new order of things.

Earlier that day Philip-Yoey had come begging for his aid.

"ELDER, THOUGH I'VE been told that K'San Drucas is dead I think there are those in the Cabal who could possibly recreate a magical link with either Marti or Chelka."

"Then do what I have always told you; kill them," Qwasigara snapped, folding his arms across his grey-furred chest. "Stop putting it off and do what is

232

necessary for our protection, because you are right. if they have the opportunity the Cabal will use those women to destroy us."

"The solution isn't that simple—"

Qwasigara snorted, cutting him off. "I know the Speir'dina woman is the chosen mate of your Khutani relative, but the big male can find another Speir'dina female, or pay our bride price and have a Sand Mountain girl—just as you did." Qwasigara smiled, showing his canines.

Phillip took a deep breath, letting it out slowly. "That's a generous offer, and I understand your reasoning, but it isn't how we do things."

"Yes, I'm aware of how you coddle your people. Did you learn your soft ways among the stars or among the Khutani's slaves?"

Qwasigara inwardly smiled. Phillip-Yoey was trying hard to conceal his growing anger, but Qwasigara could sense it. He was deliberately baiting the Khutani and wasn't sure why he was doing it. Old habits die hard maybe. "And as for the Warlinga," the wizard curled his lip with contempt. "I repeat; you need to kill them."

At last venting some of his growing frustration, Phillip-Yoey snapped, "I think you are trying to make me angry, so you have an excuse to refuse me, but that last is unworthy of you Elder. Tobrach and the other Warlinga have fought and died alongside warriors of the People, so please stop."

Qwasigara glared, but said nothing more. At last Phillip sighed. Taking over, Yoey explained, "There are reasons besides sentiment why we don't want to just kill them. First of all, Tobrach is a valued hunt leader and we are in his debt for saving my relative Dunnagh-Tani's life.

"And as for Marti, yes she is my Amsi's mate, but even if she wasn't we would want to save her. There aren't so many breeding females among the Speir'dina and we need her genetic potential if a host species is to continue to thrive on this world."

"Please, Elder," Phillip said. "I'm asking as a kinsman, and my kashallan relative and the Warlinga of Tragar and Meh'gach will also be in your debt if you help us. Isn't there a spell or something we can do to prevent the Cabal from possessing the minds of either of them again?"

Qwasigara growled deep in his throat, but at last he relented. "I will talk to Wizard Eilo. I can't promise, but we will see what can be done."

CALLING UPON THE SACREDNESS of kinship obligations, that had been a clever ploy, worthy of a true son of The People, he grudgingly had to admit. Qwasigara had reason to believe that his new relative by marriage, Phillip-Yoey, was an honorable man. But were the Khutani Makers? Instinct warned him to be wary of the Ancient Enemy. How much could the Clans trust them once this war was over? With these troubling thoughts uppermost in his mind, the wizard finally fell into a troubled sleep.

AMONG THE COLORED MISTS and chaotic sounds of the Dream, Qwasigara drifted seeking renewal. His soul craved the comfort of the familiar sites of home. Home... Without much effort he found himself standing among the red rocks of one of his people's sacred places. A hot dry wind blew across the sandy plateau spread out to the west where a glowing red sun touched the horizon. Nostrils flared he breathed in the scorched smell of hot sand and grease brush. The screech of triumph made by a bat-winged teskla as it rose with its prey from the rocks above caused him to look up and smile.

Turning his back on the view, the wizard stepped between the giant boulders that guarded the holy spring in the cave beyond. Cool mists caressed his face as he moved deeper inside, patches of glowing fungi and furry purple moss clung to the rough stone, leading the way to the holy spring. Trailing a hand over the moist walls of the cave Qwasigara breathed in its power, already feeling revived. Running a tongue across dry black lips the wizard hurried forward anticipating the renewal he knew awaited when he drank at the spring itself.

As he stepped into the little hollow Qwasigara halted, staring. He was not alone in this holy place. Where the blue water falling from the darkness above gathered to form a shallow pool, a shrouded figure knelt. Qwasigara choked down a snarl of anger, gathering himself for an attack. Who would dare defile this sanctuary without asking Sand Mountain permission? One of the Ghostland wizards might dare. A knot of fear twisted in his gut. The battle fought with the Cabals minions had nearly drained him of power; he wasn't ready to meet one of them in battle so soon—even if this place was a power source for his people.

The figure had its back to him, but knew he was there, turning to face him Tess-weh smiled. "This place is very—rejuvenating. I'm not surprised your people call it holy." Raising a delicate white hand she motioned for him to join her. <<Come, Wizard, drink, isn't that why you came here, after all? The water is very—refreshing. Its gift will aid you in future battles with the Cabal.>> she chuckled, but there was no mirth in the sound. <<And you will need all its strength—and more.>>

Qwasigara folded his upper set of arms across his chest. <<What are you doing here, Demon?>>

<<Why the same as you, Old One.>> Tess-weh motioned again for him to join her. <<I too, need its healing and empowering waters.>>

<<You don't have Sand Mountain's permission to violate our holy places with your foul presence, Witch. Go to the Khutani pools if you seek a renewal of your power.>>

Her eyes flashing a dark fire, Tess-weh snarled, <<I don't need yours—or Sand Mountain's permission. I come and go as I please.>>

<<I repeat; why are you here?>>

<<To help you survive what is coming, Stubborn Old Fool,>> she snapped. At his startled expression, she let out a mocking laugh. <<Yes I am here to help you—survive and live many more years. If you pay my price, of course.>>

Qwasigara snorted and looked down his long dog-like snout at her. <<I'm too old to play sexual games with you, Demon. I will have to take my chances with the future.>>

<<There are other things I value that I will accept as payment,>> she cooed in a low voice.

<<Like what?>>

Tess-weh motioned for the old wizard to join her on the soft moss growing near the spring. Curious yet still wary, Qwasigara crouched on his haunches facing her.

After a long silence, she finally said, <<Truly, if you refuse my gift I can offer my magics to Wizard Eilo, or to the reluctant young one who could be great among you, but you are my first choice.>>

<<And why is that, Demon?>>

Tess-weh growled impatiently deep in her throat. <<Because the obligations of a relative already bind you to the Khutani—whether you like it or not. In spite of what your experiences in the Kashallan Alliance have shown you to be true, in your heart you still have refused to let go of the old hatred that has been passed down through the generations of your people.>>

She spoke true, but Qwasigara was too obstinate to let her know that. <<Choose another then,>> he snapped back. <<I will keep to the old ways of my people no matter the cost.>>

Tess-weh growled again. <<Stubborn Old Fool!>> Reaching out before he could stop her, she plunged a hand into his spirit body and wrenched a tangled mass of power from his chest. With a cry the wizard fell back, pain and sudden loss goading him to launch an attack, which she easily dismissed with a wave of her other hand.

Too weak to try again he lay back, staring at the muddy orb of dark swirling colors on her palm. <<What's that? Give it back,>> he grumbled.

<<It's the nest of anger and bitterness that has been poisoning your heart for a long time now.>> She held it out to show him. <<Look into its depths, see the vibrant chaos of rage and hatred, intermeshed so carefully with bitterness and disappointment?>> A smile curved her full red lips as she watched the play of glowing energies along with him. <<Oh there is power here—great power. For much of your life this is the essence of the magic that has guided you, protecting your clan, giving you strength.

<<It will eventually kill you—perhaps very soon—but I will return it to you if you like. I will only offer my gift to you but once, so consider well before you decide. My gift is also a source of great power—it can sustain you as well as this poisonous crutch. I will give you what I can spare of my magic, if you pay my price.>>

As he lay upon the moss thinking, the wizard was aware of a new emptiness, longing to be filled within him. But now that it was gone from his body, did he really want that seething ball of hatred and bitterness back? Before he woke into the Physical World he must be filled with—something however... he sat up, and said, <<Very well, Demon, what is your price for your magic gift?>>

Tess-weh quenched the glowing orb with a wave of her other hand. <<When I am gone; I need you to take up my contract and protect your kinsman and the other kashallans if necessary.>>

His jaws agape, Qwasigara sat back. Never in his wildest imaginings would he have expected her to say that. <<I don't understand. Are you telling me that you will die before we achieve victory over our enemy?>>

<<That is exactly what I am telling you, Wizard.>>

Qwasigara shook his head in disbelief. <<But even with a gift of your magics I wouldn't be powerful enough to win a victory over the Ghostlanders. They are too strong for one man—even with your magic gift to aid me.>>

<<Nor will you have to battle them. That will be my task—mine and some of the big worms to accomplish, though it will cost us dearly.>>

<<In other words some of you don't plan to survive.>>

<<I learned at the battle of Red Rock that my Speir'dina host's body isn't strong enough to channel all the power needed to defeat them again. Our life is the sacrifice my H'an and I freely make to fulfill our obligations to our kin and the Khutani,>> she said quietly.

<<What must I do to pay your price?>>

<<The warriors of the Kashallan Alliance have destroyed most of the Ghostlanders' ability to threaten the Alliance for many years to come, but as long as the Elite that presently control the Cabal remain alive there is still great danger not only for the Khutani's peoples, but for the clans across the Shallow Sea as well.

<<The Sorins are coming and many will want to go home, but if the Clan warriors or the Warlinga do that before you kill off its Ghostland roots, the threat will grow anew—and be harder to kill next time. The Alliance must finish this task, even if it means spending the Sorin Season in the Ghostlands. You, Wizard Qwasigara, must use your power to convince most of the warriors to remain with the Alliance. That is one part of your payment.>>

<<And what else?>>

Her smile was secretive as she said, <<I charge you to take care of your kinsman when I am gone and no longer able to do so. My contract is to protect the kashallans from Ghostland magics, but a time is coming when their paths will split. We have chosen who we will protect and follow. You must be there to help the other when it becomes necessary.>>

The wizard thought she must be talking about Phillip-Yoey with her mention of a kinsmen's obligations, but he was unable to puzzle out the rest. <<<What must I do to help my kinsman?>>

Tess-weh stood up adjusting her veil over her scarred face. <<I can say no more now, but you will know more when it is time to aid him.>>

Qwasigara rose, too. <<Wait—where are you going?>>

<<I go to prepare myself for the battle that is coming.>>

<<What about my gift? You promised—>>

<<I keep my promises, Wizard—never fear. Drink the water here, lie down on the soft moss and refresh yourself. When you wake in the morning you will feel my gift within you, right here.>> She touched her chest and then disappeared.

Chapter Nine

Tobrach blinked up at the fabric of the med tent overhead, trying to determine what time of day it was. Carried on a make-shift stretcher and lost down a well of pain after his fight with the changeling, he remembered little of the return journey back to the Alliance main encampment.

Every part of his body still hurt, but when he woke this time at least, the pain was bearable. Taking in several deep breaths he lay back with eyes closed. How long had he been like this? And what had been going on while he'd been lying here like a lazy Begta? Trying to figure things out he drifted once more into a dreamless sleep.

Sometime later he was awakened by someone crouching by his cot and taking up his arm. His wrist guards had been removed exposing the sensitive skin underneath that was devoid of heavy scales like most of his body. This spot had been bred into his people centuries ago for a kashallan's touch, just like the one who formed a link with him now.

"Good afternoon, Hunt Leader Tobrach," Phillip-Yoey said, while extending his tentacles and inserting them into his flesh, to check on his injuries. "I saw you looking around earlier, but I was busy at the time. I taste that you are doing better today. I'm glad, because you have a visitor who has been waiting anxiously to see you."

Tobrach stared up at the kashallan, his mind still a bit fuzzy from whatever kavay pain killer the symbiont had been giving him. Not hearing that he had a visitor, he focused on the question he most wanted answered. "How long have I been lying here like a lazy Begta?"

Studying his face for a moment before answering, Phillip reluctantly admitted, "It's been seven days since the surprise attack and your wounding."

"Seven days! I need to—" Tobrach tried to sit up only to find he was as weak as an infant. He swore one of Nathan's favorite Caldoni oaths and tried again. Gently but firmly the kashallan pushed him down upon his cot.

"You aren't going anywhere—not for a few days yet. Your wounds are deep and serious. If Maker Qwaltamis and your Teh'lach brother Ikuwi hadn't helped you with their power, you might not have made it back to camp alive."

Tobrach lay back, breathing hard. He had only blurred recollections of the battle with Drucas. "The Changeling is dead—Chelka is safe from him now; isn't she?"

"Chelka is safe, for the moment." Phillip-Yoey released him from the link and placed his arm back on the cot. "And before you get too tired and drift off to sleep from the medicine I've just given you, she is here and wants to visit with you."

As the kashallan stepped back Tobrach became aware of an anxious Chelka with Warega right behind her, staring down at him. He offered her a tentative smile. "Hello, My Dear One. I hope you aren't angry with me for spoiling your chance to kill the Changeling."

Chelka's head crest rose in surprise. Crouching beside him she took one of his hands, holding it clumsily between her two bound ones. "No, of course I'm not angry. And I thank the Great Hunt Leader, that you are still alive after the battle." She released his hand to brush at the tears spilling from her red eyes. "I don't know what I would have done if-if he had killed you, My Dear One."

Tobrach snatched her hands away from her face staring at her bound wrists. "What's this," he growled, glaring at Warega. "If the changeling is dead—how dare they keep you tied!"

"It is of her own choosing to remain bound, K'San Cousin, I assure you. No one is forcing her," Warega hastily protested.

Chelka leaned over and licked a sensitive spot on his neck. "Be at peace, My Love. San Warega is right; for everyone's safety I chose, no demanded that I continue to be bound." She motioned with her chin to the strong cord confining her tail to a twist around her hips.

"But why? If Drucas is dead, then there is no need—you are free—"

"No I'm not—not yet at least. The kashallans and the Clan wizards think that someone in the Ghostland Cabal might be able to use Drucas's glyph to control me or Marti if given the chance. So for that reason I have told them to keep me bound and guarded for now."

With the mention of her friend, Tobrach asked, "Marti... I thought she was dead. What has happened to her?"

Chelka's head crest dipped with her distress. "No, she isn't dead, but knowing she could have killed Hunt Leader Tizu and maybe Kashallan-Nathan, too, she has told me she wishes she was. Every time one of the healers comes to check on her she starts crying and begs them to kill her.

"She is so afraid, My Love, so afraid she will fall under a Ghostlander's spell again. It is so terrible. Kashallan-Nathan is very gentle with her when she gets like that. I think he tries to keep her shielded and sleeping as much as he can. I hope she will be all right."

What a horrible mess, he thought. He had known survivors of the Umwira's foul sorcery before. Most ended up killing themselves after a time, if they were left unguarded and given the chance. "Yes, I hope she will be all right, too."

Tobrach could feel the kavay Phillip-Yoey gave him starting to take effect, and with it came an overwhelming wave of despair. How could he live if they had to kill Chelka after all. "I thought we would be free of Drucas and his malice if—"

"And I will be—we will be—soon—so rest now and don't worry. All you need do right now is focus on getting better—so we can go home."

THE SUN HAD DIPPED behind the jagged purple mountains when several dark figures left the Alliance main camp following a narrow game trail heading deeper into the thorn-bush. In the center of a sandy hollow between sheltering boulders they stopped when their leader raised his hand. Overhead pink ribbons of clouds streaked across a mauve sky deepening to purple.

"This is the place Tess-weh showed me in my dream," Qwasigara said. "We will conjure our magics to lure the Ghostlanders here."

Directing the two kashallans and the women to stand to one side, Qwasigara and the Red Wind wizard Eilo instructed Ikuwi and Tesulu to sweep and remove all debris from a large center area of the sand. Aju'an and Sietriga stood on guard at each end of the trail while they worked. All the warriors had come along to guard the participants from interruption from physical intruders and do other mundane tasks as needed, but it was the wizards and the kashallans that would have to do the real work planned this night.

When the area was cleaned to the wizards' satisfaction four fires were lit in a diamond-shaped pattern at north, east, south and west. Qwasigara nodded and motioned for Masonja to bring the two bound women forward to the center. Placing blankets upon the cooling sand Masonja helped Marti and Chelka lie down, then sat on the ground between them.

Kashallan-Nathan had given them each a calming medicine to help them relax and open themselves to the magic earlier. Now they lay quiescent with eyes closed and breathing deeply. Masonja laid a strong hand on each woman's belly, chanting softly as she did so.

EARLIER THAT DAY THE Begta shamanka sought out the wizards as they were discussing the coming night's proceedings. Standing fearlessly in front of them with her muscular arms folded across her chest, she stated boldly, "Why you no ask Masonja come? Kashallans got magics; wizard got magics, Masonja gots big magics, too. You need Masonja."

Qwasigara and Eilo glanced at one another. The Begta was brave—Qwasigara would give her that, but like all her kind stupid. Looking down his long nose at her and curling his lip in contempt, he growled, "Get out of here before I kill you for your insolence, woman. We have no need of a Begta's puny conjurings tonight."

Masonja didn't cringe away as he'd expected. The Begta he had known as slaves among the Clans would have run away screaming at the sound of menace he had deliberately put into his voice. In spite of his threat she remained obstinately standing her ground.

As he opened his mouth to chant a spell to punish her, his fellow wizard surprised him by asking, "I'm curious; why should we bring you tonight, Little Begta? We have the power of Red Wind and Sand Mountain and Khutani magics to guide and protect us. Your magic is nothing compared to that force. We can defeat our Ghostland enemy without you."

Still determined the Begta looked him in the eye. "Maybe, but if Umwira mans sly they beat you cuz you no thinking."

Surprised, Eilo drew back, studying her in a new light. "What do you mean, Little Begta—speak. Not thinking of what?"

Masonja made an exasperated sound deep in her throat, as if what she meant was so obvious. She pointed to the wizards. "True, wizard got big magics—very strong—" she pointed in the direction of the med tent, "and Khutani got magics, too—not so strong as wizard, but strong. But you all mans, so got only mans magics.

"Chelka, Marti womans—need womans magic too. If Ghostlander sly him put seed in womans secret place—make bad trouble later. Masonja got womans magics can protect womans. Mans magics no can do that." She folded her arms across her chest again. "So, Masonja come, too, yes?"

The two wizards exchanged glances. "I'm not sure the grey mushrooms would think of that possibility, but why take the chance," Eilo said. Then turning to Masonja, he conceded, "You have a point, Little Begta, and one we hadn't considered until now."

"All right," Qwasigara grumbled. He hated sassy Begta—especially sassy Begta females, but he also agreed with Eilo; the woman had a point. "You will come with us—now get out of here."

WHEN THE WOMEN WERE settled Qwasigara directed the two kashallans, their faces already painted with magical glyphs similar to his own and Wizard Eilo's, to take places across the circle from each other by the East and West fires. Qwasigara took a pouch of red colored sand and a small cone funnel from his bundle and began drawing a protective circle just inside the diamond of fires. While he was creating the outer ring Eilo proceeded to trace another circle, around the women. He decorated his circle and Qwasigara's with magical glyphs in black white and green.

Each wizard sang a deep-throated chant as they worked, Tesulu and Ikuwi accompanying the chant with their hand drums. As they chanted a glowing orb of protection formed around the participants as the wizards invoked the powers of the Unseen Ones to be with them and protect all within—and the warriors standing guard without their magical working.

Confined within the men's magic, Masonja sang her woman's songs and painted her own powerful runes in red powder mixed with blood upon Marti and Chelka's exposed bellies.

The magical orb complete, Qwasigara's song changed as he crouched and activated the ownership sigils Drucas had carved into the women's foreheads. When he finished the sigils glowed like an angry red beacon, even through their protective shield. If anyone had taken over the changeling's ownership of the women, the Ghostlander would now know someone was magically tampering with the bond—and come to investigate.

As Qwasigara worked Eilo sang, and then the warriors took up his song as those within the circle allowed their trance to deepen, leaving their physical bodies sitting upon the sand. Forming spears of etheric light the kashallans, their symbiont bondmates coiled like silver ropes around their chests, followed as the wizards led the way into the Dream. Together they would wait in concealment near the tempting women for someone to come.

They didn't have to wait long before a small figure surrounded by a shield of light appeared through the etheric mists. Holding out a crystal that glowed red with the same sigil as the women wore, the Ghostlander swept past the hidden threat, seemingly too anxious to secure its valuable prize to notice their waiting trap.

Stepping forward before the wizards could stop him, Nathan-Corha growled, <<Come to claim the changeling's property, Bacach?>>

The Ghostlander halted, turning to face this new threat.

Coming to stand by his relative, Phillip-Yoey bowed. <<Good Evening. I believe you may be our true adversary come at last. Can I assume you are the now deceased Barak's successor? What shall I call you, Wizard?>>

The Ghostland wizard was a slim greyish-skinned person with an oversized bald head. It had lots of wrinkles on its brow and around its sunken grey eyes. The nose and mouth were small and seem more humanoid and pinched together, unlike the jutting nose and jaw of most Timornans the Speir'dina had met. But like all other Timornans it had a four-fingered hand and was clothed in a caftan-type robe similar to those worn by the gaishinay.

For just a moment the hunters caught the taste of surprise in the creature's Psy, quickly masked by an air of arrogance and contempt. It would seem the Cabal underestimated the Alliance's knowledge of how costly the battle at Red Rock had been for those in the North.

<<You may call me Master, Khutani slave, for soon enough you and your kind will be dead or in our slave pens, as will all those in the South.>> Focusing his glare on Qwasigara and Eilo, he added, <<As will all those in the West who have forsaken the Ancient Covenant, and now oppose us.>>

Nathan-Corha let out a dry laugh. <<Master? I think not. The lands of our Alliance may be a more difficult mouthful for you to swallow than you suspect, Ghostlander Puke.>>

The wizard glanced at the circle of protection Qwasigara, Eilo and Masonja had formed around Chelka and Marti and its aura radiated with contempt. <<If all you have to defend your people are savages and Begta, Khutani slaves, then I am safe in Tiebarai. You may call me Your Eminence, until I have you groveling at my feet, if Master isn't to your liking.>>

Phillip smiled showing lots of pointy Khutani teeth. Ooh, he could play this game with the best of them. Hadn't he been such an arrogant prick himself before Timorna had shown him the error of his ways?

Hoping to anger the creature into revealing more information or making a mistake, Phillip let out a condescending laugh. He looked down his patrician nose at the smaller wizard, and said in his most irritating tone of voice, <<Eminence? That's a lofty title for such a little grey mushroom of a man.>>

The kashallans had recently become aware of this derogatory term the Clans used among themselves when referring to the Ghostlanders. For that reason he had deliberately used it hoping to anger his opponent.

Evidently the shot hit its mark. Red waves of anger rippled off the wizard's projected image. Dropping his shield, Cohbruel flung bolts of etheric fire into their collective shield in the next moment. <<How dare you!>> the wizard roared its wrath echoing through the Dream. <<I am The

Exalted Cohbruel. I head our Cabal now. As you have guessed that old fool Barak is dead—as is your pet demon.

<<I care nothing for your puny magic nor for the big worms in their puddles. No one can stop us! We will have what belongs to us—the Real People at last will triumph over all you alien invaders and your minions!>>

As the Ghostlander's Psy attack dissipated, Eilo muttered, <<I don't know if you are incredibly brave or very stupid, Khutani.>>

Qwasigara laughed. <<Maybe both, Brother.>>

Eilo chuckled. <<As are we; because we agreed to this crazy plan. But even working together we won't be able to withstand many more onslaughts like that one. The treacherous mushroom has the power of the entire Cabal behind it. >>

Grinning at each other, the circle braced for another attack, but it never came. As they felt Cohbruel gather himself for another blast a glowing snaky body encompassed them. Qwaltamis's sleek grey head lifted, its cold yellow eyes meeting those of the Ghostlander. <<You should have more respect for the 'big worms' in our puddles, Little Wizard.

<<Just like your dead changeling, your power over the brave females who have given us their loyalty is ended. It is time for you to leave.>>

Giving the unsuspecting Ghostlander no time to prepare Qwaltamis spat etheric black fire into the wizard's unguarded face. Cohbruel screamed, his image in the Dream exploding in a ball of flame. When all that was left was the stink of burnt ozone, the Maker uncoiled itself from around them, leaving a loop around kashallan-Nathan's torso. For just a moment the kashallan leaned, his head against that comforting bulk, Corha's tentacles brushing lightly over its parent's glowing hide. So many questions but this wasn't the time to ask them.

Qwaltamis gave him an affectionate squeeze but kept its yellow eyes focused on the two Western Wizards still in the link with its child.

<<Is the foul creature dead?>> Qwasigara finally asked.

The Maker rumbled a laugh. <<Probably not. He has stolen a great well of power from the others in the Cabal, but I did weaken him considerably. He will be hurting for some time to come.>>

<<That's a relief at least,>> Eilo said.

<<Don't become over confident,>>Qwaltamis warned them sternly. <<While that one has been weakened another may kill him and assume the leadership of the Cabal and pursue Barak's plan.>>

Phillip turned to the western wizards. <<After Barak's death, Wizard Qwasigara, you told me you could think of a couple Ghostlanders that could take over their Cabal. Was this Cohbruel one of them?>>

Qwasigara glanced at his fellow wizard for his thoughts, then he shook his head. <<No, he is unknown to us.>>

<<Hmm,>> Qwaltamis rumbled. <<I think we must keep alert as we continue on to Fa'Hanzoi. The Cabal isn't done surprising us, I fear.>> Looking both wizards in the eye, the Maker said, <<I must leave you soon. Do you understand the patterns of compulsion the Changeling has marked onto the women's flesh?>>

The Red Wind Wizard hesitated, then admitted, <<I have seen them before.>> Qwasigara nodded his agreement as well.

The Maker rumbled a laugh. <<And used them on occasion, too, I'll wager. My question is: Can you remove the spell's power? Do I need to help you?>>

Eilo's aura blazed with indignation. <<No, you do not, Khutani. We will manage just fine without you.>>

Still rumbling its amusement, it added, <<Yes, I'm sure you will.>>

<<But if the Changelings power is too deeply embedded in their spirits, we may not be able to rid them of his torments completely without killing them, Khutani. You must know that as well. Do you seek to blame us if the women die?>>

Serious once more, Qwaltamis said, <<No, that's not my intent at all. The Speir'dina woman is a warrior. As my child's chosen mate I have tasted her many times and I sense even now she fights for her sanity and release from the changeling's implanted magic—just as the Warlinga woman does. I think you may find it easier to rid them of the foul conjuring than with others of your experience.>>

Releasing the kashallan Qwaltamis brushed a tentacle over symbiont and host, and said to them privately, <<Summon me back if there is need, but I believe your new allies are quite capable of the working.>>

Chapter Ten

In the healing that followed their victory over the Ghostlander they weren't able to completely erase Chelka and Marti's glyph, but at Nathan's suggestion Qwasigara changed Marti's to an ancient Caldoni rune of power and protection.

Nathan traced the rune in the sand. "Is that your personal sigil of ownership, Khutani?" Eilo asked as Qwasigara drew the rune in blood to cover the changeling's mark upon Marti's forehead.

For just a moment Nathan's eyes flashed with anger, then he quieted. Based on Timorna's customs, the wizard had asked a reasonable question. "No. The rune is a sigil of protection my ancestors used. I remember seeing it painted on a few things handed down the ages in my family."

Eilo nodded. "It is a wise choice then." He let his hand hover above the mark in the sand. "I can feel its power."

Finished with Marti, Qwasigara blotted a stream of blood sliding down her face and asked, "Shall I invoke its magic for the Warlinga as well?"

"No." Aju'an said, coming over to stand by them. He took Nathan's stick and drew a mark in the sand. "This is our family glyph. You can use this to disrupt the changeling's magic. Even when she marries she will still be claimed by Meh'gach. As her twin I will always be there to protect her if I am needed."

Qwasigara nodded and began his chant of power over Chelka as he carved the Meh'gach glyph into her flesh.

Finished at last and all traces of the Changeling's magic banished, the wizards sang the songs their people used to honor the Unseen Ones and bid them farewell, as they opened the circle and released the power.

Phillip-Yoey knelt by Chelka and taking her wrist sent a restorative through the link to wake her. Aju'an crouched at her other side, so she could see him as she joined them. "Since her Tobrach couldn't be here I want her to see me when she wakes," He explained to Kashallan-Phillip.

"Yes," Phillip-Yoey agreed. "She may be disorientated at first and seeing family will help bring her back."

Sitting down beside Marti, Nathan-Corha gathered her into his arms and formed the link. It wasn't long before she opened her eyes. When Marti saw him she burst into tears, clinging to him sobbing.

Nathan held her tightly, tears streaming unheeded down his own face."Shhh, Mo Hara, don't cry. It's all over now. You are free. The Ghostlanders can't invade your dreams and force you to do anything—ever. The changelings' foul magic is gone now—and can't come back."

After a while she sniffed and looked up at him, wanting to believe him, but afraid to trust in his assurances. "How—?"

He cut her words off with a kiss. When he released her, Nathan said, "Qwasigara took away the magic in his compulsion by changing Drucas's glyph." He showed her the mark he'd drawn in the sand. "The wizard drew this in its place. Do you recognize the old Caldoni rune?"

She studied the symbol for a long moment, then said, "Maybe—sort of—I've seen it before back home on Caldon, but not sure what it means."

He chuckled. "Dunnagh can tell you more when we go back south, if you're interested. What I know is that it was used by our ancestors as a protection against evil magic. The wizards agreed with me that it's a good choice." Nathan hugged her close again Corha speaking for the first time, "Our Amla agrees with the wizards. The changeling's magic is gone.So don't cry, and don't be afraid. We love you and will keep you safe."

Against Nathan's chest Marti murmured, "Thank you, Corha. I'll try."

The sky was paling with the light of a new day when the exhausted Alliance members made their slow way down the game trail back to the main encampment.

HATING THAT HE STILL needed a wooden crutch to get around, but determined to walk home rather than being carried like some of the badly wounded, Tobrach hobbled back and forth in front of the med tent growling to himself and glaring murderously at anyone who dared pause to stare at his pitiful efforts.

Though he hated the thought that he wouldn't be there when the Alliance pressed on to Fa'Hanzoi, and eventually to Tiebarai, he recognized the wisdom that the war council made by appointing him and Chelka to head up the convoy of injured and those needed to care for them heading south soon.

"You and the other wounded will be a liability when we go North," Hunt Leader Tizu told him bluntly.

"Better you go now before the rains and the Sorins cut you off and you have to pass the Storm Season at the destroyed Te'gal or be caught in the open between here and Tragar," Aju'an added.

He didn't like it but saw the sense in the plan. He would be a liability in his present state, so there was no point in arguing about it. And at least Chelka would be coming with him.

Chelka had told him that Nathan wanted Marti to go with them, too, but she refused flat out to consider it.

KNOWING THE PARTY HEADING South would be leaving in the morning, Phillip-Yoey was placing the last jars of medical supplies in one of the packs for their trip when another rumble of thunder echoing off the surrounding ridges caught his attention. More rain was coming. He hoped they could make the long journey back to Tragar safely.

The tent fabric snapped in a random gust of wind, and on a side wall water pinged into a bucket set to catch a small leak. Outside he could hear Aju'an barking orders to a work crew tying down their supplies with heavy tarps for protection before the rain came in earnest again.

He shivered in a cold draft from the open tent flap. The rainy season had arrived in these northern lands at last, breaking the intense desert heat. What was coming was just another violent rain storm, but soon enough the rain would dry up and the winds would shift direction and blow straight down from the poisoned land of the nuclear-destroyed northern continent. When that happened, they would need to be safely underground while these poisonous Sorin Storms held sway or they risked terrible illness, mutation or death.

Walking over to the entrance, Masonja peered out into the gloom then pressed the flaps together to lock them close as the first pelting down poor of rain hit the camp. Coming slowly back to the stove where Kashallan-Phillip now sat cross legged, a cup of sourwood tea in hand, she poured herself a cup and sat down in front of him. "Storm bad," she said and took a sip of her tea.

Phillip nodded. "I'm glad the civilians and the wounded are leaving tomorrow, weather permitting." They drank their tea in silence for a time, listening to the storm. Only a few of the injured still remained on the cots arranged around the center area near the stove, and most were asleep or resting quietly.

<<Masonja seems troubled about something, Kasha,>> Yoey said when the silence between them had dragged o n to the point of being uncomfortable.

<<Yes, I sense that, too. I wonder what's wrong.>> finishing his tea he rose and poured himself a refill from the kettle. Then noticing it was nearly empty, he refilled the kettle with more water from ajar resting on the ground near the stove, added a few twigs to the brew, then took his place again facing her.

"It's quiet enough in here for the moment, but I suspect we will have some cold and wet company joining us soon. So, My Dear, why don't you tell me what's on your mind."

She had been staring at the ground, a clawed finger tracing tiny circles in the dirt, but at his words she looked up. Her golden eyes met his, yet still she remained silent.

"What is it? I know you are troubled; please tell me," he said, his voice barely heard over the raging storm.

Taking a deep breath she finally said, "Masonja don't know what to do. Sorins come and no Maker and no Masonja in Swamp to keep Begta safe with magics. Umwira mans have bad, bad magics, Masonja no want leave Phillip-Yoey. Begta need Masonja, but Kashallan need Masonja, too."

Phillip sat back stunned. She was right, of course, and he should have thought of this before she reluctantly brought it to his attention. She did need to go back to the Great Swamp before the Sorins locked everyone underground.

He had only a vague idea where his Amla Maker Tinguss was, or its eldest child Ro for that matter. With things so unsettled in the North they weren't at home in the Great Swamp—and probably wouldn't be during this Sorin Season with the Allies pushing forward into Fa'Hanzoi and maybe Tiebarai before the Blue Snows fell and cleansed the land once more of its new carpet of poisons.

Phillip-Yoey took one of her hands and squeezed it tight. "Of course you must go, and the Begta hunters like Dado should go with you as well, to see you get home safely."

She snorted at his suggestion that she needed the hunters to protect her, but nodded her agreement. "Begta no want go Ghostland town. Begta afraid. No want be slave to bad Umwira wizards. Happy go with Masonja."

Feeling his eyes moist with unshed tears, he slipped his tentacles under her skin and made the link. "I understand their fear and they are right to want to go home."

Love and sadness as well as other unnamed emotions were suddenly flooding his awareness, Phillip swallowed hard before he could continue. "I was just a lost and frightened man when I came to your village. You helped me so much and I will be forever grateful to you and your mentor for showing me the way and helping me find my Yoey and my true calling," Phillip told her. "We will miss you, but don't be sad. It is the right thing for you to do."

She studied him with her knowing yellow eyes. "What kashallan do if Masonja go? Yoey young no have big magics. Maybe Masonja stay."

Phillip shook his head and leaned forward to plant a light kiss on her forehead. "No, My Dear, you need to go. I know in the past you have always been there to guide and protect me, but you need to leave. I will have to rely on my Western Clan relatives to advise and guard me when we go further north."

When she still seemed dubious he laughed. "I know Qwasigara can be a bit crabby at times, but I am a relative now, and he takes kinship obligations seriously. I'm sure I can count on him if I need to. So don't worry, My Dear, truly. I will be fine. And I will see you when I come back to the Swamp when the Blue Snows have come and gone. So keep everyone safe for me."

Masonja might have argued more but the tent flaps were pulled apart vigorously at that moment as Nathan-Corha and several other soaking wet figures hurried inside and quickly resealed the flaps behind them.

"Hope you two got something hot in that kettle," Medic Ruan called out as he shook the water off his poncho and hung it on a tent pole by the entrance.

"It's probably only sourwood tea so don't get too excited," Nathan grumped.

Ruan laughed as he headed for the stove "I happen to like the brew."

Nathan made a face but took the cup Crowis offered him nonetheless.

"How bad is it out there?" Kashallan-Phillip asked as he rose to check on a patient.

"Bad enough," Nathan said. "Hopefully our guys can get started south tomorrow, because this far north the Sorins come on earlier and harder than they do in the Yeyen or the Swamp."

"Then we need to get moving, too," Ruan said as he brushed his damp curly hair off his face. "Or at least we should move people and supplies out of this low area by the water. The river out there is rising."

"Yeah, Ogwy, and I think Goro have already suggested that to the Hunt Leader," Nathan said. "I saw some of our guys moving supplies further up the slope earlier this afternoon."

"No worry," Masonja said. "Rain go away tonight. Sun come back for trip tomorrow." The people standing or sitting by the stove nodded, accepting her prediction without question. "Masonja keep everybody safe."

Crowis, with his cup halfway to his mouth, stared. "Masonja, are you going back to Tragar with the injured?"

"Not Tragar," she corrected. "Begta and Masonja go Great Swamp. Begta need Masonja's magics. Masonja keep Begta safe during Sorins."

Nathan nodded. "That's probably a good idea. I heard from my parent that the Makers have Tinguss off babysitting—whatever that means—I didn't ask. But with Phillip-Yoey going north with the rest of us I'm sure the Maker will be joining us at some point."

He sipped his tea, made a face, then changing the subject he turned to Crowis. "You could probably go with them, too, Crowis. They could use an extra medic, most like. You've done well here, so I'm sure your sister won't mind if we send you back to Tragar for the Storm Season."

For just a moment a spark of excitement glowed in Crowis's eyes, then he shook his head in negation. "Thank you for your kind words, Kashallan-Nathan." He dropped his eyes and took a deep breath. "I'll stay with my Teh'lach."

Ruan chuckled, and stood to add more water to the pot on the stove. "He doesn't want to take you up on your offer, Nathan, because he would miss talking to Nurse Kitha, right Brat?" Overhearing Ruan, the cousins and Athala joined him in his mirth.

"No! That's not why—well maybe it's part of the reason—sort of," Crowis protested, making his Teh'lach brothers laugh all the harder. Desperately he glanced at Phillip-Yoey pleading for help.

Phillip hid his own smile behind his cup rim. He was sure that underneath all that brown fur the young man was blushing furiously with embarrassment. Everyone had noticed how he followed Kitha around whenever he could, and had started to tease him about it.

"Oh leave him alone, all of you. He's my best student and he fancies continuing his studies while he can."

Phillip saw the look of silent gratitude in the Avairei's eye. There was another cause behind why Crowis couldn't go back to Tragar, but for whatever reason Tess-weh must have warned him to keep silent about his becoming her Cha'Han. Crowis could no longer head south till she released him, than Nathan could have fought the Umwira in their last battle.

AS MASONJA HAD PREDICTED, the next day broke clear and sunny, a whisper of a breeze blowing up the narrow valley from the south to welcome the travelers on their way. Nathan walked up the slope away from the army's camp to where Aju'an stood watching the retreating column, now not much more than a dark blur strung out along the swollen river.

Aju'an was aware of his presence, but continued to stare down the valley. When the column passed from view around a bend in the river he finally spoke, "I sent his bones with Chelka. With no heir—the family will want them—in case I—"

"Varrod's death was a great loss not only to your family, but to all of us, but you're gonna make it back, Aju'an," Nathan said, trying to comfort him. "I feel it."

Aju'an turned to him, his head crest raised. "Have you had a sending, Holy One?"

Did he know that Aju'an would survive and return to his wife, father and his clan, or was he saying that just to reassure a hurting friend? Nathan shrugged. "Sort of," he hedged.

Aju'an accepted his assurance without comment. At last he said, "It will be different when I get home, however. Without Chelka to frustrate everyone with her woman warrior's antics and Varrod calling me out with word and tail slaps when my smart mouth might get me into trouble—it won't be the same at all."

No it wouldn't, Nathan thought, suddenly missing Dunnagh intensely. It wouldn't be the same for any of them.

Both men fell silent after that lost in their own thoughts. Leaving Aju'an alone to his grieving a while later, at Corha's urging Nathan patted Aju'an's shoulder and headed back to camp. As the symbiont reminded him they had work to do. There were still patients to check on and medical supplies to make and pack.

Nearing the outskirts of their camp, a man carrying on his shoulder a heavy basket of fuel for the nightly fires stepped out from the thorn brush and stood waiting for him. He was one of the new Ghostlanders that had joined the Alliance after Te'gal was destroyed. Tall and muscular with whip scars crisscrossing his chest, he looked vaguely familiar, but Nathan couldn't place him.

Nathan stopped a few paces in front of him. "What can I do for you—sorry, I don't remember your name."

Setting down his basket, the man straightened and faced him boldly. "My name is Nieshu." He took a deep breath and then blurted, "I wasn't born in a crèche or always a slave, Exalted. I want to learn how to fight and join one of your warbands."

Nathan resisted the urge to let his mouth drop open in surprise. Instead he motioned for Nieshu to pick up his basket and then fell into step with him as they continued back to camp while he considered the proposition. "You say you weren't always a slave what do you mean by that—what were you then?"

"Not all slaves are born and bred in a crèche, Exalted. My family are trades people. The men make some of the finest glassware in Tiebarai and our women make fine beaded and embroidered kaftans for some of the Ruling Families."

Shocked Nathan stopped abruptly, causing Nieshu to come back. "Wait a moment," Nathan said. "if that's true, what by all the Gods were you doing at a place like Te'gal digging masa root;?"

Unable to keep the bitterness out of his voice, Nieshu snarled, "Because my older brother is a fool!"

Reaching out a hand Nathan took Nieshu's and inserted his tentacles. The man flinched then steadied. "Go on; tell me more."

Nieshulooked down at the kashallan's tentacles in his flesh, took a deep breath and continued, "My father and older brother made several powerful enemies in the Cabal when they backed the wrong political faction. In order to save my favored brother's life, instead of letting the fool pay for his stupidity my, oh so noble father, forfeited my sister and I in exchange.

"We were given as slaves to a wizard benefactor in Barak's Cabal. My sister went to one of the city's pleasure houses. And me," he snorted a laugh. "Not having the 'right' temperament to be used as a servant among the elite, even though I can read, I was sent to Te'gal to work in the fields."

<<He is telling us the truth,>> Corha said. <<He hates his family and the Cabal for what they did to his sister—and to him.>>

"You can read the Northern glyphs, eh?"

Nieshu nodded. "I can read, yes, though my knowledge of the glyphs is of a more practical nature like shipping manifests and other documents dealing with trade. I don't know much about poetry and literature."

"The army doesn't have much use for poetry at the moment, so not to worry about that. Have you traveled much on your family's business?"

Nieshu dropped his eyes and scuffed a dirty foot in the dirt. Remembering earlier warnings Nathan made to them about lying, he said, "I traveled some with older siblings on family business trips between Tiebarai and Fa'Hanzoi, but I was still too young to make any trips on my own before I became a slave."

He would definitely have to talk to Tizu—and maybe his Amla bout this one, Nathan decided. Recognizing that whatever Nieshu's personal motivations, the man might have valuable information to give Command as they traveled further into the Ghostlands. Coming from an upper tier family in Tiebarai Nieshu would have a different perspective on affairs in the North than they might get from the gaishinay. If the man could be trusted, Nathan would like to keep him close as an adviser both to himself and Command.

"Are there others among those who joined the Alliance that like you might be interested in learning to fight?" Nathan asked as he retracted his tentacles from the man's arm.

Nieshu thought about it for a moment then said, "Maybe. We have talked amongst ourselves, but I don't know how serious the others are about wanting to learn."

Resuming his walk back to camp Nathan said, "I will speak to the Hunt Leader on your behalf. If he agrees we will find someone to begin your training, and anyone else who wants to join the warriors."

Nieshu smiled showing lots of teeth. "Thank you, Exalted. I will tell them."

"Mm, my name is Nathan, or if you like Kashallan-Nathan. There's no need to call me Exalted, all right? You and anyone else who is interested, come find me tomorrow evening after the meal and I will have an answer for you," he said as he stopped by the Med Tent.

Nieshu bobbed his head, still smiling. "Nieshu," Nathan called as he walked away. "Tell them too, that signing up for weapons training doesn't mean anybody gets out of doing other work assignments. Weapons training will be in addition—got that?"

"I understand, Kashallan- Nathan," Nieshu said and quickened his pace into the center of the encampment.

Part Three
Chapter One

Cursing its bad luck and the incompetence of underlings, the Ghostland wizard Zuhan huddled in the tiny cave among the boulders further up the narrow river valley from their destroyed base. Ze was now waiting for the changeling and the few others who escaped the enemy's attack on their real base to come back from their scouting mission and report.

Zuhan had lost zer's precious eye shields, and might have died during the escape, but fortunately for the wizard Drucas's Second had found zer soon after the Khutani's slaves attacked. Sanglaz and another of Drucas's men, knowing that their own survival might depend on zer's magic they quickly gathered up the wizard and a few supplies and escaped the carnage by fleeing back down the trail towards Fa'Hanzoi.

Then, thinking they were safe at last, the warband with the wizard in tow had come out of hiding only to be discovered and attacked by their own crazed monsters also fleeing the Khutani's hunters. They had lost about half their remaining warriors before the crazed beasts had been driven off.

Leaderless and hungry for blood, the remnants of the Great Avenger's horde was heading towards Fa'Hanzoi. They dared not follow too closely in the monsters' wake. Yet they couldn't delay too long or the Khutani's hunters might find them with equally disastrous consequences. And for that reason ze had sent the sniveling changeling scum to gather other stragglers and spy on the enemy's movements. But that had been quite some time ago, the wizard fumed. What was keeping them?

The sun had disappeared behind the purple ridges to the west when Zuhan heard their return. Peering out the cave mouth in the pink light of afternoon Zuhan saw Sanglaz and three of his men dragging a couple slaves with rope tethers around their necks heading up the slope. With relief ze noticed the slaves were carrying gathering baskets. Food had been scarce in the past few days. Hopefully something edible was in those baskets.

Stepping out of the cave Zuhan waited, impatient to hear their report. Coming up to zer, Sanglaz pushed one of the slaves to his knees at the wizard's feet, then put clawed fist to his chest in salute. "We caught these two sneaking away from the Enemy's camp. This one saw us but did not run. I'm thinking the Puke is sorry it joined the enemy army. Maybe wonders how he can serve the Cabal before I kill him."

With a hard slap of his tail to the man's shoulders the slave fell forward with face in the dirt. "Isn't that so, Cowardly Scum? Truly you are loyal to the Cabal and you beg the Exalted's pardon, Yes?"

"Y-yes-ss," the slave stammered. "I had no choice the Khutani made me swear—I didn't want to—" the slave broke off as another slap of Sanglaz's tail sent him sprawling.

Zuhan held up a hand before the changeling could do more damage. "Don't lie to me, Slave, if you want to live. How could a Khutani make you swear to them? There are no deep pools near here to contain a creature as large as one of those foul aliens."

"Don't need deep water, Exalted, two of the new aliens have Khutani nesting in their bodies."

Startled Zuhan looked up and met Sanglaz's eye. Did the Cabal know about this—and if Cohbruel did, why didn't the arrogant scum tell them before sending them with the horde? Sanglaz met the wizard's look and nodded. "It is possible," he confirmed. "The Alliance had a kashallan with them when they took Riath.

"Whether they are from a mutant strain from the West, or a new alien species as some claim, the Khutani it would seem have found a species that can host their foul symbiont children. It is entirely possible that one or more are with this army."

That might explain a lot, Zuhan thought, trying to control his mounting anger and frustration. Too bad Drucas or this one hadn't thought to warn them of the possible danger, before they had sent the Great Avenger with the warriors to attack the enemy camp.

Taking a deep breath to center, ze focused his attention more carefully on the kneeling slave. Using his magical sight, Zuhan became aware of the slave's tiny muscle spasms and the tremors he was trying hard to conceal. A cruel smile touched the corners of zer's thin lips.

The creature was going through the first stages of crivo withdrawal. The slave was hurting and ze could help him—if the slave had the information they needed to gather before heading straight for Tiebarai. Because after the major disaster that had just cost them much of the Ghostland army, they would need something with which to bargain for their lives. Ze was sure of that.

Making zer voice a soothing, hypnotic murmur, ze said, "Are you in pain, slave? Have your new masters been limiting your dose of crivo?" The slave's head shot up and Zuhan saw the pleading in his eyes.

"They have no crivo or malloneen. The Khutani say it is bad and we must stop using it."

"Poor creature, no crivo at all? What do they expect you to do when the craving is bad like now?" Zuhan asked, suddenly curious.

The slave shrugged. "If it gets bad one of the kashallans will put his tentacles in us and the Khutani will make the hunger go away—for a while."

Zuhan saw the slave shiver and zer smiled widened. "But you don't like the Khutani touching you, do you? So you wait until the hunger is bad—very bad—like now, hmm?"

"Yes-s, Exalted." Eyes pleading the man stammered, "Please, Exalted, will you help me?"

"Perhaps." Zuhan stepped back into the small cave. "Come in here so we can be more comfortable and we will talk about it. If you please me with your answers I may help you."

"NATHAN, WAIT UP A MOMENT," Phillip-Yoey called when he saw the other kashallan cutting through a row of tents nearby. Nathan paused and waited for him to catch up.

The evening meal was over the sun having gone down behind the western mountains some time ago. Everyone was busy with last minute chores before settling in for another restless night. Noticing the frown on Phillip's dark face as he came up to him, he asked, "Something wrong? You look worried."

Phillip chuckled. "I'm that obvious, am I?"

"What's going on?"

Phillip nodded. "Yes, I am worried. The cousins have been talking to me, but I've heard fragments of the talk elsewhere—warriors shutting up when they see me—but it seems like a sizeable number of the men, Clan and Warlinga alike, want to go home before the Sorins lock us underground for the Storm Season."

"Yeah, I've heard the talk, too, and so has the Hunt Leader."

"Nathan, they can't do that," Phillip blurted. "I don't like the idea of staying in the Ghostlands any better than the men, but we can't go back until this is settled. It would be a disaster—"

"I know," Nathan said, cutting him off. "I'm just on my way to the meeting Tizu has called to talk with the rest of command about this very problem. He probably sent Chang to find you, so come with me now if you want.You can tel—" Nathan broke off staring at something—or someone over Phillip's shoulder.

Phillip turned and saw one of their new Ghostland recruits, standing with eyes cast down waiting for them to finish talking.

"What is it, Chadaz? Is your craving getting bad? You haven't come to me in a while. I think it should be about time for me to help you."

The man shook his head without looking up. "Not bad yet, Exalted. I am getting stronger—don't need so much help now." The man hesitated, then said, "But my companion Danik is bad sick and one of the gaishinay is asking for help, too. Gaishinay with hurt eye say come find kashallan." He glanced up briefly, then hastily dropped his gaze again. "You come, yes?"

Nathan muttered a curse and sighed. A note of frustration coloring his voice, he grumped, "You guys have got to stop waiting until the craving is so bad. I've told you no one is going to hurt you. You need to come to us with your problem sooner." Never taking his gaze from the ground, the man nodded and waited.

Phillip laughed and put a hand on Nathan's shoulder. "Go on, find out what Tizu wants; I'll see to this one's friend and stop by the gaishinay's tent after that."

Nathan nodded, and still muttering under his breath stalked off. When he disappeared around a large tent, Phillip-Yoey turned to the man next to him. "All right, Chadaz, is it? Let's find your friend."

"Yes, Exalted, I am Chadaz. Come, I will take you to Danik."

"I know it isn't a Ghostland custom, but just my name, Phillip-Yoey will do," the kashallan said as he fell into step with the man.

Startled Chadaz glanced up, then quickly dropped his gaze. "Yes, Exalted." Phillip sighed.

To his surprise instead of heading to the Teh'lach encampment to which most of the new members of the Alliance had been assigned, Chadaz headed up the slope out of camp. Not far away from the light and fires Phillip-Yoey stopped, suddenly wary of going any farther with this man. "Chadaz, I thought you said your friend and one of the gaishinay were sick with the crivo hunger? I assumed they were both nearby. Where are you taking me?"

The mauve sky overhead was deepening to a purple the shadows of the thorn bush around them dark and menacing in the advancing night. "Not far," Chadaz said. "We were gathering fuel for the evening's fires when he got bad sick—couldn't walk—cramps so bad. Gaishinay see me when I go for help. She say come too. Danik not far, please come."

<<Kasha, I don't like this,>> Yoey said. <<I know he has given the Alliance his oath, but we don't really know this man.>>

<<You're right, Shalla. Let's put him in the link and see what is really going on here.>>

Looking around with all senses alert, he said, "Chadaz, if your friend Danik was so sick why didn't you carry him back to camp to get help?"

Chadaz shrugged. "Please, you come help, yes?"

"No," the kashallan said and snatched up the man's arm and jammed in his tentacles to form the link. "It would be dangerous to leave a sick friend out here alone, so why did you do that? What are you really up to?"

<<Kasha he tastes—>>

Then everything happened at once. Phillip was distracted by a loud groan from behind a nearby thorn bush. He turned in that direction, and then a dark cloth was flung over his face. He opened his mouth to call out an alarm, and then he was falling, sinking into blackness.

As consciousness left him, he heard a strange voice say, "Quickly now, tie him up and gag him before the Khutani wakes. Get the slave to carry him. We need to get away from here before he is missed."

Chapter Two

When Nathan arrived at the central fire pit, the camp's leaders were already there and waiting for him. To his surprise present was not only Command, but representatives from each of the Teh'lachs. Muttering an apology to the group around the fire he took a place between Ross and Chang.

As Nathan settled Chang murmured, "Where is Phillip-Yoey?"

"He'll be along," Nathan said. "A couple of our new recruits needed help with their crivo problem. We got stopped on our way here." Chang nodded then both men focused their attention on the space by the fire as Qwasigara finished his opening prayers and the Hunt Leader rose and took up the speaker's carved bone that the wizard handed him.

"I called everyone here tonight, because I'm aware of the gossip going around camp," Tizu began. "I know that many are talking about deserting the Alliance—and a few already have left. It's time to speak about your concerns and discuss them out in the open."

There were a lot of whispered conversations from the men standing in the shadows, but nobody ventured forward to take the speaker's bone. Tizu waited, slapping the bone lightly against his palm as he surveyed them.

Sighing, he finally continued, "Granted, we have had a bad time of it. Everyone has dead to morn. The victories we have achieved have come at a great loss to all our peoples, Warlinga, Clan Warriors, even the Speir'dina all have suffered.

Standing, a Warlinga said as he waved away the offered bone, "You have said it yourself, Honored Hunt leader. We have won great victories over our Enemy. Why not go home now. Surely they are defeated."

Head crest flattened Warega took the bone from Tizu and faced the assembly. "That's what K'San Tobrach's noble uncle thought, too and look where it's got us," Warega growled. "I was with the noble K'San when he took his hunting packs into the Ghostlands a generation ago. We achieved great victories over the Enemy—like now, but we never went far enough. We never cleaned out the underground nests of the vermin. And so they have always come back to raid our lands, kill our people and steel our children."

Warega handed the bone back to Tizu and took his place next to Aju'an in the circle. Tizu considered the bone in his hand gathering his thoughts before speaking again. At last he said, "Yes we have won two great victories. The Ghostland wizards are hurting. They have lost many of their monster-bred warriors and it will probably take years for them to fully recover and threaten us so forcefully again.

Tizu glared, his voice hardening as he continued, "But they will threaten us again—all of us. And the next time they come for us, they will come to kill and destroy everything in our lands and anyone they believe could possibly oppose them in future. There will be no mercy granted, no escape from that reckoning, believe me –no escape for any of us."

Stepping forward Lubwey took the bone Tizu offered him. "We can't afford to be complacent now. This war isn't over yet. We can't just leave and go home to sing our victory songs and think the threat is past. They will come for us again as my Teh'lach brother says. This is our fight, not our children's. We must finish this and protect their futures."

"Our families' future is it, Blue Stone Man? I say there will be no future for them if we don't go home to hunt and care for them during the coming storm Season," a Red Wind warrior shouted angrily. "If we stay in the Ghostlands when we go back there may be no one left alive to welcome us or sing our praise songs. Only corpses may be there to greet us if we don't go now."

Taking up the bone Ogwy stood and faced Tizu. "You speak of the Ghostlanders needing time to recover, Hunt Leader. I say we need that time, too. I say we go home for the Sorins then take up the war path again in the next Sun Season—or the one after that. When we are strong again."

"And give them a chance to prepare for us? Leaving this unresolved will give everybody time to recoup and regroup. And I don't want to keep doing this year after year. We need to finish this now," Nathan said.

"Even if that means going underground and making a base for ourselves in one of these northern towns, we need to finish this –once and for all.

Because nobody will be safe on this world until the Cabal in Tiebarai is dealt with."

Qwasigara had been silent during the meeting so far. He rose, stepped to the fire and took the bone Nathan handed him. As a wizard of great power and the eldest among them the private arguments and murmured conversations going on in the shadows quieted as the Elder took the bone.

Before he began, he raked them with hard black gaze. "The Khutani is right; we must finish this. The Storm Season is when the Cabal are the most powerful. Think on that, Lazy Begta. Did they leave us alone last year, hmm? Even with their warbands crippled they still have great power. Will our families be safe even if we go back to them? They name us traitors. Are you so stupid to think they won't come back to finish what they started. Have you forgotten Red Rock so soon?"

Touching the Sand Mountain glyph on his face with his free hand, he said, "Sand Mountain will go north to fight the Enemy. We must all trust that those back home who agreed to care for our families will keep their word and do so—"

"I will not sneak away in the dark like a coward. I will keep faith with my kinsmen and the Alliance as my Elder has said," Tesulu cried, jumping to his feet. He gave Ogwy a scornful glare. "I too, have a new wife waiting for me across the Shallow Sea."

Before Ogwy could rise to that challenge, Qwasigara growled something and made a cutting gesture with his hand and Tesulu hastily sat down again.

Into the silence that followed, Nathan said, "Elder, if you think your people would accept Khutani help, I could ask Phillip-Yoey to see if some of his pod, who now have kinship ties to the West, could be sent to the People to assist them in preparing for the Storm Season while the warriors are away. They could help fill the nets of sea hunters if they would be willing to accept Khutani aid."

"That is an interesting proposition, Khutani," Eilo said. "We shall have to think about it and get back to you or Phillip-Yoey. So far when Qwasigara and I have used our gifts to check on the people in the West all has been well."

Goro let out a rasping laugh. "And perhaps when we take Fa'Hanzoi we can send them even more good things," he said.

"Speaking of Phillip-Yoey, Nathan," Chang murmured. "Shouldn't he be here by now; where is he?"

Nathan glanced around the council circle but saw no kashallan. Where was he indeed? "Not sure what's keeping him."

"Do you want me to go look for him? This council may drag on for a while yet. Where was he going; do you know?"

"When I was on my way here one of the new guys, Chadaz by name, stopped me while I was talking to Phillip. He said his friend Danik was bad sick with the crivo hunger and so was one of the gaishinay. He said that Cochinna told him to go find one of us to help them out. Phillip said he'd do it and then come along to the council. But that was a while ago; I don't know what could be keeping him."

"I'll check with Cochinna and let you know what's up," Chang said as he rose and slipped away into the night.

Watching Chang leave Ross turned and asked, "Trouble?"

"Not sure. Phillip-Yoey said he was coming; Chang went to see what's keeping him."

SENSES ALERT, CHANG headed for the gaishinay's area. As he drew near, the sounds of laughter and someone playing a musical instrument drifted out to greet him. Remaining in the shadows he watched the people gathered round the fire.

Jojo was there, of course, as were most of the gaishinay and some of the armachda who weren't on duty. In a nest of pillows Cochinna sat with the musical instrument cradled in her lap. Everyone seemed relaxed as if they were having a good time.

But there was no Phillip-Yoey. Well maybe he finished here and had gone back to the Med Tent. His co-husband didn't care much for meetings—especially of a military nature, Chang knew. He would check there next.

Easing further into the shadows before someone noticed him Chang went to the Med Tent. Chang's lips curved into a smile. His co-husband was probably sitting by the stove, a cup of sourwood tea in hand. In full instructor mode he was most likely engrossed with another lesson in Timornan medicine for the medics and forgot all about Tizu's meeting.

Brushing aside a tent flap Chang stepped inside the tent and looked around. The stove radiated an inviting warmth, a lantern giving off a welcoming green light hung from the ridge pole, but aside from a sleeping Warlinga on one of the cots the tent was empty. Starting to get really worried now, Chang swore, spun round, and nearly ran into Timma and Crowis just coming through the door flap.

Crowis gasped and stepped back wide eyed. "Brother-in-law you scared me."

Timma met his mentor's eye calmly, but Chang could tell he was troubled about something. "We saw someone opening the tent flap and hoped it was Phillip-Yoey. Have you seen him, mentor? Is he up by the council fire?"

"No, he is not. When did you see him last?"

The two Avairei glanced at one another, then Timma said, "It was still light, after the meal I guess, I wasn't really paying attention." He glanced at Crowis, inviting his comment.

"I saw him talking to Kashallan-Nathan and one of the new Ghostlanders—I don't know his name, earlier, before the big council." He shrugged. "That's the last time I saw him."

"We were just out looking for him," Timma added. "We were supposed to have a lesson tonight, and he was going to make some more yellow kavay for me. I'm always running low."

Chang swore a vile Caldoni oath and pushed past the young men and ran back into the night, Timma and Crowis hurrying to catch up.

At the gaishinay fire Chang was greeted with welcoming shouts that quickly died when they saw the grim expression on his face. Crouching beside Cochinna, he said in a low voice, "Honored Sa, did you send one of the Ghostlanders to look for a kashallan, because one of your gaishinay was sick tonight with the crivo hunger?"

Studying his face with her one good eye, she shook her head. "No, Warrior, I did not."

"No one among us is sick with the hunger," Janixa confirmed.

Chang stood up and faced the people by the fire. "Has anybody seen Kashallan-Phillip this evening—or a man called Chadaz?" a chorus of no's and headshakes answered his question.

Swearing under his breath as a knot of fear tightened even more in his gut Chang glared at the off-duty armachda, and spat out, "We got trouble—big trouble. Kashallan-Phillip is missing. Lann Gheal, pair off and start a search for Phillip-Yoey and that damned Ghostlander. Boughthy, you and Owyn there go alert the sentries. We may have intruders in camp. Everybody keep sharp and call out at the first sign of trouble." Leaving the Avairei behind, Chang raced back to the council fire.

Hurrying to Nathan's side, he opened his mouth to tell him what he suspected, but Tizu had seen him come back and recognized the grim expression on his armachd's face.

Holding up a hand to stop the argument in progress between two Clan warriors, he demanded, "What's wrong, Armachd? Report."

Chang automatically saluted and said, "Phillip-Yoey is missing. Nobody has seen him since just before this council began. I've started a search for him and the Ghostland recruit he was last seen with. So far we can't find either of them."

Chang's news created an uproar, with everyone shouting out questions and reaching for their weapons. During the turmoil Qwasigara sat as rigid as a statue, his expression grim, but inside he was boiling with rage. Why hadn't he foreseen this possibility?

The demon had warned him to take care of his kinsman—was the Khutani really stolen out from under their noses—how? And if so, was the Ghostlander that powerful, or had they grown too lazy and complacent since their last victory?

Eilo put a hand on his shoulder returning his attention to the council where Hunt Leader Tizu was balling orders and a certain amount of order had been restored. Patrols of warriors were being dispatched to various parts of the encampment to search, see who was missing, and look for signs of intruders.

<<I have sent my spirit searching for the Khutani,>> Eilo said into his mind. <<I can find no trace of him nearby.>> he motioned with his lips to

the Sand Mountain sigil on Qwasigara's face. <<As a kinsman your bond with him is stronger than mine. Can you sense him?>>

Qwasigara shook his head. <<No, I cannot and that troubles me. He is lost within some foul conjuring.>>

"Then one of the Cabal wizards must be near—the filthy mushroom," Eilo spat. He might have said more but at that point a Speir'dina named Rhys stepped into the firelight and saluted the Hunt Leader.

Folding his arms across his chest, Tizu growled, "Well?"

"As best we can tell so far, Hunt Leader, three people are missing: Phillip-Yoey, a new recruit name of Chadaz and another man named Danik. Nathan took us to where he'd left Phillip-Yoey with Chadaz. The tracks were too jumbled to follow him while in camp, but I may have found the place where they went into the thorn bush."

"Can you follow their trail, Armachd?"

Rhys mopped his brow with his sleeve and refused to meet the Hunt Leader's eye. "I'm not sure, Sir. I can feel it—sort of—but it's like trying to catch a fish in muddy water. I touch it, try to grasp it, and then in the next moment it slips away again. What I do know is thatseveral people were waiting for them in the thorn bush, but some kind of Psy is blocking me, Sir, from knowing who or how many. I'm sorry. Maybe Nathan-Corha can tell us more—" Rhys broke off and turned around, his mouth falling open when he didn't see Nathan behind him.

"Yeah, where is the crazy amadan."

"He was right behind me when we got here—"

"Great, that's just fuckin' great," Tizu growled. "Now we have two missing shit for brains kashallans! And where's that damned Tess-weh, anyway. I thought she was supposed to be protecting them! Rhys pick a patrol and—"

Putting a hand on Qwasigara's shoulder, Eilo said as he rose, "I know you want to go on this hunt, but it's best you stay and search within the Dream. I am younger and can endure the chase more easily. I will do this for you, Brother. I will take Tesulu, the Speir'dina and that stubborn young Blue Stone man with the powerful gift. Together we will break through the Ghostlander's illusions and find him."

Tizu broke off what he was saying when he saw the Red Wind wizard stand. "Hunt Leader, I will head up this patrol, if you agree," Eilo said. "We suspect a powerful Ghostland wizard is behind this abduction and your warrior's failure. I will take your Speir'dina tracker, but let me also choose some clan men with magics to go with me on this hunt."

Chapter Three

His thoughts in turmoil, Nathan followed Rhys and the others back to the edge of the council fire, then slipped back into the shadows. That treacherous Ghostlander! He wasn't going to let him get away with this. He would find him and give him the most painful death he could imagine. Pain, oh yes, he would teach him the true meaning of pain!

Snagging a lantern from an unoccupied tent, Nathan retraced his steps to the faint trail Rhys had found leading back into the thorn. Kneeling down, he placed his hands on the dry ground, Corha extending its tentacles reaching for the faintest trace of Phillip-Yoey's passage.

He was in danger of losing another he had grown to care for. Nathan found it hard to concentrate and allow Corha's Khutani senses to dominate their shared awareness his emotions were in such a maelstrom. Finally heeding Corha's mounting frustration, Nathan closed his eyes and took several deep breaths, searching for calm.

Sometime later Corha finally said, <<I can taste him, Kasha, but his flavor is very faint and mixed in with many others.>>

<<Can you taste him well enough to follow, Shalla?>>

<<I can try,>> the symbiont said hesitantly.

<<Good let's go then. They already have a big head start,>> Nathan urged, and without waiting for his bondmate to answer he headed off into the brush.

<<But shouldn't we wait for the warriors?>> Corha said.

<<I'm sure a patrol will follow us soon enough,>> Nathan said. <<You don't want those damned Umwira Pukes to get away with taking our Amsi do You, Shalla? We need to find him and teach them a lesson, right?>>

<<Yes, but it's dark now and—>>

"You should listen to your bondmate, My Jewel, the thorn is a dangerous place at night for one alone—especially a kashallan alone."

Startled, Nathan's head jerked up from the faint sign he had stopped to examine more closely by lantern light. Seeing Tess-weh with Atahru by her side standing in front of him he straightened and faced her. Not this time, he thought. He wasn't going to be put off by her "protect kashallans" bullshit. And where was she when Phillip-Yoey was taken, anyway? Damn her! Finding a convenient target for his pent up rage at last, he snarled, "Where is he, Demon?"

She chuckled and folded her arms across her breast. Only her mocking eyes showed above her veils. "Well on his way to Tiebarai by now, I suspect. If the wizard who took him doesn't kill him with his arrogance or neglect on the way, he will make it there in reasonably good condition."

"You bitch," the kashallan snarled and lunged for her throat. "You knew this was going to happen!"

With a flick of her power she froze him in place, his body rigid as stone from the neck down. "Yes, I saw the possibility in your future."

Feeling like he was going to explode Nathan strained against his confinement, even though the sane part of his mind knew it was futile. "Then why didn't you stop it, treacherous bitch?"

"Because I couldn't

"Couldn't? Or wouldn't> You swore an oath to protect us is this how you keep your word? I should—"

"Want to spit black kavay in my face, Khutani Slime? If you try, I will gag you as well," she warned.

When he quieted, she continued, "And don't tell me how to fulfil my contract with you, Khutani Slimeworm," she snarled, her eyes flashing dangerously. "Would you rather it had been you the changelings and their wizard took instead? Both of you together, unguarded—so very tempting, it could have been you, not Phillip who walked into their trap. Think on that, My Treasure, when next you want to scold me for how I keep my contract. How would you have liked that, I wonder? With your anger and your warrior's arrogance, would you have survived the journey?"

And with his capture the Enemy would have also gained access to at least one star weapon. That was a sobering thought and one he hadn't considered until she brought it to his attention. If Tizu hadn't called the damned meeting—if he had decided to go with Chadaz...

Phillip-Yoey—Amsi...

Hating the tears threatening to unman him he choked out, "Why?" He swallowed hard but no more words could get past the lump clogging his throat. Instead he stared, the pleading for an answer plain in his eyes.

Removing the veil that covered the lower half of her face, she came close and allowed him to see the ugly, puckered skin and burn scars that now covered much of her face.

Nathan's jaw dropped in surprise. He had heard from Phillip-Yoey that she had almost died in a battle with the Cabal of Ghostland Wizards somewhere across the Shallow Sea, but since her return with the clan warriors he had rarely seen her and never had he seen her unveiled. The beautiful woman Tessa that he had fallen in love with during their capture and enslavement at Sulas Keep was gone.

Reaching out a hand she caressed his cheek, her eyes suddenly soft, and this time it was the human woman Tessa who spoke. "Take a good look at me, my Heart and then maybe you will understand—and maybe one day forgive. My human body isn't strong enough to channel all the power needed to protect everyone and destroy all our enemies.

"My bondmate saw that in our future there would come a time when I would have to make a choice. We have only enough power left for one more battle before our time is ended, and we are no more."

Leaning forward Tessa cupped his face between her hands and kissed him tenderly full on the mouth, then drew back to study his face once more. Her voice sad with regret, she said, "I chose you, My Love, and the Alliance. I'm sorry about Phillip, but if he heeds the advice we gave him he will survive his ordeal and you will find him again in Tiebarai."

Unable to keep the note of bitterness out of his voice, he said, "Yeah, tortured and half-dead, like I found Dunnagh-Tani?"

Tess-weh jerked back as if he had slapped her. "Careful how you speak to my H'an, Ungrateful Slimeworm! We have told you that if he is clever and remembers what I've told him you will see him again. Don't pressure me further on the matter," the demon screeched.

"What we do to protect Speir'dina and this precious Alliance of yours will kill my H'an and some of your slimy relatives, too, so don't criticize me for what I do. Sacrifice! We all must make sacrifice if your people are to survive on this world."

Turning her back on him she motioned imperiously at her slave. "Atahru, pick him up and carry him back to camp. Put him on a cot in the med tent and then return to me.'"

"I can walk myself if you release me, damn it," Nathan grumped. He knew he had pushed her—maybe too far and now was paying for it.

"I think not, My Jewel. You need a little lesson in gratitude and humility."

Still as stiff as a board, the Wa'chassey'ul effortlessly picked him up and started back to camp.

"So when are you going to let me loose?" he shouted back to her.

Her mouth twitched in a smile. "When I think you have learned your lesson, and won't put yourself in danger again."

"All right, all right, you've made your point. I've learned my lesson; I'll behave. Ouch! Atahru she didn't say bring me back to camp all bloody. Watch where you are going!"

Nearly back to the Med Tent they were spotted, and the cry rang out that at least one of the missing kashallans had been found. Someone ran to tell Tizu and the wizard. Those who weren't out searching, stood around gaping at the spectacle he made, being carried like a big piece of firewood over Atahru's shoulder.

Raising his head Nathan glowered. "Don't you people have anything better to do? I'm back. Go on, get out of here!"

Murda laughed. "Guess you were a bad boy, Nathan-Corha, running off like that. Did Tess-weh spank your bottom for you, too."

"Laugh while you can, Amadan," Nathan grumbled. "I'll laugh later when you're doing double duty digging privy holes from here to Fa'Hanzoi."

That brought another chorus of laughter from the onlookers. And damn it all, here came Jojo sticking his pocket recorder in his face and asking how it felt to be ensnared in a demon's magic?

"Are you in pain? Can you feel anything? How long are you going to be like that?" Jojo burbled, keeping pace with the silent Atahru and holding the recorder up to Nathan's face. "Any comments for the folks back in the Yeyen?"

In the Med Tent, Atahru laid him on a cot by the fire and stood for a long moment gazing down at him. Noticing that a worried Marti had come up to stand on the other side of his cot the Demon said, using Atahru's voice, "I give him into your care now. Take care of him for me, Speir'dina. Keep him safe as best you can." Acting through her slave, Tess-weh touched his cheek one last time. "Good bye, My Jewel."

"Wait! Aren't you going to let me up now?"

The demon laughed. "Later."

When Atahru was gone Marti grinned and sat down beside him. "Is your cock as stiff as the rest of you?"

"Oh shit don't you start too," Nathan grumped.

Marti laughed and laid a blanket over him. "That was pretty stupid of you to go running off like that, you big amadan."

"Yes I guess it was," he admitted."I wasn't thinking clearly. I was too worried about Phillip-Yoey. Have they sent out a patrol to find him yet?"

"Yeah, Wizard Eilo is leading it. He took Rhys, Sietriga, Tesulu and a few others that have good Psy with him. The Elders say a powerful Ghostland wizard took Kashallan-Phillip/"

"Yeah, that's pretty much what Tess-weh told me, before she got mad. But I doubt if they have much luck"

"Has Tess-weh gone to bring him back then?? Tizu asked. "Crazy demon, I thought she was with us to keep things like this from happening." Unnoticed, Tizu and Qwasigara had come up to his cot and heard the last of his conversation with Marti.

"Yeah, that's what I thought too," Nathan said. "She said something about having to make choices, but I couldn't make sense of most of it."

"Well we'll just have to ask her when she comes back with Phillip."

"Excuse me, Kashallan-Nathan, Wizard, Hunt Leader," someone said and cleared his throat.

Tizu turned and saw Crowis standing behind him with gaze cast down, his hands nervously crumpling the folds in his stained kilt. "What?"

Crowis swallowed hard and then said, his voice barely above a whisper, "You can't ask her, because she isn't coming back, Hunt Leader."

"Hey Brat, come away and let the grownups talk," Medic Ruan called from across the tent. "I still need you to read and sort these jars for me."

Crowis glanced over his shoulder and turned to go back to his task, but Tizu stopped him. "You're Phillip-Yoey's brother-in-law, right?" when Crowis nodded, he said, "How do you know that? Did Kashallan-Phillip tell you something about her plans?"

Tess-weh not coming back! Was she going to leave him like this—forever? By all the gods of Caldon and Timorna was she really that mad at him? Was he going to have to be carried on a stretcher all the way to Tiebarai just so she could make sure he wouldn't do something stupid again?

<<Don't be silly, Kasha, she wouldn't do that,>> Yoey said. <<Tess-weh loves us. We will probably be soft by morning.>>

<<Love, eh? She has a damned funny way of showing it,>> Nathan grumped.

"N-no, Hunt Leader, Phillip-Yoey didn't tell me anything—he doesn't know, I think."

"Who told you she was leaving then?"

Lifting his head and staring them straight in the eye, Crowis said, "Tess-weh told me herself, Hunt Leader."

"And why would she do that, Priest?" Qwasigara growled. "Speak true or you will suffer for it."

Crowis took a deep breath and bowed to the wizard. "I am speaking true, Elder. She told me, because back at Tragar I swore an oath to serve her, when she has need of me. She left Ata Doyan at the keep because I am her Cha'Han now."

"What! Why didn't you tell somebody?" Nathan said."

Crowis shrugged. "She didn't want me to tell anyone, but Phillip-Yoey knew—or guessed—and maybe Moraga knows, too." He shrugged again.

"Exactly what did she tell you, then?" Qwasigara said, his expression thoughtful. Recalling what the demon had told him herself, he believed the young man.

"Not much, Elder. She just said she was leaving to prepare for a great battle. And when it was time she would call upon me to serve her one last time. When I performed that service for her then she would free me."

Chapter Four

In the paling light of a new day, the kashallan was unceremoniously dumped off his captor's shoulders to fall in a heap onto the stony ground. Hurting everywhere and trying to catch his breath around the gag still clogging his mouth, he warily glanced around.

Over the sheltering boulders behind which he now lay the day was dawning with its usual rosy glow, but to the north-west black clouds were massing jagged green lightning, a warning sign of the storm's growing fury. The storm was a bad one, he recognized the signs, but thankfully not heading their way.

Kashallan-Phillip had been awake for some time as they traveled through the darkness. Flung over a man's muscular shoulders, he'd been painfully aware of their progress, blood trickling from countless small cuts made by thorns as they pushed their way through the worst of the snarl. Unable to protect Yoey from the weight of his human body pressing down on the symbiont's coils, he'd experienced the full force of his bondmate's agony along with his own as the thorn scored his flesh.

Pulling himself up to a sitting position at last he surveyed his captors for the first time. Five or six Changelings and Ghostland officers were building a small fire and doing other camp chores. Looking past them, he saw a small slim creature dressed in a dirty kaftan sitting cross legged in the sand near the fire. Ah, a wizard, and probably a powerful one, he thought. That would explain how they had managed to capture him so easily. The wizard must have taken over the mind and body of the one called Chadaz and sent him back into the Alliance camp to cause whatever mischief possible before being discovered and killed.

And it was just his bad luck that he happened to run afoul of the creature. Finding the two kashallans talking together unguarded must have seemed an irresistible prize. And with that realization he couldn't suppress a shudder the

Enemy could have dealt the Alliance a terrible blow if both he and Nathan had been captured or killed.

The work the recruits from Te'gal offered the Alliance was sorely needed after the losses they'd suffered, with so many gone the Ghostland recruits were needed to carry heavy supplies and help set up camp, but maybe it hadn't been such a good idea to allow the former enemy to join them—especially with their crivo addictions to complicate matters.

Crivo addictions... Two of the freed Ghostlander slaves they'd brought with them from Te'gal sprawled on the ground next to him. The one called Chadaz, the one who'd been carrying him and another. He guessed that one was his friend Danik, no doubt. Whether they had betrayed the Alliance willingly or had been forced to when they were captured he didn't know at this point. What he did know, however was that both were in almost as bad of shape as he was himself right now.

Easing his protesting body closer to the one called Chadaz he reached out with his bound wrists and tried to insert his tentacles into the man's arm to check on him.

"He betrayed you, you know," a cool voice said from over his shoulder. 'Why would you want to help him? Or do you plan to kill him, if I let you, Slimeworm."

Phillip-Yoey sat up and eased himself around to face this new threat. He'd become aware some time ago that there was a magical aspect to his gag and bindings, otherwise he could have released himself during the night and escaped. <<Was he a willing participant or did you merely take advantage of his vulnerability, I wonder?>>

The wizard chuckled. "Does it matter? The result is still the same."

<<It matters to me.>>

The wizard shook his head and clicked his tongue in a dismissive manner. "Such a sentimental creature I wouldn't have expected such a merciful nature from one such as you, Khutani—or is it your new host that has the tender forgiving sensibilities."

The kashallan remained silent studying his adversary with care.

At last goaded into more talk by his relentless stare, the wizard folded his slim arms across his narrow chest and looked down his nose at his disheveled captive.

"Answer one question for me; I am curious. I see the clan markings on your cheek and shoulder. Are you indeed a product of one of the Western Wizard's breeding programs as Barak always claimed, or are you another foul alien species the more moderate among us say the slimeworms have lured to our world to host their symbionts?"

<<What do you think, Wizard?>>

"I think that whatever the truth is, the result is unnatural, loathsome and disgusting. You condemn us for enslaving our semi-intelligent masses, but are you any better, Khutani? Isn't this creature which contains you within his flesh your slave? Doesn't he do whatever you and the Makers want him to do?"

The kashallan gurgled a laugh around his gag. <<Not always,>> Yoey chortled. <<My Kasha can be most stubborn at times like the rest of his kin.>>

<<You probably won't understand this,>> Phillip said, speaking for himself. <<It's not like it was before the plague. The kashallan bond—at least with me and my kin, is a partnership between equals. Symbiont and host, we each have our own special gifts we bring to the union. We work together to fulfil the charge we were given at our making."

The wizard snorted. "Your charge, it is to destroy us, yes?"

<<No, it is not. Our charge as a kashallan is to work towards the healing of this wounded world that calls herself Timorna.>>

"Pretty words, but history doesn't agree with you." The wizard hissed his eyes flashing with pure hate. "You want to destroy us. You always have and it is no different now."

<<The Maker who is our parent didn't agree with that long ago decision. I was created to try and heal that old wound as best I can.>>

"Enough of your jabber—all lies—I will hear no more of it." Whirling suddenly around he nearly bumped into one of the changelings waiting for him to finish. "Well," Zuhan snarled. "What do you want?"

"W-we have prepared you a meal, Exalted Wizard Zuhan," the changeling stammered. "K'San Sanglaz wants to know if you would eat now?"

Without answering Zuhan stalked away and resumed his place by the fire, taking up the bowl he was offered.

The kashallan watched the men eat. None of the men by the tiny fire offered him or the exhausted slaves any food or drink. When the day grew hotter, Yoey said, <<The food they were eating didn't look very appetizing, so I'm not sorry to skip it, but we are getting very thirsty. I wish we had some of that water.>>

<<I'm sure by now our people know we are missing. With our wizards and armachd Rhys searching for us we will be rescued soon, so don't give up hope, Shalla. Truly we will be all right,>> Phillip soothed, trying to cheer himself up as well.

As the sun grew higher in the sky, Phillip took note of the fact that the wizard had no eye shield. He had torn a piece of cloth from his robe and had wrapped it around his eyes to protect them from the glare. That was probably why they were staying hidden in the rocks instead of moving on, because surely the enemy knew they were being followed.

Maybe he could use his adversary's near blindness to his advantage if a future opportunity arose. Unfortunately the changelings didn't suffer from such a malady, as Yoey pointed out to him. So the wizard's blindness might not matter.

<<Though the wizard and the changelings might not know that the Speir'dina have night scopes so the darkness won't hide them from our hunters,>> Yoey added hopefully.

In late afternoon the men made preparations for the night's trek, grabbing a hasty meal before leaving. Deciding to risk it, Phillip said, <<Are you going to give me some of that food and water I see your men have and let me fix my injuries or do you plan just to bring a corpse back with you to Tiebarai—for that's where we are going, isn't it?>>

Coming to stand over him again the wizard studied him carefully for a long moment before answering. "Ye-ess," ze said slowly. "We are going to Tiebarai, but whether you come with us as corpse or a living creature is up to you—in part."

Phillip's eyebrows rose at that remark. <<Oh? Well I have no plans to spit black kavay in your face at the moment if that's what you are worried about if you ungag me. You have my word on that.>>

He let out a mental chuckle. <<What would be the point? The changeling who is in charge over there would kill me for my effort in the next moment, so I see no advantage to the kill—at present.>>

"Ah, but can I really trust you, Khutani? It was not so in the past."

<<I have given you my word.>>

"Your word. The word of a Khutani how trustworthy is that I wonder?"

<<As trustworthy as a creature who feeds innocent children poisons that enslave their minds and bodies for the sake of their own selfish hunger for power, Wizard Puke? We must both have a matter of trust here, otherwise kill me now and be done with it.>> Yoey snarled.

<<Yoey, please,>> Phillip cautioned his bondmate privately. <<I know we are hurting right now and you are frightened—I am too, but there's no point in provoking him. Calm yourself, Shalla, please.>>

The wizard considered him for a long moment, then directed one of his warriors to remove his gag and give him and the two slaves food and water. "You are right, bringing you back to the Cabal alive would be my preference, but if you try to escape, I will kill you."

When he had eaten and drunk all the water they would allow him, Phillip held out his bound wrists. "Will you untie my hands so I can put yellow kavay on my wounds?"

The wizard thought about it for a while, then nodded his agreement. "Untie him," ze told one of the changelings as ze stepped back to a safe distance. "I am curious.""

When he was untied and feeling had come back into his hands and feet, the kashallan held up a hand and spat a yellow glob into his palm and plastered the goo on every wound he could reach. Unable to curb his natural tendency to teach, Phillip said, "When the kavay dries, in a few moments, it will help heal the wound and act as a protection from further injury or infection."

"Hmm, and can it do other things, too?"

"Not the yellow kavay, but I can make other kavays that will perform other healing tasks," he explained. Glancing at the two slaves being driven to their feet with curses and slaps of the changelings' tails the kashallan asked, "May I be allowed to help them, too? I'm sure it will be a long night for them and they will need to be fit, or one or both of us may be walking the rest of the way to Tiebarai."

"Ye-ess, you have a point. See to them, but be quick about it. We need to get moving."

Speaking softly to the slaves, Phillip-Yoey did what he could for them. It wasn't much he knew. His own reserves were very low from rough treatment and lack of food and water, but he did what he could and they seemed grateful for his efforts.

When it was time for him to be tied up again, he hopped onto Chadaz's back and wrapped his legs around the man's middle. "Tie my hands and feet around him if you're worried about me running," he told the warrior. "If Chadaz has to carry me over his shoulders it will be uncomfortable for both of us and slow you down. This way is better."

The warrior glanced at the wizard and when the Ghostlander gave his consent he proceeded to tie his hands and feet around the man.

Chapter Five

In the growing twilight they slipped out of the rocks, and headed North through a maze of dry canyons and rocky hillsides covered here and there with twisted thickets of sourwood and purple thorn.

It was rough ground—Phillip's abused body could attest to that. Up ahead riding piggyback on Danik's back, the wizard used his night vision and magical light to lead the way. In the rear, one of the changelings with a thorn broom brushed out any physical signs of their passage. The wizard was taking no chances, also surrounding the fugitives with a magical shield, which he could see if he allowed Yoey's senses to dominate their shared awareness.

When Phillip felt all hope of escape threatening to desert him, Yoey reminded him that their magical imprint would remain for a time on the back trail—even if the physical sign was erased, but the symbiont agreed it would be that much harder for the Alliance hunters to follow. Both bondmates hoped that one of the Clan wizards was with them.

<<Shielding us, guiding, it must be taking a lot of the Puke's magical energy to do all that,>> Yoey mused a while later. <<I wonder how long ze can keep it up before ze collapses?>>

<<Now that is truly a comforting thought and one to look forward to, Shalla,>> Phillip said with a mental chuckle.

Leaning his head against Chadaz's back, the kashallan closed his eyes and tried to nap. He would need to conserve his strength and be ready to take advantage of any opportunity when it came.

"THIS IS WHERE I LOST the trail, Elder," Rhys said as he squatted just past a scuffed patch within the thorn.

Eilo crouched and put his hand to the ground and allowed his magic to flow into the soil. The rest of the patrol drew close to hear. After a while he released his magic and smiled at the armachd. "The Ghostland puke that took the Khutani is a clever and powerful wizard—more than the others the Cabal sent with the Hoard. You did well, Speir'dina, to find this at all."

Rhys blushed "Thank you, Elder. Can you discover more from this disturbed ground than I could; will we be able to follow their trail?"

A muscular man with tips of grey starting to show in his fur around nose and mouth, and vigor in his step in spite of advancing years, Eilo was considered by his peers to be a "young elder." That meant, in practical terms, that he had things to learn, but could also keep up with warriors half his age for a task like their present one.

Eilo rubbed his jaw and considered the problem. "I can, with a little help from you and the stubborn one over there." Eilo pointed with his lips to Ikuwi watching them his expression apprehensive.

Rhys turned and studied the warrior as well. Puzzled he turned back to the wizard, and asked, "I'm not sure what you mean, Elder."

"He means he wants us to share our power with him, so his magic will be strong enough to find all the mushroom's traps and break through his illusions," Ikuwi said answering for the Elder.

Eilo scowled at the cheeky young man then nodded. "You have explained it quite well, warrior. Do you agree?"

Ikuwi dropped his eyes and nodded. "I let a Khutani Maker share my mind and body, how could I do any less for one of the People?"

"This time I won't need such a deep sharing. I will only want to draw upon your power if I have need. Do you agree?"

Ikuwi let out a long relieved sigh. "Yes, Elder it will be as you say/"

Eilo next turned to Rhys awaiting his answer. "And you, Speir'dina?"

Rhys shrugged. "I want to help, but my people don't usually make such a deep sharing. I don't know how it is done." Rhys took a deep breath before continuing. "And to be honest I'm a little bit frightened by such a communion," he admitted.

"As well you should be. To entrust yourself into the hands of the wrong person might mean enslavement or death." Eilo allowed himself to study this alien man carefully with his magic for a long moment. Finally he said, "You have a powerful gift, Speir'dina warrior. But what you have learned to use from your kin among the stars is only a small portion of what you could do.

"You and this stubborn one," he smiled at Ikuwi, showing his canines. "You both have strong gifts. If you let me teach you, become my apprentices for a time, you could be great among your peoples."

Rhys's mouth dropped open in surprise. Eilo waited, still smiling. Finally he said, "I shall have to think about your offer, Elder. That is an interesting possibility I might consider, once this war with the Ghostlanders is over—and we both survive."

"You speak true, Warrior, if we survive." Then hoping to sweeten the deal even further the wizard added, "And we will find you a pretty sweet-tempered Red Wind girl for you to marry as well."

Sietriga and the other Clan warriors gathered around them smiled, making some suggestive comments. Rhys blushed a deep shade of pink and cleared his throat. "Thank you; that too is a generous offer which I will have to think about—later. But for right now should we stick to the important matter here—finding Phillip-Yoey and the rest of our missing people? How can I share with you my magic, as untrained as I am?"

"I will begin by using Ikuwi; he already will know how to open himself to me and aid me," Eilo said. "Watch us with your magical sight as best you can. When he tires I will come to you for assistance, yes?"

Rhys took another deep breath and nodded. "Yes, all right.'

HOLDING OUT ANOTHER bone charm to warn against magical traps, Eilo and his hunters kept up a steady pace throughout the rest of the night. The wizard had been right, Rhys thought. The Ghostlander must know what a prize he had when he captured Phillip-Yoey. It didn't take a genius to figure out that they were heading back to Tiebarai, and the mushroom was doing all in its power to hinder their pursuit.

Time and again they had to stop and retrace their steps. Once they were led into a small box canyon where rocks along the canyon's rim were set to fall on the unsuspecting traveler if the magical wards were triggered.

When the trap was pointed out to him by the wizard Rhys was grateful the Red Wind Elder was with them. Even if he had sensed it with his sight he might not have discovered the trap in time.

True to his word, Eilo told them to watch with their gifts and took the time to explain to the young men what he was doing as he triggered the Ghostland magic from a safe distance so it wouldn't hurt an unsuspecting animal or hunter in future passing that way.

Most of the time the Ghostlander's tricks weren't so elaborate. Small illusions meant to slow them down, but even the warriors were able to recognize most of them by using their own war magics.

After a series of such petty illusions, Rhys commented, "These last tricks feel—different from the earlier obstacles we've encountered."

"They are," Eilo agreed. ""One or more of the changeling pukes travelling with the wizard created them."

"Does that mean he is tiring, Elder?" Ikuwi asked hopefully.

Eilo smiled. "Yes, that is exactly what it means. Well done, Students."

"Then if we keep going we may catch up to them soon," Tesulu said.

"Hopefully that is true, Warrior, but keep alert. Even though the Ghostlander is tiring, the mushroom may still have a few tricks to surprise us with when we come closer."

THE ALLIANCE CAMP SPENT a restless night, everyone on edge and worried about their missing people. Hunt Leader Tizu had everyone up soon after dawn and packing up camp. Grim-faced he strode into the med tent to check on his remaining kashallan. To his relief, Nathan was sitting by the stove and puking up kavay into an impatient Timma's medicine jars.

Finishing the last of the yellow kavay containers, Nathan-Corha handed the jar to Timma and looked up as Tizu stopped in front of him. "Any news from the search party?" Nathan asked.

Tizu shook his head. "Qwasigara says they found the trail and are following, but the Ghostlanders are setting traps and playing games with them, so it's a slow business. He says Eilo is hopeful though."

Nathan grunted and got to his feet. "What do you want me to do? Ruan says we are moving camp."

"Yeah, we are. I had planned to move us further north anyway—no point in staying here any longer. The hunters will have a shorter distance to go to find us if we keep moving. It's obvious the fugitives are going north—though I doubt they will risk Fa'Hanzoi. The new recruits they captured would have told them we were planning on taking it. They will probably skip it and head straight to Tiebarai."

"Yeah, that's what I'd do in their place," Nathan said. "Who knows what we will find when we get to Fa'Hanzoi, with the last of those crazed monsters getting there before us. The wizard leading them probably wouldn't want to take a chance on that. So what do you want me to do?"

"Right now I need you to take charge of Medical." When Nathan opened his mouth to argue, Tizu snapped, "I know you don't want to, but with Phillip-Yoey gone, you have to. Timma and Williams can help you, so you won't need to do it all."

Tizu grinned. "It will keep you out of trouble, maybe, and since there's no one else to make kavay medicines you are gonna be spending a lot of time in the med tent anyway, so you might as well take charge."

Focusing his eyes on Nathan's middle he said, "Am I right, Corha? Can you keep your big amadan of a bondmate in line and doing the job I need done?"

Corha laughed. "I will try, Hunt Leader. And you are right, we will need to make lots more kavay with my Amsi gone."

ON THE MORNING OF THEIR third day of travel the fugitives were forced to take cover quickly when a scout Sanglaz had sent to check behind them came hurrying back to them with the news that several of the crazed monsters from the defeated Hoard were on their trail.

"Do you think they are looking for direction and wanting to join us?" Zuhan asked as he slid down off the slave's back.

"No, Exalted, Ram says they are hungry and on the hunt for meat," Sanglaz said.

"They probably have picked up a blood trail. I warned you to let me put kavay on Chadaz and Danik's open wounds," Phillip interjected. "I'm sure if I can smell the blood so can those creatures. What an irony if you were killed and eaten by your own creations gone rogue."

With a curse, Sanglaz slapped the still bound kashallan sitting on a nearby rock hard with his tail, causing him to fall heavily on his side. "Keep silent, Khutani Slimeworm, or I will feed you to them and be done with it."

Phillip slowly sat up, making several efforts with his bound hands to right himself before he accomplished his goal. "If you do that, however, your reception when you get to Tiebarai may be far more unpleasant than you are hoping for."

The Changeling stood over him with teeth bared, barely able to contain his fury. "What do you care, you will be dead?"

Phillip shrugged. "I don't care, actually; I'm a dead man whatever happens. Painful but quick death by the teeth and claws of some of your creatures will probably be a kinder death in the end than what the Cabal may have in store for me once we reach Tiebarai."

"Shut up, the pair of you," Zuhan snarled. "I can't think with all your noise!" the wizard sank wearily onto a nearby boulder and rubbed a hand across his face. At last without looking at either man he said in a tired voice, "K'San Sanglaz remove the ropes from around his hands. The shackles on his feet can stay. He has a point—damn him."

"I can't make medicines without food and water. You will have to feed me first," Yoey bargained.

"Do as he says," Zuhan said and closed his eyes.

Muttering under his breath, the changeling directed one of his men to fill up their water containers at the creek they had passed not long before.

"How far behind us are they?" Zuhan asked without opening his eyes.

"About three sun-marks, Exalted."

"I need to eat a little and rest for a time, then I will use my power to deal with them."

"I will have one of my men bring you and the Khutani some food, Sanglaz said as he glared at the kashallan.

Taking the food offered him, Zuhan bit off a portion of the tasteless dry meat and chewed. Swallowing, he asked," What of the Alliance hunters, are they still following?"

Still smiling at the kashallan, the changeling said, "If they are, they are at least a day or two behind us. My men and I detect no sign of them. Maybe the Hoard have taken care of that problem for us."

<<Do you think that's true, Kasha?>> a worried Yoey asked.

<<I doubt it, Shalla. Qwasigara or the Red Wind wizard—or maybe both of them—are with the hunters coming for us,>> Phillip assured his bondmate. <<If the changeling's men can't find them that just means they are hidden under a powerful illusion. That's all.>>

Chapter Six

As another day dawned, Rhys could see how the land they were travelling through was changing. The narrow maze of canyons and hillsides of thorn thickets and boulders was opening out into a flat barren plateau dotted here and there with deep gullies, high mesas and eroded rock formations. To the north and west another range of purple mountains lay, a grim barrier on the horizon.

Pausing at a high point in the trail, Rhys asked, "how far is Fa'Hanzoi or Tiebarai from here?"

Coming to stand beside him Eilo surveyed the country ahead of them stroking his chin. "I have not travelled to either place, but what I know from our warriors' accounts Fa'Hanzoi will be somewhere to the south and west at the mouth of an inlet of the Shallow Sea. There is a well-marked trail at the edge of the desert that we can follow when we get near."

"Mm, I'm glad to hear we won't need to cross that desert. Finding and carrying enough water for all our people might present a real problem."

Eilo snorted a laugh. "At this time of the year we will face the opposite problem. Like back home this flat land will easily flood with a big storm. That is why the trail goes around much of the desert, though to cut straight across would be faster."

Rhys grimaced. "Too dry or too wet a forbidding place at any time of year. Where is Tiebarai then?"

Starting to turn away the wizard paused and pointed to the northern horizon. "In those mountains." At Rhys's horrified expression, Eilo laughed again. "The path to that place goes underground not far after the trail forks near Fa'Hanzoi. We will have to catch up to our prey before then. Once in the tunnels it will be nearly impossible to find them without being captured ourselves."

It was later that night after the hunters had allowed themselves a few hours badly needed sleep that a band of monstrous warriors the fleeing Hoard left behind attacked.Focused mainly on the trail of their quarry they hadn't been paying enough attention to their surroundings as they should.

Bursting through the veil of their own clever illusion the blood thirsty warriors were upon them in moments as the Alliance hunters rounded a bend in the trail. Screaming blood-curdling war cries the hideous creatures charged them from the slope above while others of their number attacked from behind.

Surrounding the wizard, the Alliance men formed their usual triangular fighting units and began picking off their adversaries, fountaining blood and charred body parts soon forming a gruesome barrier around them. But unlike before when they'd fought these fearsome creatures, the Ghostlanders weren't running away or backing down. It wasn't long before several Alliance hunters sported wounds, and the smell of their fresh blood seemed to goad the enemy's frenzy to a higher level.

Eilo grimly tried to aid the warriors as best he could by channeling his power to them. Finally paying attention to what the Ghostlanders were actually screaming about, he shouted, "Speir'dina, don't burn them with your star weapons. Make them bleed and then just stun them. These fiends are crazed with hunger. If they see the bodies maybe they will leave us alone and attack the easier prey." It took a moment to get his message across, but when they understood. Rhys and Sietriga did what he suggested.

Leaving a trail of mangled bodies and the remnants of their attackers fighting over the spoils, the Alliance hunters managed to escape during the melee. Putting as much distance as possible between themselves and the monsters, it was nearing day break when they stopped in a thorn thicket to rest and take stock of their injuries.

Tesulu and Rhys pulled out jars of yellow kavay from their belt packs and began plastering everyone's wounds with the gelatinous goo.

"We should have stayed to kill them all. They might attack some of our people next, coming up behind us," Sietriga grumped, then swore as Rhys plastered a thin coating of kavay on a long gash down his arm.

"I have already warned my brother wizard of the danger," Eilo said as he put some of his own herbal preparation on Ikuwi's chest. Motioning to the com unit on the blond warriors belt, he added, "Call them yourself if you want to be sure they understand the danger."

"Where are they, Elder do you know?" Tesulu asked.

"They have moved camp and are following us at a slower pace."

"That's good we won't have to go all the way back to the river when we take care of these Ghostland vermin," Sietriga said.

Knowing that the fugitives would probably conceal themselves during the heat of the day the hunters decided after a short rest to continue on.

"We are still too far behind them," Tesulu argued when Rhys suggested a longer break. Noticing Rhys's eyes flick to the Elder, Tesulu stammered. "Of course, Elder, if you need more time we can stay longer. I'm sure we will catch up to them soon either way."

Eilo snorted and got to his feet. "I'm fine, Sand Mountain. And you are right we need to press on."

During the day that followed the hunters crossed the erratic trail of the Horde several times. Torn up ground and picked clean carcasses gave more evidence of the monsters' passage.Fearful of another ambush or of getting too close, the hunters took the time to make sure the creatures were some distance ahead and still heading north.

As Rhys stopped to crouch by a particularly gruesome find he placed a hand upon the bloody ground to read the sign. Noticing a shadow fall over his shoulder after a time he glanced up.

Eilo was standing beside him also looking down at the mound of mangled bones, bloody and chewed. "They are attacking and eating the weakest of their number," Eilo said, his expression grim. "What did you learn when you touched the ground with your power?"

"I could tell it was Ghostland monsters that were slaughtered here, but I couldn't be sure who had attacked them."

"You would have known with a bit more time," Eilo assured him. "I was able to know sooner, because I have earlier knowledge of how these creatures are raised and trained. From the time they hatch they must fight to survive. It is their nature to kill and eat the weak, both among themselves—and among the peoples their keepers send them to attack. They are always told that the Enemy is too weak to let live."

"Then they will be a truly formidable force once they arrive at Fa'Hanzoi," Rhys said and rose to his feet.

"Are these some of the ones that attacked us, Elder?" Ikuwi asked as he came up to them.

"No, I don't think so. That vermin was running away from this force perhaps to keep from being eaten. That is why they were heading back towards our people in the hope of picking off stragglers, I think."

"Then I definitely will have to alert Command when next we come into range," Sietriga said and reached for the com unit at his waist to check its power.

Eilo and Ikuwi exchanged smiles. Command already knew with the use of "Timornan technology."

LATER THAT DAY THE wind picked up, blowing sand and other loose debris into their faces, making it nearly impossible to find any sign of their quarry's trail. As night fell the purple clouds that had been massing on the horizon let go with a downpour of bone-chilling rain to add to their confusion and misery.

Throwing polli-fiber ponchos over their heads they continued on for a time, but finally realizing they had lost their quarry's trail, Eilo called a halt at last. With forks of the green lightning booming overhead Tesulu pointed to a rocky overhang just ahead and the hunters hurried up the slope to huddle under its uncertain shelter.

At the back of their overhang was a hollow in the rock, not much bigger than a man, and over the wizard's protests the warriors lined it with an extra, only damp blanket, and insisted that Eilo go inside and rest. Rhys and Ikuwi huddled just outside to shield him from the rain and give him a little extra warmth, while Sietriga, Tesulu and the rest of the patrol huddled together and took what shelter they could find underneath the dripping overhang.

Though their shelter wasn't much, barely keeping them somewhat dry, they were grateful to be under the ledge and on higher ground, when during the night the cliff above turned into a cascade of muddy water and debris, tumbling past their hideaway and onto the lower ground below in an angry flood.

ZUHAN HATED TO ADMIT it even to zerself, but the constant travel with little food and water while also keeping them safe from the Enemy with zer's conjurings was draining ze to the core of zer's being. But ze couldn't stop because the Alliance hunters were still following—and they had a powerful western wizard, or two, with them—curse them to the Pit of Poison Fires!

Zuhan's thin mouth curved into a cruel smile. Ze had managed to divert the stragglers of the Hoard pursuing themwhen they came too close, however.In a display of power and promises of easy prey if they would only turn back to find the gift ze left for them. That, of course sent them running back towards the Alliance hunters.

With another storm coming, ze hadn't detected the Alliance followers in a while, so maybe those foul creatures he had diverted their way had taken care of zer's problem.Zuhan's grin became wider, thinking about it.

Judging that the Alliance was too far behind to worry about for the moment, he decided that their little cave shelter was a pleasant place to rest during the heat of the day. And when he saw the storm clouds massing again, ze was even more grateful for the shelter.

"A bad storm is coming," Zuhan said to Sanglaz as ze studied the south-western sky from the mouth of the cave. "We will stay here till it passes. Direct your men and the slaves to gather water, and fuel for a fire tonight. And we are almost out of food, so someone needs to go hunting," the wizard grumped. "I can't conjure on an empty stomach."

Sanglaz dipped his head crest in acknowledgement of the order. Glancing over at their prisoner, he asked, "And what about the Khutani? I don't want to leave you alone with him with so many of us doing tasks that will take us away from this place."

Zuhan waved a careless hand in the kashallan's direction. He was sitting with his back against the cave's wall, his hands and feet once again tied after he'd been taken off Chadaz's back. His eyes were closed, pretending to sleep, but Zuhan knew he was faking and hearing everything they were saying.

"Don't worry about him. Leave him tied up; I will gag him with my magic if you are that worried about my safety. I will be fine; he isn't going to bother me while I rest."

The storm bringing on an early twilight, Zuhan stood once more at the mouth of the cave and watched as the angry clouds drew near. Forks of jagged green lightning shot through the dark mass heading their way. Suddenly there was a loud boom and then somewhere overhead. chunks of broken rock;tumbled down the slope out of sight. The damp air stank of burning ozone, dust and rotting thorn. This beast of a storm was going to be a bad one; ze could feel its mounting power.

It was always like this, ze knew just before the rains stopped and the winds shifted to blow down from the Burning Lands of the northern continent. And the power deep in the wizard's core thrummed as ze attuned itself to the alluring call. It wouldn't be long now; a couple eight-day cycles at the most.

They needed to be gone from this accursed desert before that happened. And to do that Zuhan might need to make sacrifices. Turning back into the cave ze considered the motley bunch of companions ze had collected since their escape from the Hated Enemy. The Khutani, of course, Sanglaz and the best of his men ze would have to keep, but some of the others, and, alas maybe those pitiful slaves might have to be killed. They could use the meat on the trip and they would need less water that way.

And they were going to need all the water they could carry, because they were going to make a run straight across the desert plateau to the underground entrance that would lead to Tiebarai. With the Horde ahead of them and the Alliance behind, they couldn't afford to take the safer and longer trail that skirted round the dry plain.

But first they needed a little distraction to occupy the Alliance and their damned meddling wizards. Yes, something to slow them down and lessen their chances of making it to a safe refuge like Fa'Hanzoi at all. And the storm out there could be persuaded, with the right conjuring, to give them just such a challenge.

Ah, but was ze strong enough by zerself to tame the Beast and force it to do zer's bidding? Perhaps, but it would be easier with more life force to augment zer power. Zuhan stroked zer pale chin, contemplating zer's options.

The Khutani could give zer all the power Zuhan would need, but without Thaufda or one of the other substances use to master an unwilling mind and body, the Khutani would fight him every step of the way, so there was no point in even trying with him. No, ze would have to make a blood sacrifice to the Storm, so one of the others would have to be killed. Turning back into the cave ze gathered the power and began the preparations for a mighty conjuring.

Chapter Seven

It had been a long march that day, the light was fading; everyone looking forward to a hot meal and some rest. Then Qwasigara shivered as a blast of cold wind slammed into his back. He glanced toward the south-west where angry black clouds were massing. Blowing straight across the Shallow Sea the mounting storm was picking up water and debris jagged shafts of green fire slashing through the cooling air, heading their way.

Another blast of cold wind hit him, flinging grit into his eyes. Storms like this were natural at this time of year, a warning of the Sorins to come, but this storm—felt different. It was coming on fast with an unnatural malice behind it that suggested a wizard's conjuring was directing and enhancing its power.

Turning to one of the young warriors assigned to him for the journey, he said, "Athala, go tell the Hunt Leader we need to stop soon and brace for a bad storm. It is going to be trouble." As the youth hurried off to find the Hunt Leader, Qwasigara returned to studying the sky.

Like the storm that had blown up out of nowhere and had tried to drown them in their boats when they were on their way to Red Rock, he detected a magical element in its making. But who was behind it, the Cabal? Possibly, but a better and closer agent would be the unknown wizard who now had Phillip-Yoey. A storm at this time of year would be a natural occurrence. One wizard alone *could* use his magic to direct and augment its force without an overwhelming effort on the Ghostlander's part, especially if that wizard sucked power from his travelling companions, like the changeling warriors.

When Athala raced up Tizu had already seen the brewing storm and was directing his men to set up their shelters on the slopes above a particularly wide space in the trail. Thankfully they were out of the maze of canyons through which they'd been traveling for the past few days, so the danger of being caught in a flash flood had lessened.

"Athala," Tizu called over the rising wind. "Get your crew together and tell our guys to unpack as little as possible and tie down everything they can," he added as another gust of wind went whirling past.

ZUHAN GAZED INTO THE crystal pendant ze wore around zer neck and smiled at the tiny figures trying to shelter in their flimsy dwellings from the fury of his conjured tempest. Didn't they know it was hopeless? Ze laughed as another cloth cover tent collapsed and blew away in the wind, its occupants scrambling to find cover before they were blown away, too.

Outside the cave where they sheltered a booming crack of thunder sounded. Dropping the pendant to zer chest Zuhan stepped to the cave's entrance and looked out. Rain was coming down in pounding sheets of water, tiny rivulets turning into roaring streams in moments, rushing down the slope to form a muddy stream on the trail below. Uprooted thorn bush and other debris hurried by in the swift current. Overhead the wind howled demonic voices singing with their newly-found freedom.

Stepping out the entrance Zuhan ignored the wind and rain that was tearing zer kaftan and soaking zer to the bone. The wizard laughed and raised zer hands and threw back zer head drinking in its magnificence. "Yes, Hated Enemy, feel the true might of Ghostland power and die!"

QWASIGARA LISTENED to the chaotic voices howling in the wind outside the flimsy shelter the Speir'dina's tent offered to the mix of people huddling inside it. He didn't need a Khutani coiled in his middle to taste their fear. From somewhere out in the darkness he heard a woman scream and men shouting, but the wind distorted the sound so much that he wasn't sure it was real or only the wailing of the spirits trapped within the chaos of the tempest.

Though he hated to admit it, even to himself, he wished that sassy Begta witch was still with them. He had little affinity for weather magics. He had drawn a circle of protection around this shelter and two others nearby, but he was hard pressed to do even that. He needed help.

As if in answer to his unspoken need Nathan-Corha sat down beside him. "How are you doing; can I help?"

Qwasigara snorted a laugh and took the kashallan's hand, closing his clawed fingers around his wrist. Nathan jerked back and tried to pull away, but the wizard firmed up his grip. Then his eyes bugged wide when he felt the wizard drawing on Corha's Khutani power. "You are right, with my brother wizard and my strongest warriors with the gift, off hunting, I do need help." Qwasigara grinned, showing his canines. "So I guess that leaves you, Khutani—since you so kindly offered."

Nathan muttered a curse, then he relaxed and allowed the wizard to link with him. "Warn me next time," he grumped. With his now enhanced power the wizard was able to increase the diameter of his shield, but he wasn't sure how long he could keep this up.

Later as the wind's intensity increased, the wizard said, "Khutani, I'm sure you've guessed by now that this isn't a natural storm. It has been strengthened either by the Cabal in Tiebarai or the Puke with the help of his changelings that stole Phillip-Yoey. This far from the river where we last saw your kin, are you able to contact one of the Makers to help us?"

Nathan's answer was lost in a great roaring sound, and the cloth over the tent's polli-fiber frame suddenly ripped free from its mooring and flapped away into the night like a giant bird of prey. Through the rain and streaks of pale lightning they saw the swirling mass of a funnel cloud picking up rocks and debris in its boiling mass as it tore a path of destruction down the hillside on which they had made camp.

In their minds Qwasigara and the kashallan heard the Ghostlander's gloating laughter. As they watched in horror, people and their precious supplies were picked up and hurled here and there, their screams mingling with the unleashed chaos demon's song.

The wizard still clutching his wrist, Nathan pushed them to the ground, and tried to make them as flat as possible. Overhead the metal camp stove, shooting sparks from the open door in its side, hurtled past the spot where they'd been sitting just moments before.

<<Amla, come quick! Please help us,>> Corha cried, its fear threatening to overwhelm Nathan's reason.

WITHIN THEIR COUNCIL chamber deep in the bedrock, the Makers had come together to discuss their plans. The Sorins were coming and the Alliance warriors intended on capturing one of the Ghostland underground towns, something that had never been done before.

<<I say we can't kill them all. As your own child has savored, Qwaltamis, not all the peoples in the Ghostlands carry the ancient taint,>> Gladdris argued. <<Some have even sworn their oath of allegiance to the Kashallan Alliance. And many more may also do so if given the chance.>>

The pod writhed, the water glowing with phosphorescent fire and the bitter flavors of their uncertainty.

<<You are getting as troublesome and argumentative as your old partner Tinguss,>> Dievris growled, spitting the sour flavor of its displeasure into the soup of their communication.

<<Oh, want to lock me up, too, like you did my Amsi?>> Gladdris challenged. <<I am merely stating my opinion and I have a right to do that, Amsi Dievris, even if you don't agree with it.>>

<<Amsi, please,>> Meyagus pleaded, vomiting up a soothing spice into their communication. <<Nobody is locking anyone up. Everyone keep calm. We need to talk this out and make a plan to help our warriors.>>

<<We need total victory over the Hated Enemy once and for all,>> the scarred Maker Sherigus said. <<And to do that we need to destroy them. This time we need to kill each and every one, not just drive them into the poisoned lands like we did before and hope they will die.>>

<<And maybe if we hadn't driven them away into the Ghostlands but let them stay in the Yeyen and mingled them with our own bred species, as Tinguss wanted, then maybe we wouldn't have had these long years of warfare.>> Gladdris said.

<<Don't start that old argument up again,>> another Maker complained. <<What is done can't be undone.>>

<<Speaking of our wild cousin,>> another asked. <<Where is Amsi Tinguss? Why isn't it here?>>

Qwaltamis rumbled a laugh. <<Our Amsi is babysitting, as the Speir'dina would say.>> Savoring the pod's confusion, Qwaltamis laughed again. <<Our troublesome Amsi is caring for my young as well as its own, and I think some of yours, Gladdris, at Tragar, am I right?>>

<<Yes, since we had to leave Sulas my young were there in the care of K'San Tobrach and some of the priests from Sulas who didn't go with Dunnagh-Tani to Ticca, even before the Alliance was formed.>>

<<And I hear our Amsi has another project to keep it busy and out of trouble,>> Meyagus burped the sweet flavor of its amusement into their sendings.

<<Do tell, Maker,>> someone said swallowing down a large mouthful of the sweet nectar.

<<I persuaded Tinguss to convince its child's mate to conceive his child—and that of her other mate a fierce Speir'dina warrior. We need their genetic codes so our Amsi was agreeable, but the female is nearing the end of her fertile years, so the pregnancy will be a difficult one. Tinguss agreed to do this, and in turn I agreed to keep its child safe,>> Qwaltamis explained.

Dievris and Sherigus rumbled their laughter. <<That was very clever of you Amsi, Dievris gurgled.

Suddenly Qwaltamis's head shot up, hearing its child's frightened wail. <<What is it, Amsi?>> Gladdris said.

<<Trouble, terrible trouble! My child is in great danger as are all our warriors. We must go to them. Now!>>

CROWIS AND KITHA WERE huddled close in the med tent not talking, just holding each other for warmth and comfort. He could see Kashallan-Nathan go to the wizard and sit beside him. The wind moaned, the fabric of the tent billowing then flattening against its frame as the storm gained fury outside. The medics and their helpers as well as many of the gaishinay were also huddled nearby.

The warriors had pitched their shelters within a stand of sturdy thorn and sourwood trees to act as more of a wind break, but Crowis had the uneasy feeling that the Alliance was being singled out by the storm—which was crazy—it was just a bad storm, wasn't it? The voices he was hearing were Justin his imagination, right?

Then a while later, in a howling gust the cloth covering overhead blew off and he and Kitha were being lifted through the darkness into the air. Instinctually holding her tighter, he felt the storm whirling them round and round as it sucked them higher and higher into its vortex.

This was the end—he knew it. Looking into her beautiful frightened face, he knew he loved her more than life itself. "I love you so much, Kitha, will you marry me?" he shouted, but the wind tore his words away and he wasn't sure she heard him. Holy Mother Timorna he wasn't ready to die! I'm too young—well if I have to go at least my dear one is with me, he heard himself babbling within his mind and held on to her even tighter.

Once again he heard demonic laughter, but this time the voice had a familiar cadence. <<You are right, my Treasure, it isn't your time, and I still require your service to me. So I will have to do something about that meddling wizard,>> Tess-weh said.

The two Avairei next felt a violent swirling motion that pulled them into the calm of the tempest's central core. And then with the wind's power no longer supporting them, Crowis realized with horror that they were falling, the air being sucked from their lungs. Just before an impact that might have broken their bones, they slowed and landed with a jolt in a hollow of sand and plant debris. Overhead the storm still raged, but in their little hollow only the cold rain continued to pelt them. Finding barely enough energy to pull some of the rotting debris over them for some extra warmth, Crowis held Kitha close, and allowed his weariness to float him away into sleep.

STILL REVELING IN THE storm's power Zuhan was engrossed in the destruction zer malice had released upon the Enemy when a bolt of etheric power from an unknown source slammed into zer's spirit, breaking the magical connection and sending the wizard sprawling in the mud at the cave's mouth. When Zuhan's head cleared and ze raised zer head, a glowing, bare-breasted alien woman in an embroidered green kilt was standing over zer, an armed Clan warrior with a sigil of power on his forehead standing at her side. His hard eyes trained on the wizard's men, sitting round a small fire, he seemed to be daring them to try and interfere.

<<Your meddling, Wizard, is interfering with how I meet the obligations of my contract to the Alliance. I can't allow that to continue.>> Crouching over the wizard, with a delicate pale hand she reached into his chest and pulled a glowing orb of power from zer's chest. Zuhan screamed, nearly blacking out with the pain.

With a mirthless smile curving her red lips, the woman stood holding out the orb on her palm to show zer. In the next moment it fragmented into shards of light that disappeared into the storm.<<If I have to come back, Ghostland vermin, next time I will take all your power, so have a care if you think to cross me again. Leave the warriors of the Alliance alone.>>

From deeper in the cave a weak voice called, <<Tess-weh, please, help me!>>

Looking in his direction her expression softened, but she made no move to go to him. Her voice when she spoke was thick with emotion and tenderness. <<I'm sorry, Khutani. Remember what I told you and all will be well both for you and the Alliance in the end. Good bye, My Jewel.>>

Returning her attention to the now sitting up wizard, she said in parting. <<You may keep this one—for a while, Wizard. If you manage to hold on to him all the way to Tiebarai, he may prolong your living for a time—a short time.>> chuckling to herself she and her companion disappeared back into the storm.

<<OH, KASHA, OUR AMLA is here and bringing many more K'amsi to help us,>> Corha shouted into Nathan's mind.

Glancing up into the storm, Nathan and the wizard saw several snaky creatures with bat-like wings out stretched speeding to the aid of the Alliance. Etheric power flowing out of their open mouths, the Makers managed to direct the storm away from the Alliance encampment, turning what was left of its force back upon the one who had sent it.

In the lessening wind and rain the kashallan felt the presence of their Amla surrounding them in its coils. <<Rest easy, My Child,>> Qwaltamis said into their minds. <<The Ghostlander who attacked you will not do so

again I will stay near from now on. We will meet in the physical world when you come to Fa'Hanzoi.>>

As he felt the connection fade, Nathan shouted, <<Amla, wait! You need to tell Maker Tinguss that a Ghostland wizard has captured Phillip-Yoey. You and the other Makers must help him, too!>>

Had the Maker heard him? He wasn't sure.

Chapter Eight

After the storm's fury the night before the day broke rosy and clear. The wind that had been a howling beast now caressed Hunt leader Tizu's face with a seductive warmth, bringing with it the smells of broken grease bush, sourwood and carrion.

Pulling aside a twisted jumble of torn tent cover and broken polli-fiber poles off a mound of storm debris, he stared down at the lifeless body of a young armachd. Who? Crouching he turned the body over to reveal the bloody face. Brushing away debris and locks of dirty brown hair, Tizu stared at the tranquil face of Vili, one of the youngest of his armachda. The lad had finished his training and joined Lann Gheal just before the Dymarian rescue mission that had left them stranded on this crazy world.

Tizu didn't know much about the lad or his family connections. Vili hadn't given him any trouble, nothing to make him stand out in the Hunt Leader's mind. He carried out orders without complaint, as far as Tizu knew. In fact, he only knew him at all, because Ross had entrusted him with the care of the corps' icons, the Lann Gheal swords. The crossed swords had been the corps' symbol ever since Lann Gheal's founding in the ancient past.

The young armachd had been excited and proud of the honor he'd been given, Tizu recalled. And now it had probably killed him, for still clutched in his arms, even in death, were the swords encased in their water-proof coverings.

Hearing footsteps coming up behind him, Tizu glanced over his shoulder then returned his contemplation of the fallen armachd.

Her dress ragged and muddy, Cochinna had still taken the time to wash her face and hands and twist her silver hair into a knot on the top of her head, before seeking him out. Though Nathan assured him her wounded eye was getting better under her protective visor, it still lay covered with a kavay patch.

Coming up beside him she remained silent, also contemplating the young man. She had seen him glance in her direction as she approached, he knew she was there and was content to give him time to speak or not as he chose.

They remained like that for a long time before Tizu at last spoke "I've been a warrior and commander in Lann Gheal for more than thirty years, but the enemies we fought among the stars never prepared me for what I would face on this world. Magic, Psy and hatred so strong that it can change the course of a natural storm. There are times like now," he told her, "that I feel so helpless, so out of my element."

Hoping to offer compassion and sympathy by her touch, Cochinna took his hand and squeezed it gently. "You are doing the best you can, Hukiyo, and that is all anyone can ask of another."

He patted her hand with his free one and swallowed hard. "Ah but will that be good enough, I wonder?"

"It will, Hukiyo, truly it will. Your men love you—all the Alliance warriors love you—and that is amazing to me." He stared at her incredulous. She laughed softly and squeezed his hand again. "Yes it is true—even the western savages are growing to respect and love you, I believe. And that truly is a marvelous accomplishment, because in the past they have never taken directions easily or for long without deserting and returning to their lands across the Shallow Sea.

"The warriors bred and controlled by the Cabal in Tiebarai have always maintained power by exerting pain and fear of pain to accomplish their goals. And to keep the people compliant they administer drugs to everyone, so no one dares rebel. It is an evil system, but very efficient."

She allowed him to think about it for a moment before continuing. "Before meeting your people I never dreamed another way of living was possible, but I see it every day and I am humbled by it. Don't give up, My Friend. You and the Speir'dina can offer all of Timorna hope for a better future."

Crouching she took the wrapped swords from their dead guardian's arms and held them out to him. Tizu took them still staring at her face. "These are the symbols of Speir'dina power and triumph—and I'm sure have been an inspiration to your people through other desperate times in the past. I am sorry that the young man died protecting them, but in some way I think he understood how important his sacrifice would be."

Tizu gazed at the bundle he now cradled. "As always, My Dear, you offer me good council. You are right, we won't forget his sacrifice. We will carry his bones on our death strands. And," he grinned, "I'll get that fool of a Dymarian Jojo to compose a song in his honor."

Tucking the swords under his arm, he took her hand and started back to their make-shift command center. "I need to get back, see how much damage the storm has done and plan our next steps."

"Then I will leave you now and see how my own people are faring. I know you will be busy, but come to me later I will have a meal prepared for you when you want it."

"Thank you, I will look forward to that," he said as he released her hand and strode over to the Command where Ross and Nathan were already waiting for him.

THE HOT SUN ON HIS face finally woke Crowis. Then noticing that Kitha was no longer cradled in his arms, he sat up, panic starting to twist his gut into knots. Where? Oh, Merciful Mother Timorna, if something had happened to her while he lay asleep he would never forgive himself.

Then he saw her sitting on a boulder not far away. Rising to his feet and brushing off the debris clinging to his fur he crossed and sat beside her. Tentatively putting an arm around her shoulder, he said, "Why didn't you wake me?"

A tiny smile curved her lips as she turned to him, but he also saw the fear in her eyes that she was trying hard to hide. "I would have soon."

Crowis glanced at the position of the sun overhead. It was getting late. They needed to figure out where they were and get back to the Alliance camp before nightfall. They would be tempting prey for this land's many predators alone and unarmed as they were after dark.

"Have you any idea where we are?" she asked as if giving voice to his thoughts.

Crowis shook his head and got to his feet, pulling her up beside him. "No, the storm could have carried us anywhere."

They seemed to have landed on a hillside thick with thorn bush and sourwood. But there was no sound of men and camp activity on the breeze, and he could see little but the sky over head through the tangled mass of thorn bush.

Crowis wasn't experienced with natural lore, but from the little he did know, he suspected they had two choices. They could climb the slope and try to find evidence of the Alliance from a higher vantage point. Or they could head down slope and try to pick up their trail near a stream.

He glanced at his love, her braidlets snarled and ragged, her dress dirty and torn. She looked up at him, her eyes telling him she trusted him to take care of them—no matter what. He hoped he was up to the challenge.

Crowis glanced in every direction, studying the density of the bush and the steepness of the incline. Which way would be easier on his companion, he wondered. Kitha had been keeping up with the column since they left Te'gal, but she was no warrior used to the hardships of the war trail. Well neither was he, but he had been taking part in their nightly training ever since coming to Tragar and being forced to go north with the army—a fact for which he suddenly was grateful.

Knowing they would need to find water as the day's heat increased, and deciding the slope looked a bit less formidable heading downward, Crowis took her hand and headed in that direction.

Their progress was slow without a big knife or some other way to cut a trail through the brush, and he worried they might not find the camp before night caught up to them. Midway through the afternoon, when he knew she was tiring, he stopped by a hollow in the rocks that had collected a sizable puddle of rain from last night's storm.

Cupping his hands he showed her how to drink. The water tasted of grit and the minerals leached out of the rock, but it was wet and it would keep them going for a little while longer. He wished they had something to carry water in, just in case they didn't find any more later. But that was a wish unfulfilled. All he had was a small bone knife and a couple jars of kavay in the belt pouches at his waist and Kitha didn't even have that.

The day dragged on and they were no closer to finding the Alliance. Maybe he had made a bad mistake and they should have headed for higher ground instead of getting themselves lost in this maze of bush and rock. Without food and little water Crowis could feel his own energy reserves waning and suspected Kitha was in no better shape.

As the sun was dipping behind a western ridge of mountains their luck seemed to run out. From within a thick cover of thorn, a six-legged beast that seemed to be all teeth and claws charged them.

Grabbing Kitha's hand Crowis raced for a pile of boulders a little way down the slope. Climbing atop the highest of the rocks, Crowis quickly snatched up a handful of stones and began throwing them at the beast, shouting and swearing Caldoni curses at the creature at the top of his voice. When he ran out of ammunition, Kitha quickly handed him more.

Several of his missiles hit their mark. The creature howled in pain and frustration, but backed out of range snarling.

When the beast gave no further signs of an attack, Crowis sank down on the boulder to catch his breath. Kitha sat down beside him, still cradling a handful of fist-sized rocks in her lap.

Now what were they going to do, he thought. They were trapped in these boulders with no idea where camp was—and night was coming on. Soon enough they would run out of nearby missiles to throw at the beast.

Together they warded off two more attempts to kill them by the hungry creature, but it was almost dark and they were running out of stones. Well, he wasn't going to let the foul creature have his love, Crowis decided, grimly. He would give himself to the beast first. Tess-weh would just have to find another to swear to her service. He was going to protect Kitha at all costs.

"Kitha?" Crowis tore his gaze away from watching the edge of their sanctuary and kissed her. When he let her go she looked up at him with wide frightened eyes. "I love you and if we get out of this mess by some miracle will you marry me?"

Kitha gasped. She thought about it for a moment, making him wait on her answer. At last she said, "I think I love you, too, Crowis. You have been so good to me, a stranger among you, but what about your betrothed that is waiting for you back home?"

Damn! Who had told her about Grasina? That might explain why she hadn't encouraged him, when everyone in camp knew how much he cared about her. "My betrothal is my mother's idea not mine. For political reasons she wanted me to marry a girl that is related to one of the first kashallan's wives." He let out an ironic laugh. "Well, it turns out I'm related to a kashallan anyway without getting married. Though I'm not sure my mother is going to approve of Phillip-Yoey when we eventually get back."

Kitha gave him a tentative smile. "Your brother-in-law is a good man, I think. He also has been very kind to me."

"Yes he is, though I couldn't see it at first," he agreed. "But I think my reluctance to marry the girl was why I took Adnim up on his stupid bet to come north with the army—maybe."

"But what I do know is that it was the best thing that ever happened to me, because I found you. So I will ask again. Will you marry me?"

"I wouldn't mind if you please your mother and marry the girl. I could just be your special gaishinay if you want."

"No, that's not what I want. I want you for my wife and only you," he declared, still looking into her eyes.

"Then my answer is yes—if we survive—" she broke off as a loud roaring came from a thicket of sourwood a little ways down the slope. Kitha shivered and drew a little closer to her chosen protector.

A moment later Atahru walked out of the thicket, bloody spear in hand. Wide-eyed, Crowis and Kitha stood. Gazing at them with his otherworldly stare, he motioned for them to climb down off their boulder and follow him. Using his Speir'dina knife and his spear, the Wa'chassey'ul slashed a path for them through the brush.

Refusing to answer any questions Crowis called to him, he led them down the slope and along a muddy wash, then up and over another hill. When it was becoming too dark, Crowis shouted for him to wait, because they could no longer see him in the dim light and they might get lost again.

Finally understanding their difficulty he held out his hand and a glowing orb appeared in his palm, which he tossed into the air to perch over top of his head. Then he started moving again, without turning to see if they were following.

Sometime in the quiet hours just before dawn they stepped through a last barrier of thorn and saw the glow of the Alliance campfires below. Waving them on, Atahru stepped back into the bush and was gone, before they had a chance to thank him.

Stumbling with weariness the couple staggered down the slope where they were first challenged by a sentry and then greeted with joy by the few still awake to meet them.

Chapter Nine

In the twilight the day after the great storm, the Alliance hunters were following a game trail up the slope from a ravine still choked with debris and raging muddy water when Ikuwi, who had been trailing the patrol to cover up their passage raced up to Eilo and Tesulu.

"Elder, War Leader," he shouted over the roar of the flood when he caught his breath. "The enemy we chase is behind us not ahead."

"What, Lazy Begta, how can that be?" Tesulu growled.

Unperturbed by the insult Ikuwi shrugged. "Maybe they wanted a longer rest because the mushroom is getting tired. But I tell you true; they are behind us."

"Did they see you, Young One?" Eilo asked. If this was true then they had no time to waste on debating the matter.

Wiping a wisp of his mane out of his eyes, Ikuwi shook his head. I don't think so. I had my shields in place long before I spotted them. I doubt if they saw me."

Motioning for the patrol to follow him, Eilo led them farther up the slope where they could still see the trail, but they could talk without shouting over the noise made by the flood.

When they were hidden behind the thorn with a look out posted nearby, Eilo turned to Ikuwi and said, "Now describe to me exactly what you saw."

"I didn't dare get too close but what I saw was about five or six warriors—mostly changeling bred, but there was at least one northern man among them as well. Leading the way was a Ghostlander—the wizard, I think. He was being carried on the back of another man—maybe one of the missing slaves. With only the faintest of shields in place to hide them, they were making their way slowly, picking their way carefully and not in any hurry, as if they weren't worried about being pursued."

"Maybe he thinks the storm finished us off," Rhys suggested.

"That is one possibility," Eilo conceded, "or maybe he is too weak at the moment to be as careful as he should be."

Picking up his spear Tesulu smiled. "Then this is the perfect time to kill the vermin."

Eilo nodded but held up a hand to stop him when the Sand Mountain warrior would have left to attack them. "Continue your report, Ikuwi. Where is the Khutani? I assume they still have him, yes?"

"Yes, they still have him, Elder. They have tied his hands and placed a rope collar around his neck that is connected to a leash which one of the changelings carries. If the Khutani is too slow, he jerks hard on the leash, making his prisoner stumble and choke."

Ikuwi's words were greeted with angry murmurs until Eilo held up a hand to quell the noise. "How far behind you are they?"

"Not far, a half of sun-mark or less."

Eilo pointed with his chin to Rhys and Sietriga. "Speir'dina, take your weapons and night glasses and find places on the trail where you can see them as they appear. I will take care of the wizard. Try to get as many of the warriors as you can—especially the one holding the Khutani's tether. Tesulu, you take the rest of the men and rescue the Khutani."

STILL RECOVERING FROM zer fight with the other-worldly creature that had drained zer power, Zuhan was in a foul mood, hitting the slave with zer fists when he was slow about obeying his orders and screaming at the warriors, before they were finally underway the next evening. It was a good thing that the storm and the remnants of the Horde had taken care of their pursuers, because ze needed more time to recover.

Unfortunately for the fugitives, they found once out on the trails that an unplanned result of the storm was the flooding and damage apparent to the trail north they should be following. Several times they had had to go around a mound of rock and debris that had slid down the hillside to block their path. Or a bit later they might have to backtrack and find another way around a swollen creek.

It was full dark and they were spread out along a narrow path overlooking another flooded gulley when the man just ahead of Zuhan burst into flame, and fell into the turbulent water below.

"Back go back," someone shouted, but the path was narrow and as Zuhan turned another warrior in their rear also burst into flame. Trapped, they were trapped! How could this be? Then he felt the presence of a powerful western wizard in zer mind and ze was fighting for his life.

AS THE CHAOS EXPLODED around him Phillip-Yoey grabbed onto his tether and jerked the rope out of his guard's hand. As the man lunged for him he burst into flame. Startled, Phillip stepped back, slipped on the muddy edge of the trail, and then plummeted helplessly over the edge and into the maelstrom.

Tesulu saw him fall and raced over to the edge of the path, barely dodging a well-aimed spear aimed at his middle. He shouted the kashallan's name, but there was no response and no dark head emerged from the muddy water.

KNOWING THEY WERE OUTNUMBERED and the damned wizard was nearly unconscious from zer battle with the enemy, Sanglaz called for his remaining men to run and not fight them. If they wanted the damned Khutani that bad, they could have him. He would take his chances with the Cabal if they got to Tiebarai.

Deciding they might need the wizard later he ordered one of his men to take up the limp body and race for the shelter of the concealing brush downstream. Then whipping the slave hard with the end of his tail he forced the weary man to follow. As food or to carry the wizard they would need him, too.

A SHORT TIME LATER Eilo joined Tesulu at the edge of the trail, also staring down into the frothing water. "The Ghostlander was defeated. We almost had him safe among us. And now he is gone," Eilo said, his voice thick with emotion. "Crazy Khutani, I will miss him."

Tesulu grunted. "I will, too. It will be hard to bring the news of our failure to the old one."

"But he may not be dead," Ikuwi protested, coming to join them. Remember he is part Khutani, he can breathe underwater like the Dhuura."

"That is true, Young One, but look at that water," Eilo said. "There is a swift current and it is full of floating branches and other debris. Any creature would have a hard time surviving in that."

"What do you want to do, Elder?" Tesulu said. "Shall we go after the changelings and the wizard?"

"No, I think not," Eilo said, stroking his jaw. "The wizard is no threat, his power is too weak now to bother us. And with the Khutani gone there would be no point. We will go back, find our camp and report."

"Elder, please," Ikuwi pleaded. "Let me take my Teh'lach brother Chuunga and follow this flood for a while, see if a live Khutani or his body turns up. We are all going north; we'll find you in a few days, with or without him."

Eilo looked at Tesulu who nodded. "All right, but you had better keep in touch with me, young One, and don't take any risks. That wizard may recover and the Changeling leading them I sense has a great well of power to draw upon as well."

BY THE AFTERNOON OF the next day, the Alliance Command had a better idea of how much damage the storm had caused them. "We've lost more than half of our food supplies and some of our off-world weaponry—as well as most of the fire jars we had left from what we made last Sorin season at Ticca," Ross reported, his expression grim.

Damn, that could become a real disaster, Tizu thought. There was no way to replace their off-world weapons and they might need all they could muster, especially if the Cabal decided to hit them with some of their own salvaged technology.

"...A number of our people are still unaccounted for," Ross was saying. He shrugged. "Some of them may still turn up. A few wounded have already straggled back into camp. Timma, Ruan and Williams are treating them as best they can."

"Casualties?" Tizu asked.

"Hard to say, Sir. As we uncover debris we keep finding more. I won't have a full report for you until later."

Tizu grunted. "Do the best you can. We'll need to take stock and get moving as soon as we can manage it. We have to make it to Fa'Hanzoi as soon as possible now."

Ross grimaced. "Yeah, before another damned wizard takes it into his head to blow us off the map."

Hungry and desperate for a Sorin refuge, he pitied any Ghostlander that got in his way. Tizu snorted, his expression as grim as his armachd. "Yeah, we have no choice now, no matter what's waiting there for us. We take Fa'Hanzoi, or die in the attempt."

The End

Tales of the Kashallans is continued in book Nine, the final book in the series.

Don't miss out!

Visit the website below and you can sign up to receive emails whenever Celu Amberstone publishes a new book. There's no charge and no obligation.

https://books2read.com/r/B-A-YGQM-FEEHC

BOOKS 2 READ

Connecting independent readers to independent writers.

Did you love *Treacherous Campaign*? Then you should read *Taste of Memory*[1] by Celu Amberstone!

TASIMU is a youth who can call down the power of the northern lights to win a rock-throwing contest, but he is also a boy troubled by the mystery surrounding his birth. Others taunt him, claiming that he isn't truly human. Before he can discover the truth, gold is discovered on tribal land, and soldiers from the Empire come north with orders to remove his people from their northern home.

Taste of Memory deals with issues of family breakup, ritual abuse and cultural disintegration as these tribal people are forced to become refugees, stolen away from their ancestral land. But it is also a story where love for one's family and people triumphs over a need for selfish desires and personal power. This is the first book in the *Tales of Tasimu* series by celebrated author Celu Amberstone.

The Dreamer's Legacy is truly an interesting book. It takes a familiar story of the colonization of Indigenous people, and gives it a new and exotic twist. Celu Amberstone has fashioned a truly original take on aboriginal storytelling - it teaches, entertains, and mystifies.

- Drew Hayden Taylor (author of *The Night Wanderer: A Native Gothic Novel, Motorcycles and Sweetgrass*)

An original and gripping story. Amberstone transports us to a sad, wild land that is not of our world to tell a heart-warming story from another culture and another time.

- Dave Duncan (author of *The Seventh Sword, A Man of His Word, A Handful of Men*)

Merges the mythic aboriginal world with the grim realities of cultural disintegration. The Dreamer's Legacy is a compelling read.

- Eileen Kernaghan (author of *Wild Talent: a Novel of the Supernatural*)

Also by Celu Amberstone

Rituals
Blessings of the Blood: A Book of Menstrual Lore and Rituals for Women
Deepening the Power: Community Ritual and Sacred Theatre

Tales of Tasimu
Taste of Memory
When Memory Dies

Tales of the Kashallans
The Dream-Chosen
The Hunted Kashallan
The Outlawed Bond
Uncertain Refuge
Prey of the Umwira
Blood Magic's Snare
Kashallan Alliance
Treacherous Campaign

Standalone
Refugees and Other Stories

About the Author

Celu is of mixed Cherokee and Scots-Irish ancestry. Celu Amberstone was one of the few young people in her family to take an interest in learning Traditional Native crafts and medicine ways. This interest made several of the older members of her family very happy while annoying others.

Legally blind since birth, she has defied her limitations and spent much of her life avoiding cities. Moving to Canada after falling in love with a Métis-Cree man from Manitoba, she has lived in the rain forests of the west coast, a tepee in the desert and a small village in Canada's arctic. Along the way she also managed to acquire a BA in cultural anthropology and an MA in health education. Celu loves telling stories and reading. She lives in Victoria British Columbia near her grown children and grandchildren.

About the Publisher

Kashallan Press is an independent publisher releasing books by author Celu Amberstone. Among her books are critically-acclaimed works now re-released by Kashallan Press, and new works showcasing her talents in writing both fiction and non-fiction.